Historical fiction
CW01669010

STANDING AT THE EDGE OF ORDINARY

LISA-MARIE AINLEY

Copyright © 2025 Lisa-Marie Ainley
All rights reserved.

ISBN-13: 978-1-9191717-0-8
(ISBN:1-9191717-0-8)

For you, Little Bird.

"The moment you abandon belief or principle for the approval of others,
you have assisted in the persecution of your own freedom."

A DEBT TO PAY

Harriet Blackthorn was a woman of formidable intellect. In a time of sweeping progress and ingenuity, when the great men of the world were rising to power, she could have bested them all, but for one small problem.

Harriet was a woman.

Raised on Latin and logic, she had long held the opinion that in a society afflicted by poverty of thought, education was wasted on determinedly unintelligent men. It could not compensate for a lack of natural intelligence and common sense. Nor could their breeding compensate for good manners.

She closed her eyes, lulled by the gentle rocking of the carriage—the hypnotic rhythm of iron wheels against the road. Deep in her own thoughts, she resided in that wonderful portion of the brain where memories cling to the present with potent force, determined not to be forgotten.

She thought of her father—how thoroughly he had loved her. He would have given her anything she wanted, had she ever asked. But she had always been content with his affection and her books. She touched the ring he'd given her, spinning it around her finger.

The carriage lunged violently as the wheel dropped into a rut. The movement wrenched her into the present, and she clutched the toddler in her lap. They had arrived in town, and business awaited.

Harriet alighted the carriage and lifted Lillian out, setting her on the pavement. She walked with purpose, punishing the ground underfoot. Lancaster, she thought, was a terribly inconvenient place: ill-suited to the needs of a pedestrian. It was as though it had been built on a rolling sea.

Fallen leaves were sodden with rain and slippery underfoot in the narrow cobbled streets. It was late September, and the first signs of autumn were long past. A granite sky scowled over the town, and damp wrapped itself around her. She shivered now and then, partly from the cold and partly from the shock of that morning's post.

Aggie had brought it to the breakfast table with her usual cheer. "Here you go ma'am, just the two today," she said, handing her the envelopes with a wrinkled brown hand.

Aggie was slight and sinewy, but had the strength of a woman half her age. She'd been Harriet's nurse, housekeeper and the only motherly figure she'd ever known.

The first of the letters had the British Army seal. She'd hesitated before breaking it. Her husband's letters had never thrilled her. They were littered with dutiful affection, but they had never loved each other—not really. She hadn't seen him in almost three years, but that didn't matter. All she had ever wanted was right here with her.

When she saw the address written in an unfamiliar hand, she had known immediately.

> *Dear Mrs Blackthorn, It is with regret and deepest sympathy....*

Arthur was dead—taken by fever in India.

She'd opened the second letter. A solicitor. Debt. Tremendous, crippling debt.

She still couldn't believe it. How could he possibly have left debt? Her father left her a sizeable fortune, but in truth, she knew very little about it once it passed into her husband's possession. Surely he hadn't squandered it all. He couldn't have.

The clock at the town hall struck the hour. It ticked on, knocking seconds dead at the moment of their birth. But that was life, she supposed; relentless, inevitable.

For the first time in her life, she was at a loss for words, her course of action unclear. The sensation was novel to her and altogether uncomfortable. Her father had prepared her for many things in life, but not this.

Lillian smiled up at her. She was the one exception to Harriet's dispassionate manner. The only one she'd ever loved without restraint. The first and only person to break through Harriet's ironclad exterior.

My poor darling, Harriet thought. She was too young to understand she'd just lost a father whom she had never met.

~

MARKET STREET soon came into view. A neat row of almost identical shops with smart bow windows. Painted signs hung on metal chains, jutting out into the street like pointing fingers. They appealed to Harriet, and she always walked the extra distance to come here rather than go to the untidy shops she passed along the way. If a shopkeeper didn't see fit to keep his shop presentable, then a satisfactory standard of work inside was most unlikely.

They entered Mrs Petty's shop to order Harriet's mourning attire. A bright-eyed, stout woman was behind the counter. Her red hair fizzed about her in a little cloud. "Good morning, Mrs Blackthorn. Are you well?" She said in a heavy northern accent. "And how's you, little missy?" She beamed at Lillian, and leaned over the counter to pinch her cheeks. "Is someone going to get a nice new pretty dress today eh?"

"No, Mrs Petty. I'm afraid we're here on a more sombre business."

"Oh, I'm sorry to hear that, Mrs blackthorn. Now't too serious, I hope?"

Harriet covered Lillian's ears. "I received news from India this morning that Mr Blackthorn has sadly passed." She delivered this news as calmly as if she were discussing the weather.

"Oh Lord! Oh, dear Lord! What happened my dear? Was he killed in battle?" She looked almost hopeful, Harriet thought. As though such circumstances would have made it all the more thrilling.

"No, nothing so honourable. He contracted a fever." Harriet explained.

"Oh, Mrs blackthorn, you poor thing, and that sweet child. That dear, sweet little child, to be left without a father. Good Lord!" She splayed a hand over her heart in a theatrical gesture. Mrs Petty looked so distressed that anyone might have thought it was her husband.

Harriet let her finish before removing her hands from Lillian's ears.

Mrs Petty took her measurements in the fitting room, where mannequins stood like sentinels, guarding the mysterious world of cloth and haberdashery. It was a cave of wonders. Scraps of lace and linen were strewn about the floor.

Lengths of ribbon wound their way around furniture legs, and strands of glistening gold embroidery thread caught the light. Beads of unimaginable colours spilled from tiny wooden drawers like jewels, and bolts of colourful silk stood in every corner of the room.

She flitted about like a trapped bird, offering Harriet tea, biscuits and too much sympathy—none of which she found useful—but accepted with grace all the same. That sort of attention always made her uncomfortable. She never knew how she was supposed to react to it.

Mrs Petty took her order with meticulous attention to detail, making a list of the articles required. The silk was expensive. Too expensive now, so Harriet settled on the bombazine.

"A very fitting choice," Mrs Petty said, her eyes crinkling at the corners. "Much better than the silk. I always think it shows a deeper sense of loss."

Harriet bristled. As much as she liked her, she was not interested in Mrs Petty's thoughts on the matter. She was even less concerned with how deep a sense of loss was portrayed by her garment choice. She hated that a person should have to wear black to signify to the rest of the world that they had suffered a loss. It felt like advertising your emotions on the outside, and in her opinion, that was not where they belonged.

Nevertheless, she wasn't brave enough to renounce the concept of mourning dress. For now, her clothing would have to portray the devastated and grieving widow. The idea made her stomach clench.

She'd known Arthur for most of her life. He was a friend of her father's, and when the time came that her father proposed him as a husband, she considered him an agreeable match. He had a respectable income, as well as a large estate, albeit entailed. He came from a good family and was a decorated

British Army officer. She knew nothing of love or the silly foibles that preoccupied other girls her age.

Despite having no inclination toward matrimony, she accepted him to please her father. At just seventeen, she'd known nothing of the trials of marriage and what it meant to a woman's independence.

They had only been married for three months when Arthur was posted to Delhi, India, and so she'd spent the majority of her married life, including childbirth, without him. In short, she felt nothing greater than a mild fondness for him. Any esteem in which she'd previously held him now dissipated under the weight of her situation.

When the fitting was done, Mrs Petty dispatched a boy to Mr Moorby's for the necessary items. She promised to have one simple dress and veil completed for Harriet to collect in two days' time. The rest she would deliver upon completion. Harriet paid the deposit and bid Mrs Petty good day.

Lillian had been very well behaved during their transaction. Harriet was astonished at the level of restraint the toddler had shown in such a treasure trove of objects. As a special treat, she took her to the sweet shop before they continued any further.

They crossed the street to Marven's, and Harriet lifted her up to look in the window. Lillian's eyes grew wide with wonder when she pressed her tiny nose to the windowpane. She wriggled with excitement, and gold ringlets bounced about her shoulders.

The old man inside peered at them from half-moon spectacles. Wiry, disordered eyebrows framed his sallow face. He looked down his long nose at them, then motioned impatiently for them not to touch the glass pane.

Lillian gave a snort of laughter that fogged up the glass

with her warm breath, and the old man's eyebrows shot up in horror.

They entered the shop, and Lillian squealed, delight apparent on her face as she took in the countless rows of sweet jars. She bounded off toward the back wall to inspect them.

Harriet closed her eyes and breathed in the sweet scent of childhood. The overwhelming smell of sugar came first, sweet and sickly. Then a full-bodied vanilla and toffee, the tang of lemon, fresh bright strawberries, cold sharp peppermint and the bitter snap of liquorice. She remembered buying humbugs as a little girl not much older than Lillian. Fattening her cheeks with sweets so that she could hardly close her mouth. How her father had laughed at that.

She bought a penn'orth of humbugs in memory of him, some pear drops, because Aggie liked those, and Lillian chose a bright, cherry red lollipop. She waved it about like a magic wand in between licks and Harriet laughed, thankful for the momentary release.

~

By the time they reached Castle hill to see the solicitor, Lillian struggled to keep up her mother's brisk pace. Harriet carried her the last few yards and set her down on the wooden bench in the waiting room.

Mr Oglethorpe had been the family solicitor for several years and was a trusted friend of her father's. She took the letter to him, with the intention that he might suggest what could be done regarding the outstanding debt.

The letter stated that the debt was owed to a Mr Piggot of the East India Company, to whom Mr Blackthorn had lost several games of cards with particularly high stakes. She wasn't aware that he gambled and was suspicious of the claim. The letter, however, made reference to the existence of a note authorising the debt. According to the letter, the note was written in Arthur's hand and was at the offices of Swainson and Goodier for her to evaluate if she so wished.

"Good Heavens Mrs Blackthorn, what a pickle," said Mr Oglethorpe, his whiskers bristling. "Eight hundred pounds! I can't imagine what would take possession of a man to indulge in such a thing." He shook his head and his drooping jowls flapped. "I must say, it's outrageous, quite outrageous."

"Quite so, Mr Oglethorpe. I was terribly shocked by it." Harriet said.

"Yes, yes, I can see that it would be quite distressing for you." He paused, studying her, and then continued. "Is it your intention to see this note, bearing your husband's signature?" He raised one bushy eyebrow as he asked.

"Do you think I ought to authenticate it? I mean, if I found it wasn't in my husband's hand, do you suppose there's anything could be done to repudiate the claim?" She brightened with hope at the possibility.

Mr Oglethorpe cleared his throat. "Oh no, no, that's...not what I meant. The note would be legally binding in most courts, especially when the creditor is a man of Mr Piggot's standing. I'm afraid, considering his rank and the ramifications if such a course were to be undertaken, I very much doubt anything could be done. I strongly advise you against such actions. I merely thought that it might settle your mind perhaps, to see it for yourself?"

Not surprised by his answer, she was no less disappointed when he gave it. "In that case," she said, "I don't suppose it would be beneficial to see it. I shall have to let it stand." She sank deep into the chair and sighed, as though she might breathe out the disappointment in one long breath.

The room was dimly lit and smelled of beeswax. It stirred a memory of her father at home in his study. A room much like this one, the walls wrapped with glossy wood panelling and lit with warm firelight. She remembered Aggie, much younger then, waiting by the door to put her to bed. The smell of her father when she'd climbed onto his lap to say goodnight—warm and soapy, and the comfort she felt with his strong arms around her. Her chest ached at the memory.

Mr Oglethorpe coughed and cleared his throat again, bringing her attention back to him. He offered her a sad smile, and they set about the business of discussing her options. They drew up a list of her dispensable belongings and their monetary values; the sum of these assets falling far short of the amount owed to Mr Piggot. After careful consideration, they decided the only feasible option was to sell the house and furniture. Since Arthur's estate was entailed, it could not be sold, and in the absence of a male heir, would pass to his cousin, Edward Blackthorn.

Harriet had never had much of a relationship with Arthur's family. He was an only child and his father was already dead when she married him. When she gave birth to Lillian, her mother-in-law had visited to see the baby but, disappointed it wasn't a boy, had never returned. There would be no financial help from them. There would be no help from anyone.

Mr Oglethorpe set a date for the house to go to auction in two weeks' time. Better to deal with such matters efficiently. "I'm dreadfully sorry for you, Mrs Blackthorn. There really ought to be something done to protect women from this sort of thing. They're seldom victorious in matters of law. I'm afraid it's most unfair." He smiled at her with genuine empathy.

"Thank you, Mr Oglethorpe. I appreciate your kindness

and your good counsel as always." She shook his hand and returned to the waiting room to fetch Lillian, who was fast asleep on the bench.

Outside, the sky had dulled to pewter, and the wind tugged at Harriet's shawl as she stepped from the solicitor's office with Lillian sleeping against her shoulder. She carried her through the streets, her arms aching from the weight of what lay ahead.

Behind every closed door, a life went on unchanged. She could no longer remember what that felt like. She had done what needed to be done, and the finality of it pressed against her ribs like a slow suffocation. The house would be gone in two weeks. She did not know where they would go, only that they could not stay.

A LAST GOODBYE

The fortnight preceding the auction date passed quicker than any other in Harriet's life. Her calm and collected demeanour was fraying at the edges. The last two weeks had felt strange—unnatural. As though she were stuck at the turning of the page between one chapter and another.

There had been no funeral as such, just a small remembrance service held in Arthur's honour. What was left of it, that is. His family did not attend, despite being informed by Harriet. There would be no headstone, no monument erected in his memory, where a widow or a daughter could lay flowers. It was as though his life had evaporated, with no more ceremony than steam escaping from the kettle.

She had no idea what would become of herself and Lillian, and she was unaccustomed to such uncertainty. It became impossible to visualise what their lives might look like in the next few months.

She had made all the necessary preparations for their departure on Sunday. The furniture was packed and sent to the auction house, excluding a few choice items, which were still necessary. It had brought a handsome sum at the sale last week, enough to see her through a few months at least, provided the house also made its expected price. Two beds, a breakfast table, three chairs and a washstand were all that remained now. The rest of their belongings were packed into two tan leather portmanteaus and a large trunk.

She stood in the parlour, staring out at the inky night as it glared back, wild and ill-tempered. Trees hunkered down and turned their backs to the wind, their boughs groaning and branches whipping and lashing about. A few remaining leaves clung with defiance to the outstretched fingertips of twigs.

Rain fell in a ceaseless torrent, hurling itself against the window in great fat drops. They stuck in place for a single moment, then with a quiver, as though they were overcome with the effort, trickled downward in little rivulets, shining bright and silver against the glass.

It rained so often that Harriet had grown accustomed to the continuous patter of raindrops in this damp patch of England. It was comforting at times—familiar. *Nothing will be familiar now. Perhaps not ever again.*

Aggie wandered in and came to stand next to her. Her hair was a halo of wiry black-grey curls that looked like a hat of steel wool. For as long as Harriet could remember, she had combed her hair through with the cold tea left in the pot.

"It keeps the colour strong," she would say.

The strange ritual had always baffled Harriet, but Aggie's hair was a half dozen shades darker than other women her age.

She placed an arm around her shoulder with a soft sigh. "Everything will be alright, you know. I can feel it, and you know how my feelings are," she said, "I always know."

"Oh, Aggie, I don't know what to make of all this." Harriet

raised her hands then let them drop limp against her sides. "Imagine if we knew in our adolescence how life would thwart our plans, make merriment of us. Would we continue on, do you think, determined as we are with the arrogance of youth? Or would we surrender right there and let fate make of us what it would?" Her shoulders dropped. "I don't understand. What's the use of making provisions for a life we have so little control over? It seems so useless."

"Come now, don't lower your spirits with all your fancy talk about ifs and buts and maybes. It's never done anybody any good. You know you remind me so much of your mother when you're like this."

Harriet turned to her, surprised. "Was my mother unhappy?"

"No, no, I don't mean that. She was happy enough. It's just... sometimes she'd get to thinking too hard and get all melancholy like. You're just the same when you're thinking too hard. You get this far-off look about you. Like you're somewhere else. She was just the same. Her head was often somewhere else."

They stood in thoughtful silence for a while before Harriet asked, "Aggie, why were my mother and her family estranged?"

Something like panic crossed Aggie's face. She hesitated and wiped her palms down her apron. "What did your father tell you?"

"I never asked him," Harriet said.

"You mean to tell me in all these years, you never asked your father?"

"No, I suppose it never occurred to me to question it. I just accepted it." She looked at Aggie with wide, pleading eyes.

"Well, you know your mother wasn't from here?" she began.

"Yes, Father did tell me she was Spanish. That much I know."

"That's right. That's where your beautiful golden skin came from." She smiled lovingly at Harriet.

Harriet knew from her mother's portrait that they looked alike. They had the same honeyed skin, the same green eyes and high cheekbones. She'd often been told she had her mother's effortless grace. Aggie always said she had a way of looking at a man that made him wither under her gaze.

"Her people," she continued, "were an ancient family line. They didn't want their daughter to be the wife of a businessman. He was below her station, and they didn't take kindly to him." She smiled at some private memory. "But she loved him so much she'd have died before give him up."

Harriet couldn't imagine loving a husband so completely.

"They warned her—your grandparents—that if she married him, they'd cut all ties with her. Told her she wouldn't like it here in England—that the English would never accept her. They were right in that respect. You know how cruel folks can be. You've seen it yourself. She used to say her skin was a shade too dark for polite company." Aggie trailed off with a wistful smile. "But never mind all that now. Don't be too much longer to bed. You look awful tired," she said, rubbing Harriet's arm before she left the room.

She was right. Harriet was tired, but she couldn't sleep now. She wanted to make sense of her mother's blind love for her father. But how could she? She'd never been in love. It saddened her though, to learn that her mother was cut off from her people by their own impoverished ideals.

She knew her father wasn't known to society in his early years. He was a successful businessman though, making his fortune early on in the cotton mills of Bolton. As a result, they lived in as much luxury as the landed gentry and socialised among the ranks of high society. They'd been tolerated as a respectable family but never truly belonged. Polite society never accepted those without the proper heritage.

Harriet lived amongst the upper class, but she had a greater affinity with her staff than the society she inhabited.

She walked through the house with slow, deliberate steps, memorising fine details, atmospheric touches that kept a memory vivid and alive. Perhaps she might draw comfort from them at some unknown time in the future. She often committed things to memory this way—stored them neatly away—like filed papers.

This house was filled with happy memories. Memories of Aggie, of herself and Lillian. They were an unconventional little family, thrown together by circumstance but bound by love and loyalty.

It was strange to see the house so bare, stripped of all the things which made it theirs. Paintings and pictures that once adorned the walls, were no more than squares of darkened wallpaper, never touched by the light. Windows were no longer dressed in their fine curtains, carpets were rolled up and taken away. It was hollow, cold. Nothing but an echo of the life it once held between its walls.

Their luggage waited in the hallway. How could the sum of their lives fit into such meagre space? Twenty years, a marriage, a child—all reduced to three bags.

A stack of old newspapers lay atop the bags. She peeled off a sheet and took down the clock in the hall to wrap it. The paper smelled musty and old. She looked at the date: Saturday, July 23rd, 1853. Not so very old then—only last year. She took another sheet and scanned the page. There was an account of some domestic trouble which had occurred on Main Street and another about vagabonds at the racecourse at Lancaster Moor. She folded it with care and put it in her pocket to read later. All her beloved books had been sold, so newspaper articles would have to quench her literary thirst for the time being.

On the staircase, she tried to avoid the creaks, tiptoeing so as not to wake Lillian. Her effort was in vain as the rustle of her black dress made more noise than her footsteps. The door creaked as she entered the bedroom, and Lillian stirred.

She was curled up with her knees tucked under her chin, hair spread over the pillow. The faint glow of moonlight caught the pinkness of her cheeks, and her rosebud lips were drawn into a pout. She looked like an angel.

Harriet sometimes spent half the night gazing in reverence at the cherub-faced child in her arms. It was as if all the beauty of the heavens was laid out for her own personal joy. She whispered into the night, "My precious little jewel." She planted a kiss on Lillian's forehead and slipped her arm as gently as she could underneath Lillian's shoulders, drawing her into an embrace. Curled up in each other's arms in blissful happiness, she wished they could stay like that forever, just the two of them.

Aggie stood in the doorway, beaming like a doting grandmother, tears in her eyes. She was the most emotional woman Harriet had ever met. She cried when she was happy, when she was sad, angry, and every feeling in between.

"I've never seen such love as when you look at that child," she said.

Harriet gave a soft chuckle. "Love," she said, "It's a funny word, isn't it?"

"What do you mean, child?"

"Such a small word to mean so much. So infinite and indefinable a feeling as this could never be rendered into ordinary words. It defies definition, defies logic."

Aggie shook her head. "There you go again with your

fancy talk. It's not for ordinary folks like me. I swear, sometimes I think you're speaking another language." She chuckled. "Why, if folks ever knew just how much sentiment you're capable of, they'd never recognise you."

Harriet narrowed her eyes in mock menace. "Then know that I expect your discretion, Madam." They both laughed.

Aggie didn't want to leave them when they moved, but Harriet could no longer afford her salary and couldn't allow her to continue unpaid as she'd suggested. It wouldn't be right. The faithful old lady insisted on spending the last night with 'her girls' and tomorrow she would move in with her brother. For the first time in Harriet's life, she would be without her.

"Come, Mrs Blackthorn, let's get you out of that dress. You'll be a sorry sight come tomorrow morning if you fall asleep in them stays." She shuffled over to the bed and took the pins from Harriet's hair, teasing it out until it spilled down her back like black ink.

"Oh, Aggie, I do wish you would just call me Harriet. It's ridiculous that you address me so formally one minute and call me 'child' the next."

Aggie stiffened as she started to unlace the corset. "Absolutely not. I never have, and I never will," she said. "It wouldn't be decent and proper. What would folks think if they heard your housekeeper calling you Harriet? No, my child, it wouldn't do. It wouldn't do at all." She nodded her head as though she agreed with herself, and that settled the matter completely.

Harriet breathed in, filling her lungs as the whale boned casing peeled away. "Then what did you call me as a baby, Aggie? You must have called me Harriet then. You couldn't very well have called me Mrs or Madam, could you?" She showed her a triumphant grin. "Did you call me Hattie as my father did?"

"I did not." She said. "That was your mother's pet name and your father's privilege. But it wouldn't have made any difference to me whether he'd named you Betty or Bill or any other name, because I only ever called you Darling. But you're a married woman now."

"I'm a widowed woman," Harriet corrected.

Aggie leaned in close and lowered her voice. "All the more reason that you should be addressed proper."

Harriet smiled. There was little point in pressing the matter any further. She'd seen Aggie dig her heels in plenty of times over the years and knew well how this ended. She surrendered dutifully and offered up her cheek for the goodnight kiss she knew would follow before going to bed.

"Goodnight, my little darling." Aggie said with a wink as she pecked her on the cheek.

"Goodnight, Aggie."

A WOMAN OF ILL REPUTE

Sunday morning dawned just as dreary as the day before. The only sign of the sun having risen at all was a faint pinkish hue poking through the clouds to the east. Even that was almost swallowed by the sullen greyness.

The coach arrived at nine, and Harriet stepped outside, taking one last look at her home. She closed the door and placed her palm against the warm wood, then climbed into the coach with Aggie and Lillian. They set off for the Sunday service at St Luke's.

Harriet sat by the window, looking out at the river as they crossed the stone bridge to Main Street. Dirty brown water snaked underneath them and away onto the horizon. The tide was in, so the river was wide, swollen to the tops of its banks. Meagre light glimmered on the rippled surface.

She didn't like this part of town, but it was the closest church to them and it was where Aggie's brother lived. Harriet wanted to see her off with a proper goodbye after church this morning.

Main Street ran along the banks of the River Lune. The

houses stood in tight little rows, as though they were linking arms with each other. Their faces were hard and well-worn, but clean. Weather-beaten women in aprons competed in an endless battle to boast the cleanest entrance to their dwelling place. Always on their knees, they scrubbed hard at the stone steps, wiped windows and swept at the dust and straw that blew about, with great stiff brooms.

The coach rolled to a halt, and the coachman opened the door for Harriet. Stepping out into the cold morning air, she shivered. The atmosphere enveloped her like a wet blanket, dampness permeating her bones. She took in a sweeping view of the street, usually full of grubby children and horse dealers, houses full of working men and women. It was different today.

Everyone was turned out in their Sunday clothes, their children scrubbed red and blotchy. Boots were wiped clean, and women donned their best shawls and bonnets—not a dirty apron in sight. Even the gypsies had blackened and polished their boots and wore neckties, their little girls sporting ringlets and ribbons in their hair.

Harriet watched as they filed into church, imagining what sort of people they might be. What did their daily lives look like? How did they conduct themselves in private? There were often newspaper reports of arguments and brawling in this street. Harriet secretly found them an entertaining read. In the way one might view a curiosity at the fair. A kind of spectacle. Wonderfully entertaining, from the other side of the glass.

Most of her class viewed the working people as one entity; a mass of bodies enclosed by some invisible boundary. They never entertained the idea of its being otherwise. But as Harriet sat among them, she could see the individuals of that great flock. Each with their own story, like her, and she wondered how much of what she read was really true. After all, it was universally acknowledged that newspapers were notoriously biased. They were always painting one party or another in a false light.

Aggie startled her with a discreet jab of her elbow as they made their way into the church. "Quick," she whispered, "sit down before that infernal bleedin' woman beckons us over. She's making straight for you."

It was too late. Hortense Watson had already slithered over. A woman whose piety was rivalled only by her self-importance, she moved like a viper and was equally venomous. Everything about her was sharp—her long nose, pointed chin and slanted eyes. She had a way of tipping her head back so that she looked down from under half-closed lids. It gave an impression of distaste for everyone she spoke to.

"Good morning Harriet, it's lovely to see you." She said in her nasal tone. "We were all so sad to hear about your—" she paused as if searching for the right word, "situation." The word hung between them, swollen with accusation, and the snake's eyes gleamed.

So she knows. Harriet offered her a tight smile and glided into the pew before her. Aggie and Lillian followed, and Hortense seated herself at the end, hands folded neatly in her lap.

As the congregation settled in, a hushed murmur rippled through the nave, and Harriet noticed people looking toward the back of the church. An elegant lady in exquisite dress walked up the aisle and looked about her for somewhere to sit. The murmurs silenced in her wake, as though rendered mute by some invisible force. She paused two or three times, at pews with empty spaces, but the ladies in the aisle stared straight ahead, refusing to acknowledge her.

How incredibly odd. Why are they behaving in such a way?

They all pretended not to notice her. She then approached

Harriet's pew, and Hortense gave her the same reception, raising her chin and staring straight ahead.

Harriet couldn't believe she was bearing witness to such unchristian acts and in church, of all places. She lifted Lillian onto her knee and beckoned the woman to sit beside her, leaving Hortense obliged to stand to let her pass.

The woman smiled and thanked Harriet in a delicate French accent. It wasn't the pretentious tone of Parisians she'd met, but softer. More southern, perhaps, but she couldn't be sure.

Harriet paid no attention to the service. She couldn't concentrate—couldn't stop looking at Hortense. She wore the sternest of expressions, and her back was poker straight. Her foot tapped furiously, as though she couldn't quite contain her annoyance.

After the final prayers, when everyone stood to leave, Hortense leapt to her feet and exited the church like a horse bolting from the starting gate.

The French lady took Harriet's hand and kissed her knuckles. "Merci Madame," she said, "I will not forget your kindness." She smiled at Lillian and left before Harriet had a chance to say anything.

"Well," said Aggie, "what on earth was that all about?"

"I have no idea, but it certainly upset Hortense, did it not?"

They didn't have to wait long to discover the reason for such odd behaviour because the viper was waiting outside.

"Oh, Mrs Blackthorn, what an unfortunate mistake to make. I *do* hope you will recover from this dreadful faux pas with your reputation untarnished." She smiled with malevolence.

Harriet's brows knit. *What does she mean?*

Hortense continued. "I do *so* hate to see a good woman's downfall." The words slid from her acid tongue.

"What faux pas?" Harriet retorted with barely disguised impatience.

"Why, that unfortunate business in church before the service. Decent women like ourselves should never be seen in the company of a woman of her character. I must admit, I was surprised when you allowed her to sit by you. But then, perhaps you're unaware of her..." She paused again then lowered her voice. "Reputation." The word sat for a moment. "Perhaps if the other ladies are of a forgiving nature such as myself, they might overlook your error. But you know how easy it is to lose your place in society." She smirked, and Harriet fought the sudden impulse to slap her.

Hortense drew herself up to her full height and raised her chin. Fangs bared and slick with poison, she leaned in close to Harriet's ear and hissed. "She is a woman of ill repute." She placed special emphasis on the last two words.

Harriet looked at her with an expression one might wear when regarding a maggot wriggling in a rancid carcass. Her voice was calm—warm even—which only sharpened the sting. "Good day to you, Hortense. And in the words of our good book: may the Lord pour upon you the riches of his mercy and his grace. For you are in greater need of it than most."

Hortense's mouth hung open as Harriet marched past, with Lillian and Aggie following like ducks. Harriet had never been so furious on someone else's behalf.

Aggie had to break into a jog to keep up with her. "Never in all my born days have I met a woman as vile as Hortense Watson," she said. "She makes my blood boil. And that holier than thou attitude. How she can sit in God's house and be such a hypocrite I'll never know."

"Hypocrites are often clothed in righteous robes, Aggie."

Aggie crossed her arms over her chest. "Well, I can't abide her. She's a rotten piece of work, she is. You showed her though, didn't you? Wiped that nasty grin off her big old snake's head. Hmph," she said, her mouth set in a grim line of displeasure.

"Who was she—the French lady?" Harriet asked.

Aggie shrugged. "Whoever she is, she's made enemies in all the wrong places."

~

AGGIE WAS STILL RANTING when they arrived at her brother's front door. She was just raising her hand to knock when a voice from behind them called out, "Aggie. I'm here."

John broke into a trot, which did little to alter his speed of approach. It only shook him about and seemed to make harder work of the distance remaining between them. He arrived, red faced and breathless, bending double with hands on his knees. "I saw you—coming out—but—I couldn't catch up," he wheezed, raising a finger as if to say, give me a minute. When he finally composed himself, he beamed at them and knelt down to speak to Lillian.

"Now then, little 'un," he said, "shall we go inside and see what we've got for you? I think I might just have something a little bit special. What d'you say?"

Lillian nodded and squeezed her fists tight.

"Morning, ma'am," he said to Harriet with a nod, then he pulled loose the ribbons of Aggie's bonnet. Aggie laughed and batted his hand away.

Harriet hadn't seen them together many times and was surprised by how they interacted as brother and sister. She hadn't expected their childish playfulness and the happiness it inspired in them. She couldn't remember the last time she'd laughed with such freedom.

John Morrison's house was welcoming, homely, and

considering he lived alone, very tidy. One window struggled valiantly to illuminate the modest space. The flagstone floor was swept clean, and a small tufted rug lay upon it, in front of the hearth. Two high-backed chairs with padded cushions flanked the fireplace, and a number of brass trinkets adorned the mantel. The fire blazing in the grate cast flickering shadows on the whitewashed walls as the flames danced about.

They passed a pleasant morning, with easy conversation and copious amounts of tea, drunk from thick rimmed, earthenware cups. Aggie had made her signature orange sponge cake, and they ate it whilst John told Harriet tales of their childhood and Lillian played on the hearth-rug.

Once again, Harriet thought of her affinity with these simple people and how much closer they felt than anyone else in her life. Most of her acquaintances offered little more than polished exteriors, with nothing underneath. But these people were whole, full of life and kindness. They displayed a quiet dignity in their unassuming manner—something that could not be replicated at will, and very few people in her circle possessed.

She lost herself in this easy atmosphere, gazing into the fire, watching sparks scatter as they flitted up the chimney. Now and then, a curling tendril of smoke peeled away and escaped from the fireplace, hanging in the air and making John's cough start up again.

"I'm awful sorry, Mrs Blackthorn," he coughed again. "Fire blows back terrible when the wind gets up. But there's now't can be done to set it right, short of mastering the weather. And I'd be a more capable man than most if I could master the weather, wouldn't I? Happen I wouldn't need to worry about making my own fires at all." He slapped his knee with a broad, freckled hand and laughed at his own humour. He looked to

Aggie to join him in his amusement, but she too was gazing into the fire.

Her eyes were unfocused, distant. Tears threatened to burst their banks and roll down her cheeks. The cup of tea in her hands was cold and untasted. She had by degrees withdrawn into herself as the time for Harriet's departure grew nearer. She sighed and looked down at her cup.

Harriet and John locked eyes and held their breath as the tears, which threatened only moments ago, spilled over, sliding unabashedly down her face.

"Oh my dearest darling girls," she said, "it breaks my poor old heart that we should be parted after all these years. I don't think I can bear it." She pulled a handkerchief from her sleeve and blew her nose noisily. "What are my idle hands to do without you two to look after?" She gave a shuddering breath. "And what shall my old eyes rest upon if not your faces? You're the two dearest creatures in the whole world to me." She broke into another round of sobs.

Harriet shifted in her seat and fidgeted with the buttons at her throat. She was used to seeing Aggie's outpourings of emotion, but she still didn't know how to handle them. She placed her hand over the old woman's and rubbed her thumb back and forth across her knuckles. "Come now, Aggie, compose yourself or you'll make yourself ill. We won't be so far apart that we cannot visit each other often. You must take comfort in that, surely?"

"Yes, of course," she said between sniffles, "but it's hardly the same. I've never been parted from you, not one solitary night since the day I laid eyes on you. All pink and wrinkled, and come screaming into the world. 'Tis a miserable business."

"A little tot of something stronger might calm her nerves, d'you think, ma'am?" John asked, his eyebrows knit together with concern. He looked as much afraid of setting her off again as Harriet was. "Could you take a little tot of brandy, our Aggie?"

"Aye, that'll do, John. Thank you."

When Aggie had drunk her brandy and was finally settled, they said their goodbyes. With a last embrace and a heart that ached more than she'd expected, Harriet took her leave of the only mother she had ever truly known.

THE GUEST HOUSE

As the carriage rolled into Dalton Square, Harriet glanced out of the window at her temporary home; a large building with a sign over the door which read "Guest House" and underneath "Proprietor Mrs E. Carter."

Emily Carter's guest house was her kingdom. In Lancaster, she dominated the field of hospitality. Other establishments only aspired to reach her level of respectability. Ruthless in her ambition and unrivalled in her thoroughness, she ran a tight ship. She kept her own accounts, bought the kitchen supplies herself and inspected the brass doorknobs daily. It would not do for a greasy fingerprint to spoil the immaculate entrance. If she could ask her guests not to wrinkle the bedsheets, she undoubtedly would have.

The house itself was a proud sandstone building of four floors. Its blank face stared out across the square, its rows of windows like unblinking eyes. Stone pillars flanked its glossy black doors, and eight crescent-shaped steps spilled out onto the pavement like a dog's lolling tongue. The rest of the square was made up of gentlemen's houses, all similar in style—four storeys high with double doors, but Mrs Carter's was the only one with a stone portico, lending the building an air of superiority over the rest.

Harriet went inside and made a swift survey of the interior. It was tasteful and classical in style. From around the edges of woollen carpets, a chestnut-coloured wooden floor shone so highly polished, she dared not step on it. Pictures in gilt frames hung on painted plaster walls, pale blue in colour. The furniture was French in style, carved with intricate patterns, and long velvet curtains framed the windows, spilling onto the carpet in pools of thick fabric.

She noticed a palm in a blue and white pot, its large fronds reaching high up and arching overhead. It reminded Harriet of her own palm and the china pot, which now graced someone else's parlour. The thought pinched her, and she tried to push away the sour feeling of discontent.

Mrs Carter introduced her to some of the long-term residents in the household so that she might be more comfortable when they took meals together. There was a newlywed couple who usually took their meals in their apartment, but everyone else, she was informed, took breakfast and dinner as a group.

Harriet wasn't sure she was ready to make polite small talk with strangers but didn't relish the idea of eating alone either. She assured Mrs Carter that she could be expected at both breakfast and dinner, providing the other residents didn't take issue with a child being included at the dinner table.

"Nonsense!" declared an old gentleman to whom she'd just been introduced. "I for one, would be delighted to see you both there. It's about time we had some young life in this household. You can sit by me, little one, and I'll tell you some stories." He gave Lillian a wink and patted her like a small dog. She treated him to her best smile before moving to hide behind her mother's skirts.

After their introductions and a swift tour of the house, Mrs Carter showed them to their rooms. Their bags were brought in, and a tray of tea sent up with a small selection of sandwiches and cakes, which Lillian devoured.

They took an apartment on the third floor overlooking a neat walled park. There were three rooms: a bedroom, sitting room and a bathing room, with an enormous copper bath. The sitting room faced east to west, running the entire length of the building. It had tall arched windows at both ends, thus offering her the benefit of seeing both sunrise and sunset.

Sunlight flooded in every morning, illuminating the room with an orange glow as it peeked over the silhouetted rooftops of the city. That was a treat indeed. Harriet loved to watch the sun come up. The apartment, she thought, was a perfect stepping stone until she decided on a long-term plan.

It was a shock at first—having to do things for herself. Little things, like fetching her own towel and drawing her own bath. She never knew how difficult it was to dress without help. How on earth was a lady to tighten her corset strings alone? It was impossible. The entire ordeal was exhausting, and she usually found herself panting and hot by the time she finished.

When ordering her mourning attire, she hadn't accounted for fastening the buttons herself. All but one dress buttoned at the back, and since Lillian was far too little to fasten buttons, she had to do them herself. Each day she spent many minutes with one arm stretched over her shoulder, the other reaching upwards to fumble with ineffectual fingers. It was her first experience with intense frustration, and it brought home the urgency of her situation. She must find employment.

Harriet looked for work every day, scanning advertisements in the papers and publications, asking at local businesses, but weeks passed and she found nothing. She needed work soon. The money she had wouldn't last much longer.

She slammed today's paper on the table and walked to the window. *I need air.*

A few moments later, she stepped out into the square, closing her eyes, and drawing in a deep, calming breath. The air was sharp—crisp—and her breath hung in white clouds when she spoke.

Lillian, with a bright red nose and glowing cheeks, giggled at the visible moisture clouds. They walked a little way and took a seat on one of the iron benches. The metal was cold and struck through the many layers of petticoat and dress. She wished she'd brought a blanket to sit on.

Lillian climbed onto her lap and put her head underneath the black veil on Harriet's hat. It wasn't long before she fell asleep, her cheek pressed against the steady rhythmic rise and fall of her mother's chest. Harriet leaned her head back, enjoying the sunshine on her face. Putting a hand into her pocket, she felt the sheet of newspaper she'd kept on her last night at home. She took it out and unfolded it, smoothing out the creases.

> ***THE LANCASTER GAZETTE Saturday 23rd July 1853***
>
> ***A Bunker's Hill Row-*** *Ann, wife of Robert Airey, wheelwright of Bunker's Hill, Skerton; and Ann, wife of Thomas Willock of Main street, Skerton, carver, were charged with assaulting Ann, wife of Thos. Redhead, also of Bunker's Hill...*

She scanned the lines of text.

> *On Tuesday 12th, the defendants, having oiled their tongues with a little Jamaica Water, proceeded to the complainant's house and called her such names as although the complainant scrupled not to repeat them in court, decency forbids our printing...*

Harriet chuckled at the appalling behaviour, but she read on, eager to hear the result of the women's drunken debacle.

> *Airey and Willock made use of filthy and disgusting language, and Airey shook her fist in Redhead's face, saying she would kill her if she was to go to the door....*

Harriet couldn't help but laugh at the thought of the three Anns and their rum-fuelled disagreement. She shook her head and folded the sheet back into her pocket. She was still smiling when she looked up to see the lady from the church approaching.

"Mrs Blackthorn, I believe?" She said in her musical French accent and extended her hand.

Harriet tried to stand but was spared the effort as the lady bent to reach her.

"Good morning. I'm afraid we didn't have the pleasure of an introduction when we met last. I am Harriet."

The woman kissed her on both cheeks through her black lace barrier, and the unprovoked contact left Harriet slightly off-kilter.

"Delphine de Matthieu," she said. "It is wonderful to see you again. I have looked for you these past few weeks, but I did not see you in church again. Do you live close by?"

She went back to that church after what happened?

"I did, but I'm afraid I don't currently have a permanent

residence," Harriet said. "I'm staying at the guest house across the square until I find somewhere to live."

"Oh, I see," said Delphine. She looked confused, or perhaps concerned; Harriet couldn't tell.

"Would you like to join me for some tea inside? It's bitterly cold out here, and I can hardly see you through my veil." Harriet said, nodding her head towards the guest house.

Mrs de Matthieu cocked her head and considered her. "Why don't you take it off?"

Harriet sucked in a breath. Why didn't she take it off? Her hand moved toward it instinctively, then she hesitated. People would talk. People like Hortense. "I'd rather go inside," she said. "Lillian's getting cold."

"Oui, oui, of course. You must take the little one inside. It is very cold," she replied, and they walked back to the house.

The morning passed with ease as they drank tea in the shared parlour, revelling in each other's company. She stayed well beyond the prescribed fifteen-minute limitation of polite visits. They found they had much in common—well matched in both their education and opinions. Before parting, they agreed to meet the following week to take a walk together. Harriet was very much looking forward to it.

When she wasn't looking for employment, Harriet busied herself with other matters. There was much paperwork regarding Arthur's estate—legal matters which required her to return to Mr Oglethorpe's offices. There were domestic tasks like clothes to be washed and stockings to be mended. These menial tasks kept her mind from her worries.

The problem was when she was at leisure, in the moments when Lillian was asleep and her work was done. That was when she failed to convince herself that things would get better. The evenings were lonely and stretched long into the night. Her meandering thoughts gathered like fog at the edges of day. In the small hours of dusk and dawn—when the world was sleepy—her disquiet magnified, unwilling to be ignored.

She missed Aggie and their simple conversation, the comfort that only comes with years of familiarity. She missed her house and her possessions, the stories they told, like tangible fragments of the life she used to know. The few belongings she did have were scattered around the apartment. A photograph of Arthur, a small portrait of her father, a silver trinket box which had belonged to her mother, but even these familiar things could not replicate the sense of home she attached to Aggie.

She belonged nowhere. The things surrounding her now were someone else's memories: a borrowed life. It was like wearing someone else's shoes. She picked up the photograph of Arthur and scowled at it before setting it face down on the table. It was a petty act of displeasure, she knew, but it felt good in the moment.

Because of his behaviour, her status was no longer equivalent to her upbringing. She was less than equal. This lack of consideration for his family sat heavy in her chest. How he could gamble away their entire fortune, she would never understand. Worse than that, her father's fortune, that he had worked so very hard for. An honest working man who had carved out his own path, made his own fortune, and provided a wonderful life for his family. Everything he'd worked for, Arthur had frittered away without a second thought for her or Lillian.

If Lillian had been a son, they would be living at Herdwick House now. But for whatever reason, the world did not see fit to honour women as it did men. It would have been a wonderful home for them, had it not been tied up by the rules of entailment.

A better man than Edward would have allowed his cousin's widow and daughter to live out their days in the comfort of their family home, but Edward was no such man. A rapscallion whose intellect fell short of his ambition. Would she have begrudged him any less, had he been a righteous and morally upstanding man? She couldn't say with honesty, but his shortfalls certainly rubbed salt into the wound.

She stared out of the window across the city, and the view matched her mood. Church spires, towers and jagged rooftops punctured the taut line of the horizon. The sky was angry, a molten fiery red that throbbed and intensified the longer she stared at it. She knew it was fruitless to rage against what couldn't be altered, but when everything practical has been actioned, what is there left but to feel? It was a new state of being for Harriet. One she did not like.

A sudden and sharp rap on the door startled her, and Mrs Carter announced that there was a man here to see her. Harriet wondered if it might be Arthur's family after all. Perhaps Edward had come to take them to Herdwick House. But he wouldn't know she was here, would he?

A GENTLEMAN CALLS

Mrs Carter poked her head into the room. "There's a gentleman caller here to see you Mrs Blackthorn."

"Who is it Mrs Carter? I'm not expecting anyone."

"It's a Mr Hardcastle." She handed Harriet a calling card with the name embossed in fine black script. "I've never seen him before, but I've heard tell they're the new tenants at the big house over in Skerton." She paused, scanning the room and, finding no-one else, continued in hushed tones. "They say he came here under a bit of a black cloud, he and his family. From down south, but no one seems to know what happened." She imparted this useless scrap of gossip voluntarily, as was her habit, and gave a little nod when she'd finished.

In the short time she'd been there, Harriet had grown accustomed to Mrs Carter's unusual qualities. Once having established an individual as a definite patron of the guest house, she dropped her well-bred British accent and returned to her native Lancashire dialect. She shrugged off the majestic air, indispensable to her in attracting the right clientele, and set about befriending her guests so that she might procure some gossip.

"Shall I send him up then, Mrs Blackthorn? Will you receive him in your apartment?" The gleam in her eye showed a little too much excitement for Harriet's liking.

"No," she said, "I'll receive him downstairs. Please tell him I will be along presently. And can you ask the maid to sit with Lillian?"

Mrs Carter nodded and left the room disappointed. Harriet shook her head at the thought of Emily Carter's encounters with new customers. The grave dignity and upper-class accent were wholly believable to strangers, but a source of great comedy to those who already knew her.

She headed downstairs to greet her mystery caller. It was an unusually bright morning for November. The sun streamed in across the breakfast room with such ferocity that Harriet had to shade her eyes when she entered. The brilliant light behind him threw Mr Hardcastle so completely into the shade that she could only see him in silhouette form.

He stood and offered her a clammy hand, introducing himself as Caiaphas Hardcastle.

"Pleased to meet you, Mr Hardcastle." She replied.

A long, crooked nose pointed to a pair of thin lips which lay just underneath it. His eyes were weak and watery and sat much too close together to lend the impression of honesty or sincerity to his expression. It was the face of a lean and sickly man, incongruous with the broad figure standing before her.

"Forgive me Madam, for the intrusion, but there's a matter of urgency in the proposition I intend to put to you."

We're not wasting any time with pleasantries then—straight to business.

"I'm led to believe you are an exceptionally learned woman, Mrs Blackthorn. In fact." He paused. "I have it on good authority that there isn't a man this side of the country equal to your scholastic achievements." He watched her as the weight of that sank in. "I have two children in desperate need of an education."

"I see," said Harriet. "And on whose authority you have acquired this information?" Whoever he'd spoken to knew about her education. By the time she'd reached twelve, her intellect had surpassed that of every governess her father had employed. He had to hire a retired professor to teach her instead.

Mr Hardcastle placed his elbows on the arms of the chair and pressed his splayed fingertips together but did not answer her question. "We arrived here only recently, and our governess could not accompany us." His head tilted to one side. "And so, alas, I'm afraid my children will become quite feral." He arched a thin brow. "Am I correct in my assumption that you are looking for employment?"

Harriet spoke slowly. "I am looking for work, that much is true. But—"

He interrupted her mid-sentence to continue his line of inquiry. "Then might I hope you'll consider the position?"

Something about him bothered her. Apart from being interrupted, which she did not appreciate, there was something else. The way he drew out his words, played with them, like a cat taunting its prey.

"Well, I must tell you Mr Hardcastle, that my abilities have been somewhat exaggerated. Besides, it would be highly irregular to take a widow as a governess." She smoothed the folds of her skirt, unsure of what to do with her hands.

"As for your exaggerated abilities Mrs Blackthorn, let us not be too modest. Your reputation precedes you." The words dripped like honey, but there was cruelty in his smile.

"I also have a child of my own Mr Hardcastle. What would

I be expected to do with her whilst I gave lessons?" Harriet asked, not sure what she wanted the answer to be.

"I would be more than happy for your child to attend lessons along with my own, and so you see, the problem is quite removed. She would not need to be parted from you at all." He paused, and something passed across his features that she could not interpret. He considered her for a moment and then added, "I do apologise for the rushed manner of my proposal Mrs Blackthorn. I rather feel that I have accosted you with it, but time really is of the essence."

In the five minutes she'd been standing in the room with Mr Hardcastle, she had returned his every comment with a reason that his idea wouldn't work. She'd searched for weeks, hoping and worrying about finding work, and here it was, offered to her on a plate. A respectable position like this was not easily found and even less likely to be as accommodating to her situation. *I must be quite mad.*

Unconventional as it was, the thought of not being parted from Lillian appealed to her enough to ignore her unease. She was in no position to turn up her nose at such an opportunity.

"And the salary, Mr Hardcastle?" She asked.

"How very direct of you Mrs Blackthorn," he said, smiling again. The smile did not register any warmth in his eyes and did little to brighten his sallow complexion.

"Well, Mr Hardcastle, since you are so eager to settle the business quickly, I see no benefit in either of us dragging it out. It's better, I think, to be direct, especially in matters of business."

He watched her for a long moment, then laughed as though the idea of a woman in business was ridiculous to him. "I think we're going to get along rather well Mrs Blackthorn. Board and lodgings are included with the position, and the salary is forty pounds a year, paid at a rate of sixteen shillings per week, with two weeks unpaid leave."

It was far less than she'd ever had to live on before, but it was a great deal better than nothing. "Very well Mr Hardcastle, I accept."

"Wonderful! I'll send the carriage for you on Friday, then you'll have the weekend to settle in before you start." He concluded their business with another clammy handshake and turned to leave.

Harriet stared at the spot where his hand had touched hers and wiped it on her dress more forcefully than she'd meant to.

MRS CARTER ACCOSTED Harriet on her way upstairs. "Everything alright Mrs Blackthorn? Was your visit with the gentleman satisfactory?"

"Yes, thank you," she said, not intending to indulge Mrs Carter's insatiable appetite for tattle.

"I thought you'd want some tea," she said, lifting the tea tray as though Harriet couldn't see it until then.

"No thank you. I have some errands to run." She took a step forward and then thought better of it. She knew the barrage of thinly veiled attempts to uncover information would only cease upon the fulfilment of said quest. "He came to offer me employment as governess to his children," she said, resigning herself to having this conversation. "I have accepted the position, and I will be leaving on Friday." She watched the news soak in, and Mrs Carter came to life like a parched plant, newly watered.

"Oh, I see. Well now, that is news indeed. Should we celebrate with this nice pot of tea then?" She said, evidently still hoping to be invited in for more.

"No thank you. I really must go out." Harriet left her on the stairs and went back to her apartment. She gathered Lillian and buttoned her into her coat and bonnet. They were already late to meet Delphine.

She tried to summon some excitement to tell her the news, but found it more difficult than she would have liked. Something pulled at her from the corners of her mind. A thought, not fully formed but gathering substance. Necessity pushed it aside.

"I have good news!" She said with as much enthusiasm as she could muster. "I've found employment quite out of the blue. A gentleman came to see me this morning and offered me a position in Skerton. I'll be moving there on Friday."

"Well, that's wonderful news. I'm very glad for you." Delphine said. She looked genuinely pleased. "And what is the nature of your employment?"

Harriet looked down at her hands. "I shall be working for the Hardcastle family." Her enthusiasm was almost spent already.

Delphine looked confused. "In what capacity?"

"Well, I'm to be governess to their two children, and Lillian can join in the lessons." Harriet winced as she said the words out loud, the reality of it only now setting in. *I'm going to be a governess. A servant.*

Delphine studied her. She looked as though she were struggling to find something to say. "Oh, I see."

Her reaction did little to ease Harriet's discomfort. "I'm aware that it's a little unconventional, but Mr Hardcastle was quite sure of it." She didn't know if she was trying to convince Delphine or herself. "And I'm afraid the period of grace my funds afforded me is nearly at its end. I have no choice but to accept the offer."

Delphine's brow knit into a frown. "Hardcastle. The name seems familiar, but I cannot place it. Is it a local family name?"

"No, I do not think so. I believe the family moved here recently, although I don't know where from. The little I have heard is from idle chatter and not to be taken seriously." Harriet said. She should have gained a more thorough understanding of her new employer before accepting his offer. She remembered what Mrs Carter had said and turned the thought over in her mind. "Under a black cloud." But then her gossip was usually unfounded and probably best forgotten.

"Is it what you want?" Delphine asked, feeding Lillian a large piece of cake. "I believe it is a rather solitary lifestyle."

Lillian opened her mouth and smiled, crumbs escaping down the front of her dress.

It was not what Harriet wanted to hear, and she wondered if all French women were so straightforward. Delphine simply asked whatever she wanted to know, without flourish or ceremony, just direct and personal questions. Harriet had never encountered such forthrightness in her circle.

She wondered what Hortense had heard about this lady. And if there *was* anything untoward, was there any truth to it? Perhaps Hortense found her familiarity with strangers crass and unrefined. She'd heard of people losing their reputations for similar things. Some based on rumours with little more substance than Mrs Carter's.

One could never quite tell with Hortense. She was always so ready to impart her malice. With the right poison, she could easily taint the opinion of the masses, infecting all those who were otherwise inclined to a more sympathetic view. Once a sense of impropriety had been awakened, Hortense was deft in communicating it to the rest of the flock. There it spread like fire among dry leaves.

In any case, Harriet couldn't muster enough negativity to dislike her new friend. She'd always taken people as she found them and wasn't going to change that now. She'd make up her own mind about Delphine. And besides, she was so very lonely.

"Harriet?"

Harriet looked up from her plate, startled. "Oh, I'm sorry. I must have drifted into my thoughts."

"Good heavens, have I become so tedious as to put you half to sleep with my conversation? This will not do. I must engage in something utterly scandalous right away." She laughed like a child, and Harriet felt her face redden.

"Oh, Harriet, I'm only teasing. There's no need to be embarrassed." She smiled, a wide, easy smile that lit up her face with genuine warmth and affection.

For all her directness, there was something about Delphine that drew Harriet in. She wanted to answer her questions. She was so frank and sincere, and she listened when Harriet spoke to her—really listened—cared even, about what she had to say. There was a softness in her expression, a magnetism in the way she smiled. Her laugh was like the tinkling of tiny bells, like the faeries Harriet had seen in picture books as a child.

Delphine reached across the table for Harriet's hand. "I am merely concerned for your happiness, that is all. If you are pleased, then I'm delighted for you."

"Thank you. I'm afraid only time will tell if I'm suited to the lifestyle, but I've always had a passion for knowledge. Even in girlhood, I understood the power of it—the advantages it afforded to men—so I'm certain I'll enjoy teaching.

"Well, then it sounds perfect for you." Delphine raised her teacup in a toast. "To knowledge," she said, and this time, they both laughed.

It felt good to laugh. Harriet had been struck with such a pang of loneliness since her sudden upheaval that the desire to have a friend was overwhelming. She needed a confidante, someone to share thoughts and conversation with. She had plenty of acquaintances, and there had always been Aggie of course, but she was more of a mother figure to Harriet. She had never had a friend—not really.

Both herself and Delphine seemed bereft of any relationship resembling a sisterly alliance. The loneliness of one soul called out to the other, recognising in it a kindred spirit.

LUNEBANK HALL

By Saturday evening, Harriet and Lillian had settled into their new home. Their dwelling places had diminished in size with each move until their circumstances were now reduced to a single room. It was however, a very pleasant room. Light and spacious, with a large wooden bed and three windows of generous proportions, from which she could see the river. The walls were painted white and the floorboards unpolished, but Harriet liked its simplicity. She didn't need finery to be happy. She was content to be with Lillian and thankful for this new opportunity.

A wardrobe stood opposite the bed, and a chest of drawers knelt squat beside it. On it rested a large earthenware jug and bowl. They were old, and the glaze was cracked, the way mud does when there's a shortage of rain for some time. It was chipped around the base and no longer watertight, the porous clay exposed underneath. When she picked it up, it left a ring of damp on the dresser.

There was a fireplace on another wall and a bookcase. Not an empty bookcase, but four entire shelves, packed with neat rows of books. Glorious, wonderful books. What was in the books was a matter of complete indifference to Harriet. She was so delighted at the prospect of having reading material other than newspapers. There was even a high-backed chair so that she could read by the fire.

They spent the first day unpacking and made some paper flowers from the old newspapers she'd kept, stringing them along the walls to add cheer to the room. Lillian loved them and reached up to touch them every time she passed by in her mother's arms.

There was just one item of furniture missing that Harriet thought necessary. A small table or desk to write her letters on or to set down a plate or cup. *I'll search the secondhand furniture shops in town at the earliest possible opportunity.* The thought pleased her.

It is strange how quickly a person's sense of finding pleasure adapts to its circumstances. The more restricted they became, the more she found pleasure in new and simple things. Small, unnoticed things. The smell of a book's pages, or a match newly struck, the feel of summer grass under foot or even the simple pleasure of a string of newspaper flowers.

Harriet lifted the sash of the middle window, and cold air billowed in. She rubbed her arms and shivered; the air sending ripples of discomfort over her skin as it erupted into goose bumps. The hour wasn't late, but the sun had already descended below the horizon, and she could pick out one or two bright stars already among the violet clouds.

She thought about Aggie, a mere three hundred yards away on Main Street. So close, but a world away. How excited she would be when she found out they were living in such close proximity. Harriet hadn't had a chance to tell her yet, but she would make the short walk to visit her tomorrow.

Upon arrival yesterday, she'd been introduced to the children and, of course, the lady of the house, Mrs Hardcastle. She seemed agreeable enough, a woman not much older than herself, about five and twenty years, with rose-tinted cheeks and a shy smile. By looking at them, Harriet estimated that there were perhaps ten or fifteen years between Mr and Mrs Hardcastle. But their natures gave the impression of a more substantial age gap.

Mr Hardcastle was confident—decisive. Mrs Hardcastle, on the other hand, was a timid and twitching thing. She flitted about the place like an insect, never staying in one place for too long. Her movements were sharp and uncertain. She seemed somewhat troubled by a lack of understanding and looked to Mr Hardcastle for guidance when she was addressed by anyone else.

Perhaps she's shy and relies on his encouragement to speak, Harriet thought. It made her seem considerably younger than him, like a child. It was as though her sense of self was completely reliant upon her husband.

Harriet knew all too well that husbands were not to be relied upon and thought to herself that poor Mrs Hardcastle had yet to discover this.

There was a tap on the door, and a young voice called her name. "Mrs Blackthorn?" It was unsure, like a question. "Are ye there?"

"Yes, do come in," Harriet said, not moving to open the door.

"It's only me—Maria. I've brought up your supper for you and the little 'un." She nudged open the door with her elbow and came sideways into the room, holding an enormous wooden tray. Her arms were spread wide to reach the handles, and she had to bend forward to accommodate its weight. She was petite in stature and rather frail-looking. Too frail to carry such a large and heavy tray.

Harriet looked from the tray of food back to Maria with confusion. "I assumed that Lillian and I would take our meals in the kitchen with the rest of the staff."

The young maid's face paled. "Did you not take your vittles in your room yesterday, ma'am?" She said.

"Well yes I did but that was a singular occurrence because we arrived after your usual mealtime. I intended to join you downstairs this evening."

"Oh no Madam, that's not the way 'tis done here."

Harriet just stared, waiting for some further explanation.

"You mustn't eat with the likes of us," Maria said, "you're not a servant ma'am, you're with the master's children you see, so you must be like the genteels, not like us." She looked down at her tray. "T'other lady always took her vittles in her room."

"So we are to eat alone?" Harriet asked, "In our room?" How could she have been so stupid? Of course she wouldn't be allowed to socialise with the servants. She ought to have known that. In truth, she knew little about the life of a governess, other than that they were usually spinsters.

Maria offered a meek smile, and Harriet took the tray from her, setting it down on the bed.

"Thank you Maria, it was very good of you to bring it up. And you know you shouldn't speak of yourself that way."

Maria offered no sign of understanding.

"When you said 'the likes of us'. It's not right for a woman to reduce herself like that. You're a respectable young woman, are you not?"

"Of course, ma'am," Maria answered and gave a small curtsy as if to demonstrate her respectability.

"And are we not all God's children and, as such, equal?" In that moment, Harriet thought she believed that.

Maria said nothing.

"Then why should you consider yourself unworthy of eating in any other person's company?"

Then Maria laughed without humour and clamped a hand over her mouth. "Beggin' your pardon, ma'am, but where have you come from? We're not people here. People with thoughts an' feelings an' ideas of our own. We're just staff. No use in thinking of it otherwise 'cause it shan't ever be different." She shrugged her shoulders, smiling without happiness. "I'll leave you to your meal." She bobbed another curtsy and closed the door behind her.

The room felt emptier than it had before. Maria's view of the world was alien to Harriet. She couldn't imagine ever treating her staff like that. Her father never had. *It seems I have overestimated my worldliness.*

She woke Lillian and gave her something to eat. The food was good. The meat was plentiful, and the gravy rich and tasting of wine. She tried her best to eat it, but she had no appetite. It stuck in her throat, refusing to be swallowed down without enormous effort.

Of course, she hadn't expected to dine with the Hardcastle family. She was not so naive as that. They wouldn't embrace a paid member of the household as an equal, despite her former station. She had, however, looked forward to being a part of the family unit the staff created for themselves. It never occurred to her that she would be placed above the rest and excluded from that community as well.

This was an unexpected revelation: that there was in fact another place in society. A place between worlds that was neither one thing nor the other—somewhere in-between the lines—with a different set of rules entirely. In the ridiculous hierarchy of society, she alone appeared to inhabit this unique station.

She realised then that, with all her education, she still had much to learn about life. It wasn't only her physical circumstances that had changed but her entire world. Her station lowered, social circle emptied, finances diminished and Lillian's prospects for the future irrevocably altered. She was outcast from society, the idealised perception of leisurely womanhood, cast off like an old coat.

Her own naivety mocked her. *I'm a child,* she thought, *nothing more than a stupid child.*

Sinking onto the bare floorboards, she wept bitter tears until her eyes stung and her nose reddened.

Some time later, when she finally stilled, spent and exhausted with the effort, she crawled into bed beside Lillian and fell asleep.

~

THAT FIRST MONTH at Lunebank Hall was difficult for Harriet. Though she'd expected hardship, the loneliness still surprised her. Aggie and Delphine became the two bright spots on which she centred her thoughts. She saw them most weeks and looked forward to their meetings with relish. They were the only company she had and helped enormously in keeping up her spirits. By degrees, she adapted her expectations and came to find satisfaction in her work, if not happiness.

Mrs Hardcastle had warmed to her, although at times, seemed a little dubious, but her two young charges were manageable and took to instruction better than she'd hoped. In fact, she rather enjoyed the teaching. She was kept busy most of the time. The days were full and passed quickly.

Lillian loved being with the other children, and Harriet enjoyed seeing her laugh and play.

As the nights drew in, December arrived with cruelty. It was the coldest Harriet had ever experienced, and the shortened daylight made for long and solitary evenings. Winter flexed its icy fingers across the landscape, stilling water and turning skeleton trees to glass. Silver crept along the ground like spilled paint, and any foliage still living, bent low to the ground, frozen in silent worship.

A keen wind from the east brought sleet and freezing rain that bit the flesh. It pursued Harriet into her chambers at night, rattling windows and blowing down the chimney. She did her best to keep the room warm with the modest fire, but the ceiling pitched high above her head, and drew upward what little heat she managed to generate.

She'd saved enough money to buy a table and a small amount of coarse fabric to make curtains. They kept out the draught from the window casement, which helped, but did not prevent ice from crossing the glass threshold. It stole in like a thief, marking the panes with intricately woven patterns of leaf and vine, painted with shards and splinters of ice.

Sometimes, she was so cold she thought she'd wake to find the same sparkling foliage etched upon her skin. If the room did on occasion get warm enough, the ice on the inside of the windows melted and dripped off the windowsill, leaving little pools of water on the floor.

When Christmas came, she found relief in the company of her old friends. Delphine invited them to spend Christmas Day with her, and she would have liked to, but she could never refuse Aggie.

Aggie and John were both leaving soon after Christmas, headed for the Northeast. John had taken up a position there as resident blacksmith on a very large estate in County Durham. Aggie had acquired a respectable position in the household, and they were to live in a fine cottage on the grounds of the estate.

She hadn't seen Aggie so animated for a long time, and she

was pleased for them both, but could hardly bring herself to think of their leaving.

"You'd love it if you saw it you know," said John. "It's just like our Aggie always wanted when we were little childer." He looked so happy when he spoke of it. "It's a fine house with five rooms and plaster on the walls. There's a kitchen garden for her to grow her own vegetables, and there's a bed a'front with flowers in it, all fancy like what the gentry have."

Harriet stole a glance at Aggie and saw that she was beaming at her brother. "It sounds wonderful, John," Harriet said. "I'm sure you will both be very happy there."

"Aye, and I'll tell you what else. I'm going to plant a big red climbing rose over the door just like you wanted, Aggie." He winked at Harriet. "It's going to be that grand, she'll be proud as punch to have visitors to come and take tea with us. Won't you, old lass?"

Harriet didn't know which was more endearing, John's effort to please his sister or Aggie's obvious pride in him.

They all attended the Christmas Day service at St Luke's, where Hortense thankfully kept her opinions in her mouth. The peal of bells from the church was beautiful. It called the parishioners out of their houses like a swarm of ants abandoning a nest. Everyone was smiling, shaking hands and wishing each other peace and good will. The children were boisterous and full of the joys of the season.

After the service, John joined a number of his friends in visiting the neighbours to drink to a 'Merry Christmas' and wish each other all the joy and happiness they could muster.

"Get on with you, John, be out from under my feet while we get the dinner sorted," Aggie said, swatting him away with a tea towel.

John only grinned, saluted her and went on his way.

She flitted around the kitchen all morning, cutting and

peeling, roasting and boiling. Harriet was hardly given a task to complete, so concerned was Aggie that everything must be just to her own liking. There had never been such fretting over a pudding as Aggie did that morning. She tended to it constantly to make sure it hadn't boiled dry—peeling back the cloth and pressing the top to see if it was firm. After that, she tied it back up and placed it on the stove, watching it as though it might get up and run away when she turned her back. She worked herself into such a lather about it, her cheeks glowed red and she had to mop her brow every few minutes with the skirt of her apron.

By the time John came back, everything was ready. The table was laid with a white cloth and their mother's best china. They feasted on roast beef and mashed potatoes, stuffing and rich golden gravy, applesauce and carrots. It was a feast fit for royalty.

They each had a cracker to pull, with a hat and sweets inside, wrapped in brightly coloured paper. This was Lillian's favourite part of all. She squealed and clapped her hands at the loud bang the crackers made.

When the pudding was ready, Aggie, still fretting, untied the cloth and peeled it back. Then, placing a plate over the top, she flipped it upside down with a flick of her wrists, turning it out onto the plate with a dull thud. She lifted the bowl ever so slowly, praying to the god of puddings, that it would not stick or break apart. The bowl came off clean, and the muslin cloth peeled away to reveal a perfectly domed pudding.

Aggie sent Harriet back to the table to take her seat whilst she made her grand entrance. She wished the pudding to be beheld in its full majesty when it entered the room, ablaze with lighted brandy and crowned with a sprig of berried holly.

Setting it on the table, she beamed like a mother showing off a newborn babe.

"Oh, Aggie, what a grand pudding tha's made our lass. She's a beauty," John said, rubbing his rough hands together.

Aggie said nothing, only smiled wider and continued to serve up her culinary masterpiece with great ceremony. Before taking a bite of her own pudding, she watched the faces of her companions, studying their expressions for clues, willing them to voice their approval.

John was first. He leaned back in his chair and rubbed his broad belly in appreciation. "Finest pudding as was ever made to grace the tongues of men, our Aggie."

Aggie, sufficiently pleased with John's poetic homage to the pudding, smiled and ate her own.

When they'd eaten and cleaned away, they sat in front of the fire with a little sherry each and talked of Aggie and John's plans for their new household.

"Oh, I do wish you could come with us, my lovelies," Aggie said, squeezing Lillian in a fierce embrace. Lillian wriggled free of the old woman's kisses with squeals of laughter and bounced straight into John's arms. He kissed her too, and she gave Aggie a sly grin, knowing she provoked the Aggie's jealousy.

"Oh, you little rascal. There'll be no more kisses for you!" Aggie shook her fist in mock rage, and Lillian dissolved into giggles again, pleased with the fuss she caused.

Harriet smiled, wishing the day would last a little longer. She wasn't sure her heart could take this separation. She feared the silence that would follow, the hollow space they would leave behind.

CAIAPHAS

Harriet wrote to Aggie and John regularly and awaited their replies with anticipation, eager for news of their new lives. She hoped, for Aggie's sake, that it was all she'd hoped for.

She'd noticed recently a blossoming friendship between Mrs Hardcastle and Hortense. It was a strange and unlikely pairing.

Hortense had first called un-announced one day in February when Mrs Hardcastle was sitting in on the children's English lesson. The lesson was being held in the morning room, as the schoolroom was acquiring a fresh coat of paint, and so this was where Hortense was received.

Harriet knew Hortense well enough to expect her disapproval at such an informal reception. She was right. It was apparent in her indignant expression, her stiff posture. She even recoiled from the children, regarding them with distaste as she entered the room.

After the two ladies greeted each other, Hortense turned to look at Harriet.

With a nod of her head, Harriet said, "Good morning, Hortense."

Hortense cleared her throat. "Mrs Watson, if you please."

So, this is how it's to be?

Evidently, she was still smarting from the church fiasco last year, and her forked tongue had not retired. The demotion in Harriet's station was going to be her primary source of ammunition. "Of course, Mrs Watson," Harriet managed through gritted teeth. She dreaded the influence Hortense might exert over the anxious and timid Mrs Hardcastle, and what that might mean for her life here.

Mrs Hardcastle so readily accepted instruction from other people, she would be a lamb to the slaughter in the hands of that woman.

Hortense continued her abasement of Harriet with each visit. On one occasion she leaned in to whisper to Mrs Hardcastle, her voice still audible, and said, "It surprises me, Mrs Hardcastle, that you have taken a widow as a governess. Very brave, I must say."

Mrs Hardcastle twisted her handkerchief. "Oh?"

"Personally, I would not have the courage to do something quite so..." She used her trademark weighted pause. "Unorthodox." She sat back in her chair, letting her statement steep for a moment in Mrs Hardcastle's mind.

The latter looked bewildered. "Unorthodox?"

"Oh yes, quite," Hortense said.

Mrs Hardcastle's confused expression did not alter, so she continued.

"You see, the problem with a widow is this. She is a woman with all the experience of matrimony, if you understand my meaning." She glanced sidelong at Harriet. "Yet she exists outside the bounds of its constraints, and *therein* lies the danger." Her eyes held a wicked glint. "It is well understood that any poor unsuspecting man would have little defence against such sinful and feminine wiles."

Mrs Hardcastle did not react with the horror Harriet expected, but she did look distinctly uncomfortable, if a little confused.

Hortense seemed to sense that she had mis-stepped and quickly righted her course. "But of course that is nothing you need to worry about, Mrs Hardcastle. Such base inclinations need not be considered in a household of your standing, and your husband of such fine character, I'm sure."

And there it was. The poison, the seed of doubt, imparted so effortlessly with such devastating potential. Harriet burned with silent fury. How easily Hortense had reduced her entire womanhood to something indecent. *It's not enough that I must embrace the role of widow; now I must bear shame for having been married at all.*

Mrs Hardcastle wrung her hands, opened her mouth as though she made ready to answer, then swallowed, pressing her lips into a tight smile. She glanced back and forth between Harriet and Hortense, who—having discharged herself of her primary commission—looked delighted at how it played out.

Hortense then proceeded to regale Mrs Hardcastle with her latest gossip. Some newspaper article concerning an event in Devon, where a strange set of hoof prints had appeared in the snow in all kinds of unaccountable places. On the tops of houses and such. The locals thought they were the footprints of the devil.

Her enthusiasm in retelling the story confounded Harriet. She'd never have thought Hortense would be taken in by such a sensational and ridiculous story. She could hardly believe she'd given it credit enough to be repeated.

Mrs Hardcastle's reaction, however, was not a surprise to her. She looked as though she might faint with fear.

Poor naive lamb. The shock of this would probably render her ill for days.

In time, Hortense inserted herself firmly into Mrs Hardcastle's company. She visited every week, bringing information procured with the specific purpose of undermining Mrs Hardcastle's delicate equilibrium.

Harriet learned that she herself was sometimes the subject of such conversations. Often the noise of the children interrupted the flow of dialogue, and it fell upon her ears in fragments. It was from these fragments, however, that she discerned the following: Madame de Matthieu had an infamous reputation; Harriet had been seen meeting with her; and of course it would affect the good name of Mrs Hardcastle's household.

She also learned of the danger of women in possession of great beauty. According to Hortense, they were wicked women with sinful natures, known to use their charms to purchase indemnity from all culpability. If beauty were synonymous with wickedness, then surely Hortense would be the most beautiful of all.

By March, Mrs Hardcastle had begun to withdraw into herself. She became tense and agitated, suspicious. She attended every lesson and watched Harriet with searching eyes. Whenever they spoke to each other, Harriet could see unasked questions there. She tried to be open and friendly with her, but the more Harriet tried, the further Mrs Hardcastle retreated. Apart from the lessons, she avoided Harriet completely.

Mr Hardcastle, on the other hand, made certain to be in Harriet's vicinity frequently, which only added to his wife's suspicion. He appeared in the schoolroom on occasion, developing a sudden interest in his children's lessons. He approached them in the garden when she took the children for outdoor recreation, or in the stables when she and Lillian went to pet the horses. He always gave the impression that it was quite by accident that he had chanced to happen upon them.

Harriet never believed him, but she couldn't say why. The reason eluded her, playing about the fringes of her conscience, just out of reach. He was always respectful, cordial in his address but there was something else she couldn't identify. Something apparent in the holding of a handshake for a fraction too long, a coincidental journey in the same direction.

Sometimes there was a moment—just a flicker—when his gaze lingered too long, not on her eyes, but on her mouth. She blinked and it was gone, but the unease remained. He made frequent invasion of her personal space, always standing just closer than propriety allowed. But she noticed he did that with everyone. Perhaps that's just the way he was. It didn't seem fair to judge him on so little. She wasn't disposed to entertain bad opinions of people, especially those based chiefly on conjecture.

~

ONE NIGHT IN THE SPRING, Harriet awoke in the early hours with a sore throat. She tried drinking water, but it felt like swallowing gravel. She tried not swallowing at all, but that only increased the urge.

After making sure Lillian was sound asleep, she went downstairs to get some milk and honey. Aggie always swore by the remedy and administered it to them on many occasions. The concoction would soothe her soul as well as her throat, bringing her the comfort of a cherished memory.

She took a candle from the nightstand and padded along the passage to the kitchen, fearful of disturbing the household.

The candle flame guttered as she walked, casting eerie shapes along the walls. Shadows stretched out to her, then contracted as she passed, flinching back from the light.

When she entered the lower passage, she saw, emitted from the kitchen doorway, a faint yellowish glow which varied in its intensity, like a candle flickering. *Someone must be in the kitchen. Probably the housekeeper.*

The housekeeper held no fondness for her and would not appreciate being disturbed.

Harriet's gait faltered as she considered whether to continue or turn back. She half turned the way she'd come, then thought better of it. *Why should I care for her comfort? She certainly doesn't care for mine.* She entered the room, her shoulders squared with newfound courage. The floor was cold and hard under her bare feet, and she regretted not putting on her slippers. There was a candle on the table, but she could see no-one in the vast kitchen, only the dancing flame atop its wax pillar. The candlelight seemed too afraid to reach into the corners of the room, not stretching much further than the table.

"Who's there?" She asked the darkness. She waited a few seconds before asking again, "Hello? Who's there?" She heard a movement and the sharp intake of a breath.

Then a voice cut through the air. "Harriet."

Mr Hardcastle leaned forward from a chair in the corner, the light illuminating parts of his face only, whilst others remained in near blackness. The effect was ghastly, and Harriet stumbled back in surprise.

"Good grief, Mr Hardcastle, you've given me the shock of my life." She pressed a hand to her heart and felt it race beneath her palm. "When no one answered the first time, I thought the room quite empty." She laughed—not properly—a short, nervous sound.

"I'm sorry to have given you such a fright, Harriet. Come sit down; you must be quite overcome." He rose and pulled out a chair for her.

"Oh, no, it's alright really, I'm quite recovered."

He wasn't sorry at all. Why hadn't he answered her? Why had he stayed silent, watching her from the darkness?

"And what are you up to, padding around the house barefoot in the early hours?" His tone was teasing and threw Harriet further into confusion.

"I—I came down for some milk and honey. My throat is a little sore." She cleared her throat and rubbed at her neck as if to demonstrate the problem.

"Then you are unwell, Harriet. I must insist you be seated and allow me to tend to you. Come sit here and I'll fetch your milk and honey." He took her carefully by the arm and directed her into the chair with a gentleness she'd not thought him capable of.

She had not witnessed in Mr Hardcastle's character any inkling of care or tenderness toward his wife and children. There was a coldness in his civility, an aloofness. The strangeness of his manner now was a stark contrast.

He brought the potion and sat beside her whilst she drank, watching her with eager eyes as she drained the glass.

"Thank you, Mr Hardcastle," she said. "It's good of you to put yourself to such trouble on my account." The syrupy mixture relieved the burning as coated the back of her throat.

"It's no trouble at all. Tell me, do you often float about the house, haunting people in the middle of the night?" He asked. "You looked quite the spectre in your white chiffon." He waved a hand at the billowing nightdress spilling from her robe. A minute violation of her privacy.

She readjusted her dressing gown, pulling it tight around

her. "No, I don't usually come out of my room at all in the night." *I wish I hadn't.*

"Perhaps you should." He rocked the chair back on two legs and stretched out to his full length, crossing his legs at the ankle. He locked his hands behind his head, elbows out. The gesture was arrogant: a display of masculinity to make her look at him. "I often find myself down here in the wee small hours, and you would be a pleasant distraction from a long and solitary night."

This doesn't feel right. Keep the conversation light.

Her spine prickled, and she resisted the urge to shiver. "You have trouble sleeping then, Sir?" She grasped for a safe and neutral topic.

"Caiaphas," he answered.

Harriet stared blankly at him.

"Call me Caiaphas."

A sickly tingling sensation covered her skin, and the hairs at the nape of her neck rose like hackles. It was only now that she noticed the empty whisky bottle on the table. *He's drunk.*

"I could not, Sir. It would be most improper." She fumbled for something else to bolster her argument. "My position in your household doesn't grant me such a liberty." She saw the flash of irritation in his eyes.

"Your position in my household requires you to do as I see fit." His voice was calm, but his eyes blazed. "If I command you to use my name, you are obliged to take the liberty, are you not?"

Command me! Even in marriage, Arthur had not been her master. She'd never had to obey any man against her will.

But this was different. She was indeed obliged to obey this one. Trying to keep her voice even, she drew upon all her courage. "If you command it, Sir, then I will address you as you see fit."

He was emboldened by the whisky, pleased with his own mastery. Silence hung between them as he watched her with intensity, a smirk pulling at the corners of his lips. Then he rose to his feet abruptly, sending his chair screeching across the stone flags.

Harriet flinched and felt the wall at her back, her anger dissolving into panic. "I must return to my chamber now. Lillian might wake and find me gone."

"Of course," he said, all smiles and kindness again, "if you are quite recovered. Goodnight Harriet."

"Goodnight," she said, deliberately omitting any form of personal address.

The omission did not escape him. He stretched his arm across the doorway and blocked her exit.

He's going to make me say his name.

He leaned close to her ear and lowered his voice to a gravelly whisper. "Goodnight, Harriet."

She swallowed. "Goodnight, Caiaphas."

He smiled and moved aside to let her pass.

Harriet ran all the way back to her room and slumped to the floor, her back pressed against the door. She'd left her candle in the kitchen in her haste to leave, so she sat in the dark, wondering what had just happened. *What did he want? Was he just being friendly, or was that something else? Is this how men behave in private?* She didn't know. She had no experience —nothing to compare it to. She only knew how wrong it had felt.

AFTER THAT NIGHT, she eluded him with diligence, hoping he'd been drunk enough to forget what happened in the kitchen. But when he did eventually cross her path, he still insisted she call him Caiaphas. His manner, though, returned to normal—polite, courteous and nothing further happened that was out of the ordinary.

With no variation in regularity to mark the passing of the weeks, Harriet forgot her uncomfortable encounter and began to feel that she'd been too hasty in her judgement. After all, many a gentleman had behaved less than honourably under the influence of whisky.

Time often did that to memory. As the distance from an event increases, the recollection loses its potency. It loses focus, the details diminished. We lose confidence in our capacity to remember, questioning the legitimacy of our own knowledge. Nature embroiders pretty details into the mind's eye, softening the picture of our truth. The painful and ugly truths, then, are not so hard to look at anymore. Perhaps it is the body's way of dealing with pain.

Harriet wondered if she'd misinterpreted his behaviour and unfairly attributed to him a character he didn't deserve. Even though she'd felt uncomfortable, he hadn't actually done anything wrong. *Had he?* He hadn't touched her. He hadn't used lewd or foul language. What then had he done? What would she say if she told anyone? "He brought me milk and honey and asked me to use his Christian name."

It sounded ridiculous.

As the memory faded, so too did the last traces of winter. The days were longer now, bright and warm enough to hold a lesson or two outdoors. The land put forth tendrils of fleshy green foliage, and crocus bulbs and daffodils poked their heads above the ground. Ferns uncurled majestic fronds from their crowns, and the earth gave birth to new life.

Harriet took walks outdoors and taught the children the names of wildflowers and how to identify a tree from its leaf or its bark. She and Lillian even ventured into town with

Delphine, taking tea together on her days off. They wandered around the park, airing their views on everything from political matters to the latest style of hat to make its way across the channel.

The more she saw of Delphine, the less credit Hortense's accusation held. In truth, she no longer cared. She saw only a dignified and compassionate lady and was becoming increasingly attached to her new friend.

Delphine was her senior by some years—not enough to separate them by a whole generation—but sufficient to inspire confidence in Harriet that this magical being was both wiser and more worldly than herself. Harriet viewed her with the frank admiration of a little sister.

Mrs Hardcastle was now less vigilant in her shadowing and no longer attended all the children's lessons. There was still one point of contention between the two women. That was Harriet's use of the word 'Caiaphas.' The outrage Mrs Hardcastle displayed when she first heard it slip from Harriet's tongue was bordering on comic. She confronted Harriet in the bravest act she'd committed since Harriet arrived.

Harriet told her politely but firmly, "I'm afraid I have been instructed—no, commanded by your husband to address him in this manner."

"Liar!" Mrs Hardcastle said, then clapped a hand over her mouth. Her eyes went wide as though she couldn't believe what she'd blurted out.

Harriet offered no resistance, but waited for her to continue.

"He would never ask you to do that."

Harriet saw it in her eyes—her conviction crumbling in the face of Harriet's calm and passive expression.

"Mrs Hardcastle, I do not care for it any more than you do, but unfortunately, we are obliged to bear it. As husband and employer, he is both your master and mine." The words tasted bitter in her mouth.

Mrs Hardcastle walked away, and Harriet wondered if her suspicion would be roused again. She wasn't sure how much longer she could endure living under her constant scrutiny.

As it turned out, it would not be for very long.

AN ALTERCATION

On a Tuesday afternoon in April, there occurred an altercation between Caiaphas and Harriet which rendered her resignation inexorable.

It was a warm day, the sun drying up the dew by nine o'clock in the morning. The children had completed their lessons for the day and Mrs Hardcastle had taken them for a stroll in the park. Lillian was playing with Maria in the kitchen and Harriet had some free time. She took her book to the shelter at the other end of the garden for an hour's peaceful reading.

The shelter was an unusual building, like a small bandstand. Hexagonal in shape, it had six stone pillars and a domed slate roof, with ornate iron fretwork around the edges. It reminded her of a painting she had seen once, of St. Peter's Basilica in Rome. There was an opening at the front, between two of the pillars, and a stone bench wrapped around the inside.

Ivy wound its tentacles up and around the pillars until it reached the ceiling. It clung there, poking its fingers under slates, searching for the light outside. One or two tiles had come loose from the foliage pushing its way out, but the overall effect was still beautiful.

She took a blanket to sit on because, although the air was warm, the stone was still very cold. It clung to winter with defiance, refusing to give up its frostiness the way old houses do, only heating up when they had stood in the blazing sunshine for at least three months.

The air stirred and the soft scent of narcissus drifted over on the swell of the breeze. Little birds sang in the ash trees overhead, a sweet, delicate song of spring. Winter had felt so long, she'd almost forgotten what it was like to hear birdsong.

No one ever used this quiet spot besides herself. It felt like her own little piece of the world. When she wasn't reading, she liked to sit here watching the willow sweep its branches across the pond, kissing the water's surface. Even the softest of breezes fluttered its million tiny leaves in a soft hush like the faint whisper of silk.

She opened her book—borrowed from the shelf in her room. Poetry. Love poems, to be precise. Broken hearts and lamenting souls, passions, sacrifice and yearning. She'd read all the books except this one, which she'd discarded as a weak and fickle thing. But now she'd grown curious. Having never experienced the passion or lament it spoke of, she was intrigued. Perhaps it was possible to experience them through the words of others and feed her heart with the nourishing verses.

She'd read but two or three pages when a shadow crossed the floor at the edge of her vision. She looked up to see what bird or little animal had strayed into her quiet nook but was disappointed to find Caiaphas.

"Oh!" she said, annoyed at his sudden appearance. "Good afternoon."

He watched her, but said nothing. His eyes were bright with menace, and she knew in an instant he was fuelled with whiskey. He looked deep into her, as though he tried to read her thoughts. Then his gaze retreated and roamed across her, cold and horrid on her skin.

She shuddered as if the wingtips of death had brushed against her—feather light. She wondered how the whiskey would affect him this time. Would he stay right at the tip of propriety, never quite doing anything that would stand up under confrontation? Or would this time be worse?

He stepped into the shelter's shade and leaned against a pillar. "Good afternoon." He was a master of ambiguity. A look passed between them—the sort of look where both parties silently acknowledge a disquietude. There was something visceral and crude in his gaze. The smile cut into his face like an open wound.

"How vibrant you look in this light, Harriet. It becomes you."

She didn't reply.

"Tell me, Harriet…is it the breeze that coaxes out the flush upon your cheek—or the contents of your book?" He stepped forward. "I do hope you're not reading anything inappropriate," he said, arching an eyebrow. He swiped the book from her hands and turned it over to read aloud. "Come to me in sweet delight, that we might be tonight, as one in body and soul." He laughed without mirth and slammed the book closed. "Tut, tut, tut," he waggled a finger at her, "quite scandalous."

Harriet's face reddened.

"Do you dream of a lover, Harriet? Do you want to be loved?" The words were slurred.

He's intoxicated.

Her eyes darted about for an escape, and she moved backwards, but he caught her at the waist and pulled her close. She froze.

"I could love you Harriet," he said into her hair, pressing his face against the side of her head. His breath brushed over her with a sickening hush, and sour whiskey filled her nostrils.

"Please, sir—let go of me. You're quite insensible." She still clung to propriety, but this new boldness alarmed her, and she struggled against his grasp, pushing with both palms against his chest.

His grip tightened. "I could show you what it means to be loved by a man. Don't you long for the touch of a real man?" His voice was low and mocking as he crooned in her ear. "You know what they say about widows don't you? Once they've had it, they can't do without it." He ran the pointed corner of the book along her bare arm. "Don't fight me, Harriet. It only makes me more determined." He lowered his mouth to her neck, and she jerked backwards.

"Take your hands off me, you animal." She snatched the book from him and slammed the hefty volume into his right temple. Knocking him off balance, she broke free of his hold and ran toward the house.

A shrill voice echoed across the garden. "Caiaphas?"

Eleanor Hardcastle stood on the steps, ashen-faced and trembling, her hands cupped to her mouth.

Harriet stopped midway across the lawn. From a distance, their altercation could easily have been misinterpreted.

"What are you doing, Caiaphas?" Eleanor said, disbelief painted all over her face. She started to back away as he advanced toward her, striding past Harriet with a glare.

"Eleanor, go inside." He barked the words at her like a vicious dog. A bead of blood bloomed on his temple. It glistened in the sun like a fat red ruby.

Harriet felt a grain of satisfaction when it ran down his cheek.

"Eleanor, this woman has made advances toward me that are wholly inappropriate." His chest heaved. "Now go inside, as I instructed, and I will handle this."

How dare he try to pin this on me?

Both women locked eyes. The air was heavy, weighted with expectation. Then, a look of clarity passed across Mrs Hardcastle's face, and Harriet knew she understood. She'd known all along.

Harriet continued to walk toward the house, Mrs Hardcastle nodding to her as she passed.

"Where are you going?" Caiaphas shouted.

"To pack my things. I will be leaving today."

"You will leave when I say so, Harriet." He lunged toward her and spun her by the elbow. "You're under contract. If you wish to leave, you will work out your notice as required." He spat on the ground at her feet.

What a vile specimen of man.

Something broke in Mrs Hardcastle then, and she screamed at him.

He dropped Harriet's arm, turned very calmly to his wife, and struck her with the back of his hand.

She fell to the ground like a crumpled flower.

Caiaphas strode out of the garden without a second's pause.

Even the birds had stopped singing.

~

AN HOUR LATER, Eleanor sat in Harriet's room, tears dropping into her lap. They soaked into the light grey silk of her dress, a patch of darkness spreading out beneath them. She listened in silence to Harriet's version of events, then stared down at her hands. "This isn't the first time," she said quietly.

"What do you mean?" asked Harriet.

"It's happened before." She squeezed her eyes shut against the memory. "He was...familiar with our last governess. There was a scandal. It's the reason we moved here." She dissolved into tears. "I thought this time would be different. He promised." She dabbed at her eyes. "But what can I do? He's my husband, I can't leave him. I've nowhere to go."

"Don't you have family?" Harriet asked.

"I cannot go to my family. I married him against their wishes. They warned me he was a cad. My father hated him. My mother was distraught when I told them I was married." She shook her head again. "They cast me out. I cannot go back."

Harriet handed her a handkerchief and continued to pack her belongings. She was leaving in the morning at first light. Eleanor had paid her salary until the end of the week and given her a bonus of five pounds. Harriet wanted to refuse it—her dignity wrestling with necessity—but she couldn't.

"Come with me," she said to Eleanor, "leave him and we'll find work somewhere else. Somewhere new."

Eleanor looked at her like she'd uttered a vulgar word. "Work? I couldn't possibly. No, I must stay." She straightened her back and mopped her tears with the crisp lace handkerchief.

The thought of work must have offered her some perspective on the situation that Harriet failed to understand. At this point, her capacity for commiseration was strained to its limit. She couldn't imagine any work awful enough to stop her escaping such dire circumstances. *If I were you, I'd sooner be a kitchen wench than stay here with that monster of a man.*

Footsteps in the hall interrupted their business, and Maria

burst into the room, red-faced and panting, with Lillian in her arms.

Harriet took her and pressed her to her chest. *Thank God.*

"He's delirious drunk, ma'am," Maria said. "He's looking for you both, and his temper's fearful. He's already hit Jeremy, and he's kicked a panel out of the schoolroom door." Her eyes were wide, and she trembled like a small child. "Should I fetch someone, Mrs?" she asked, "someone to help?" She was on the brink of giving way to tears.

Mrs Hardcastle shook her head. "There's no one to fetch Maria."

They heard him then—crashing around in the lower rooms, knocking things over. Doors slammed as he made his way through the house, and heavy furniture scraped on wooden floors. There was a smash and then a sound like the tinkling of bells—a glass perhaps, or the whiskey bottle, finally empty. He shouted—the words slurred—like he was losing steam.

The three women huddled behind Harriet's door, listening with ears pressed against the wood. Once or twice they thought they heard him approach and stiffened. What were they going to do, should he reach the door?

Harriet tasted the threat of sickness at the back of her throat. Her stomach groaned and clenched. *Just how violent is he? What lengths will he go to in order to stop me?*

He did not come upstairs though, and after twenty minutes, the noise abated. They held out for a few minutes of silence before cracking the door open a fraction, whilst holding their breath.

No one.

No—wait...someone? Footsteps!

Harriet slammed the door, and they pressed their backs against it, hearts pounding and eyes closed in silent prayer.

Then came a timid knock and Jeremy's loud whisper. "It's alright, miss, it's me, Jeremy. He's fell asleep."

Relief washed through them, tense muscles relaxing. Harriet admitted Jeremy and gasped when she saw his face.

One eye was closed, the lid sealed shut by a purple swell of blood blooming beneath it. It bulged from the socket like a ripe plum, bruising spreading out by the second. It looked as though the lightest touch would have split the skin and sent it peeling back to reveal the flesh underneath.

He explained to them that Caiaphas had eventually worn himself out and collapsed in the dining room. But not before he'd piled the dining table and chairs and a sideboard behind the door to barricade himself in. The staff had watched this from the second door at the other end of the room. In his drunkenness, he must have forgotten the dining room had more than one entrance.

Harriet and Lillian crept down the servant's staircase and out into the courtyard with their bags whilst Eleanor sent Jeremy to bring the carriage around. There was no way Harriet would spend another night under his roof. Not even under contract.

Caiaphas was too intoxicated to realise his own coach and horses were helping her to escape. By the time he came to his senses, she would be long gone and his carriage back where it belonged. The rest was up to Eleanor.

~

THERE WAS JUST enough daylight left for Jeremy to get her to the guesthouse and return the coach before dark. He assured her that one eye was sufficient to drive, and they set off at a brisk pace. When they arrived in Dalton Square, the horses were panting, nostrils flaring and lathered in white, foamy sweat.

He leaped down from the driving seat and opened the door for Harriet. "Sorry about the rough ride ma'am. Just thought we'd better hurry," he said.

"Of course, Jeremy, I'm much obliged to you." She stepped out of the carriage, grateful for his arm. Her nerves had abandoned her, and she was unsteady on her feet.

She left Lillian in the carriage and walked over to the looming black doors of the guest house, praying Mrs Carter might have a room. With a trembling finger, she rang the doorbell and waited.

Mrs Carter appeared in the doorway with a shawl loosely draped over her shoulders.

"Yes, Madam?"

"Good evening, Mrs Carter. I wonder if you might have a room available for the night? I'm afraid Lillian and I find ourselves quite at your mercy," Harriet said.

"Sorry, no rooms tonight." Her tone was clipped.

"I don't mind if there isn't a cot—we can bed down on the floor. You see, circumstance has forced us to leave suddenly, and we've nowhere else to go."

Mrs Carter's face hardened. "I have no rooms tonight," she repeated.

"Please—a servant's room, a broom cupboard—anything?" She tried to steady the desperation rising in her throat, but her voice betrayed her.

"Not for the likes of you, I haven't. I've heard all about your antics in that household, Madam." The superior air, the accent, the majestic tilt of her head—Mrs Carter seemed inches taller than she was. Whatever she'd heard had inflated her pride and sharpened her cruelty.

"I'm afraid someone has misinformed you, Mrs Carter. I assure you that the matter regarding my departure was not of my doing. The fault does not lie with me—Mrs Hardcastle will vouch for that. Please, Mrs Carter, you know me. Haven't you a morsel of pity? Will you turn me out into the cold on the strength of a rumour? And a small child in hand?" She pleaded with her now, panic fully fledged and fluttering in her stomach.

"I'm sorry, Madam, but I can't help you. I have no reason to doubt Mrs Watson's word. She is of impeccable character and not in the habit of misinforming people."

Harriet fell silent, her arms dropping to her sides. *Mrs Watson? She has blackened my name? Surely even Hortense would not stoop so low as this.*

"But—"

Mrs Carter closed the door.

The click of the latch rang out in the square like the shot of a rifle and Hortense had pulled the trigger.

Harriet stared at the door. *What on earth has she said about me?*

THE LONGEST NIGHT

This was Harriet's first glimpse of the rotten underbelly of the great British upper class. Somehow she sensed it wouldn't be her last. A sickening sense of dread crept over her.

"Where to now, ma'am?" Jeremy shouted from the carriage. "We'd best be on our way sharpish. If I'm not back soon and master wakes up, he'll have me other eye."

Jeremy's voice startled her, and she turned away from the guest house. "Go, Jeremy, you must go back. I'll find lodgings in town." Her voice held more conviction than she felt, but she couldn't have that brute lay his hands on the poor boy again. Her conscience wouldn't allow it.

"Nay, ma'am, I can't leave you here in the street." He climbed down from the carriage again and beckoned her to get in.

"Please, Jeremy, do not trouble yourself. We'll be alright, I assure you." She lifted Lillian from the carriage. "Now go before he wakes and finds you missing. Oh, wait!" She turned back. "My trunk, Jeremy. Would you keep it for me, and I'll send for it when I'm settled?"

"Of course, ma'am. I'll store it in my quarters, then he doesn't get wind of it. Are you sure you don't want taking somewhere else?"

"No thank you. Please go."

He touched his cap, nodded and then he was gone.

She watched the back of the carriage dissolve into darkness as it disappeared from view. She didn't move—just stood there—her ears strained upon the sound of the hooves melting away.

Eventually, she gathered her wits and set off to try somewhere else. She knocked on the doors of every respectable lodging house she knew—and some which were not respectable at all. The latter were full of drunks and whores, and rumours had reached the rest.

She could have asked Jeremy to take her to Delphine, but she was proud and the friendship was new. What if Delphine didn't believe her? What if she didn't want to be tainted by the lies and rumours? It was too late now. She had no way of getting there, and it was too far on foot.

As the hours ticked on, the city became less inviting. Drunken men roamed the streets, spilling out of taverns and into the alleyways. It wasn't safe. She had to get out of the town centre quickly. Finding no other option, she turned toward Delphine's house.

The road was all uphill, and Lillian was heavy, making progress very slow. After thirty minutes of hard walking, she reached the summit of the first hill, only a mile from town, and could go no further. She'd never make it to Delphine's. She could think of no other solution but to seek shelter in some hiding place close by. Somewhere they would not suffer the indignity of being discovered in the morning.

The thought of being discovered made her stomach lurch. She imagined the constable finding them huddled in a doorway like two beggars. The pathetic image of a mother and child, cold and hungry, not stirring the embers of his stony little heart.

She remembered the old quarry then—further along the road. It boasted a maze of hills, tracks and little nooks where they could rest for the night. The place was deserted, having closed down long since, so the chance of being found was slim—not that anyone would be looking. There wasn't a person in the world would even know she was missing.

A sob escaped her lips. *Oh, Aggie, why are you so far away?*

Stumbling through the iron gates of the old quarry, she looked around for somewhere suitable to lie down. Half the land was covered with grass; the rest was sharp rock and patches of sticky red clay. She found a spot where a great scar cut into the side of a mossy bank, a stone jutting out overhead. It was as good as they'd get tonight.

The ground was sponge-like, soft with moss. It smelled earthy and strangely medicinal, like something she had smelled at the apothecary. It was already damp with evening dew. By morning, she'd be soaked through and chilled to her bones. She took off her petticoat and spread it out on the ground to offer Lillian some protection from the damp. They were sheltered from the wind at least, and thankful it wasn't raining. *There's little else to be thankful for at this point. Dry weather is something at least.*

She looked at Lillian, blissfully unaware. *Thank God she's too young to remember this.*

Sleep did not come easily to Harriet that night. Unaccustomed to the sounds of darkness, she started at every noise and wrapped her arms tight around Lillian. Like hope and despair, they clung to each other for warmth.

An eerie stillness crept in as the city below settled into slumber. When the west eventually swallowed up the sun, darkness ushered in its night-song. Leaves swished and fluttered in the breeze, a dog barked somewhere in the distance, water dripped from the rocks above, and unknown insects called to each other across the land.

For a long time, Harriet just stared at the sky. The moon was full and brilliant. Its loyal army spanned the sky—a million lights—time's history laid out in a glittering map. Echoes of past lives, distant lands, stories untold.

She wondered if her father were up there looking down on them. What on earth would he think? Would he be disappointed? She wondered what God thought too. Her father always told her there were both good and bad people in the world, but only God could decide which was which.

He was wrong. There are only the right people and the wrong people, and it isn't God doing the deciding.

Her faith had not withstood this injury. It poured out of her like blood, ebbing away until she was emptied of herself. Everything she'd ever believed about the fundamental goodness of people—about the world at large—was nothing more than a child's fairytale.

~

IT WAS the longest night Harriet had ever spent. She was never so happy to see the sun's first rays claw at the inky blackness, staking its claim on the morning sky. She watched it rise, the sky ablaze with vivid colours. Scarlet, gold, violet and puce pushing upward as though lifting off the heavy blanket of night. She'd never seen a sunrise quite so beautiful.

They were high enough to see the river too, snaking

through the town like a great black eel. *It's breathtaking. How beautiful the world would be if it weren't for the people in it.*

Reality shot through her as her stomach growled. She hadn't eaten since breakfast yesterday. They needed to get moving before the rest of the world awoke. Finding food was her priority, and they'd have to head back into town to get that. From there, she could take a coach to Delphine's. Or even Morecambe. The seaside town was only seven or eight miles away and full of lodging houses. No one knew her there, so any rumours were unlikely.

The market traders in town would be setting up soon. They weren't so particular as the landladies about the reputation of their customers. Most of them were men whose grace was better earned with coin than with conscience. One woman's money was as good as the next.

Lillian was not yet awake and would ordinarily sleep for another hour or so, but necessity forced her to hasten.

She rolled up her mud-stained petticoat, put it into her bag and, with the dreaming child in her arms, left their hiding place. Her arms ached already, and her legs weakened with every step, but the thought of Lillian being hungry strengthened her resolve. She'd have managed without food herself, but she hadn't drunk either. Her head ached from dehydration, and it wasn't long before weakness overcame her.

I don't feel well. She wiped beads of sweat from her forehead. *Oh no, I think I'm going to faint.*

Halfway down the hill, she swayed, and the pavement seemed to rise up to meet her. She set Lillian on the ground and knelt for a moment to steady herself. As she closed her eyes and breathed deeply, she heard the crunch of wheels rolling over the gravelly road behind her. She kept her head lowered, hoping they would pass without paying attention to her, but the wheels slowed, coming to a stop at the kerbside.

She reached for Lillian, barely clinging to consciousness, and heard the click of a carriage door and the swoosh of silk skirts.

Delphine's voice cried out in alarm. "Sacre Dieu! Harriet? What happened?" She fell to her knees beside Harriet and lifted Lillian from her arms. "Are you hurt?" She asked, looking them both over with a rapid eye.

"No," Harriet said, breathless. "Just...weak." She fought hard to stay alert, but her eyelids felt heavier with every breath.

"Henri descend vite! Ici, aide-la a monter dans la voiture." Delphine shouted to the coachman.

"No, please." Harriet held up her hand. "I can walk." She tried to get to her feet, but stumbled to the ground again.

"Harriet, you are quite insensible. Henri, if you please." Delphine stepped back and motioned for her man to put Harriet into the carriage.

He scooped her up like a small child and placed her onto the soft velvet cushions inside.

Delphine followed, with Lillian in her arms.

"Retour a la Maison, Madame?" Henri asked, assuming their previous journey was now abandoned.

"Oui, s'il te plait."

The driver hopped back up to his seat and clicked his tongue at the pair of grey mares pawing at the ground with impatience. He spoke to them in French, and they turned under his expert command, in a tight half circle, heading back the way they had come.

Harriet rested her head against the window with her eyes closed, taking deep, steadying breaths. She felt sick and weak, too weak even to be appalled at the spectacle she'd just made of herself. That would come later. For now, she concentrated on not losing consciousness.

She fumbled with the brass latch on the window and opened it wide, sucking in the air in great gulps. "Water. I need water," she said.

Delphine hammered on the roof of the carriage and shouted to Henri. The carriage stopped, and Henri appeared at the door with a silver hip flask.

"Je suis desole Madame. Je n'ai pas d'eau, mais j'ai un peu du vin?" He offered the flask to Delphine, who held it to Harriet's mouth, urging her to drink the sweet wine.

She drank greedily, the ruby liquid soothing her parched lips. It went some way to reviving her, and she managed a weak smile at the obliging young man. "Merci Henri," she said, and closed her eyes again.

Minutes later, a piercing shriek catapulted her into consciousness. She reached for Lillian instinctively, but Delphine put a finger to her lips to quiet her and nodded toward the window, indicating that the sound had come from outside. When Harriet leaned over to see what caused the commotion, she saw they were passing by the County Lunatic Asylum.

The asylum van stood at the gates. Its big doors gaped open like a yawning mouth. A young woman was being rough-handled by two attendants, screaming at them as they dragged her from the van.

She was dressed in a grubby garment the colour of weak tea. The sleeves forced her arms to cross over her protruding belly and fastened behind her in a tangle of buckles and clasps. Tears streaked the young woman's face, leaving white tracks on her dirty skin.

Harriet gasped as the men jostled her about. "What are they doing? That girl is with child! They mustn't treat her so roughly." She looked at Delphine in horror.

They dragged the young woman a few steps further,

obscuring Harriet's view. She looked at the van. A tiny hand was the only other sign of life from the moveable cell, its bony white knuckles clinging to the bars of the window.

"Is it always like that? Shouldn't we do something about it?"

Delphine studied her. "Have you ever been inside an asylum?"

"No, I've never had cause. Have you?"

"I have." Delphine's voice was flat, her eyes somewhere far away. "It was the most hideous thing I've ever witnessed. Young women, brimming with youth, are stripped of their vigour—branded lunatics by men—rendered liable to the accusation by a moment's mutiny in their otherwise obedient natures." She kept her gaze toward the window. "They're suppressed and tormented in the name of science—diagnosed without proper foundation for the claims. Shut up in tiny cells without daylight or company. When they give birth, their babies are torn from them without pause. No goodbye kiss, no stolen glance of a cherub face to see them through the lonely nights. Not even a hope to cling to, that the child might find itself in a better place. All babies go to the workhouse."

She looked back at Harriet then. "And after years of this treatment, when the women are mad with grief and untethered from reality, wild-eyed and drooling at the mouth, the men say, 'Look, see for yourselves. These women are insane.' It's a place where misery and defeat walk the halls hand in hand, where souls go to die. They shrivel up like poisoned weeds, nothing left but a husk that once held life."

Incensed at the treatment of the patients, her passionate outburst seemed too personal for someone not intimately acquainted with the matter. *She must have known someone who was committed. A family member perhaps, or a friend.* Of course

Harriet could not ask her. That would be inconsiderate at best.

They passed the rest of the journey in silence. The air felt thick enough to slice.

When they arrived at Delphine's home, Henri guided Harriet inside, where two maidservants took her to a bedroom and drew her a bath.

Clean but exhausted, she climbed onto the bed and finally slept.

GREENACRE

Harriet awoke to find two figures sitting at the foot of the bed. Delphine was reading from a children's storybook, with Lillian curled up on her lap like an enormous cat. Enraptured by the colourful illustrations, every so often Lillian turned to gaze in wonder at the exotic lady who read to her.

Harriet cleared her throat and pushed herself up against the pillows. Her visitors rushed to the bedside, fussing and fretting.

"Mama!" Lillian threw one leg up onto the mattress in an attempt to scale the side of the bed. She clawed at the bed linen for purchase.

Delphine lifted her up with a giggle and sat her on the pillows next to Harriet, where she enveloped her mother in an embrace so fierce it could have strangled a bear.

"How do you feel?" asked Delphine.

"Much better, thank you. I'm so sorry about all this. I've caused you such inconvenience." Harriet stared at her hands.

Delphine lifted her chin and looked her in the eye. "Firstly, young lady, I'm furious you did not come straight to me if you were in trouble. I've made inquiries since you arrived, and I've a vague idea of the story. Why on earth didn't you tell me?"

Oh no. Who has she spoken to? What have they told her?

"Secondly," she continued, without giving Harriet time to reply, "you are my friend, and this is what friends are for."

"But it's too much," protested Harriet.

"Too much? Too much to scrape you off the pavement and give you water? Good God, Harriet, have you not a friend in the world who has shown you kindness before today?"

Harriet flushed, seeing the pity in Delphine's expression. She thought of Aggie again, so many miles away—the only friend she'd ever known. *Aggie would love Delphine.*

"I must get to Morecambe to find lodgings. I don't want to impose on you. You've taken such trouble on my account already." She folded back the coverlet to swing her legs off the bed.

Delphine skewered her intention with one look. She shouted something towards the door, but Harriet's mind was too exhausted to keep up with her rapid French. She must have called a servant because within minutes, a girl appeared holding a silver tray with a bowl of steaming chicken broth and two slices of bread and butter.

"Eat," Delphine said. "You need to regain your strength. It's plain food, but it will see you back to health."

Harriet picked up the spoon and then looked at Lillian. Before she could voice her thoughts, Delphine had already understood.

"She's already eaten. Don't worry, your little angel is well fed."

Harriet sank back into the pillows, smiling and relieved. The soup was good—simple but nourishing. It warmed and soothed her from the inside as she relished the comfort of the big soft bed she lay in.

"What did you find out from your inquiries?" she asked Delphine, not entirely sure she wanted to hear the answer.

"I sent Henri to speak to their staff. Some young man—Joseph or John or some such name—"

"Jeremy?"

"Yes—that's the one. He told Henri Mr Hardcastle was mad drunk and had tried to force his attentions on you. He said you'd escaped, and he took you to town, but I'd rather hear your side."

She told Delphine all that had happened since they last saw each other—especially Hortense's part in it.

Delphine was furious. Harriet hadn't thought it possible for someone so refined and graceful to display such turbulent ferocity. It sounded all the worse for being articulated in French. They were such furious speakers at the best of times. What surprised her the most though, was the loyalty she showed towards Harriet: her genuine concern.

"I might have known that awful woman would have a hand in this," she said. "She'll have the priest dragged from the pulpit next, so she can preach her doctrine on the impurity of women."

Harriet laughed without mirth. "I can't believe a woman could behave this way toward one of her own. It's not the sort of behaviour I'd expect from a woman of her standing."

"Pah! Standing indeed. Standing has nothing to do with it. Goodness is an indiscriminate quality, Harriet. It holds no regard for wealth, age, class or any other boundary. Unfortunately, you'll find that goodness is more often found in the gutters than the banquet halls."

"Yes, I suppose that's true," Harriet said.

"Of course it's true. People make the choice to be good or

bad. We're all born equal in the spiritual sense. We all have a choice to make when it comes to what sort of person we aspire to be. Think about it. Are the wanderings of your mind not subject to the same peculiarities as any other person? Of course they are." She didn't wait for Harriet's response but answered herself instead. "The only difference between our class and the lower ones is that our thoughts are checked by our tongues. Our passions are tempered by propriety. I'm afraid, my friend, that you have much to learn about the ways of the world."

I can't argue with that.

She stood to exit the room and then added, over her shoulder, "And don't even think about leaving until you're fully recovered. I won't have it."

~

GREENACRE WAS the most blissful place Harriet had ever been, and with each day that passed, she became more attached to it. It felt as though time worked differently there than everywhere else, slipping away unnoticed. Like the stories she'd read of faerie realms, where people spent a day only to return home and find that years had passed. Sometimes she wondered if she'd ever want to return to the real world at all. She didn't think any amount of time at Greenacre would ever be enough.

To her delight, Delphine implored her to extend her stay, and their friendship strengthened in those few short weeks—sharing confidences, experiences and developing a bond between them that Harriet could only describe as sisterly.

If she were brutally honest with herself, she was a little worried that whatever indiscretion caused society to snub Delphine, it would now add weight to the rumours about herself. Being friends had been one thing, but living under the same roof was quite another. People would undoubtedly tar them both with the same brush now, but what choice did she really have? Circumstance rendered her indiscriminate, and she had little choice but to accept Delphine's hospitality.

Now that she'd experienced such generosity and compassion from her host, she felt guilty for her earlier concerns—for a more loyal and genuine friend she could not have imagined.

They were walking in the gardens to the front of the house, enjoying the early afternoon sun. A row of cherry trees lined the walkway, their buds fat and ready to burst into sweet pink blossoms. Lillian ran ahead, pausing to pick up cones, daisies and stalks of grass, among other things. She collected fallen leaves in varying stages of decay and presented them to her mother with glee.

Harriet accepted them solemnly, as though they were precious treasures—like a cat bringing in a dead mouse, proud and expectant of praise.

Delphine was enacting her latest battle plan in the campaign to keep her guests from leaving. Since Harriet was unschooled in such arts, any attempt at a diplomatic refusal fell short, and she was left utterly defenceless against Delphine's charms. A barrage of weak and pleading excuses were all she had to her aid.

"If I stay here any longer, you might come out here one day and find I've taken root on your lawn like a tree," Harriet said. "I think my feet are sending out little roots as we speak. If I stand too long in one place, I might never move again."

"Harriet, if I thought it would make you stay, I would attempt to plant you myself." They laughed. "I could decorate you at Christmas time with pretty ribbons and baubles."

"I would need some kind of decoration if I were to be stuck there forever in my widow's weeds. I'm certain you'd tire of the view if I remained a large black blot on the landscape."

Delphine tutted, rolled her eyes in a most undignified manner and said, "Hmph, widow's weeds. Dreadful things." She wrinkled up her nose in distaste. In Delphine's opinion, mourning attire was for people who were mourning, and since Harriet was clearly not mourning her husband, she should give it up immediately. "You should take them off. You're far too young and beautiful to walk about like a black shadow all the time. I would not wear them at all if I were a widow, and you said yourself you hate them."

Harriet put a hand on her chest in mock outrage and erupted into giggles. It felt good to laugh. She'd never been so at ease with herself, so in tune with her company, and all without effort.

Delphine was still something of an enigma. Steadfast in her morality, yet utterly unconcerned with following the rules of society. Resolute in her determination to do what pleased her. Her entire personality was paradoxical.

"Wouldn't you worry people might judge you if you were to forgo the proper mourning dress?" Harriet asked.

"What people? I have no concern for the opinions and judgements of people. There is only one judge, Harriet. C'est absurde!" She always slipped back into her native tongue when her passions were excited—the English language incapable of expressing such tremendous outrage.

Harriet had learned she was prone to these frequent outbursts—endearing, fiery, impossible to argue with.

"What could people say about you or I that they have not already said?" Delphine continued. "Besides, if you forwent mourning dress, who would see you here but me?"

She made a valid point. Harriet had not left the premises

since she arrived. And truthfully, why would she want to? *It's heaven here.*

"Are you worried about that detestable woman, Hortense?"

"Well…she has proved capable of making my life very difficult. I'd rather not supply her with any more ammunition in her campaign against me."

"How I would love to give that woman what she deserves. I'd be happy to avenge you if you'd only let me. She is a monster." Delphine crossed her arms like a sulking child.

"My dear friend, do not let vengeance sow its gnarly seed in your breast, for hatred corrupts the soul, and yours is far too precious to me."

"Prettily said, Harriet, but my hatred is justified."

"Even if it's justified. We must not submit to vengeance or ill feeling of any sort. It isn't proper." She hesitated. "Besides… I think Hortense is misunderstood."

Delphine arched an eyebrow, but Harriet continued slowly.

"When a person says something vicious like she does, we assume it comes from a place of spite and malice. But I don't believe they are the cause. Rather, they are the effect. I believe the cause is something quite different. It comes from a deep-seated unhappiness—a gnawing unsatisfaction in a person's soul, that reaches out to nourish itself on the happiness of others. Like a starving child reaching out its hand to steal a loaf of bread. Don't you think that might be the case with Hortense?"

Delphine snorted in disgust. "I think you're trying too hard to be a good Christian. It's alright to be angry at someone. You deprive me of my amusement."

She had a way of looking at you from the corner of her eye to see if her stern expression had convinced you of her indignation. Then a grin spread wide over her face and told you she was in jest. There was always mischief behind her hauteur. She also had a tendency to jump from one subject to another without warning, as she did next.

"It will be your birthday soon. You will stay, oui?"

Phrased as a question, Harriet knew it was not.

"We'll take Lillian to the travelling fair to celebrate. We can have a picnic. C'est une bonne idée, non?" She clapped her hands together the way Lillian did when she was eager and smiled. It was warm, inviting—a smile that begged not to be disappointed.

"I will stay," Harriet agreed, knowing that to do otherwise was futile. And truly, she had no desire to go. She had yet to decide what to do next.

Delphine was a woman skilled in the art of achieving the satisfaction of her own desires. Harriet had never been a fan of women who used feminine wiles to get their own way. However, when such a skill—usually intended to manipulate men—could even be successfully wielded against members of one's own sex, then she had to admit her admiration.

That, Harriet thought, was a skill indeed.

A PROPHECY

On the morning of Harriet's birthday, the sun shone magnificently, filling her bedroom with softly diffused light through the closed curtains. She awoke for the first time in weeks, free of the anxious dread that had plagued her. She was lighter, happier—hopeful, even, that life had dealt her all its blows and she might have a smoother journey from here on.

Lillian and Delphine skipped into the room with a breakfast tray and a small posy of wildflowers that Lillian had picked herself. Among the buttercups and wild bluebells were fistfuls of grass that she dropped onto the tea tray before Harriet could catch them. They scattered over her toast, mingling with melted butter and sticky marmalade.

"Happy b—b—" Lillian attempted, then looked to Delphine for a prompt.

They must have been rehearsing this.

"Birthday," Delphine offered gently.

"Bir-day. Happy Bir-day, Mama." Lillian pursed her lips and stretched her little neck, reaching up for a kiss.

"Thank you, my darling."

Delphine handed her a beautiful card, adorned with a crescent of embroidered flowers and a handwritten verse. Harriet read it aloud. "Warmest birthday wishes to my very special friend. May this be the gladdest of days, joyous and true. May its pleasures be bountiful, its skies be blue. Most important of all, may God bless you." She looked up with a tear in her eye. "It's beautiful. Thank you both."

Delphine smiled at her and sighed. "Twenty one," she said. "You're still a babe."

The morning passed in a flurry of excitement as they prepared for the day ahead. They arrived in Morecambe just before lunch and spread out their picnic on a grassy bank facing the sea. The view of the bay was spectacular, framed by the outstretched land on either side. It looked like a picture postcard.

The air was cool, its scent briny and fresh, and seagulls circled overhead like vultures, waiting for crumbs to be thrown aside. Now and then, a particularly bold one would swoop down to steal a morsel from the outspread blanket. It made Lillian squeal and giggle.

When they'd eaten their fill and lazed a while in the sun, the sound of distant music caught their ears—light and lilting, like a call from another world. Harriet shaded her eyes and smiled at the movement on the horizon—the fairground. She heard the faint whirring of the carousel stirring to life and a waltz playing.

The sudden stilling of Lillian's movements and the look of glee on her face told Harriet she'd heard the sound and understood it was something good.

"Do you want to go to the fair?" Harriet asked her.

Lillian pointed in the direction of the music. "Fair," she

said, and squeezed her hands together, barely able to contain her childish excitement.

Harriet had never been to a fairground before, and her own excitement was no less childlike than Lillian's. She stared in awe at the massive structures standing along the promenade. "Helter Skelter," one sign announced in bright gold letters. Its tower rose into the sky a good thirty or forty feet, striped with red, cream and gold. A yellow slide wound its way around it from top to bottom, and children queued up with smiling faces to hurtle down it in burlap sacks. They screamed with delight all the way down.

Adjacent to this stood a row of swing boats suspended in the air by ropes. Children and adults alike enjoyed these. Courting couples faced each other, heads thrown back with laughter as they soared through the sky. Brothers and sisters shared swings, squealing with joy, wide smiles on their faces.

They weaved through the bustling crowds, and Delphine led them to a small tent with a purple satin curtain drawn shut across the entrance. A man stood outside, one leg crossing the other at the ankle in lazy repose, a thumb hooked loosely into his pocket. He held a watch in his other hand, which he stared at with intent. He looked up from under his peaked cap and smiled at their approach. He straightened, tucked the watch into his waistcoat, and greeted them.

"Good morning, ladies, and the warmest welcome to our humble fair. Right this way please. Enter and let Madam Lenora unlock the secrets of your destiny." Tipping his cap, he made a dramatic bow and winked at Delphine.

Insolent young man. How dare he.

Delphine giggled beside her.

"What is this?" Harriet asked, turning to her giggling friend.

"This, my dear, is the art of palmistry. We are going to have our fortunes told."

Harriet groaned. She couldn't think of a more ridiculous pastime. It baffled her that an intelligent woman like Delphine could be so disposed. She'd noticed that Delphine had an inclination toward superstition. At times, it caused her to give credence to all manner of myth, legend, and unexplained phenomena, but she never thought she'd be taken in by such nonsense as this. Nevertheless, she took part to please her friend.

They took their seats at a small round table covered with a white satin cloth. On it stood a large glass orb on a silver stand and a group of tapered candles of varying height and thickness—some eight or ten inches tall and some almost burnt down to the wick. Thick blobs of melted wax dripped onto the shiny fabric, and the flames danced in the glass ball's reflection, casting moving shapes and strange shadows on the tent walls.

Lillian curled up on her mother's lap, fingers gripping Harriet's arm, and stared wide-eyed at the old woman facing them. Her skin was dark and lined with deep wrinkles. Her eyes were pale and watery, the pupils frosted over, and it occurred to Harriet that she might be blind.

For the first few seconds, Madam Lenora said nothing, only stared at them with blank eyes, then she took Delphine's hand and turned it over. She said a lot of things that Harriet expected—vague, noncommittal statements which could easily apply to anyone. Her accent was thick and difficult to understand—eastern, Harriet thought—perhaps Russian or Polish. She couldn't place it, but it added to the old woman's air of mystery.

It wasn't difficult to tell from Delphine's style of dress, and the fact she had money to spare for such nonsense, that she was a lady of wealth. The old woman could probably tell from Delphine's manner and deportment that she was of high birth. It was simple enough if you paid attention. Harriet thought she could make a respectable effort at fortune telling herself.

Delphine, on the other hand, did not appear the slightest bit sceptical of the woman's supernatural abilities, and was delighted with her reading. She turned to Harriet and said with obvious glee, "Your turn."

The old woman regarded Harriet with a keen eye. "No," she said and stood abruptly from the table.

Everyone turned to her in astonishment.

"What do you mean?" Delphine said. "We have paid for two readings."

"See the man outside. He will return your money."

Delphine tried again. "Please, won't you do the reading for my friend?"

"No reading," she repeated and shooed them away with her hand.

Harriet and Delphine exchanged glances. *What's the meaning of this refusal?*

She hadn't wanted her palm read—but now that she was being so vehemently refused, she needed to know why. She looked into the woman's face, and Madam Lenora narrowed her eyes.

Her hair glittered in the candlelight as a silver curl slipped from beneath her headscarf. She held Harriet's gaze for far longer than was polite before giving a slow, deliberate nod. "Very well. I can see you're headstrong, young sprite. But I warn you, I do not give false readings. I say what is shown, and you will not like it." She waited, holding Harriet in her steely gaze.

Harriet nodded and held out her hand, palm up on the table. She did not take her eyes from Madam Lenora's.

The old woman batted it away with impatience. "I don't need that. That's nothing but theatre. It's for show."

Harriet withdrew her hand and placed it in her lap, fiddling with the wedding band that still rested there.

"What is your name—your family name?"

"Blackthorn."

"Like the tree. It's not a good name," she paused, "do you know what it means?"

"I do not."

"It means strength, perseverance, but strife too. A name touched by secrets and sorrow. Your soul is marked." She fixed Harriet with a solemn look before closing her eyes again. "I see a shadow born of violence." She opened her eyes to look at Harriet, her voice softening. "Do you understand?"

"Yes." *Not really. She speaks in riddles.*

She nodded her head toward Lillian. "She bites the hand that feeds her. She will dance in another's shoes, and the next will bring you sorrow."

Harriet interrupted. "My child?"

"Yes."

"I've heard enough," Harriet said, drawing Lillian closer to her. She stood, knocking back the chair. "I will not suffer your foul prophecy."

Madam Lenora didn't flinch. "Sit down, lady."

Harriet hesitated, suddenly aware she was making a scene.

"I warned you—I speak plainly. I tell you only what I see, and once I start, I must finish."

Delphine cleared her throat, rising quickly. "Oh, I think that's quite enough for today, don't you? Thank you, Madam Lenora." She laid a hand on Harriet's arm. "Let's get some air, shall we?"

The old woman slid two silver coins back across the table. "I don't take money for bad readings."

Harriet glared at the coins and left them on the table.

Outside, Delphine was filled with remorse and apologised profusely for casting such a shadow over her birthday, but Harriet had composed herself by the time they left the tent. Despite her distaste for the experience and her absolute refusal to believe in nonsense, it had rattled her. The old woman had stirred something—an ominous feeling she couldn't shake.

Mr Oglethorpe was waiting at Greenacre when they returned from the fair. The butler explained that he'd insisted on staying—his business, he said, was a matter of great importance.

Harriet entered the library, where Mr Oglethorpe waited by the fire. He stepped forward with surprising eagerness, a rare smile playing at his lips.

"Good afternoon, Mrs Blackthorn. I trust I find you well?" He took her hand in both his and shook it with vigour.

"Yes, I'm quite well thank you. I believe you have something important to speak to me about?" She fiddled with a loose thread on her sleeve. *What could he want? Another debt? No—he looks* far *too pleased for that.*

"Indeed, I do, Mrs Blackthorn. I have some wonderful news for you."

Wonderful? It wasn't a word she'd heard him use before, and she couldn't imagine anything wonderful happening to her at this point.

"But first, allow me to wish you many happy returns of the day." He gave a little bow before turning to the fireplace to take down a large velvet pouch from the mantel. He held it out to her. "When your father made his will, God rest his soul, he stipulated that these were to come into your possession on the day of your twenty-first birthday."

"What are they?"

"Go ahead, take a look," he said, beaming at her.

She opened the bag and gasped.

Mr Oglethorpe chuckled. "Your mother's jewels, my dear."

"I didn't—I never knew she had any." Emotion swelled in her throat, and she fought to steady her voice. "Well, Mr Oglethorpe, this is a wonderful surprise indeed. Quite unexpected."

"Now that you have them in your possession, there are some papers to sign. If I might trouble you for a few moments longer, then I shall leave you to your celebrations." He retrieved a sheet of paper from his leather satchel, then took out a pen and a pot of ink. "It's merely a receipt to prove they have passed from my hands to yours—just a formality."

Harriet signed the paper and asked Mr Oglethorpe to join them for dinner. He declined politely and went on his way, still wearing the silly grin, which looked so out of place on his usually serious face.

When he left, she opened the bag again and stared in amazement. A glittering mass of precious stones and metals winked at her from within. Her heart fluttered at the sight. She never knew her mother had possessed such beautiful jewellery, and she wondered if Aggie knew about them too. *How lucky that my father thought to keep them from me until now. If he'd given them to me when I married, Arthur would have probably gambled them away.*

She knew deep down that she'd still have to part with them at some point. Fine jewels and pretty ornaments did not fill empty stomachs. But at least it would be on her terms—for the benefit of herself and Lillian—not him. *The money could secure lodgings until I find proper employment—*

perhaps even enough for a small house, if I'm careful. I'll have to be.

At last, she might make her own way in the world. All she had to do was break the news to Delphine. She waited until the following week. The conversation did not go at all as Harriet had imagined.

"You would leave me now, after letting me fall so completely in love with this little girl?" Delphine nuzzled into Lillian, who was sleeping on her lap. "You would be so cruel as to take her away?" She leaned in and whispered over Lillian's head, "What a wicked, wicked woman your mother is," smiling all the while. She cast Harriet a sly sideways glance.

Harriet flung up her hands in exasperation. She could tell Delphine wasn't taking her seriously—she was still smiling.

"I thought we were a family now," Delphine added for good measure.

They did feel like a family.

We are a family. The thought caught Harriet off guard, and her conviction faltered. "Delphine, I cannot, in good conscience, allow you to go on providing for us. It simply isn't right." She had to make Delphine see this from her point of view. She took a breath. "I need to reclaim something of myself."

"Pour l'amour du ciel, Harriet! C'est ridicule! I could not spend the money I have in this lifetime—what use is it when I cannot help the people I love? Would you prefer I were alone with my fortune and desperately miserable?"

"Very well," Harriet said, raising her chin. "I'll make a deal with you. We will stay, but under the condition that I pay rent as a lodger. And I need your assistance to sell this jewellery."

Delphine's lips parted to speak, but Harriet was quicker.

She raised a finger, firm and calm, to silence her bemused friend. "Stop. I won't have it. These are my terms. This is the only way I will agree to stay. It's important to me, Delphine. Now, will you help me or not?" She couldn't allow her to win this one.

Delphine considered Harriet, and something in her expression changed—like something new had just occurred to her. "Very well. I'll help you, but if you want a fair price, you'll have to wait a little while longer. There's only one man I'd trust with such business, and he won't be back here until the spring. Do you think you could wait until then?" Her eyes sparkled.

"I suppose I'll have to."

Once again, the delightful Madame de Matthieu had managed to have her way.

Harriet chuckled under her breath. *How does she always win?*

STRIKING A DEAL

By mid-April the following year, when the air had turned soft and sweet with spring, Delphine finally announced that her trusted buyer had returned to town. He was able to see them the next day, and Delphine sent word that they would meet him at four o'clock.

Harriet took the jewels from their pouch and admired the way they caught the early evening light—casting flashes of colour along the walls of the room. There was a handsome bracelet of gold filigree vines, set with rubies and emeralds to resemble red roses and green leaves; a beautiful opal ring; and a diamond brooch, among various other pieces.

Her favourite piece was a large sapphire pendant suspended from a chain of pearls. The brilliant blue stone was the size of a quail's egg, surrounded with rows of sparkling diamonds to form petals. Images of her mother swirled in her head. Long-forgotten pictures in photo frames—a painting in her father's study—her mother staring out from the canvas in eternal youth. A small plaque had been underneath the painting, inscribed with 'Henrietta Francisca de Borbon y Cabrera.'

She was wearing this necklace in the painting. I always thought it was the painter's embellishment. But it's real. Did she dream of passing this to her little girl one day? Did she even know I was a girl?

Her mother had died before she had the chance to hold her. It was strange to think she'd never known her mother's touch, even for a brief moment. Now, Harriet could not pass these treasures to her little girl either. She must sell them to provide for their future, whatever that might look like. Everything in the pouch was of substantial monetary value. The workmanship of each piece was incredible. But their value to her had nothing to do with money. The cost of selling them was far more personal.

She scooped them into the pouch before Delphine could catch her admiring them. If she realised the personal value held in that velvet pouch, she would refuse to help her sell them. Already she'd caused such a fuss, and Harriet hadn't expressly told the truth about them. She'd been deliberately vague, stating only that they were from family members she'd never known. It wasn't exactly a lie.

At three o'clock sharp, they set off to Lamb's field to meet their potential buyer. She'd never heard of Lamb's field before, but she discovered it was much less a field, and more, a dusty patch of land with very little grass to commend it as such. It was situated near the church she'd attended with Aggie, and was one of the stopping places used by the gypsies who travelled there every spring.

Harriet had expected to meet a gentleman jeweller, with a reputable business and proper premises but Delphine informed her no such thing existed, and she trusted her judgement.

Delphine strode into the camp like an exotic bird, bright

glossy plumage waving about in her hat—oblivious to the spectacle she created.

Harriet felt the eyes of each and every inhabitant. A tall man leaned against the wagon they were headed towards. His cap was so low over his brow that Harriet could hardly make out his face, but she knew the stance. Legs crossed at the ankle, thumb hooked into his pocket, weighing his watch in the other hand.

It's the man from the fairground. She cast her eyes about for the fortune teller, but didn't see her. *Good. I'm not sure I could take another melancholy prediction of what life has to offer me.*

This time, his greeting was neither humble nor gentlemanly. His demeanour was entirely different. They were in his territory now—and he didn't need their custom, or their money—they needed his.

Harriet was uneasy with this shift in dynamics, this transfer of power. Her confidence ebbed with each step toward him. The status that had afforded her confidence and safety previously was now gone. But then, status probably meant nothing here. She held tight to Delphine's arm.

"Evening, ma'am," the man said, offering his hand to Harriet and taking off his cap. "Charles Shaw."

"Evening, Mr Shaw," she said, trying to steady her voice as she shook his hand.

His dark eyes were clear and honest; his smile sincere. And the handshake—firm but brief. His hands were warm and rough from work—not like Caiaphas.

He turned to Delphine, amusement playing across his lips. It was the sort of smile a person tries hard to suppress, but their features betray them. He never took his eyes off her. "Evening, Delphine."

"Good evening, Charlie," Delphine said.

They're better acquainted than I realised. Interesting.

He led them up the wooden steps of a wagon, intricately carved and painted inside with reds, greens and golds that glinted in the candlelight. There were tiny cupboards everywhere, with bright brass hinges and latches. One even had a glass front with grapes etched into the glass. Velvet curtains hung from the windows, and heavy brocade cloth lined the ceiling. She'd never seen anything like it.

It was the only one in the camp, so heavily embellished. The other homes were roughly put together tent-like structures, with rain-streaked sheets draped over them. Some sat on the ground, others on carts and drays, but all were somewhat alike. *I wonder if they're cold at night. Or if they leak when it rains. How many people live inside them? Where do they keep their belongings?*

She forgot her own troubles momentarily, feeling suddenly very fortunate for the life she'd lived so far. *But how on earth are these people—with so little—going to buy my precious jewels?* Her hand tightened around the velvet pouch.

Presently, they were joined by a young woman who brought them tea. She and Mr Shaw shared a brief communication in a language Harriet did not understand. The woman handed him a jeweller's loupe, then left them to their business.

Harriet opened the pouch and placed the items on the table with trembling hands. The atmosphere felt thick with anticipation.

Mr Shaw waited until she'd laid out all the pieces, then inspected them with careful consideration, making notes on a scrap of paper. He lit a cigarette and drew on it whilst he worked.

It was widely known that gypsies were uneducated—Harriet had certainly believed so—but here was Mr Shaw, writing things down in elegant script. *Good for him! It seems Mr Shaw is a bit of a dark horse.* She glanced at Delphine, who was scrutinising him as though she had her own jeweller's loupe. Her hands were clasped in her lap, thumbs rubbing against each other in agitation. It was something Harriet hadn't seen her do before.

When he finished his examination of the jewellery, Mr Shaw leaned back and regarded Harriet with an unreadable expression. "You've got some fine pieces there, Mrs Blackthorn." He tipped his head back and took a last draw of his cigarette before flicking it with precision out of the open door. "Do you know what they're worth?"

"Well, Mr Shaw, I believe that's what we're here for." Harriet said, sounding more acidic than she'd intended.

He tilted his head to one side and looked at her. "I believe what you're here for is to find out what I'll pay for them. What I asked you is, do you know what they're worth?"

There was no malice or sarcasm in his tone, but she still felt foolish, regardless. She cleared her throat. "No, Mr Shaw, I'm afraid I don't."

"I see." He leaned forward, placing his elbows on his thighs, and clasped his hands together. "Never tell a buyer, you don't know the worth of your wares. You'll be robbed."

Splendid. He thinks I'm a fool.

"I have a rule, Mrs Blackthorn, and that rule is not to conduct business with people I do not trust, or who don't trust me." He paused, wearing the same unreadable expression. "It never ends well." He pointed to Delphine. "But my friend here enjoys the privilege of my trust, and she has also vouched for your name. The question is, Mrs Blackthorn, do you trust me?"

A privilege, he says. The arrogance of men! And Delphine is my friend! Something unfamiliar stirred within her. Was that jealousy? She pushed it down. "My friend has also vouched for you. So yes, I do." She placed special emphasis on the word 'my'.

Mr Shaw smiled, amused.

She shifted in her seat. *And now I've added petulance to my list of failings.*

"I'll speak plainly with you, Mrs Blackthorn. Your jewellery is worth four hundred pounds."

Harriet gasped.

"It is not, however, worth four hundred pounds to me. The best I can offer you is two hundred and fifty."

She looked at Delphine for guidance, but Delphine just smiled. Two hundred and fifty pounds was still an immense amount of money. *That's six years' salary working for the Hardcastles.*

"Take your time," he said, which only served to fluster her even more.

Her mind raced. She didn't want to appear at the mercy of her youth and inexperience, but she was. *Delphine said I'd have to barter.* She took a deep breath. "I need three hundred and fifty." *There, I did it.* She smiled and waited.

Mr Shaw rapped his hand on the table. "Three hundred and not a penny more. Take it or leave it."

Perfect. "Very well, Mr Shaw, we have a deal." She thrust her hand out to him, praying he didn't spit on his, as she'd seen so many working men do.

He didn't. He reached down to unlatch a small cupboard under his seat, but paused to look at Delphine. He seemed to pose some question in his look, which she answered with a nod, then he opened the door and brought out the largest purse of gold sovereigns Harriet had ever seen.

She struggled to keep the shock from her expression. *Who are these mysterious people? Keepers of magic—fortune tellers, who say so much by saying so little?* She looked at Delphine in wonder. *How do you fit into all this? Communicating with winks and nods and knowing looks.* She watched Mr Shaw count three hundred sovereigns into a burlap purse.

He handed them to her. "I'll escort you both home."

"There's no need, Charlie," Delphine cut in, placing a delicate hand on Mr Shaw's arm. "I've brought my footman with me. He will see us safely home."

"Does he know why you've come?"

"Well, of course. I told him we needed extra protection."

"Then he knows you have a lot of money in that purse."

They stared at each other, engaged in some kind of battle that Harriet didn't understand.

"He also knew we had a lot of jewels on the way here, but we arrived safely under his care, did we not?"

"I will see you home." He repeated it with a force under which Delphine wilted on the spot—her mighty powers of persuasion rendered utterly useless.

It had been a most peculiar evening. A night of revelation from beginning to end. An awkward silence rose between them on the journey back to Greenacre. Mr Shaw rode with them in the carriage, his horse saddled and tied behind the coach for him to ride home. There was something Harriet couldn't quite put her finger on. Like she'd stumbled unaware into somewhere she wasn't meant to be—gained a forbidden knowledge that bound her inextricably to them.

When they arrived home, Harriet thanked Mr Shaw again, and he helped her down from the carriage.

"Will you take supper before you head back, Charlie?" Delphine asked. It was the first thing she'd said to him since they set off.

"No, thank you. I must get back. I've other business to attend to."

Her smile faltered just enough for Harriet to notice.

“Another time,” he said, “I promise.” He winked, tipped his cap and mounted his horse in a graceful and practised movement.

Harriet went inside, leaving Delphine on the steps. It felt like an intrusion to witness their goodbye.

Delphine didn’t come in until Charlie disappeared around the bend and into the tree line. She didn't take supper that night either.

CONFESSION

"Good morning," Harriet said, finding Delphine in the breakfast room the next day. "Did you sleep well?"

She sat by the window, eyes trained on the winding road that she'd watched last night for so long. She turned and smiled when Harriet entered. "Yes, thank you. I didn't feel quite myself last night. I apologise for my bad manners." She took Harriet's hand and pressed it to her lips. "I know how you hate to eat alone. Forgive me."

"There's nothing to forgive, but are you feeling better? You seemed so...melancholy."

"I'm fine. I was just a little out of sorts." She smiled then, and her voice brightened like a lamp suddenly lit. "Now, tell me, are you happy with how things went last night?"

"I'm delighted."

"Then, since your finances are restored, you're going to stay?" Delphine clasped her hands together and beamed at her.

"You realise I've already been here almost a year. But yes, so long as you accept my payment for board and lodgings, I'd love to stay with you. I do still intend to have a place of my own though, so it won't be forever."

"As you wish." She leaned in conspiratorially. "You know, when word gets out that you're now rich as well as single, we may have to barricade ourselves in to keep out the callers. We might have all manner of undesirables vying for your attention."

Harriet let out a nervous laugh, unsure if Delphine was joking.

Delphine couldn't hold her serious expression for long. She burst into a peal of laughter so loud it brought the footman hurtling in to check if she was alright.

When the laughter subsided, Harriet cleared her throat and hesitated for a moment, fishing for the appropriate words. "Mr Shaw is quite the character, isn't he?"

"Yes, quite."

Her answer gave nothing away but Harriet was certain there was something between them. She couldn't say what, but there was definitely something. She'd felt it—a silent acknowledgement passing between them when they were together. She probed a little further. "I suppose he would be considered handsome by those who paid attention to that sort of thing?"

Delphine glanced sideways at her and smiled. "Since it's so out of character for you to pass comment on a man's appearance, I can only assume that you're fishing for information."

"No—just making conversation." *I'm a terrible liar.*

"It's written all over your face, mon cherie."

Harriet filled her plate with French pastries. "I don't understand why they live like that," she said, thinking out loud.

"Who?"

"The gypsies."

"What do you mean?" Delphine set the teapot down and knocked the top from a boiled egg with a flick of her knife.

"It surprises me, I suppose, how they live. Mr Shaw had more gold than most people see in a lifetime, so why do they choose to live in such poverty? I'd always assumed they had no choice."

Delphine's hand stilled halfway between plate and mouth. A piece of egg white trembled on the spoon. "Poverty? They live exactly as they wish—as is their tradition. Circumstance is not always dictated by necessity. Perhaps poverty means something different to you."

Harriet shrank. "Oh—I didn't—I mean…it seems such a difficult life to choose. I did not mean to speak ill of them." She rubbed her temples. "I have offended you."

Delphine smiled and took another bite of her breakfast. "No. I'm not offended. But that isn't what you really wanted to know, is it?"

Harriet blushed. *Am I really so transparent? And I've managed to offend my only friend before she's even had her breakfast. This is not shaping up to be a great day*. She pushed her plate away, not hungry now, and wondered how she might redeem herself.

Delphine stood up and placed her napkin on the table. "Come with me; there's something I'd like to show you." She led Harriet out into the kitchen garden.

Harriet followed like a pup, half eager, half nervous. They walked to the southeast corner of the vegetable garden, and Delphine lifted a thick curtain of ivy from the stone wall. It moved aside to reveal an arched wooden door. She took an iron key from her pocket and turned it in the lock. The door swung open, and Delphine paused. She looked once more at Harriet, then entered.

It was a small, private garden, about thirty feet long and twenty feet wide. High walls on all sides cut a neat oblong patch from the sky above them, and a large chestnut tree stood in one corner. Jasmine and honeysuckle clung to the walls at intervals, and bushes arranged in neat clumps bordered the gravel pathway winding its way through.

Warmth hung in patches between the dappled shade, and small birds hopped about to bask in the sunny spots. It was almost silent except for the occasional call of a sparrow, the gentle hum of a bee, and the soft splash of running water somewhere in the distance. Sounds from outside the wall struggled to permeate the air within, as though some mysterious force protected it from the outside world.

She followed Delphine to a small niche, where a trickle of water fell from the mouth of a stone cherub set into the wall. She turned to thank Delphine for sharing this magical place with her. And then she saw it—the reason they were here.

Directly across from where she stood, on a patch of bright green lawn, stood a tiny stone cross with a doll at its foot. Harriet's stomach lurched. She drew a sharp intake of breath and stood very still. *It's a headstone—a child's headstone.* She took in her surroundings again. *This isn't a garden—it's a graveyard.*

Delphine was watching her. She sat down on a bench at the edge of the lawn without speaking.

Harriet sat down beside her, wringing her hands. *What do I say under such weighty circumstances?* She was too inexperienced for this calibre of conversation.

Delphine spoke first. "Ten years ago, Charlie—Mr Shaw, that is, and I were to be married." She paused, glancing at Harriet. "We were very much in love, but we faced a lot of difficulties. You see, both our families frowned upon the union. We were from such different circumstances—different worlds. We were both of full age—we didn't need anyone's permission, so we decided to marry in secret."

Harriet put a hand on Delphine's arm. "You don't have to exp—"

"No!" She cut Harriet off. "I want to. I need you to know."

Harriet nodded.

"Charlie got a special licence, so the banns didn't need to be read in our village. When the day came, I was so excited I could hardly keep still. I told my driver he didn't need to wait for me as I was coming home later with a friend. It was a warm day, but I had to wear a cloak to hide my wedding gown. I'd made it myself from fine gossamer and lace—it was beautiful. I had a posy of jasmine because it was Charlie's favourite, and I hid it in a basket with my veil until I got to the church. When I took it out, I had crushed some of the delicate petals. I remember the scent filling the church as the day got hotter."

She closed her eyes and breathed in as though she could still smell it. "I waited for what felt like a long time. I thought at first something had delayed Charlie. The vicar came out of the vestry every so often wearing a hopeful expression, and I would just shake my head. After a while, he tried to make me go home, but I was determined my Charlie would come. Then I started to worry something terrible had happened to him—that he might be hurt somewhere—unable to reach me. Perhaps he'd changed his mind and didn't love me after all. Although I couldn't bring myself to truly believe that one."

Harriet hardly dared to breathe lest she disturb her.

"Well into the evening, I sat in that pew, watching shadows grow longer and the light turn pale and silvery, but he never came. It wasn't until my parents came looking for me, worried sick, that I found out what had really happened."

Harriet released the breath she'd been holding. "I'm so sorry." She didn't know what else to say.

"When I got home, I learned he'd managed to send word to me, but not before I'd left that morning. The note was still sitting on the tray in our hallway. No-one had paid it any attention." A single tear slipped down her cheek.

"It turned out he'd been arrested and hauled off to jail the night before. I remember my knees giving way and my mother shrieking as I fell. You see, he'd encountered some trouble in London a while back. He was only nineteen at the time. His younger sister worked as a maid, close to where his family were camped. She'd come home in a frightful state one night, with torn clothing and a bloody face. She said the master of the house had forced himself upon her and taken her virtue."

Harriet gasped and covered her mouth.

"Charlie set off to kill him there and then, but his family stopped him—begged him to reconsider. They knew he'd be caught and hanged. They kept a tight rein on him for two days and might have succeeded, only his sister drowned herself—couldn't bear the shame she felt. He went mad—they couldn't stop him. He went to the house and beat the man bloody. He didn't stop until he was sure he'd killed him. They packed up and disappeared in the middle of the night."

"How awful," Harriet said, emotion tightening her chest.

"But the man he'd beaten wasn't dead and knew who he was. Charlie had been running for almost five years when the law caught up with him the night before our wedding. It wasn't murder, but it was still a serious crime, and against a gentleman. They made an example of him—seven years' transportation to an Australian colony, and when he eventually came back, he had a wife." She laughed bitterly.

"He wrote to me afterwards. Once to tell me he was sorry

—that he loved me, and once to say goodbye—because they'd forced him to take a wife. I never told him what he'd left behind."

Left behind? What does she—? Oh....

"She was born five months after he left. My sweet little angel. She never took a single breath."

She looked at Harriet with the wide, innocent eyes of a child—like she couldn't believe it herself. They were both silent for a beat.

Harriet reached across and laced her fingers through Delphine's—a silent show of unity. "I don't know how to comfort you. I don't know the right things to say."

Delphine looked at their conjoined hands and squeezed. "You don't have to. This is enough."

"What about your family?"

"My father was so disgusted with me, he packed up his belongings the moment he found out. My mother wanted to stay, but he wouldn't hear of it. They went back to France and left me here. I was completely alone when I gave birth."

Harriet shivered. *What sort of mother could abandon her daughter to such a fate? I thought myself worldly, but I've experienced neither euphoria nor wretchedness. I've known nothing but mediocrity—a half-life.*

Delphine sniffled. "Do you know I couldn't bury my baby in the graveyard? My beautiful, innocent child, who never knew a day's sin. They offered me a shared grave on a patch of unconsecrated ground, with some poor family whose father had taken his own life." Her voice was hollow. "As though we were burying our family pets, and digging one hole was more convenient."

The light left her—like a room plunged into darkness when a candle blows out. She didn't sob or wail. In fact, she did not move at all, only stared at the little cross, a stream of tears slipping down her cheeks.

Speaking was impossible—Harriet couldn't swallow the lump in her throat. So she held her in silence, stroking her hair and kissing the top of her head until the tears stopped falling. *How does she find the strength to go on?* Ten years had passed, and still her pain was as raw and new as though it had just happened.

After a while, when Delphine seemed to come back to herself a little, she sat up and wiped her face. "Charlie must not know."

"Of course," Harriet nodded, "but can I ask why you never told him?"

Delphine shrugged. "He was gone—it was too late. And what was the sense in both of us dying inside? I thought it was kinder to spare him the pain."

"Oh, Delphine, you've suffered this alone all these years, to spare someone else?" She turned that over in her mind. *I've never witnessed such sacrifice. How does she bear it?* "Why do you still keep in touch with him? Surely it's painful for you to see him this way. Wouldn't it be kinder to yourself to put some distance between you?"

Delphine gave a short, mirthless laugh. It burst from her, unbidden. "Distance is no match for memory. He will always be here," she laid a hand over her heart, "no matter the distance I put between us. To answer your question, it is painful to see him—almost unbearable. But for that brief moment when he looks at me—I'm free." She wore an expression Harriet could only describe as reverent.

"There is no other freedom for me, not even from memory. I've tried banishing his memory—pictures, trinkets—anything connected to who I was and what I've lost. Only to walk down the street and be assailed by scents and sounds, vehicles of memory, which transport me back in an instant—the smell of jasmine, a baby's cry. There is no escape for me except through him."

"I understand," Harriet said, but she didn't—not really. How could she? "So last night, the young woman who brought us tea, is that—?" She caught herself. *I shouldn't have started that question. Too late.*

"That's her," Delphine whispered, "his wife."

"I see." *So this is why Hortense treated her with such disdain. The congregation in church that day. They knew.* She tilted up Delphine's face and looked at her empty and watery eyes. "Why didn't you tell me before now? You shouldn't have to carry this alone."

"I didn't want you to leave. You're the first person to show me kindness since it happened—the only friend I've known in such a long time. I was afraid you'd shun me too."

Her vulnerability sliced through Harriet. "I'm not going anywhere," she told her. "You were the only person in the world who was there for me when I needed you. Now let me be here for you. You don't have to bear this alone." She took her handkerchief and dabbed at Delphine's tear-stained face. *How many people carry such secret tragedies under the surface I wonder? How did I miss this? I haven't paid enough attention to notice my friend's pain. I've been so focused on my own—which is nothing beside this.* Guilt gnawed at her.

Beneath the exterior she presented, Delphine was more world-weary than Harriet had realised. She harboured none of Harriet's girlish naivety in her conception of the world. She was considerably richer in character than the painted butterfly she appeared to be. This woman knew pain and disappointment, had suffered loss and cruelty, yet she still showed more kindness than anyone Harriet had ever encountered.

She looked at Delphine, seated on the bench.

An exquisite being, shattered like crystal. The damage irrevocable.

Harriet knelt to place a kiss on the little headstone and led Delphine back inside. Both were broken perhaps, but stronger now than they were apart.

NEWS FROM DURHAM

Harriet watched her friend slowly withdraw from the world. It was as though, after years of holding in her secret pain, releasing it had rendered it uncontrollable. Even when it passed and the pain subsided, it would inevitably return at some point to reopen the wound in an endless cycle of torment. Sometimes it passed in days or hours, and sometimes it took weeks.

Harriet tried to fill Delphine's days with pleasant distractions. If she had no time to become lost in her thoughts, perhaps she wouldn't dwell on the pain. She also became acutely aware of showing affection to Lillian in Delphine's presence—careful not to flaunt a mother's love before one who had lost it.

She took her on endless walks around the countryside—dragged her to flower-arranging lectures she paid no heed to. They wrote letters, read books, and even sewed a new tablecloth. They laboured over it for hours on end, embroidering delicate blooms and vines onto the fine linen—all in the name of distraction.

They were sitting in the drawing-room one afternoon, working on the tablecloth, whilst Lillian played hide and seek with the maid. The room was quiet except for the puk, puk, puk, of needles puncturing the taut surface of the embroidery hoop. The silence had all but driven Harriet mad until Delphine suddenly threw down her work and declared she was done.

"I cannot do this. You have to stop!"

Harriet blinked in surprise, her arm frozen in an outstretched position—needle in the air. "Stop what?" she said. "What's the matter?"

"This!" Delphine spread her arms, gesturing to the tablecloth laid out across the carpet. "All of it! This incessant execution of meaningless, time-filling tasks. I can't bear it a moment longer!" Her voice cracked and failed her at this point. She covered her face with her hands and started to cry. "I'm sorry."

Harriet set down her embroidery and went to her. "You have nothing to be sorry for." She stroked her hair as Delphine buried her face in her shoulder. "It is I who should apologise. I thought that by keeping you busy, I might take your mind from your troubles, but I can see now that was a mistake. I'm sorry if I've made it more difficult for you."

Delphine sniffled and blew her nose. "It doesn't work like that. I need to feel the pain for it to pass—not ignore it, nor trick myself into forgetting. It must run its course."

"I understand," Harriet said, though it was difficult to fathom. *I'm not sure I'll ever understand this. I don't understand why people can't be clear about what they want or expect. Particularly at times like this.* It had been her first encounter with a sadness so absolute, and she still had no idea how to handle it. But in time, she learned—found the balance between comforting and allowing Delphine space to heal. She picked up little clues from Delphine's behaviour, her tone or expression. It was a valuable lesson—one she deigned not to forget.

Harriet learned much about herself in those few months. For the first time, she'd seen a soul laid bare, and it altered her in a way she didn't fully comprehend. She realised she'd been trying to hide Delphine's pain because it made *her* uncomfortable. Now she must learn to sit with it and not shrink back. That was hardest of all.

Delphine became her emotional point of reference—a comparison in which she found herself lacking. *How petty and spoiled I've been about the changes in my fortune and status. How little I've mourned my husband? Poor Arthur, did he not deserve at least a drop of sorrow at his passing? How callous of me not to afford him even that?*

It was amid this revelation of self-deprecation that she received another blow. News came from Durham of Aggie's death. John wrote to her and told her the terrible news. She'd caught scarlet fever from a child in the village. The child was one of three who died in the same week. *It cannot be true. She can't be gone. Not Aggie. I haven't even had the chance to visit her yet.* She shook her head and read the lines again. *How is it possible that a few marks on a piece of paper can bear the weight of such tragedy—deliver such life-altering circumstances?*

It had been eighteen months since she spent Christmas with Aggie and John, but time had passed so quickly she barely noticed it. *Now it's too late.* She pictured her standing there with her pudding and tried desperately to remember their last conversation. *What did we speak of? What did I say as we parted? Did I tell her I loved her?* She couldn't remember.

She ran to her room and rifled through the writing desk to find their last correspondence. She tore off the ribbon from the stack of letters, sending them sprawling over the carpet, and scanned the pages. The most recent one she found was a fortnight ago. She read and re-read the words as though she could read her back into existence, running trembling fingers over the name at the bottom of the page. 'All my love always, Aggie.'

The emotional barriers she'd so carefully begun to dismantle were shaken to their foundations and crumbled around her. Her tears fell and mingled with the ink on the paper, spoiling the writing. She dabbed at the mess with her sleeve, afraid the precious words might disappear forever.

Delphine was calling from somewhere down the hall. "Harriet! Harriet?" She burst into the room, her voice bright with excitement. "Harriet, you'll never guess wha—" She stopped mid-sentence and stood still. "What is it? What's the matter?"

Harriet looked up at her. "It's Aggie. She's gone."

Delphine crossed the room—and just like that, their roles reversed once more.

~

THE LETTER from John had been delayed, and they had to travel to Durham that very day in order to make it to the funeral. Delphine accompanied her, and Lillian stayed at home under the care of Mrs Drummond, Delphine's housekeeper. It was the first night Harriet would spend apart from Lillian.

They took the first train up to Carlisle, where they changed to another that took them east, across the country. Harriet had not travelled by train for some time, yet nothing had changed. She still loathed the rickety, rackety sound of the wheels as they gathered speed on the track—the piercing whistle and hiss of steam. The carriage lurched and swayed, and brakes screamed as they pulled into each station. She gripped the leather handle that hung from the ceiling and leaned her head against the window, watching the banks of the railway whirr past, their trees and hedges a blur of green.

The countryside was a patchwork quilt of gold and green, divided up by stone walls and timber fences. Some fields were filled with cattle like splotches of black and white paint on the grass—some had flocks of sheep that moved about in clouds, like the seeds of a dandelion clock. Wind moved over the grass in silvery ripples, shimmering in the afternoon sun. The scenery soothed her—the simple earthly beauty in nature, and its autumn colours. She closed her eyes and thought about Lillian. It felt strange not to have her close by—like she was missing a vital part of herself.

"Are you alright?" Delphine said. "You look pale."

Harriet opened her eyes. "Yes, I'm fine, just thinking about Lillian."

"I know you don't like to be apart, but she'll be fine. Try not to worry. Mrs Drummond has been with me for a long time, and she is wonderful with children. And Tilly is there; she adores her."

"I know, I just don't like it."

They drifted back into easy silence, then Harriet remembered Delphine bursting into the room this morning. "What was it you came to tell me this morning?"

Delphine looked at her, blank as a sheet of paper.

"This morning when you came to my room. You were calling my name all through the house."

"Oh—oh yes. I didn't get to tell you, did I? Well, it seems trivial now." She waved her hand. "It doesn't matter."

"Whatever it was, you were in a hurry to tell me at the time. Please tell me; it will take my mind off the journey."

Delphine considered it for a moment before she spoke.

"Very well." She leaned forward. "When I was in town this morning, I ran into Emily Carter from the lodging house."

Harriet bristled.

"Well, you know how she likes to gossip. She couldn't wait to tell me there had been some trouble between the Hardcastles and Hortense." She paused again and waited for Harriet's response.

"Go on."

"Apparently, Mr Hardcastle persuaded Hortense to introduce him to her husband, intending to involve him in a grand investment scheme. By her account, they had become quite friendly and visited each other often."

"Hortense and Mr Hardcastle?" Harriet said, astonished.

"No, no, of course not." Delphine waved her hand impatiently. "Mr Watson and Mr Hardcastle."

"Really? That is surprising. Mr Watson is rarely seen out of the house," Harriet said.

"Why not?"

"On account of his ill health. He suffers bouts of melancholia, and I was told he's largely confined to his bed." None of this made sense to Harriet.

"I wasn't aware of that," Delphine said. "Has he some injury or wasting disease?"

"Oh, no, nothing like that. It's his weight. The man's as fat as three pigs." She said it so plainly, and without a trace of humour, that Delphine burst into laughter.

"Alright, where was I?" she continued. "Oh yes. Well, about a week ago, Hortense paid a visit to Mrs Hardcastle, but she wasn't at home. Mr Hardcastle, however, was at home and had behaved less than honourably towards her. I don't know what happened exactly, but a big row ensued between the two families."

"Oh, that is unfortunate," Harriet said.

"Unfortunate? I'd say she's had a taste of her own vile poison if you ask me. But that's not all." Excitement sparkled in her eyes, and she moved to the edge of her seat. "After they'd fallen out, Mr Watson naturally sought a way out of the investment, but Hardcastle had tied up his money with shares in the Royal British Bank. When the bank collapsed two days ago, it took the Watson's fortune with it. Hortense and her husband are ruined. Their entire fortune gone."

Now she had Harriet's attention. "Everything?"

"Destitute," Delphine said with satisfaction.

"What devil lives in that man? I do not know how he gets away with it. I'd have thought one word from Mr Watson would leave Hardcastle's reputation in tatters." She shook her head. "I've never known a man so destitute of principle."

"He hasn't quite gotten away with it. According to Mrs Carter, his wife has left him and gone back to her family."

Harriet smiled. "Good for her. She's finally seen sense and left the wretched man. Although it's hardly a felicitous consequence." Perhaps now Hortense wouldn't be so quick to judge others either. She might even feel some regret at having spread the vicious gossip.

"It seems Caiaphas has finally burned every bridge," Delphine said.

Harriet didn't answer. She felt no peace in the knowing. Men like Caiaphas didn't disappear—they lingered, festering in the dark.

~

JOHN WAS WAITING for them at Newcastle station, with a small dog cart and pony. He took Harriet in a crushing embrace that expressed everything he felt about the loss of his sister. He tipped his hat to Delphine, then helped them both into the cart without a word.

Harriet knew him too well to think it was a product of bad manners. He and Aggie were very much alike. She could see that the sheer force of raw emotion had him choked up so much he couldn't have uttered a word without breaking down.

They had travelled a good three-quarters of the twelve mile journey to Waldridge before he managed to speak. He cleared his throat and announced in a strangled voice, "Not far now, ladies. Just another three miles or so."

The rough wooden slats of the dog cart seat were a far cry from the plush velvet cushions she'd become accustomed to in Delphine's carriage. Every bump in the road caused a new ache, but reaching Aggie's house would render the whole scenario undeniably real, and she wished there were another fifteen miles still to travel.

Even though she knew better, she'd half expected Aggie to be there on the platform, or standing in the doorway when they arrived home. *How strange it is—what the mind clings to. How ridiculous our thoughts are in the privacy of our own minds, unchecked by sense or reason. Grief makes fools of us, chewing up our logic and spitting it out.*

They travelled the last three miles in weighty silence. It didn't seem appropriate to converse about trivial things like the weather, or how John liked his new home. She couldn't think of anything to say if she'd wanted to. All she could think of was never seeing Aggie again. She'd lost her mother, her father and her husband, and Aggie was the one person who had stayed constant throughout her life. She anchored her in a way that no-one else ever had.

Aggie had been her touchstone. Her home. She couldn't even imagine a world without Aggie in it.

"It'll be smoother travelling from here on, ladies," John said over his shoulder.

"Are we almost arrived?" Harriet asked.

He gestured with the whip towards a stone archway above them. It marked the entrance to the Waldridge Manor estate. A row of stately poplars flanked the lane for a few hundred yards, where they ended abruptly on the crest of a hill. The view opened out below, displaying Waldridge Manor and what looked like a small village. The evening sun burned through the clouds in one or two places, casting immense shafts of light down into the valley basin, illuminating it like a stage lamp.

"It's incredibly beautiful," said Delphine.

"Aye, that it is." John slowed the horse's pace almost to a stop. "Our Aggie loved this view. She made me stop here every time we came back from town, just so she could take it all in." His voice cracked again, and he snapped the reins, sending the horse on its way.

Harriet looked down at the village, trying to appreciate the beauty as Aggie would have done, but all she could focus on was the church steeple—tall and black against the green hills. It demanded her attention, jutting out spitefully like a pin stuck in a giant map—this is where you will bury your friend.

FUNERAL

The smithy stood at the edge of the village and was closest to the manor house. There was a smart cottage attached to it with flower beds on either side of the door and a rose climbing up over the doorway. It was long past the flowering season, but Harriet knew without a doubt the blooms would be red. Her heart gave a tug inside her chest as she thought of Aggie's proud smile when John had told her about the cottage. It looked just as he'd described.

I wish I could have seen it without the black crepe wreath hanging on the door.

A plump woman with a blotchy face greeted them and led them into the house. Harriet did not know her, but the woman introduced herself as Aggie's friend. She sniffled and dabbed her eyes with her apron as she spoke to them.

Aggie never mentioned you in her letters, but you speak of her as though I were the stranger.

The house was filled with mourners: women of all ages flitting about the house like a swarm of black flies. One made tea and handed out pieces of Aggie's orange cake.

Harriet longed to stop her. *Put it back. You can't give that away. Don't they understand there will never be another one?*

John appeared at her side. "She's right in here," he said, as though they were being shown into the drawing room for a visit. There were people in the room already, and John addressed them all. "If you ladies would be kind enough to give Mrs Blackthorn and her friend a few minutes' privacy."

The ladies in question filed obediently out of the room where Aggie was laid out.

The coffin stood on two wooden biers, and white linen was draped all around the room. At either end of the coffin stood two candlesticks, enormous pillars of brass, each holding a lighted candle, and the room was filled with flowers. No black was inside the house. The mirrors were covered, and the window was open. Everything was just as it should be, but there was no black—just as Aggie wanted.

Harriet felt Delphine's hand at her back.

"Are you ready, Harriet?"

"No. No—I cannot see her like that. I cannot."

"Hattie, you must. You must say goodbye now, or it will forever be a source of regret to you. I am here if you need me, but you must try."

Hattie.

She'd never called her that before. The pet name her father had called her—what her mother might have called her if she'd lived. What Aggie might have called her if only she'd allowed herself to.

Delphine's simple act of familiarity was too much for her to bear. She could no longer hold back the tears. She made no move to dry them, but let them drip from her chin, soaking the breast of her mourning frock. She took a deep breath and stepped forward to look at her sweet, kind Aggie one last time.

It wasn't the first time she'd seen someone in death, but she was still shocked by the coldness. Even though there were other notable indications of death—the mouth downturned where there should have been a smile, the eyes sunken, skin pale and waxy—it was always the touch which upset her. She still never expected them to feel quite so cold. It was the most unnatural thing one could ever witness.

Aggie was so bright and joyful; she cared so deeply—showed so much love and warmth. How can a person like that feel so icy to the touch? If anyone was still unwilling to accept death in the madness of their grief, then surely one touch of that cold flesh would be potent enough to dispel any doubt.

HARRIET TRIED to get some rest that night, but she couldn't. After a couple of hours of fitful sleep, she tiptoed barefoot down the stairs to spend her last few hours with Aggie in the peace and quiet of early morning.

Weak sunlight filtered through the white linen over the window, bathing the room in an ethereal glow. It created an atmosphere of peace and tranquillity that she had never before experienced. The candles still burned, clear wax dribbling down their sides and falling to the floor in a wreath around the candlestick base. She watched it cool and turn cloudy, then creamy white as it hardened and set. *Aggie would be less than pleased to see wax making a mess on her polished wooden floor.*

She bent down and tried to scrape it from the wood with her fingernails. It was too hard and thick to remove. She looked around for something to aid her, but seeing nothing, began scratching at it with both hands. *She won't like this. I must get it off.* Then she felt a hand on her shoulder and heard the gentle rumbling of John's deep voice.

"Leave it, my pet. It doesn't matter." His mere presence brought a calm with it.

"But she won't like it," Harriet said, then checking herself, added, "I mean, she wouldn't have liked it."

John took her by the arms and lifted her to her feet. "Come now, compose yourself. She wouldn't want to see you in this state. Why, she always told me you were strong as iron. I don't think she'd ever seen you cry." He took a wrinkled handkerchief from his pocket and dabbed at the tears on her face. "Come on now, there's something I need you to do for me—for Aggie."

Harriet nodded and tried to compose herself as John left the room. *How shamefully I've crumbled in the face of such dignity.*

He returned a moment later with a large bowl of liquid and a comb. They exchanged a look that needed no words, and she understood they were going to comb Aggie's hair with cold tea. Harriet lifted the thin gauze veil from Aggie's face.

Laying there in silken sleep, her favourite prayer book in her resting hands, she was dressed in her Sunday best instead of a shroud, as had always been her request. She always said that the first act of devotion made to the Lord on a Sunday was the presentation of oneself at church in one's best clothing. She wanted her final journey down the aisle to be no different.

John stood in silence, holding the bowl of amber liquid in his large hands, as Harriet dipped and combed.

I cannot fathom the strength it must take to show kindness to others when his own heart is breaking. She'd met many a gentleman with polished manners and cultured conversation, with titles and money to commend them. John had none of these things, yet he was more gentlemanly than anyone she'd ever met. John had kindness and compassion. He had morality instead of pride—knew the value of things without a price. He loved quietly, steadily, without prejudice. He didn't preach his moral code—he lived by it. *Society could learn a lesson or two from this man: the kind of man who makes no distinction between his troubles and yours.*

He had executed everything perfectly for the funeral, just as Aggie would have wanted. The service was not expressed with its usual rigid formality but was personal and comforting. Harriet could tell that the vicar had liked Aggie. He spoke of her with such warmth and affection.

At the house afterwards, there was none of the stifled, awkward conversation which often ensued at wakes. A rapid succession of commonplace remarks which meant little or nothing to the person in receipt of them. Instead, people shared stories of her—remembered her with genuine affection. They laughed, and they cried, and Harriet couldn't imagine a more beautiful way to say goodbye to her dearest friend.

AN UNLIKELY OPPORTUNITY

Harriet grew restless in the months following Aggie's funeral. Although her jewellery had brought a princely sum, she knew it wouldn't last forever. Every day she spent at leisure, she could feel their security slipping away. Lillian's future was uncertain, and she had to provide for that uncertainty. *What if she never marries? What would happen to her when I'm gone? We must have a place of our own—somewhere she can call home no matter what happens.*

She decided it was time to look for work again—not in the way she'd done before—a desperate bid for whatever she might turn her hand to. This time she had the luxury of choice. Their circumstances were no longer critical, so she could afford to wait until the right situation presented itself.

It did so in the most unlikely of places.

During the summer of Lillian's fifth birthday, Harriet and Delphine took her on a trip to the Lake District. It was the first time Harriet had taken a holiday since she was a child. She loved the raw beauty of the land there, and as much as she disliked the hustle and bustle of busy places, she appreciated the anonymity it afforded. No-one here knew her name—her story, or any other story a person might attribute to her, be it true or false. Here they were just an ordinary family.

They had enjoyed four days of glorious weather, picnics and countryside rambles, and on the fifth day, they took a ride on a steamboat on Lake Windermere. The Dragonfly was the largest steamer on the lake, and according to the ticket seller, the fastest. She was painted white, and her wooden floorboards shone like polished glass. A slender funnel rose from the deck and puffed out clouds of white smoke like a giant cigarette. At the stern was a small brass band, which struck up a raucous rendition of 'The Girl I Left Behind Me' whenever they passed the other boats on the lake.

This was to the great amusement of the passengers and Lillian, who was very excited about the whole thing. She had never been on a boat before and was completely enthralled. After a quarter hour of asking questions and talking incessantly about her experience, Lillian was taken by Aunt Delphine for a turn about the deck, giving her mother a few minutes of peace.

Harriet stood against the railings, watching the boat glide through the water. The afternoon sun was low for the time of year and glinted gold on the ripples disturbing the sheet of black water. A small boy caught her eye, about ten yards to her right: pink-cheeked with a mop of hair the colour of straw. He was climbing up onto the railings to look at the water. He was perhaps three or four years old, his face still dimpled and round, his movements not quite coordinated. A young girl accompanied him—his sister, maybe—and a rotund woman of about fifty.

Harriet studied her plain style of dress, and the way she addressed the children. *She must be the governess or perhaps the nurse.* She was fussing over the girl, scolding her, levelling her collar and straightening her hair, and the little boy appeared to have escaped her notice.

It set Harriet's nerves on edge to watch him. The railings were slick with green algae and spray, and his tiny leather-soled shoes struggled to find purchase against it. She had unconsciously been creeping forward, towards him from the moment she saw him.

By the time his foot slipped, she was just within reach to grab him by the collar as he slid between the bars and off the deck. She grasped his clothing firmly at the back of his neck, but he was suspended above the water, and she feared he might very well choke before she could pull him back up. In her rush to grab him, she had thrown herself onto the floor and was now stretched out upon her stomach along the deck.

The nurse, eventually hearing the commotion, reached over Harriet to help pull the boy up. She only made matters worse and pushed Harriet closer to the edge of the boat. Harriet felt her skirts slither overboard—her left leg followed, then the other—until she too hung over the side holding on with only one hand. The woman ran away, screaming for assistance.

Harriet tried to tighten her grip on the railing, but her palm, dampened with sweat, slid down the post little by little. She felt the water pulling at the fabric of her dress, seeping its way up the heavy cloth, and dragging her further down. She struggled to hold both their weights, and the boy slipped further into the water. She tried to hoist him upwards, but he screamed and thrashed, making it almost impossible to hold on to him with one hand.

"Quick, over there!"

She heard voices and the clomping of heavy boots and then a man jumped overboard with a great splash. He had a rope tied around his middle, giving him two free hands to grab the boy and push him up onto the deck. He soared through the air as though he were weightless—like a salmon leaping from the river. A thousand droplets of spray followed him, catching the sun so they glittered like jewels.

The man then put one arm around Harriet's waist and signalled to the others to pull them up. She was hauled onto the deck with an unceremonious wet thud. Exhausted and shivering violently, she closed her eyes and breathed hard. Someone covered her with a blanket, but her wet clothes clung to every inch of her. The blanket only pressed the coldness in tighter. *At least the boy is saved. Thank God!*

Passengers grouped together to see the unfortunate and soggy individuals who had been rescued. They cheered, clapped and scolded simultaneously, some congratulating her on her bravery and others condemning her for her stupidity in attempting such a rescue. *Unbelievable! Would they rather I'd watched him drown?*

The captain turned the boat around immediately, returning everyone to shore. The boy's parents, a Mr and Mrs Davenport, insisted that all involved see a doctor at their hotel. The last thing Harriet wanted was to be poked, prodded and examined by a doctor, but after a hasty introduction to the Davenports—who would not accept no for an answer—Harriet agreed to see Dr Brownsword.

He prescribed a very hot bath, various tonics and herbal remedies and at least a week's bed rest. She was happy enough to accept the bath and a clean, dry dress, but a week's bed rest was a little excessive. *A few cups of hot tea were all I needed. That's what Aggie would have prescribed, and she's never been wrong in all the years I've known her.*

Mr and Mrs Davenport were incredibly grateful for Harriet's part in their son's rescue and insisted on hosting a simple dinner to honour her that evening. They were joined by Mr Davenport's aunt, Lady Clarissa Montgomery, who was staying with the family for the season.

The simple dinner was more like a small banquet, complete with a string quartet. It was a lavish affair that better lent itself to showcasing their fortune than their appreciation. She'd never seen such an excessive and ostentatious display of wealth. They held the meal in the hotel's banqueting suite, and there was enough food and wine for forty to fifty people.

The table was adorned with fresh fruit and flowers, and Mrs Davenport wore so many jewels, the effect was almost blinding. Each time she moved, her diamonds picked up the candlelight and scattered it about the room in fragments. She smiled at Harriet—not with affection—but eagerness, excitement even. Like a child hoping for praise.

Whilst living with Delphine, Harriet had become more in tune with the subtle nuances in character that people displayed quite by accident. *Aggie could always hear the unsaid—read the unwritten.* She studied people now, watched their expressions, their movements, tone of voice, anything that gave away clues to their hidden truths. She often removed herself from company—present in body—but absent in mind.

Delphine sometimes had to jab her discreetly with the elbow, or tap her foot under a table to bring her back into the room.

"Are we waiting for someone else?" Lady Montgomery asked when they sat down to dinner.

"No, we are all present." Mrs Davenport answered. Her tone was clipped.

"What about Elizabeth? Is she not dining with us this

evening?" A smirk tugged at the corners of Lady Montgomery's mouth.

Mrs Davenport shot her a cold stare. "Of course not, Aunt Clarissa. Why would the staff be dining with us? And in any case, Elizabeth is no longer a part of this household after today's debacle." She smiled apologetically at Harriet, as though Lady Montgomery were old and confused and must be excused for her impertinence.

How curious. So Elizabeth was the governess. I think perhaps she does dine with them ordinarily, but why the deliberate attempt to let slip that little secret? This promises to be no ordinary evening.

Lady Montgomery's eyes glittered, and the faintest hint of satisfaction passed across her expression.

Advantage to Lady Montgomery. She stole a glance at Delphine, who looked amused.

"How is your little boy Mrs Davenport? I hope he's recovering well," Harriet said.

Mr Davenport cut in before his wife had time to form a response. "He's a fine sturdy boy, Mrs Blackthorn." He puffed on his pipe from the corner of his mouth. "It would take more than a little cold water to sicken him. The doctor assures me he will make a full recovery in a few days."

"I'm very glad to hear it."

"It's thanks to you that we still have a son at all," he said. "We might just as easily be sitting around a wooden box this evening instead of this fine feast."

Harriet flinched as the image rose unbidden into her mind.

"We are forever in your debt, and anything we might do to be of assistance to you would be gladly undertaken." He raised a glass and stood to make a toast to Harriet.

Colour rose to her cheeks as everyone's attention turned to her, but she was spared further embarrassment by Mrs

Davenport, who was at that moment overcome with emotion, and seized by a passionate bout of wailing.

"Oh, my poor boy! When I think of that careless woman, to think I had given my children into the charge of such a mindless and foolish creature! Why we ought to have had her flogged before we dismissed her, James. She deserved no less."

Poor Elizabeth. I daresay she has no idea of the fate she's escaped. She risked another glance at Delphine, whose lips were pressed firmly in a tight line, but her eyes were laughing. *Hardly surprising. Mrs Davenport's display of distress was so theatrical it might well have earned the approval of Shakespeare himself.*

Mr Davenport moved to his wife's side, soothing her with promises of Elizabeth's ruined career as a governess. This seemed to appease her, and she soon regained her poise.

"There now, darling. You must put the whole thing behind you or you'll make yourself ill, my dear," said Mr Davenport, returning to his seat. "Why don't you tell these good ladies about the ball you're hosting next month? I'm sure they'd be delighted to attend." He looked between Harriet and Delphine with a hopeful smile.

"Yes, do tell us, Mrs Davenport. It seems an age since I last went to a ball," Delphine said.

What are you up to, Delphine? You're not remotely interested in parties.

Mrs Davenport told them everything about her party.From the gold cutlery to the names on the guest list.

I wonder if she'll be so eager to impress when she discovers she's entertaining a working woman. She knows nothing about us. We are unknown, yet she continues to flaunt her standing. And Lady Montgomery. Good grief, did she just roll her eyes?

Mrs Davenport's sort of behaviour usually indicated persons of wealth without heritage, or 'new money' as it was commonly referred to. *Perhaps that is why she's trying so hard. I would be interested to know if there's any substance to her character underneath that gilded facade. I cannot imagine entertaining anyone with a fancy dinner, if Lillian had been the one to almost drown. But then, I don't have a husband to appease.* She knew too well how a husband's will could render his wife's wishes secondary. It wasn't fair to judge her for that without knowing her situation.

Harriet looked again at Lady Montgomery. She was most definitely not 'new money'. The Montgomerys were an ancient bloodline that could be traced back for hundreds of years. A spectacular pedigree, with wealth of unrivalled proportions. Lady Montgomery was refined. She moved with grace and ease—spoke with confidence. She said little and paid much attention, and carried an air of authority for which she made no apology—not with arrogance or superiority. There was simply something in her demeanour that convinced you of her greatness, without suggesting your own inferiority.

She eclipsed Mrs Davenport like the sun blotting out the moon.

"Harriet?"

She looked up at the sound of her name.

"Are you alright?" Delphine stared at her with obvious concern.

"Oh yes, I'm sorry. I'm a little tired is all." She struggled to place herself back into the conversation, having no idea what had been said. *The party—that was it. We were talking about the ball.* She parted her lips to speak, but found the moment had already slipped away.

"Don't worry, my love. I will find a suitable replacement for Elizabeth. All will be well," Mr Davenport was saying.

They need a governess. This is surely meant to be. "So am I to understand that you will be looking for a new governess now, Mr Davenport?"

"I will indeed. It's such a bother trying to find a good one."

Mrs Davenport sighed. "Such a bother. Governesses can be such difficult creatures, can they not?" She gave a short burst of nervous laughter. "But we do need another."

Harriet felt her mouth open and words tumble out. "That I can help you with, Mrs Davenport."

Afterwards, she wasn't sure exactly what she'd said, or even why, but she offered her services to a stunned and embarrassed Mrs Davenport and left the table that night with a new job. She would often think of that dinner in the years to come—never fully understanding what possessed her to commit such an act of spontaneity. Whether it was madness, fatigue, or fate, she couldn't say—but from that moment on, her path was altered.

BACK IN THEIR ROOM, Delphine slammed the door. "What in the world was that?"

Oh dear. She was not happy; that much Harriet could tell. "You're angry with me," she said. "I understand, but let me explain."

"Angry? No, Hattie, not angry, I'm absolutely astonished! You just offered yourself up to a family of complete strangers like a prize pig to the slaughter. You don't know anything about these people!" She paced the room, too agitated to stand still. "What possessed you? You didn't think of talking to me about it? To discuss the matter even just a little—get another opinion perhaps?"

Harriet shrank. She had no defence. Delphine was right. It was an incredibly stupid thing to do, especially after how her last situation had ended. She knew she'd gotten carried away and let her curiosity lead her on.

"You're going to be hundreds of miles away, Hattie. It's Hertfordshire, for heaven's sake! If anything happens this time, I won't be rolling past in a carriage by mere chance to rescue you."

"I never asked to be rescued, and I do not wish to be your responsibility. I'm not a child." *That was a cruel thing to say. I have behaved like one.* She wished she could swallow the words back in.

"After all this time, you're just going to leave? Just up and leave in a split-second decision, with no idea who, or what awaits you. Has our friendship meant nothing to you? Have you been so desperate to get away from me all this time?" Delphine's voice cracked, and the hurt behind her anger poured out. "Please, Hattie, think about what you're doing. Don't leave. I love you both so much. You're my family now." She flopped onto the bed with her face in her hands.

This isn't Delphine trying to get her own way. She's heartbroken. "Oh, please don't cry. I love you dearly, of course I do. And I've loved every minute of our time together. But I can't stay with you forever. You know that. I've extended my stay a hundred times already, and you knew this day would come eventually."

"Yes, but not so suddenly. Not without warning," Delphine said.

"If it's any consolation, it was as much a shock to myself. I suppose I just saw the opportunity and took it."

"I don't understand you, Hattie. I don't understand what it is you want from life. You have money now, and if that runs out, you can have mine. You have the freedom to do whatever you want; what more do you need to make you happy?"

"I don't know," Harriet said honestly. "It isn't about money. I have no desire for finery or useless trinkets. It's about security. I want to deserve what I have—to earn it. I need to *do* something."

Her resolve weakened when she looked at Delphine. *I cannot allow myself to be persuaded again. Not this time.* "I want to do something that matters. To leave the world a little different than it was when I entered it. Don't you ever want more? Don't you ever think there must be something more for us than our lot? Something more fulfilling at least than embroidery and walks in the park and pretty lace parasols!"

Delphine didn't answer.

"I know you understand, Delphine."

She nodded and managed a weak smile.

"Why don't you come with us? There's nothing to keep you in Lancaster for a while—no reason you can't accompany us. We can find lodgings down there, and you can stay until we're settled. It's a beautiful part of the country; you would love it. Oh, say you'll come." Harriet pleaded with her, possibilities unfolding in her mind at lightning speed. "It would put your mind at ease to know how we are situated, and you can visit us whenever you like. Please, Delphine. I want to do this."

For the first time in their relationship, Delphine gave up the fight and agreed.

HERTFORDSHIRE

The Davenport's home was a more stately affair than Harriet expected. Her living quarters were an extensive apartment in the east wing—a far cry from the attic room she'd had with the Hardcastles. Their wealth, it seemed, had gone some way in establishing their place in Hertfordshire society, and they enjoyed frequent company. There were always callers coming and going.

For the most part, Delphine seemed happy that they were decent, respectable people. Although she retained a lingering suspicion regarding Mrs Davenport, and couldn't exactly say why. "I don't know what it is, Hattie. Reason escapes me; it's more of a feeling. I just can't take to her." She much preferred the company of Lady Montgomery, who soon proved to be somewhat rebellious in nature.

Lady Montgomery was a wily old woman who made no attempt to be other than she was. She never took advice from her nephew, rolled her eyes whenever Mrs Davenport said something to her distaste and had a wicked smile that always promised mischief. She was well schooled in the art of coercion, graceful as it was. Harriet saw much of Delphine in her personality, and it warmed her to the prickly old lady.

For the first few weeks, they stayed with Delphine, in a rented apartment in the town of Hatfield, until Harriet and Lillian were officially instated at Hatfield Manor. Delphine stayed on in the village apartment for another month, just to see them properly settled in. When the time came to part with Delphine, it stung more than Harriet cared to admit. Still, she was keen to exercise her independence and remained positive.

Delphine promised to visit them often, and they agreed to write every day so that nothing might pass without the other knowing. It was a lovely thought, but not at all practical, and lasted just shy of three months before they reduced their letters to twice weekly. It was as much as Harriet had time for in her busy new life.

It didn't take long for Harriet to grow fond of her new pupils, William and Theodora. William was only three and still in the nursery, but liked to listen in on his sister's lessons and sometimes play with Lillian. The two youngsters became good friends. He was an unassuming child of mild manner and always had a smile on his face. She noticed he thrived under any sort of female attention. *I do wonder at times if his mother has ever held him close, or kissed his cheeks. She doesn't appear to pay him much attention at all. She's always with Theodora.*

Mrs Davenport concentrated her efforts on turning out the perfect specimen of British aristocracy, but her efforts were in vain. Theodora was never going to be what her mother wanted. Harriet could see that right from the start. She looked the part, that was true—pale, creamy skin as smooth and soft as butter, raven hair braided and curled into exquisite styles. Perfect teeth, sparkling eyes, and just the right amount of pink in her cheeks. To look at her, she was a perfect

English rose, but when she opened her mouth, the illusion shattered.

Her speech was littered with quaintly turned phrases picked up from locals, her accent regional, her conversation inappropriate for a young lady. She repeated old stories and legends she'd heard with the gusto of a drunkard raving in a tavern. She tempered neither the excitement nor astonishment in her voice, and when she laughed, it was raucous.

How has she come to be so unrefined? Harriet found out soon enough. The servants at Hatfield Manor were eager to talk. It seemed she'd been allowed from a young age to roam the estate with absolute freedom. Her days had been spent in the stables, petting horses, listening to the stable hands curse, and watching the coachmen play cards and games of dice. She'd run through the gardens with wild abandon, paddled barefoot in the fountain and had not been taught even basic manners or codes of conduct.

Arabella had not hired her first governess until Theodora was ten years old, and the wildling had seen off several since then—all of them wholly unequal to the task of creating a lady from this headstrong child. That duty now fell to Harriet.

She recognised a great deal of potential in her charge. Theodora was intelligent and quick-witted but lacked discipline. She was neither rude nor ill-tempered, but her manners were crass, and she lacked proper decorum. *No matter, manners can be taught and discipline instilled—the rough edges smoothed.* What couldn't be altered was Theodora's thoroughly modern mind.

~

BY THE TIME Theodora turned sixteen, the novelty of Hatfield Manor had long since worn off. Harriet's days settled into a steady rhythm, though no two were ever quite the same with Theodora under her care. She seemed to spend as much time in search of the girl as she did instructing her.

"Theodora, where are you?" Harriet was searching for the third time this week for her pupil. *I sometimes wonder if I'm employed as a governess or a bloodhound.*

Mrs Davenport, who was now happy to be addressed as Arabella, had been no help at all. She wanted her daughter to be obedient but was not prepared to issue consequences when she was not, nor was she pleased when Harriet issued her own.

Theodora had little to no consideration for the politics involved in social hierarchy. She saw no reason, to Arabella's dismay, why she could not socialise with the children of working men and women in the surrounding villages. Nor did she understand why she couldn't take walks with the gardener's boy to admire the roses, since they were doing nothing wrong. To Lady Montgomery's delight, she held no desire to make herself agreeable to anyone whom she did not hold in high esteem.

"Here I am," came her voice from across the courtyard. The stable door opened, and she appeared into the daylight, squinting and shielding her eyes from the sun. Her hair had come loose, and her face flushed with the midday heat. She held her silk skirt bunched up in a fist as she broke into a trot across the yard.

"Good grief, Theodora! What on earth are you doing? What would your father think if he saw you in such a state? You cannot be in there alone. You're not a child anymore. Young ladies must not put themselves in situations where their integrity might be compromised."

Theodora smiled. "Don't fret, Mrs Blackthorn, my father was with me. I've been to look at the new stallion. What a spectacular specimen he is. He's got a broad chest, a neat little head and a fine topping. You should see him. He's exquisite." She was never so animated as when she spoke about her horses.

"Topping?" Harriet said, bewildered.

"Yes, you know his mane. He's got a bonny tail too."

Harriet sighed, exasperated. "I do wish you wouldn't use such common language Theodora. It's the language of stable hands, not of young ladies."

Theodora cupped her hands to Harriet's face with affection. "It's only me and you."

"You and I Theodora. You and I!"

"Alright, Mrs Blackthorn, it's only you and I. There's no-one else here to hear me."

Most of the time she was right, and Harriet found it increasingly difficult to chide this girl for being herself.

"I'm going to call him Hercules," Theodora said, as though the last minute of conversation had not taken place at all. She took Harriet's hand and pulled her toward the stables. "Come on, you need to see him."

She called to the stable hand as they entered the building. "George, can you bring Hercules out so we can see him?" They stepped inside, momentarily blinded by the sudden dimness.

"Yes, Miss Theodora, I'll bring him out right away," came a reply from the darkness. The slow clip-clop of Hercules's giant hooves echoed around the stable block as he made his way down the centre aisle. "That's a mighty fine name you picked, Miss Theodora," said George, emerging into the light.

The title would have suited either one of them, Harriet thought. She knew George was just seventeen years old, but he was as large as any full grown man she had seen. A giant of a boy, six feet tall, with sprawling limbs and powerful shoulders. He smiled wide, his pearly white teeth a stark contrast to his ebony skin.

"Isn't he magnificent?" Theodora said with a dreamy expression.

For a moment, Harriet wasn't entirely sure whether she meant the stallion or the stable hand. "He certainly is a beautiful horse," she said, just to be clear.

Hercules swished his tail to bat away a fly, and sunlight rippled over his flank as the muscles shuddered. He pawed the ground with impatience, snorted and threw his head about. George stopped him with a sharp tug on the halter, and the horse stood to attention once more.

"Don't you think he might be a little spirited for a young lady, Theodora?" Harriet asked.

"Oh no, ma'am," George said. "Miss Theodora's more than fit to handle him. Why, she's the best little rider I ever did see, and I'll make sure he's broke in good an' proper. He won't be causing her no trouble, ma'am, I promise. And I don't make promises I can't keep, ma'am."

"Of course, George, I'm sure you don't." Harriet wondered at Mr Davenport, buying such a powerful animal for this wisp of a girl. It was difficult enough to get Theodora away from the stables at any time. Now it would prove near impossible. "Come Theodora, you must attend to your studies now."

Theodora walked over to give Hercules a pat on his huge shoulder.

George stiffened as she approached and made a visible effort not to meet her eye. He tipped up his chin and stared straight over her head.

Harriet spoke to her on their way back to the house. "You know you really should be careful, Theodora. You spend far too much time with the horses, and it isn't fitting for a young lady of your standing to be so friendly with the staff, let alone a man."

"Oh, but George is a lovely young man Mrs B. He would never do or say anything inappropriate. He's my friend."

"I'm sure he is, but your blatant disregard for propriety puts others at risk. That young man was clearly afraid to be in your presence. You have inserted yourself into his place of work without a chaperone, and that leaves him open to all manner of accusations."

Theodora wasn't listening. "Did you know he's from the Caribbean? His mother and father were slaves, and they brought him here when they were freed. I wonder what it was like?"

"Theodora are you listening to me? If your father or mother found you in that building alone with him, do you think it would be he or yourself who faced the consequences? If you value him as a friend, then the kindest thing you can do is to stay away from him."

Theodora opened her mouth to argue, then closed it. Her shoulders sagged. Her eyes filled with tears. "I hate this life," she said. "It's not enough that they will choose my husband one day. Now they must choose my friends as well."

Harriet placed an arm around her shoulders. "I know, darling, I know. It isn't fair, and it isn't right, but it's the way of things, and there's nothing you or I can do about it. You'll understand when you're older." She wasn't sure why she added that last part, because she knew it wasn't true. Understanding didn't come with age—it came with disillusionment. She understood no better now than she did ten years ago.

Though she did now realise how fortunate she'd been when her father allowed her the education she wanted. Theodora wasn't so fortunate. She longed to study science and mathematics, but her mother denied her that.

"Come on. Your mother's friends will be here for tea soon, and she wants you to attend this afternoon."

Theodora winced. "Do I really have to sit in the drawing room listening to those stuffy old women? Oh, I hate it Mrs B. Please don't make me go."

"Sweetheart, it isn't up to me to say where you can and cannot go. If your mother requires your presence, then I must deliver you. And in appropriate dress, I might add." She looked at Theodora with narrowed eyes.

Theodora folded her arms and raised her chin, trying hard not to laugh. "I have no idea what you mean."

The last time she sent her to the drawing room for a social occasion, she went in a pair of men's riding breeches she'd taken from the stables. Harriet had tried hard to mould her into the daughter Arabella wanted, but found it difficult to teach her a way of life she didn't believe in anymore.

Mostly, Theodora seemed to improve, or at least she learned when and where it was necessary to play the part—quickly realising that if she behaved appropriately in public, her mother was pleased and allowed her more freedom at home. She faltered from time to time and at home, was just as wild and untamed as she'd always been.

It was difficult not to admire her ferocious young spirit. Much like her aunt Clarissa, this girl made no apology for who she was and fought vehemently to defend her beliefs. She was so much braver than Harriet had ever dared to be, but then, she had experienced little of the world yet. She knew nothing of pain or want or fear, and held a blind faith in the victory of goodness that only children can possess.

BETROTHAL

"Harriet?" Lady Montgomery called from the sitting room as they passed.

"Yes?" Harriet poked her head through the open door.

Lady Montgomery was watching William from a large window overlooking the garden. "I need to speak with you." She turned to Harriet and smiled.

"I'll just see Theodora into the drawing room, and I'll be right back." When she returned, the old lady was sitting by the fireplace with two glasses of port.

She handed one to Harriet and commanded her to drink. "Do you know why she wants her in that room today?"

"Theodora?" Harriet shook her head, not sure what was coming next.

"Have you heard the name Croydon mentioned in this house?"

"Yes, I've heard the name. There was talk of a Lord Croydon during the London season, none of it favourable."

"Lady Croydon is in the drawing room right now to take her first look at her son's betrothed."

Harriet's lungs constricted, and the air in the room suddenly felt too thin. "They've made her a match?" Her voice sounded far off and distant to her own ears. She already knew the answer. "Does she know?"

"What do *you* think?"

No of course she didn't. She would have unleashed hell by now. If it was the same man she'd heard rumours of, he was from a very old family, but a dubious reputation preceded him at best. "What is the young man's name?"

"Lord Benedict James Croydon." Lady Montgomery said. "Is that the young man you've heard tell of?"

"It is."

"Do you think she's ready for marriage?"

Harriet considered for a moment how to answer this. Lady Montgomery would know in an instant if she lied. Her features operated of their own volition, quite without her consent. The problem was, how would a brutally honest answer be received? She squared her shoulders and took a deep breath. "No. I do not."

Lady Montgomery looked at her, eyes narrowed in consideration, then gave a slow nod. "Very well. And if she were ready for marriage, what would be your opinion of this match?"

Harriet cleared her throat, injecting as much conviction as she could muster into her response. "I expect that it's an advantageous match considering the usual qualities a family would look for in a suitor."

"Advantageous for who?" Lady Montgomery's answer was quick—sharp with irritation. "You ought to tell them the truth."

"I don't understand," Harriet said.

"Yes you do. You've been here for three years. You know her better than her mother does. Do you really think for one second that they will successfully shackle that little sprite out there to a man? She will never be suitable for marriage, she isn't meant for this sort of life," she gestured around the room with her hand, "this gilded cage and all its rules. It would kill her."

If only I could tell you how much I agree. "I appreciate what you are saying, but I don't see how I can be of help."

"Tell them it's a mistake—that she's not ready." She stared at Harriet without a trace of doubt that this could be done.

"Lady Montgomery, I am in no position to say such a thing to a mother about her child. That is a family matter and none of my business. I could never—"

"But you agree?" she cut in.

Harriet gave a small nod.

"And I don't mean her mother. You'd be wasting your time there. Speak to my nephew. Explain your concerns to him. He's a rational man. He knows she doesn't need a match to bring money into the family. There's no need to marry her off to a cad twice her age."

Lady Montgomery was becoming agitated and too loud for Harriet's comfort. She closed the door lest anyone should hear in the hallway and tried to calm the old lady.

"I don't understand. If the motivation isn't wealth, then why can't she choose a match herself? Why do they insist on this man in particular?"

"His name, Harriet. Arabella wants him, for his name." Her voice dripped with loathing.

"I see." This wasn't becoming any clearer for Harriet. She'd been thrown headlong into a conversation she shouldn't be having and didn't fully understand the politics of this family. *Why has Lady Montgomery chosen to speak to me so frankly? Surely there must be someone else.*

Lady Montgomery cleared her throat. "My parents

married me to my second cousin, so that my children would still be Montgomerys—the bloodline as undiluted as possible. My husband and I had a wonderful marriage, but I was lucky. I do not agree with choosing a woman's husband for her."

"That's a very progressive view for a lady of your..."

"Age?" she cut in, raising an eyebrow.

"I was going to say station." Harriet smiled awkwardly.

"Dear child, it is only my station that allows me to entertain such views. Extreme wealth liberates one from convention."

She's right. The fabulously wealthy seemed to exist on a plane above the laws of both man and God.

"As I was saying, my parents chose matches for both my sister and I. My sister's match, however, was an idiot who made terrible investments and liked to gamble. He lost their entire fortune when my nephew was born, and they never recovered. When James was old enough, he had to work, and my sister was too feeble-minded to arrange him a match that could rectify the damage. They allowed him to marry whomever he wanted. He chose Arabella."

Harriet thought about her own marriage and how Arthur had gambled away everything too. "But I thought you were against arranging marriages? Wasn't she right to allow him his own choice?"

Lady Montgomery sighed, exasperated. "I'm against it for women, dear, but not for men. Good grief, Harriet, do try to keep up. Men aren't capable of choosing a wife for themselves. They're stupid and impulsive. You ought to know that. You had one of your own."

Harriet couldn't argue with that. She'd just never heard it put so bluntly before. Lady Montgomery always said exactly what she wanted, when she wanted, with little to no regard for how it would be received. That's what Harriet liked about her. You never had to wonder what she was really thinking.

In the past she'd been friendly toward Harriet, but only in so far as she deemed appropriate with a member of staff. They had never spoken so intimately before. Of course, Harriet knew of Lady Montgomery's disdain for Arabella, she just hadn't known why.

She took a risk with her next question. "Am I to understand then, that you disapproved of Arabella?" The question sat between them like an over-stretched balloon. Harriet waited, then Lady Montgomery's face lit up with a grin.

"I thought you'd never ask."

They called for tea before continuing their little tête-à-tête and took it in Lady Montgomery's own sitting room, where they could enjoy more privacy.

"You're an intelligent woman Harriet, and reasonably perceptive." She was a master at coupling a compliment with a minor slur. "I'm sure you are perfectly aware of my dislike for Arabella. I've made no effort to hide it."

Harriet said nothing, but fiddled with the teacup.

"My nephew has always entertained romantic notions of the world. He's a good man, but when it comes to his wife, he's somewhat blinded. When they met, she wasn't remotely interested in *him*, only his family. Arabella knew he was an only child, and that I was a childless widow, thus making him the sole heir to the entire Montgomery fortune."

Lady Montgomery paused and stared into the distance as if reliving some private memory. "She was a magnetic creature —Arabella. Incredibly beautiful and charming, so it didn't take long for James to notice her. An innocent little parson's daughter, simple and good. She played the part well—was even humble from time to time, but a girl who possesses all the powers of womanhood cannot hide them for long."

"With respect, Lady Montgomery, that's a rather one-sided account of things. Are you so certain that she did not love him?" Harriet said, offended on Arabella's behalf.

"She didn't. The moment she married him, she abandoned her father and sisters lest they should embarrass her. She doesn't even speak of them. What sort of woman does that, I ask you? Arabella is proud and ambitious, and seeks to attain her ends by any means possible. That pride and ambition have shaped every decision she's ever made, to the point where they have erased all conscience. The foundations of Arabella's principles are so deeply rooted in social avarice they will never come out. And that's why she wants to marry her daughter to Benedict Croydon. She has the money and everything it brings, but she'll never have the breeding. This match is her opportunity to be placed among the cream of society."

Lady Montgomery breathed heavily, after her lengthy outburst.

It was true, Arabella enjoyed an elevated status which did not by rights belong to her—afforded to her by association only. But this was a brutal account of a woman Harriet found to be, on the whole, nothing worse than aloof. On the other hand, she knew Lady Montgomery always spoke the truth. For the simple reason that she didn't care one jot whether anyone liked it or not.

Harriet tried to keep her opinion unbiased, but Delphine too, disliked Arabella. So here were two people whom she both respected and admired, with negative opinions of the same woman. *Could they be right?*

"I can see that you're conflicted," Lady Montgomery stated flatly. "Make no mistake, Harriet. Arabella is artful and manipulative. When it comes to being devious, she would outwit you at every turn."

That stung. *Does Lady Montgomery think me foolish?*

"Don't misunderstand me." Lady Montgomery held up a pointed finger. "I'm not suggesting you are silly, only that you are honest—pure of thought. You couldn't begin to fathom her scheming. If she makes a friend of you, it is because it serves her purpose. You would do well to remember that." She paused, watching Harriet's expression. "You will find no one in her circle who would agree with me. Not a single person will you find, with an unkind word to say about her. Do you know why that is?"

Harriet shook her head.

"Because she excels at it. Deceit and manipulation are her greatest strengths. She claims to be a good Christian, but does not live by her own moral code."

Harriet swallowed hard. Her legs felt weak. "Well, thank you for the warning. I shall certainly take care not to get too close, but I really must find Theodora now. She'll be wondering where I am."

Lady Montgomery gave a slow nod and continued to drink her tea.

As Harriet left the room, she heard her say, "Poor sweet girl. What a terrible shame." *Does she mean Theodora...or me?*

~

HARRIET WENT to the schoolroom to check in on Lillian and set up the art equipment before collecting Theodora. She wasn't much in the mood for teaching and could not bring herself to believe that Arabella was as callous and cold as Lady Montgomery insisted. *I've been a reasonable judge of character so far, haven't I? My instinct was correct when I disliked Caiaphas from the offset. When others couldn't, I sensed the goodness in Delphine. And she's proved to be an invaluable friend.* She was certain that Lady Montgomery was exercising extreme prejudice in her opinion of Arabella, and was determined not to let it sway her.

When she arrived at the schoolroom, Theodora was already sitting neatly by the window, scrutinising her embroidery hoop.

"What are you working on, Theodora?"

She looked up, startled from her intense concentration, and almost dropped the hoop. "It's a new kerchief. I've embroidered my initials on it. I thought I might surprise you," she said.

Harriet was surprised to see her engaged in such a ladylike activity by choice. "Well, consider me pleasantly surprised," she said. "May I see?"

Theodora removed the white cloth from the hoop and handed her a beautiful handkerchief of the finest cotton batiste, edged with Belgian lace. In one corner, in pale blue silk thread, was a crude attempt at the letters 'TMD'—Theodora Mae Davenport.

"It's beautiful," Harriet said. "You have much improved." *She cannot possibly know about the betrothal—she's too happy. They haven't told her.*

She beamed and bounded back toward the window. "I know you wanted me to paint this afternoon, so I was wondering if I might paint outside? If I promise to be good and apply myself properly to my work, of course." She put on her most serious expression to show Harriet that she absolutely meant what she said.

"Theodora, we are not painting the horse."

"No, no, I don't want to paint Hercules. I thought I might paint the summer house from out on the lawn."

"Very well," Harriet said, knowing the spot she would need to occupy to obtain such a view, also afforded her an unbroken view of the stables. "Gather your equipment. I will carry the easel and Lillian, you may join us to play outside." She didn't mind indulging her if it meant Theodora working voluntarily.

The truth was, Harriet would have done anything for her just then. When she looked into that beautiful young lady's face, all she could see was a child staring back. A wonderfully brave and adventurous child who had no idea what was coming to her.

BREAKING THE NEWS

Three weeks—they waited to break the news. For three whole weeks, Harriet knew about the match with Lord Croydon, whilst Theodora remained blissfully unaware. She spent every day of those three weeks on edge, waiting, wondering if today would be the day—standing by always to comfort Theodora when her parents administered the fatal blow.

Harriet knew the moment the axe fell. She could hear Theodora's cries as she thundered through the house and upstairs to the schoolroom. She appeared in the doorway, throwing it open so that it crashed against the wall, leaving a doorknob-shaped dent in the plaster.

Harriet opened her arms wide, and she ran into them. They stood in silence for a while, Theodora weeping into Harriet's chest. "Hush my sweet girl, hush now, there's no use in crying. There's nothing to be done." She kissed the top of Theodora's head.

"You knew," she whispered between sobs. "You knew all this time, and you didn't tell me."

Harriet's heart sank. She held her tighter. "I'm sorry darling, but I couldn't. It wasn't my place." She knew there was nothing she could have done, but the crushing weight of guilt pressed down upon her all the same.

"I don't want to get married."

How can they do this to her. It's too much.

"Please, I can't. Don't let them do this!" She clutched Harriet's arms, eyes wide with panic.

"Oh sweetheart, they are your parents. I have no power to stop this."

"But you don't understand. I can't, I—just can't. I don't want to marry him," she wailed. "Why must I marry now? I'm not even out yet!"

Harriet didn't know what to say to her. She could hardly make sense of it herself. Theodora was only sixteen and hadn't even made her debut.

"Can't you do something? Can't you speak to my father?" She pleaded.

"Think about what you're asking, Theodora. I'm your governess! You don't really think a gentleman of your father's station would take advice from a governess about how to raise his daughter, do you?"

"Well, he ought to. You've got more sense than all of them combined." She tore herself from Harriet's embrace then and began pacing the room. Her emotions swung like a pendulum —between heartbreak and fury—settling on neither for more than a minute at a time.

Harriet probed further. "Is it the gentleman you object to or the idea of marriage altogether?"

Theodora stopped pacing for a moment. "I know nothing about him. He's probably a dusty old duke with a lot of money. I don't understand why I have to marry at all, let alone so young. Why does it have to be now?"

Harriet didn't answer.

"I won't marry him. I won't marry anyone, I tell you. I won't. You just see if I don't." She stormed out of the room, fists clenched at her sides.

Harriet let her go. *Best to leave her be for a while until she calms down.* Her mother would be there soon to ask how her daughter was processing the news.

Arabella arrived shortly afterwards, strutting into the schoolroom like a peacock. "Is she here?" Her voice was sharp.

"No, I think she needed some time to herself," Harriet said.

"I see. Well she's not in her room either, so where do you suppose she's gone to?"

The stables, I'd imagine. "She's most probably taking some air in the garden."

"How was she? Has she composed herself?"

"She was angry with me because I knew and didn't tell her," Harriet said, trying to avoid answering the question directly.

"And why would you have told her? You are her governess, silly girl. Her father is furious. She has no idea how lucky she is to have secured such a match."

Harriet found it difficult to believe that Mr Davenport had ever been furious in his life. He was the most gentle soul she'd ever met, whose only true happiness appeared to depend on that of his children. If anyone was furious, it was most definitely Arabella. She hadn't stopped pacing since she entered the room.

"Most young girls could only dream of the life she'll have. She'll be the envy of all who lay eyes upon her," Arabella said, as though that were the most important thing in the world. She stood still and smiled off into the distance as if she were picturing the scene in her mind. "I expect you will talk some sense into her before the meeting takes place tomorrow."

Tomorrow? Good Lord. I'll never be able to calm her enough for a meeting so soon. "I think perhaps it was just a shock to her. I'm sure, given a little time, she will see things more clearly. If there is a long engagement perhaps, she will adjust to the idea in due course. She is very young, after all." *This is overstepping, but I have to try something.*

"A long engagement? Out of the question. Why on earth would we wait now that the match is secured? No, the wedding must take place as soon as possible, and I expect her to be ready."

"I see," Harriet said. "Do you know when the wedding might be?"

Arabella shot her a look of undisguised impatience. She might as well have asked what business it was of Harriet's. But she didn't. She would never be so straightforward or blunt. Arabella caught flies with honey, not vinegar.

"I only ask so that I can ensure she's sufficiently prepared," Harriet explained.

"Tell Theodora. She can expect to be Lady Croydon within the year." With that, she swept out of the room.

That left just four short months in which Theodora would be married. *I'm not sure she would be ready in four years, let alone four months.*

Theodora did not return to the schoolroom for the rest of the day. Harriet saw her outside later, standing barefoot in the dewy grass, one hand resting on Hercules's strong neck. He whinnied softly as she stroked the place just beneath his mane.

"They say I must wear lace and pearls and smile like I'm grateful," she whispered. "But I'd rather ride into the sea and drown." Hercules snorted and nuzzled her shoulder, and she pressed her face into his neck. "You understand, don't you?" she murmured. "You don't belong in a cage either."

Harriet slipped away unnoticed and waited until evening

before she approached her. She tapped on the door of Theodora's bedroom and listened for a response. There was no sound of crying. That was a good sign. She knocked again. "Theodora, it's Mrs B. May I come in?"

"Come in." Her voice sounded stiff and detached.

"I brought you some tea," Harriet said, setting the tray down on a side table. "You should try to eat something. Here, Mrs Coulson has made your favourite biscuits." She handed her a delicate shortbread laced with lemon icing and sugared violets. "If I didn't come soon, I was afraid Lillian might eat them all."

"Where is she?" She looked past Harriet as though expecting Lillian to follow in behind her.

"In bed. I had to wait until she fell asleep; I'm risking my life to bring you these."

Theodora took one of the biscuits and gave a feeble laugh despite herself. She looked up at Harriet through red-rimmed eyes and smiled.

"There's my girl."

She nibbled at the edges of the biscuit, then popped the whole thing into her mouth and closed her eyes. "What is he like?" she asked, her mouth full, "this man I'm to marry?"

Harriet suppressed a chuckle. *How am I ever going to refine this girl?* "Hmm, Lord Croydon. Well, he's a little older than you. He's thirty-two I believe."

Theodora's eyebrows shot up, and she stopped chewing, another biscuit suspended midway to her mouth.

"Okay, he's quite a bit older than you, but still a young man."

"He's older than you!"

"Mind your manners young lady." Harriet feigned outrage but Theodora didn't laugh. "That is not old by any means, although I suppose you might think differently. I've never seen him myself, but by all accounts, he's very handsome. Tall and dark-haired with blue eyes."

Theodora waved her hand. "No, I don't mean what he looks like. I couldn't care less about that. I mean, what is he like?"

Perhaps she's more mature than I've given her credit for. It seems as if she's reconciled herself to the idea. Could she really have accepted her fate after such a short-lived outburst? It certainly looks that way, but one can never quite tell with Theodora.

She had a way of throwing you off course and could disarm or disorient a person with precious little effort. Most likely, she had convinced herself it wasn't really going to happen and was playing along to humour everyone. She did that sometimes. "I want to know what sort of man he is," she said.

Harriet hesitated, combing her mind in a rapid sweep for something positive to say about Lord Croydon. By the time she'd drawn breath to speak, Theodora's hopeful expression had already crumpled. That small hesitation had been enough to tell Theodora there was something wrong. Harriet tried to keep her tone light and playful, excited even, but she knew it was a fruitless task. Theodora was too perceptive for such tricks.

"I'm afraid I know very little about him except that he seems well liked among the young ladies, and I'm sure he's a perfectly charming young man." It was a poor offering, but it was all she had.

They stared at each other in silence for what felt like the longest moment, weighing each other up, trying to guess what the other was thinking.

"My mother says I'm to meet him tomorrow," Theodora said, breaking the silence, "but I don't think I shall." The tilt of her chin said she was confident in her conviction, but her wringing hands said otherwise.

"I know you don't want to, but he's coming here all the same. He and your father have already arranged everything. There will be a formal announcement in the papers this week. Think how badly it would reflect on your father if he came here to meet you, and you refused to come down. What would that do to your family's reputation if the engagement was called off because of your behaviour?"

Harriet hated herself for saying it. It felt like blackmail, but it was true. There was nothing she could do to stop it, and the more Theodora struggled, the more difficult it would be for her.

Theodora retreated just a fraction. "Will you be there?" she asked, "if I agree to meet him?"

"That depends on your mother's wishes, but I won't be far away if you should need me."

"I'll think about it."

Harriet held her steady gaze but said nothing.

"Oh, alright, I'll meet the silly old fool!" Theodora said with a huff.

"And you will be polite?"

She nodded.

"And courteous?"

"I will be on my best behaviour." She bowed low, her words dripping with sarcasm.

"Alright then, try to get some sleep now, and we'll talk more in the morning." Harriet kissed her on the head and went back to her own room. She was exhausted from juggling everyone's expectations all at once, terrified that everything would come crashing to the ground. *How can I possibly keep both Arabella and Theodora happy when they want such different things?*

She looked at her own little angel breathing heavily on the pillow, and bent to kiss her cheek. She whispered as she stroked her hair, "I swear, you will never be put in Theodora's position. You won't have to marry at all if you don't want to. Even if it means I have to work for the rest of my life."

She hadn't been in bed an hour when the door creaked open in the darkness and Theodora tiptoed into the room. She climbed into bed beside Lillian and Harriet and fell fast asleep.

MEETING BENEDICT

Benedict James Croydon was every inch the Lord. The accounts of his physical appearance had done him little justice. He filled the room with such commanding presence that he was difficult to look at without feeling self-conscious.

Harriet knew from the deep flush that sprang to Theodora's cheeks that she noticed it too. Well, that was something, she supposed. At least if she found him attractive to look at, it was a start. If a person held no desire to be married to begin with, surely it would be even more difficult to foster a liking for someone they found repulsive.

Harriet allowed her gaze to sweep over him, making a swift evaluation of his attire. His nankeen trousers were a brighter shade of yellow than usual and too tight. They looked ridiculous, but he wore them with such confidence that lesser men would no doubt seek to imitate him. She also noted—in the four minutes that had passed since he entered the house—he had admired his own reflection no less than three times.

He offered Arabella an enormous bouquet of exotic

blooms, which he informed her were specially selected by the gardener from the hothouse in the gardens of his estate. Arabella of course, was delighted by such a lack of genuine sentiment.

"For you," he said to Theodora, and handed her a heavily ornamented trinket box filled with Turkish delight, which she despised. Had he made just the smallest effort to find out what she liked, he would have known that she loved peppermint creams and poetry books. She preferred wildflowers to exotic, and better yet—if he'd brought her a few plucked by his own hand—he would most certainly have swept her off her feet.

Still, Theodora was a forgiving girl and not at all ungrateful. "Thank you. It's beautiful," she said. She beamed at him, but he either didn't notice or didn't care. There wasn't so much as a glimmer of acknowledgement across his fine features.

"I thought you'd like it." He said without looking at her. He gave himself a congratulatory smile in the mirror.

Arabella moved to Theodora's side and took the box to look at it."Of course she likes it. You're so clever, knowing just the right gift." She crooned when she spoke to him and he lapped up the attention like a cat with a bowl of milk.

All went reasonably well whilst they made polite conversation about the weather, and how the lord's journey had been that morning. Theodora was on her best behaviour, as promised. There wasn't the slightest inkling in her demeanour to suggest she was anything other than a docile and beautiful plaything.

Probably just the way he likes them. But this isn't Theodora. What performance is this?

Polite conversation was all well and good for now, but difficulties would arise when Theodora endeavoured to enter into deeper and more meaningful conversation. He wasn't going to hold her attention for long with trifling compliments and niceties. She liked to talk of science and nature, philosophy and literature, and Harriet had the distinct impression Lord Croydon would be out of his depth. She was certain he'd never met a girl like this before.

Arabella left it to Harriet to chaperone the couple as they took a turn around the estate after lunch. The air was crisp and a cool dry wind loosened the first of the turning leaves from their branches. They came fluttering down like feathers, twirling gently to the ground.

Harriet stayed about twenty paces behind them so as not to intrude, but she could still hear their conversation.

"Isn't it beautiful?" Theodora said. "I love this time of year when everything is changing. So many colours. Sometimes when the sun is setting, the trees on the horizon there look like they're on fire."

Harriet could hear the wonder in her voice—and the disinterest in his.

"Yes, lovely I'm sure, but it gets awfully cold and wet in the country. I'm not much of a fan." He said, brushing lint from his coat.

"Don't you like it at all? I thought you lived in the country?"

"Yes I do. Quite out in the wilderness in fact, but once we're married, we'll be moving to London. I would be more than satisfied if I never saw the wretched place again."

Oh dear. That was the wrong answer. He's not doing very well.

"But where would I keep Hercules if we lived in London?"

"Hercules?"

"My horse. Father bought him for me. Would you like to see?" She let go of his arm and veered off the path, ready to cross the field to the stables. She turned back to him, glee evident on her face, but he made no move to follow her.

He watched her for a moment, then laughed heartily, as though she'd made a joke. "I've come here to appraise a filly—not a worthless stallion." He shoved both hands into his pockets, laughing at his own joke. Its implication toward her, and the negative connotation of his comment, seemed to elude Theodora.

"I cannot have my wife riding about on a beast like some country rustic. If you need to go somewhere, you shall go in a coach and four." He laughed again, shaking his head, then extended his elbow to Theodora, expecting her to fall back into step.

Harriet wanted to throw something hard at him.

Theodora regarded him with steely determination. She glanced at Harriet, weighing up the possible consequences of this moment of potential anarchy. Then very slowly, she returned to the path and walked beside Lord Croydon without taking his arm. Her stock of patience was obviously depleted.

Harriet drew in a long and steadying breath. *This is never going to work. He isn't the least bit interested in getting to know Theodora. She's little more than breeding stock to him.* He meant it when he said he'd come to appraise a filly. He may as well have picked up her feet to see that she was well shod, or opened her mouth to check her teeth.

A man like him could not begin to understand the passion for life that burned so brightly in this wonderful human being. A soul like hers would be squandered on such a man.

Harriet knew much more about Benedict Croydon than she'd admitted. He was a man who knew only excess—his passions untempered by conscience or rectitude. A man who believed in his right to pleasure and sought it at any cost. *What would a man like that do to the pure and unpolluted mind of a young girl who has barely cleared childhood?*

She could envision Theodora's whole pitiful life from this point onwards. Wrapped in silk and lace—a painted on smile—dead behind the eyes. Auctioned by her own parents for the price of an old name, and plunged into a world of unbridled decadence, with no preparation for the pitfalls it held.

An icy shiver tingled all the way down her spine. *What has made her father disregard her needs in such a way? What causes her mother to overlook her daughter's worth?*

It was bad enough to live in a world ruled by men, but women themselves were complicit in this subjugation. Harriet's thoughts spun as she tried to make sense of it. How long could womankind survive in this arrested state of development? Caged—fenced in—with boundaries of their own making. Their ambitions stunted by fear, governed by men's logic. Their actions modified by the possibility of persecution. She wished she could do something to help, but she was just as bound to her fate as Theodora was.

WHEN THEODORA STORMED into Harriet's room that evening, she already knew what was coming. "I know, I know," Harriet said, holding up her hands in defeat.

"Then I suppose that makes two of us, because everyone else thinks he's bloody marvellous. I will not marry that brute under any circumstances."

What could she say? Harriet wholly agreed with her, but she'd never seen Theodora so animated in anger.

"I agreed to meet him to give him the benefit of the doubt and meet him I have. Him and every inch of his colossal ego. If they insist on this marriage, I'll run away." She folded her arms as though that were the end of the matter.

"I see," Harriet said. "And where would you go?"

"Anywhere."

"And have you considered how you would survive? What would you do for money? Where would you sleep?" Harriet kept her voice light.

"I don't care. I'll sleep outside in the fields, in the hedgerows if I have to!" Theodora said.

She hasn't thought this one through properly. I'm fairly certain it's an idle threat. "Tell me, Theodora, have you ever been outside on a starless night? When the moon hides behind the clouds and you can't see your hand in front of your face."

"No, but I'm not afraid of the dark."

"So you're not afraid of things that move in the blackness? Unseen, unknown things. Things that crawl and creep and skulk."

Theodora turned pale and rubbed at the goosebumps erupting on her arms. "Alright, so I won't run away then. But I will not marry him." She halted for a moment whilst her child's mind sought an alternate plan. "I shall make myself so entirely disagreeable that he could not bear to marry me. He wouldn't want to spend all his time with a disagreeable wife." She stuck out her chin, a pleased smirk perched on her lips.

My poor girl. She thinks he's going to spend all his time with her. The only time she'll see that man is when he visits her bed. All he wants is an heir. "I don't think that will work sweetheart. Men do not dwell on such things as women do. If they are unhappy at home, they simply employ themselves in seeking other pleasures in other places. I can't imagine it would matter to him much if you were unpleasant. As with many matches, it is your reputation he intends to wed."

Theodora went quiet for a moment, then a slow and sickening smile spread across her face. "Then my task is lighter still. For a reputation is the simplest thing in the world to be rid of. I will cast it off with no more effort than the slipping off of a garment."

Harriet's stomach knotted.

"I will go to him in ruin." The words dropped like stones.

This one did not feel like an empty threat.

She spoke with a tenacity of purpose seldom found in one so young. Her voice was eerily calm—detached—as though it wasn't her own. She said it so simply, like she had just made up her mind to take a walk or read a book.

Harriet's eyes went wide with shock. "Theodora! What manner of talk is that for a young lady? How could you say such a thing?"

Theodora breathed heavily, her shoulders rising and falling with the effort.

"I won't hear such nonsense, and I most certainly hope you have the presence of mind to regret those words. I'm disappointed that such thoughts would even occur to you." Harriet hoped that was enough to dispel such a ridiculous notion.

They stared at each other, both hurt but not knowing how to mend it.

Harriet broke the silence. "I wish there was something I could do for you, believe me, but it is beyond my powers."

Perhaps Theodora could hear the pain behind Harriet's words, or perhaps she just gave up. "I know," she said.

THEODORA'S SECRET

A thin mist of rain blurred the view outside Harriet's window, but she could just make out the faint silhouette of someone moving across the lawn. The figure was slight —not too tall—and moving away from the house, but that was as much as she could tell in the dim light. The moon was weak, its light choked by thick clouds.

From what she could see, the figure might have been a woman. Perhaps one of the servants had heard something outside and gone to investigate. She turned away from the window and strained to see the clock face without lighting a candle—half past one.

Lillian stirred, mumbling in her sleep, but did not wake. Harriet had been awake for hours. She couldn't sleep at all. In fact, she hadn't been able to rest properly since the day Benedict Croydon made his indelible impression on Theodora. In the six weeks since, she'd learned that there were shades of his character that were more unsavoury still. Parts of his personality activated by liquor. He was rumoured to be ill-tempered and quick to react when he'd been drinking, and he drank often.

Every night she tossed and turned, unable to rest for worrying about Theodora. She would get up and pace the room to ease her restless mind—the carpet almost worn to the weave.

Recently, Theodora had been perfectly agreeable. She'd met with Lord Croydon three times since the initial meeting and had put on a performance to envy the most seasoned actress. But a performance it was. A spirit such as hers could not be subjugated into domestication in as little as six weeks. *And if it had, it would not look like this.* No, Harriet had seen what a broken spirit looked like, and this was not it. No sadness or misery marked her manner. She was neither subdued nor despondent. She would even go so far as to say Theodora looked happy—too happy.

Something did not sit right with this new attitude. Mischief glittered in her eyes, and a smirk lurked behind her sweet smile. She walked taller, with more purpose. Her speech was more decisive. There were no more idle wonderings where she allowed her mind to roam. And perhaps the most telling of all—she was not afraid. The terrified child who had once begged, cried and pleaded not to be married, was suddenly not the slightest bit afraid. What caused this new acquisition of power?

Harriet couldn't shake off the chilling words Theodora had uttered about ruining her reputation. Even though she'd made no allusion to it since, the threat lingered. Had it been a serious threat or just a throwaway comment in the heat of the moment? She couldn't have meant it, could she? What could she know about being ruined? Did she really understand the meaning of what she'd said? Harriet couldn't imagine how.

Besides, where and when would she have access to such an opportunity? Certainly not at home, and she never left the estate without her mother or Harriet. No young ladies her age visited the house, and Harriet was the only staff member she spent time with, which limited her means of securing secrecy. She'd never shown even the remotest interest in young gentlemen, and as far as Harriet knew, she didn't know any.

The only male being she seemed interested in was her horse. She'd spent more time with that horse lately than she had with people. Harriet allowed it, putting aside her usual timetable of lessons. She deserved to enjoy her time with Hercules whilst she could. After all, Lord Croydon had already made it clear she could not take him with her.

A heavy door thudded, echoing somewhere deep in the house, and Harriet glanced at the clock again—two o'clock. A few minutes passed, and she heard a shuffling of footsteps. Closer this time. She pressed her ear to the bedroom door and listened. The familiar creaking and groaning of wood as the stairs sprang back, throwing off the pressure of each step. Then more footsteps along the hallway, quick and light. And finally, the softest click of a door closing.

The only rooms in this part of the house were her own, Theodora's, and the nursery. Had that been her out on the lawn? Surely not. She crept out into the hallway and tiptoed along to Theodora's room. Every sound seemed to ring out in the darkness. With her hand upon the doorknob, she turned it, holding her breath, and nudged it open just enough to see.

There was Theodora's sleeping form, bathed in the soft glow of firelight from the dying embers in the grate. She watched the rhythmic rise and fall of her breathing. *Oh thank goodness! It could not have been her. She's sound asleep.* She stood for a minute longer, just to be certain. Theodora remained still, her breathing slow and steady. *I suppose it must have been the nursemaid. Although what she was doing wandering about in the middle of the night, I cannot imagine.*

~

THEODORA CAME to see her early the next morning. "I thought Lillian might like to come and paint with me," she said.

"I'm sure Lillian would like that very much." She was eight years old now and looked upon Theodora as an older sister. Her face lit up like a lantern every time she saw her, and she attended Theodora's lessons along with William any time they were allowed.

"What are you going to paint?" Harriet asked.

"The view from the lake. You know how I love those trees once they've turned." She smiled—the first genuine smile Harriet had seen in weeks.

"Don't forget, you have a fitting today for your wedding gown. You need to be ready for half past eleven."

"I know, don't fret, I'll be finished by then." She looked at Lillian, who was bursting with eagerness. "Come on, let us gather our things, shall we?" They breezed out of the room hand in hand, as though Theodora hadn't a care in the world.

There wasn't a quiver of doubt in her expression when Harriet mentioned the wedding gown. No wince or subtle stiffening of the spine. Not even the clenching of a hand. She didn't show a single telltale sign that anything was amiss. This was more disturbing than the tantrums. Such a stark contrast it was to the sobbing mess she'd been in previous weeks.

Harriet made her way to Lady Montgomery's rooms, trying not to bump into Arabella on the way, which was more difficult than one might expect in such a large house. They had developed a somewhat unconventional relationship since their frank conversation. They sometimes played cards together in the evenings, and Lady Montgomery regaled her with stories she'd gathered from Arabella's society circle. When it came to Arabella, Lady Montgomery watched everything and said little, becoming proficient in feigning innocence or confusion as necessary.

Harriet knocked on the door before entering her sitting room. "Good morning, Lady Montgomery. Are you well?"

Lady Montgomery didn't waste time with niceties. She took one look at Harriet and said, "Out with it. I have a busy morning."

Harriet often marvelled at her perception. She knew. She always knew when something was wrong. It reminded her so much of Aggie. "I'm worried about Theodora. Something's not right, and I can't put my finger on it. She's gone from wailing and begging not to be forced into this marriage, to accepting it with no resistance at all."

"I see. Perhaps she's decided to accept defeat and go along with her parent's wishes. She's only a child, after all. Maybe she hasn't the stamina to fight them about it on her own."

"But that's just it," Harriet said. "She *does* have the stamina. She may be a child, but she's stronger and braver than I've ever hoped to be. And if she felt defeated, she'd be...... I don't know—different. I can't explain it, but I would know. She wouldn't be this happy. Anyone would think she was in love with him from the way she's behaving!"

Lady Montgomery raised an eyebrow. "Is she?"

"Absolutely not. She cannot bear him."

"Then what's the matter with her?"

"I don't know." Harriet sighed. It sounded ridiculous now that she'd said it aloud. "I don't know what the problem is, but I'm certain there is one."

"Have you spoken to her about it? Have you asked her outright?"

"No." Why hadn't she done that? It was the most logical thing to do if she wanted to know something. She almost laughed out loud at the thought of it. *Harriet Blackthorn, the most logical person in the world, has not considered simply asking her.* She felt foolish under Lady Montgomery's gaze. "I'll speak with her today." She left the room to find the girls.

Halfway across the lawn, she saw George, the stable boy, hovering by a clump of rhododendrons. He was looking down at something in his hands, a wide, silly grin on his face.

"Good morning, George."

George's head shot up, and he thrust one hand behind his back. He touched his cap with the other. "Good morning, ma'am."

"What are you hiding there, George?"

He hesitated for a moment, then brought his hand slowly forward to reveal a crumpled scrap of white fabric. He smoothed it out flat, and Harriet saw the familiar blue embroidery in the corner. The letters 'TMD' stared up at her.

"Is that Theodora's handkerchief?"

He stared at her a moment too long before answering. His grin vanished. "Yes, Mrs Blackthorn, ma'am. I was just going to take it up to the house."

"Oh, I see. Where did you get it?"

He shifted from one foot to the other. "I found it, ma'am, out there on the grass. I was only going to take it to the house. Honest, I was."

Harriet touched his arm. "It's alright, George. I was only asking. There's nothing to get upset about." *Poor boy. He's a nervous wreck. Theodora really must keep her distance from him. She doesn't seem to understand the difficulty she poses for him—*

always going to the stables unchaperoned. She took the handkerchief and dismissed him.

Theodora and Lillian were working at their easels down by the lake. Lillian had made a commendable effort to paint the scene, but it was a painting only a mother would appreciate.

"Do you like it Mother?" She said.

"It's the most beautiful painting I've ever seen. I love it."

"Theodora likes it too. She said I have excellent technique, and she knows all about painting. Even more than you, Mother." She smiled at Theodora, trying so hard to impress her.

"Indeed she does," Harriet said. "Theodora knows a lot of things, and if you study as hard as she does, then someday you might be just as clever."

Lillian sat up straighter on her stool, her chest puffed with pride, and a satisfied smile on her lips.

"Now then, I need you to take your painting things back to the schoolroom whilst I speak to Theodora. Can you do that for me?"

Lillian frowned. "Yes, Mama."

Harriet stifled a chuckle at her disgruntled little face.

She clearly wasn't pleased about being excluded from this 'big girl' conversation. She gathered her paints and easel and stormed off toward the house without another word.

Theodora looked at Harriet with expectant eyes. "Is everything alright?"

Harriet smiled. "That is exactly what I was going to ask you. You haven't been yourself lately. I'm concerned about you."

"Oh, I'm quite alright. There's nothing to be concerned about."

"I thought you might be worried about your impending nuptials, perhaps?"

"No, not really. I'm sure everything is in order."

This wasn't going as well as she'd imagined. Harriet struggled for something that might coax her into talking about it. She fell short. "But I thought you were dead set against it?"

Theodora's head snapped towards Harriet. Her eyes flashed with fury. "Isn't this what you wanted?"

Ah, there you are. There's the girl I've been looking for. "What I want, Theodora, holds no weight here. None of this is what I want."

"But you wanted me to be on my best behaviour. You said there was nothing to be done about it. So here I am, accepting my fate like a good girl."

Every word cut Harriet to the core. "There's something else. Something you're not telling me." She hadn't meant it to sound like an accusation, but it did. "Theodora, please. If there's something bothering you, I must know. I cannot help you unless you talk to me about it."

"You cannot help me anyway, by your own admission. But there's nothing to tell. I assure you, Mrs B. there's nothing at all to worry about." She stood and smoothed her skirts, then offered Harriet an arm. "Shall we go inside to prepare for the fitting?"

Harriet pulled the handkerchief from her pocket and extended it to Theodora.

She paled.

"George had this. He was taking it up to the house for you."

Theodora stumbled over her words. "Oh...I—I wondered where that was—I must have dropped it."

Harriet took her face in both hands, searching her eyes. "I love you, Theodora, and I want very much for you to be happy. Are you sure there's nothing you want to tell me?"

Theodora shook her head.

"Do you promise?"

She nodded. "I promise."

Harriet saw it—quick, but unmistakable: a flicker of doubt. She couldn't lie whilst holding Harriet's gaze. Her eyes darted away for the merest of seconds. She was lying. Harriet was sure of it.

RUIN

Sleep did not return easily to Harriet. She spent night after night gazing out of the window into black, starless skies, wondering what she could do to help Theodora. But every night she drew a blank; there was nothing to be done—at least nothing within her power. She couldn't speak with Mr Davenport about it. A rational man he may be, but she was still staff.

The Hardcastles would have thrown her out in a split second for such a violation of social propriety. Mr Davenport probably wouldn't be so harsh, she thought, since he'd always been kind to her. Nevertheless, it wasn't worth the risk. She just wished she could account for this sudden shift of attitude in Theodora.

Something white flickered at the edge of her vision and she turned her attention back toward the window. There was the figure crossing the lawn again. The night was clearer this time—definitely a female—and dressed in a long nightdress. She hadn't heard any footsteps but thought she'd better check Theodora's room.

Padding down the hall in bare feet, she creaked open the door just enough to see Theodora's bed. It was too dark to see, so she raised her candle and entered the room. The bed was empty. *Perhaps she's gone downstairs for water, or to sit in the library because she can't sleep. She does that sometimes. It's unlikely to be her outside. Isn't it?* The knot in her stomach said otherwise.

She ran back to her room to put on her shoes and shawl, and lifted Lillian from the bed. It wasn't easy to carry her now, but Harriet didn't want to leave her alone. She didn't know how long this might take. She reached the nursery door and nudged it open with her elbow, knocking Lillian's feet against the door frame.

"Ouch," she mumbled in her sleep, and tried to draw up her knees.

Harriet whispered to the nursemaid, "Clara, I need to leave Lillian in here. I won't be long."

Clara got up and turned back the blankets on the spare bed.

Harriet didn't offer any further explanation, but left the room and ran downstairs to the front door. When she stepped outside, she stood still and listened. Nothing. She looked around, straining her eyes in the dark, but saw no signs of anyone. *Where would Theodora go? What would she be doing out here?* Then it struck her. *The horse. She must be with Hercules.*

She liked that explanation because it was innocent and easily remedied. All she had to do was find her, put her to bed, and all would be well.

She set off toward the stables at a brisk pace, her mind running through what she was going to say to Theodora when she found her. All the while, something pulled at her from the depths of her consciousness. Something was wrong. As she rounded the corner of the building, she heard Theodora's laugh and the pawing of hooves on the flagstone floor. Relief flooded her. *She is with the horse. Oh, thank God!* She paused a moment to steady her breath—the panic melting away.

A yellow glow shone from a stable on the left-hand side of the building. She crept toward it and Theodora laughed again, but just as she reached the door, she heard a rustling sound and the low rumble of a distinctly male voice. She froze, fingers stretched out toward the latch. The cutting speech she'd prepared perished on her lips. She drew in a shaky breath and pulled back her hand as quietly as she could.

What do I do? Should I scream? She looked around for something she could use to protect Theodora from her assailant. For Theodora was surely being attacked. *But then, hadn't she been laughing? No—she must have been crying.* Harriet's hand closed around the shaft of a large pitchfork, which she positioned in front of her before flinging back the stable door.

Two half-naked bodies were locked in such a passionate embrace that it made Harriet blush. This was no attack. Had it not been for the colour of their skin, she could not tell where one person ended and the other begun, but even in the half-light of the oil lamp, she could see that one was white and one was black. She screamed and the pitchfork clattered to the ground.

Startled, the lovers turned to see her, and the mass of writhing limbs disentangled. They scurried apart, eyes glittering and wild in the amber light. George grabbed his breeches from amongst the scattered straw and ran off into the darkness, barefoot, leaving Theodora to face the consequences alone.

Harriet still hadn't moved. Her breath came in short, shallow gasps, her voice barely a whisper. "What in God's name have you done?" She took a step backwards and Theodora lunged for her.

"No, please! Please don't!" She clutched at the fabric around Harriet's retreating legs. "Wait, please. They'll send him away! Please don't tell them, please!" She scrambled to her feet and tried to throw her arms around Harriet, but she held her at arm's length.

"This is madness." Harriet looked wildly around the stable, her brain refusing to accept what she had seen. The sting of tears pricked her eyes, and she struggled to swallow the lump in her throat. "Why?" She shook her head. "Why Theodora? Why have you done this?"

Theodora continued to beg, fumbling to fasten the buttons on her nightgown with frantic urgency. "I'm sorry. I—I wanted..." She looked up at Harriet with wide eyes. "I wanted..."

Harriet cut her off. "Sorry? You're sorry? Do you have any idea what you've done? Was this your plan? To ruin yourself with the stable boy! Do you really think they will tell Lord Croydon and call off the wedding?" Harriet rubbed at her temples. "You reckless, thoughtless girl. If anyone found out about this, they would think he attacked you."

Theodora did not speak.

"How could you be so selfish, to use a human being like that?"

"Oh, please don't let them send him away."

"Send him away? Are you insane? They'll hang him. You've as good as sentenced him to death!"

Theodora fell to her knees with her face in her hands.

Harriet didn't understand. If she'd ruined herself to get out of the marriage, then by design, her parents had to find out. It made little sense that she asked her not to tell them. "What exactly were you planning to do, Theodora?"

Theodora wiped her tears on the sleeve of her nightgown and sniffed. "We were going to run away."

"You and George?"

She nodded, still not meeting Harriet's eye.

"Why on earth would you run away with George?"

She raised her head now and looked at Harriet with challenge in her expression. "I love him."

Harriet couldn't think straight. She needed help from someone else. There were too many things to consider before she could decide on the best course of action. There was only one person she trusted to act in Theodora's best interests, but first, she needed all the facts.

"Theodora, if I am to help you, I need you to be honest with me."

She nodded.

"I have to know if your innocence is lost entirely."

Theodora frowned.

Anxiety sharpened Harriet's temper. "Is your maidenhood still intact?"

Theodora blushed and shook her head.

Harriet had still hoped it wasn't as bad as it looked—that the situation might be salvaged with minimal damage. Until now. That was out of the question. "Was this the first time?"

Theodora shook her head again, and her face glowed with shame.

"How many?"

She screwed her eyes shut tight and turned her head away from Harriet.

"How many times, Theodora?"

"I…I'm not sure. Perhaps a dozen or so?"

Dear God. How have I missed this? "How long has this been going on?"

"Three months," Theodora said.

Harriet's mind flashed with images; George's reaction to Theodora in the yard that day; Theodora staring out of the window smiling; George with Theodora's handkerchief;

Theodora's constant trips to the stables and a thousand other little signs that had escaped her.

"Alright. Listen to me. I want you to go to your room, get into bed, and do not leave it until I come for you. Do you understand?"

Theodora nodded. "What are you go—"

She didn't get to finish the sentence. Harriet's temper finally snapped and she shouted at her to leave.

Theodora ran, and did not look back at her.

HARRIET RAN straight to Lady Montgomery's chambers and told her what had happened.

Lady Montgomery paced the room, stopping periodically to speak to Harriet, who stood by the fire with her second glass of brandy. Her initial idea was to bring the wedding forward, in the hope that a possible pregnancy could be passed off as Lord Croydon's child. Until Harriet explained that the stable boy was black. "Do you think it likely that she is with child?" she asked Harriet. "There's a chance she may not be."

"I don't know. It's possible, but how likely it is, I couldn't say. She said it wasn't the first time."

Lady Montgomery considered this for a moment. "Then we cannot risk it. If she married him and gave birth to a black child, it would be disastrous for everyone involved." She groaned and flopped down into a chair. "Why couldn't he have been white? We could have swept this under the rug."

"What if we waited a little while longer to make sure she isn't with child? There's still a few weeks until the wedding."

"That's all well and good if she isn't, but what if she is? What do we do then? It would be impossible to break off the engagement at the eleventh hour without there being a colossal scandal."

"Then we postpone the wedding under the guise of illness and send her away to convalesce. You and I could accompany her and when she's had the baby, she can come back and marry Lord Croydon and no-one would be any wiser."

Lady Montgomery shot her a look that made her think she'd just said something absolutely idiotic. "You don't think a man as experienced as Benedict Croydon could tell the difference between a virgin and a young woman who has just given birth?"

Harriet blushed. She honestly didn't know.

"And besides, she's claiming she loves him. Do you think she'd give up a child with a man she loves to come back and marry that man? Do you think she'd willingly give up her baby, her own flesh and blood?"

Harriet let out a long sigh. "No, she wouldn't."

"And if she wouldn't, would you take it from her? Could you prize that baby from her arms and forcibly separate mother and child? Because I couldn't, and I don't think you could either. Then where would that leave us? An unmarried mother, a bastard child and a Lord still expecting a wife."

Harriet winced. She was used to Lady Montgomery being blunt, but she'd never heard her use such crass language. It was the truth though. That was exactly the way the world would see it. Marriage to Benedict was definitely off the table. "I can't see a solution to this," she said. "I just don't know what else to suggest."

They stared into the fire, the knowledge that they would have to tell Arabella gnawing at them. Then Harriet had another idea. "What if we sent him away—George, I mean? We find him another situation far away, and we tell her he ran away—didn't want her. If she hated him, she'd be more inclined to give up the baby should there be one."

Even as she suggested it, she felt as though she'd betrayed something essential—George, Theodora, or maybe just herself. The thought made her sick to her stomach, and she wished she could un-say the words.

Lady Montgomery just shook her head slowly and looked at Harriet with a sad half-smile. "I'm afraid, even in the face of disenchantment, love is as constant as the sun. She would not be so easily put off."

"I'm not sure she even knows what it is to love, let alone tell the difference between that and a girlish fancy."

Lady Montgomery smiled again. "There's nothing so proficient as the opposition of one's family, to fan the embers of a girlish fancy into a full-blown flame of passion." There was a resignation in her voice, as though she had already accepted defeat. "I'm afraid she's lost to us, Harriet. Whatever she does, this life can no longer be hers. She can marry George and make the best of it, but it won't be easy for them. They'll be outcasts wherever they go."

"But why does she have to go anywhere? Can't she stay here?"

"Arabella will never allow it. Theodora's marriage would give her access to the upper levels of society. Not only will she not have that, but she'll have the scandal of an unfulfilled engagement. Even if there isn't a baby—people talk. There will undoubtedly be rumours. Things like this don't stay secret for long. All the servants here will know already. They will tell servants from other houses, who then tell their masters, and so on. Arabella will never forgive her. Her only chance is to make a life with this young man."

"Well, what of Mr Davenport? Won't he have some say in

this? Surely he won't turn his back on his own daughter! You said yourself he's a rational man."

"James is a lamb. He will not stand up to Arabella when it comes to this."

"But you wanted me to speak to him about the marriage! Why did you ask me to do that if you know he won't stand up to her?" Harriet had had enough of secrets and lies, people with ulterior motives and hidden agendas. It was exhausting.

Lady Montgomery shrugged. "It was an act of desperation I suppose—a last-ditch attempt to stop the engagement before it was too late."

Harriet hadn't considered that Lady Montgomery might feel desperation. She always seemed so composed and in control.

She looked at Harriet quite suddenly, as though she'd had another idea. "Bring her down here. Let us talk to her and find out what's in that little head of hers."

Harriet brought her into the room. She hadn't said a single word as they walked from her bedroom down to Lady Montgomery's quarters. Her chin was set at an angle that suggested defiance, but a steady stream of tears ran down her face, dripping unheeded from her chin.

"Well," said Lady Montgomery, "let's have it. What do you intend to do? What is it you want?"

Theodora's eyes widened in surprise at this unexpected consideration of her wishes. She opened her mouth but made no sound and closed it again.

"Come on! Out with it girl! You must have had some sort of intention. Some plan you'd thought of?" She folded her arms and stared hard at her niece.

"We were going to run away."

"Where to?"

"I—I don't know," Theodora stammered.

"Well you'd better think fast because in less than two hours the sun will be up and your mother and father are going to know about this."

Theodora looked even younger than she was, standing there, twisting the folds of her nightdress.

"Does he intend to marry you?"

"Yes. We planned to be married as soon as we could."

"And how did you suppose that would happen without your father's permission? You're not of full age, Theodora, so you need your father's permission to marry. You know that don't you?"

"George said we might find someone willing… for a price." She looked down at her feet.

"You think someone would put themselves at so much risk? To lie in God's house—commit fraud against the justice of the peace—sign away his daughter to a black stable hand? You've taken leave of your senses altogether. How much money do you think you'd have to pay a man to do such a thing? Far more than George has to offer. I can tell you that."

Theodora didn't speak, but her fingers twitched at her sides.

"Let us say for a minute that you did manage to get married. Where are you going to live? Does he have a job to go to? Will there be a roof over your head? Do you realise you would lose your entire family? You'd be shunned wherever you went. Any children you have will be sentenced to a life of hardship, subjected to hate and prejudice from both sides, accepted by neither blacks nor whites. Is that a life you would want for your children?"

Theodora shook her head.

"Then let him go. You can still marry Lord Croydon, and no-one need know about this."

Theodora's hand moved instinctively to her abdomen. "I can't," she said. "It's too late."

ASYLUM

Arabella and James did not take the news well. Harriet had never seen them so outraged. For hours the house echoed with shouting and sobbing and the sound of things breaking in far-off rooms.

Harriet met Mr Davenport in the hallway that morning, his shotgun hooked over one arm. His face was red with rage and his eyes emptied of gentleness. He marched past her without a word, and headed out toward the stables.

She wasn't worried. She'd never seen him raise so much as a hand to a servant, let alone a gun. In any case, George was already gone. They'd looked for him earlier and found his bunk stripped bare. The other men said he took his things last night and left in the dark—didn't say where he was going or why. She couldn't blame him. If he'd stayed, he would have most likely died. If Mr Davenport hadn't shot him, he'd have been tried for rape and probably hanged.

There was more shouting outside. *Mr Davenport must have discovered he's too late. Perhaps he will calm down now.* Once his temper was spent, she expected he would think more clearly and deal with the more pressing concern of Theodora's delicate situation.

She did not expect what he did next.

He emerged from the stable, breathing hard and leading Hercules by the bridle. Sweat still glistened on his brow.

Harriet watched him from the front steps, wondering what he was doing.

When he was halfway across the lawn, Theodora screamed. "No! Please—no. Don't!" She came tearing down the hallway and out of the house toward Harriet.

Harriet looked back at Mr Davenport and realised what he was going to do.

Theodora barrelled into her, and Harriet clasped both arms around her waist, bringing her to an abrupt halt. "Don't look." She barely had time to spin Theodora around before the gun clicked shut and a shot split the air in two.

Birds squawked and fled from every treetop. Hercules made a strange noise somewhere between a squeal and a whinny, and stumbled to his knees with a thud. They felt the vibration of his massive body hitting the ground.

Theodora tore herself away and ran across the grass to Hercules. She fell to her knees beside him, but he was already dead. His coat gleamed in the low winter sun. Even in death, he was a magnificent sight to behold. Such a beautiful animal—such a waste of life. Theodora draped her body across his, sobbing into his shoulder and stroking his cheek.

Her father looked down at her and then at the gun in his hand. He staggered backwards as awareness enveloped him, a horrified expression on his face. Then he turned and walked away.

THEODORA DISAPPEARED from Hatfield under the guise of illness, but Harriet knew the truth. They postponed the wedding, telling Lord Croydon she was gravely ill, and had to go away for respite. Harriet had hoped to accompany her during her confinement. She imagined a little cottage tucked away somewhere quiet, where they could enjoy privacy—or perhaps a maternity home. She had heard there were such places, where young women could stay until their babies were born and could be adopted.

But it was not so for Theodora. Arabella would accept none of these options. There were too many people involved in such establishments—people who could pass on delicate and damning information to others. Instead, she sent her to an asylum that took in unwed mothers, on the other side of the county.

Images plagued Harriet day and night—of the poor young girl she'd seen at the asylum gates, the day Delphine rescued her. She couldn't help but imagine Theodora in that monstrous jacket with the straps and buckles, fighting to break free. She and Lady Montgomery tried countless times to turn Arabella from this decision, but it did no good. She insisted it was the only way to preserve what remained of their family's good name.

Harriet even wrote to Delphine to ask her advice—she knew about such things. But no-one could do anything. Theodora was too young. It was her parent's decision, and none of them could intervene, however much they wanted to.

When the doctors came to collect Theodora, Arabella pushed the papers in front of her husband, and he signed them without question. He didn't even say goodbye to her. Mr Davenport turned inward after that. He barely spoke to anyone, and if he did emerge from his study, he wandered the grounds aimlessly—spent hours standing in the empty stable where Hercules once lived.

Harriet couldn't watch her leave. She took Lillian to her room so that she wouldn't see either, but they heard her screaming. They heard her beg and plead and cry out for help. She screamed Harriet's name, and her father's. They heard the men struggle to hold her—and then, silence. They sedated her and loaded her onto a stretcher.

Lillian was too young to understand what was happening to her friend, but she cried for hours, curled up on her mother's knee. Harriet told her Theodora wasn't well, and she was going away somewhere nice until she was well enough to come home. She wished that were true. Her only hope was that Theodora would be strong enough to endure it.

She gave birth to a baby boy. Arabella said he'd been given to a family emigrating to America. That way, she couldn't go looking for him later on. *How cruel.*

Harriet imagined what she'd gone through when they took her baby away—wondered if she'd fought for him—if she even knew where he'd gone. She couldn't begin to imagine the horror of losing Lillian, nor did she want to.

"Are we to expect her return soon then?" She asked Arabella shortly after the birth.

"No, she's still not well enough."

Harriet thought she heard the telltale catch of emotion in Arabella's voice, but her face gave nothing away.

"The doctor said the strain of childbirth was just too great. Her mind has not recovered." She glanced at Harriet, her eyes welling. "They said she's quite hysterical when she's awake."

"Oh, the poor thing. Have you seen her?" As far as Harriet was aware, Arabella had not visited her daughter since the doctors took her.

"No, I cannot. The doctor said it would only exacerbate

her condition to see family members. They always advise against it."

How strange. Surely it would be better to see one's family in times of such anguish?

Harriet waited weeks, then months for news of Theodora's improvement, but none came. When she asked Arabella, the news was always the same; she was the same as last week, or her condition had worsened.

She decided to take the opportunity to see for herself how Theodora fared. On her way to stay with Delphine for her two weeks' leave, she visited the asylum. Unsure of what she'd find inside, Harriet left Lillian in a waiting room near the entrance, whilst the matron led her to a ward full of young women.

The vibrant young girl she once knew was gone. Theodora sat perfectly still at the end of her bed, in a thin cotton smock and dusty slippers. Her head bent over a small porcelain doll in her lap. Dark hair hung over her face in lank, greasy clumps, and her skin was dull and greyed. A breeze wafted over her, stirring her nightdress. It billowed and fluttered eerily against her absolute stillness.

Harriet knelt in front of her and whispered her name. "Theodora sweetheart. It's Mrs B. I've come to see you." It seemed a stupid thing to say, but she wasn't sure how to start. She noticed a stiff leather cuff attached to the bed frame and shuddered.

Theodora lifted her head slowly. Her expression was blank. There was no spark of recognition in her eyes when she looked at Harriet, only emptiness.

"Hello my love. I've missed you." Harriet said, smoothing the hair back from Theodora's face.

Someone spoke behind her. "Best not to get too close, ma'am. She bites...and spits. Quite unmanageable at times."

Harriet turned to see a portly man in a white doctor's coat. "What happened to her?"

Just then, Theodora reached out to touch her face. Harriet smiled, encouraging her. "That's right, Theodora, it's Mrs B. Do you know me now?" She kissed the palm of Theodora's hand and pressed it close to her cheek, but there was still no recognition.

Theodora drew back her hand. "My baby," she said in a whisper. "My baby." She began to rock back and forth, repeating the mantra over and over. "My baby, my baby, my baby." Her voice became louder as her agitation increased, then she stood abruptly, pushing Harriet away.

The man in the doctor's coat and two female nurses rushed at Theodora, grabbing her by the shoulders and forcing her down onto the bed. She shouted and cursed, thrashing and fighting against them as they fastened the cuffs around her wrists and ankles.

"No stop," Harriet shouted, but they ignored her.

One of them took a syringe from a metal trolley and injected her with something. After a few seconds, she relaxed and became still.

"I think it's best if you go now, ma'am. She'll be out for hours."

Harriet never told Arabella what she'd seen at the asylum. She didn't tell her she'd even been. No mother should have to witness anything so harrowing. After that, she visited her whenever she could, but it wasn't often. Theodora was always the same—unresponsive, vacant. Harriet didn't think she'd ever forget that image of her so broken. She understood now that Theodora might never come home.

She returned to Hertfordshire and took up her post as before. William would go to boarding school in a few years, and he needed to be prepared for that. It was never the same though, without Theodora. The house was colder, quieter, and her heart was no longer in it. The absence became something Harriet wore like a second skin—familiar, permanent, unnoticed by most.

Time dulled nothing. In the years that followed, Harriet carried on with quiet duty. She taught William, lowered Lillian's hems and wrote Delphine long letters. There was always another term to prepare for, an illness to nurse, another silence to endure. Theodora was spoken of less and less. William never asked where she had gone. Lillian, if she did mention her, wore the awkwardness of someone recalling a childhood dream.

The seasons came and went. The school years passed. Theodora remained locked in Harriet's memory, suspended in time, while everything else moved relentlessly forward.

LONDON SEASON

Harriet stood behind her daughter in a dressing room in London, pinning up curls that had once belonged to a child. The poised young woman in the mirror seemed strange and distant.

She remembered a spring day, not long after Theodora had gone. They were walking through the gardens at Hatfield. Lillian had turned suddenly to her and asked, "Why do you never wear gloves, Mother? You look so provincial." Harriet laughed at the time, but it hadn't quite reached her eyes.

Fifteen years old now, Lillian had grown into a young lady, with sharp cheekbones and an even sharper tongue. The sweet, loving child who clung to her skirts had vanished—her childish dreams and playthings, a distant memory.

Harriet smiled at Lillian's reflection, searching her face for a spark of the little girl she raised, but it wasn't there.

She'd once pinned up Theodora's hair like this, a younger Lillian perched on a stool, beaming at her idol. No-one spoke of her anymore. Not Lillian, nor William—not even her mother. It was as though she'd never existed. But Harriet saw traces of her everywhere; in the set of William's jaw when he was angry; in Lillian's unbridled will; in each autumn, when the leaves turned orange.

"What are you smiling about, Mother?"

She knew better than to share these memories. Lillian didn't like to be reminded of Theodora.

"I'm smiling at my beautiful girl, of course."

Seven years had passed since Theodora was taken from them. Sometimes it felt like she'd lost a part of Lillian that day too. In those seven years, she'd grown and changed in ways Harriet still struggled to keep pace with. There were days when she scarcely recognised her own daughter.

"Have you finished?" Lillian angled her head, trying to see the back of her elegant coiffure.

"Yes, darling, you're all finished." She pecked her on the cheek.

Lillian turned to look at her mother. She took in Harriet's attire, all the way down to her feet and back up. "Is that what you're wearing this evening?"

Harriet looked down at her dress, smoothing out imaginary creases and straightening her bodice. "Yes. It's perfectly suitable for dinner. Why?"

"No reason. I just wondered." She stood and left the room.

They were in London for the start of the season and due to attend a small gathering at a neighbour's house. Since Theodora's departure, Arabella had insisted they attend every London season—perhaps to keep up appearances, or perhaps in quiet hope that distraction might dull the ache of her missing daughter.

William hated it, but it was the highlight of Lillian's year. She loved the hustle and bustle of city life—watching fine ladies and gentlemen come and go—theatres and fairgrounds and all manner of entertainment. This, however, was her first proper social engagement. Harriet had sheltered her thus far from London society. She knew they would never accept her. She was the daughter of a governess. She had made one friend, though—their neighbour's daughter, Louise. A young girl of sixteen who accepted Lillian without prejudice. She reminded Harriet of Theodora and Delphine, with their indifference to class or convention.

It had been Arabella's idea to introduce the two girls. She said it would do Lillian good to have some company whilst they were in London.

Harriet had come across them in the parlour once, whispering over a fashion catalogue. Louise giggled at something Arabella had said, and Lillian repeated it with perfect mimicry. "It's not what you wear—it's what they think it cost." Something cold had shifted beneath her ribs.

She was glad Lillian had someone to talk to though. It would have been very lonely for her otherwise. The childhood friendship she'd had with William was over. He was thirteen and had different interests now. Besides, now they were older, it was no longer proper for them to be alone together.

When Louise had extended the invitation to join them for dinner, Harriet was dubious. She would have felt better if Delphine were there, but she hadn't come to London this year, and Lillian was so excited, she didn't have the heart to let her down.

She looked at herself in the mirror. *Is there something wrong with my dress?* She leaned in closer, examining the fine lines that were starting to appear at the corners of her eyes. She supposed it was to be expected at almost thirty-four.

Arabella came into the room then and closed the door behind her.

Harriet caught her eye in the mirror. "What do you think of this dress?"

She perched on the edge of the bed and cocked her head to one side. "I think it will do just fine," she said, with a saccharine smile. Her lacklustre approval did not have the desired effect.

Harriet frowned at her reflection before turning away.

Arabella patted the bed beside her. "Sit with me. I wanted to talk to you about the ball next month."

"Oh?" Harriet waited.

"It's the perfect opportunity to present Lillian. I mean, she's sixteen next month, and she really ought to have been out at least by last season, but I suppose it won't matter too much."

Harriet stared at her. "It won't matter at all, because she won't be presented at court. Arabella—Lillian and I don't belong to your world, and haven't for a long time."

Arabella spoiled Lillian with gifts and treats, and lavished her with attention. They had grown fond of each other. Lillian had even taken to calling her Aunt. Harriet had allowed it, seeing no harm in the growing bond. Perhaps it was Arabella's way of coping with the loss of her own daughter. And Lillian, besides her mother, had only Delphine. Surely, another aunt was good for her.

"How could I expect to present her to London society when her mother is a governess? She'd be a laughing stock!" Harriet said.

Arabella cleared her throat. "Well, that's what I wanted to talk to you about. No-one has to know anything about her mother. I could present her as my niece if you like." She said it as though she were doing Harriet a favour—as though the mother they were talking about were not standing in this very room.

Harriet's throat tightened. Something prickled at the back of her neck. "That won't be necessary."

Arabella stood up and smoothed her dress. "It's your choice, but you wouldn't want to spoil her chances by holding her back, would you?" She didn't wait for Harriet to answer. "This year's bachelors are the best London has seen for some time. Every mother in the city will be trying to get the attention of the Pemberton brothers. I've heard their father is insistent that all three of them must marry this year. No need to decide right away, though. Think about it," she said, with a dismissive shrug of her shoulders. "We'll wait for you downstairs."

Did she really just suggest I pretend not to exist? Have I misunderstood? Harriet felt a strange shift, like something important had just taken place, but she wasn't sure what it was. No matter. They wouldn't be coming back here. William would be going to school in the autumn, and so her role in Arabella's house was coming to its end.

When they arrived at their neighbour's house that evening, Mrs Pemberton and one of her highly sought sons were present. Girls and their mothers fawned over him, giggling and blushing. It was odd to watch Lillian interact with other people her age. Especially when it came to young men.

There was a time she used to bring her Latin books to Harriet's chair and recite aloud, seeking her mother's approval with each well-turned phrase. Now, she whispered French phrases to Arabella, and took pains to invalidate Harriet's opinions.

Lillian was sharp as a tack and adjusted herself to the atmosphere and expectations of a room immediately. She knew the qualities expected in young women. What was readily accepted—admired even—and she adopted a silliness not at all natural to her own character. She revelled in the attention it gained her.

Harriet edged closer to where Lillian stood. She appeared

to be holding court with a group of young gentlemen who were hanging upon her every word. The rest of the young ladies were huddled across the room, speaking to each other behind their fans, eyes darting between the members of Lillian's group. Harriet felt certain they were talking about Lillian. She tried to catch her attention, but she turned away.

Before she had a chance to do anything else, Arabella appeared at her elbow. "It seems they're quite taken with her, wouldn't you say?"

Harriet frowned. "Yes, so it seems."

"Lillian, why don't you play something for us?" Arabella said. "The one you played for me last week."

Lillian beamed at Arabella. "Oh, I couldn't. I'm not nearly good enough to play in public."

Harriet had not witnessed this false modesty before, nor had she heard Lillian play anything last week.

Arabella glided over to her and steered her toward the pianoforte. "You are too modest, darling. You play splendidly and you have the voice of an angel."

It was true. She did have the voice of an angel. When she sang, it was haunting. The sort of voice that raised the hair on the back of your neck. Lately she'd concerned herself primarily with such ornamental accomplishments—drawing, singing and music. Her interest in anything academic had withered completely. Harriet had done her best to educate her, but it required hard work on both sides, and Lillian had become so fond of ease, that the thought of work quite struck her through with fear.

Harriet watched as she started to play. Every face in the room was turned toward her, their expressions rapt, ears tuned to her voice. Who was this stranger? Who was this new and unfamiliar person who looked so much like Lillian on the outside? Harriet struggled to reconcile the child she knew with the actress before her.

Arabella stood at the piano, smiling at Lillian, and when she finished everyone clapped and told Arabella how wonderful Lillian was. But why were they all speaking to Arabella?

"Oh, Arabella, isn't she just delightful?" A tall, lean woman said. She reminded Harriet of Hortense, and she immediately disliked her. But why was she saying it to Arabella? And why was Arabella smiling and nodding so much? She soaked up their adoration and praise as if the credit for bringing this magical being into the world were hers.

Harriet had never craved such recognition, but watching Arabella bask in it stirred something bitter and raw. *I ought to move. Stand closer to Lillian—make my presence known.* But she couldn't move. Something rooted her there. *Embarrassment? Fear? But fear of what? Upsetting Lillian—rejection by society—or the look in Lillian's eyes that told her she was ashamed of her.*

She wasn't ready to admit any of those things to herself.

Lillian looked up at her then, proud as a peacock.

Harriet mustered a weak smile. It was the best she could do in the moment. She couldn't wait to go home.

That night Arabella did something that placed Harriet in an impossible position. "Oh, Lillian," she said, "I am so excited for the first ball of the season. I cannot wait to show you off. You're going to be sensational." She looked at Harriet and cleared her throat delicately. "Of course, if that's acceptable to your mother." She smiled without a hint of malice and took Lillian's arm. "We must hope she agrees, and then we can go shopping for your gown."

Lillian's face glowed with excitement. She looked at Harriet with expectant eyes.

How could you Arabella! How dare you mention this to Lillian without my consent? If she said no to Lillian now, she would be the villain. Harriet could almost feel the boiling of her blood. She'd never been afraid to disappoint Lillian for the greater good, but this was different. Their relationship was already under strain, and this would make it so much worse.

But Arabella knew that. She knew Harriet would have no choice but to agree if she mentioned it in front of her.

Lillian was still waiting for an answer.

Harriet put an arm around her and steered her away from Arabella. "Come, let's go to bed. It's late, and you've had a big night. We'll speak about it in the morning."

She seemed satisfied—for now. But Harriet felt the tide turn. She could think on it overnight, but come morning, no answer would feel right.

LILLIAN ENTERED her mother's room the next morning, with an enthusiasm Harriet had dreaded. Still in her nightclothes, she had been writing a letter to Delphine—anxious words about her growing concerns.

Delphine had written the day before with her own concerns. Charlie, she said, had found the man he almost killed years ago, and she was worried he'd try again. Delphine's words still lingered in her mind.

"He's changed, Harriet. There's a darkness in him now that I cannot reach. I fear he means to settle old scores, and I'm worried he might do something rash. He wouldn't say so directly, but I know what revenge looks like. Please—if you see him in London, remind him of the man he used to be."

So, Charlie was in London. She folded her own letter and slipped it into her robe pocket before Lillian could ask to read it.

"Morning, Mother. What are you doing?" She asked, her eyes bright and hands clasped together in delight.

Harriet remembered the way she used to do that as a small child, and felt the bittersweet pang of nostalgia. "I was just going to start a letter to Aunt Delphine. Is there anything you'd like me to tell her?"

"No, thank you."

"I'm sure she'd love to hear what you've been doing in London. She misses you so much."

Lillian hesitated for a moment, twirling a lock of golden hair. "I don't think you should write to her so much, Mother."

Harriet's brow furrowed. "What do you mean?"

"Well...you know, people talk," she said. "It isn't proper to be so friendly with someone like that."

Harriet stood, setting down her pen. "What on earth is that supposed to mean? People like what? And who has been speaking to you about your aunt?"

Lillian faltered, losing confidence in this new perspective. "No-one," she said, "it's just what I heard, that's all."

"What have you heard?"

Lillian looked down at the floor and shuffled her feet. "People say that she ran away with a gypsy. They say she's a fallen woman and that even her own family disowned her."

Harriet's heart thundered in her chest. How was she to navigate this little dilemma? "Who told you that?"

"It reflects poorly on me to be associated with anyone who's disgraced themselves. Isn't that what you taught me? To stay away from those who have sullied their reputation?"

I did. But not Delphine.

All girls were taught to avoid those with bad reputations. It was the way of the world. A woman could as easily lose her good name by association, as if she'd committed the sin herself. But this was Delphine! *Who here could have known? Has*

Arabella imparted this information? Does she know? "Lillian, sweetheart, who told you that story?" Her voice softened when she saw the genuine confusion on Lillian's face.

Lillian started to cry. "When Aunt Delphine came to London last year, some of the girls asked me who she was. I told them she was a family friend and they asked if she was coming again." She sniffed and wiped her eyes on the back of her hand. "They told me what people said about her. They said I shouldn't associate with her because they wouldn't be able to be my friends anymore."

Harriet put her arms around her and spoke softly into the top of her head. "Oh sweetheart, this is why I don't want you to go to that ball. We don't belong in this world anymore, darling. These people are not our friends. I know you think they are, but it's not proper friendship. It isn't real."

Lillian pulled away to look up at her. "You don't want me to go?"

"No, darling, I don't. There is no sense in your being presented because we won't be coming here again. Not after this year. William goes to school in September, and my position in this household will be redundant. We will go back home to Lancaster."

Lillian's eyes widened in horror. She pushed Harriet away and moved backwards.

Harriet reached for her, but she stepped back again, keeping the distance between them. Harriet's outstretched hand fell limp by her side.

"Then why are we even here mother? What has all this been for?"

"Lillian, you know why we are here. This is my work."

"But why? I don't understand why you debase yourself by working here like this when you don't have to?"

The words hit her like a slap. "Debase myself?" Her voice

came out louder than she expected. "I work so that you aren't bound to a husband by necessity. So you can live as you please. I work for your freedom." She clenched her fists at her sides.

"But I want a husband. I don't want to be old and alone. I don't want to live your life!"

"I'm not asking you to Lillian. I'm trying to make sure you have the choice. Don't you understand how precious that is? For a woman to have the means to choose her own fate? Don't you think Theodora would have done anything for that freedom?"

Lillian's face emptied of emotion. "Theodora had choices, Mother, and look what she did with them. She chose her fate, and now she's living with the consequences." Her tears stopped as though turned off at the switch. "Women like her are doomed from the start," she said with a chilling calm.

"That is your opinion of the young woman you've loved and admired? And your aunt Delphine, who took us in when no-one else would—who has been a good and true friend to us all these years. Is she also to suffer this cruel and apathetic judgement?"

Lillian adjusted the lace at her wrist. "Delphine is lucky. Most women in her position never recover their reputation."

Harriet noted the omission of the word 'Aunt'. It stung, but there were bigger things at stake just now.

"She ought to be grateful you still speak to her."

Harriet couldn't speak—couldn't breathe. She watched Lillian turn and walk away, moving with an elegance that had once been foreign to her. Only then did she notice Lillian's new dress—one she had not bought her. The same blush-pink silks and satins Arabella had ordered from the dressmaker on his last visit.

She sat by the window in her night robe until well past

noon, her thoughts so rapid she couldn't concentrate on just one. There were so many bits and pieces of new information and unexpected opinions. Parts of Lillian that were completely foreign to her. *Where has all that anger come from? Such hatred for people she has loved so dearly.* One overarching thought kept recurring, pushing itself to the forefront of her mind again and again. Arabella was somehow responsible.

She washed her face, dressed and combed back her hair into a neat bun. She was determined to have this out with Arabella before things got any worse. Marching down the hallway, she met Arabella coming toward her. Harriet was startled, so concentrated was she on how this conversation was going to play out. The scene had played over in her head all the way down to Arabella's room, and now she was quite thrown off course.

Arabella smiled. "I was just on my way to see you."

"Is that so?"

Arabella put an arm around her. "Yes, I wanted to apologise for last night."

Harriet frowned. This was not what she'd been expecting.

"That whole business about the ball." She waved a hand as though it were all very trivial. "I ought not to have said anything about it in front of Lillian. Not until you'd made up your mind, I mean. It was frightfully careless of me. I was just so excited about it after our lovely evening." She took Harriet's hand in hers, turning her around to face the direction she'd just come.

Harriet flinched at the unfamiliar touch.

"Oh, I do hope you'll forgive me. I shouldn't have overstepped. It's your decision, and I'm sure Lillian will understand, whatever you decide. She's a bright girl."

Arabella knew perfectly well how Lillian would react, and

it wasn't with understanding. She had, however, skilfully defused Harriet before the conversation even began.

How could she argue with someone who was apologising for their actions? She had little choice now but to concede. "I would appreciate in future that you don't discuss social engagements with Lillian without my express approval." She said, sounding less stern than she'd intended.

"Of course, dear, of course. In fact, I was thinking if you don't want Lillian to attend the ball, we could perhaps take her to the opera instead. Just the three of us. What do you think?"

Harriet considered this. *It might soften the blow.* She hadn't fully made up her mind about the ball until her conversation with Lillian this morning. After that, she certainly wasn't attending. The sooner she got Lillian away from these people, the better. *A trip to the opera might be a good alternative.* "Very well, the opera it is. When did you have in mind?"

"Perhaps we could go on Friday? They're playing Offenbach's Orpheus in the Underworld."

"Alright, but don't mention it just now. I'll tell her myself."

"Of course." Arabella's mouth widened into something meant to be a smile, but it fell short of being pleasant.

Has she realised she overstepped with Lillian? She was so adamant to have Lillian on the London scene. It's unlike her to give up so easily. Something in her apology felt contrived—forced.

BOILING POINT

On Friday afternoon, Harriet went to Lillian's room to clear the air. Things had been frosty between them since their argument and had gotten even worse when Harriet told her there would be no debutante ball. She hadn't told her about their trip to the opera yet—she was saving it as an olive branch. Harriet hoped they could have a fresh start, and an evening out would be a lovely way to celebrate that.

When she reached Lillian's room, the door was slightly ajar. She heard voices from within—Lillian's and Arabella's. Harriet stiffened. She wasn't sure why she was eavesdropping instead of walking straight into the room, but something in her gut held her back, keeping her on the wrong side of the door.

The voices were muffled and difficult to understand but she picked up snippets of the conversation—odd words here and there.

"...won't allow it..." That was Lillian.

"...can't be persuaded..." Now Arabella.

She held her breath and moved closer.

"...introduce you...my niece......mother...need to know..." Arabella again.

She heard enough to fill in the gaps. Arabella was still talking about presenting her at the ball. Against Harriet's wishes. As her own niece. Harriet could barely hear them now above the roar of blood in her ears and her own shallow breathing. Her instinct was to barge in and confront Arabella, but Lady Montgomery's words rang in her ears: *"Make no mistake, Harriet. Arabella is artful and manipulative. When it comes to being devious, she would outwit you at every turn."* This would require more finesse.

She backed away as quietly as she could, hoping they didn't hear the soft shuffling of her velvet slippers as she retreated. *I cannot believe what I've just witnessed. Her blatant disregard for me as a mother. Why? Is it grief? Is she missing the things she would have done with Theodora? Is she so desperate to be mother to a young lady again that she doesn't realise what damage she's doing?*

Whatever the reason, her focus seemed to be driving a wedge between Harriet and Lillian by undermining her. Trying to convince Lillian of that would be near impossible; she gave way to nothing that lay contrary to her convictions. Arabella had drawn a film across her eyes, and Lillian now saw the world only through her lens. Seduced by the glamour and ease of a life that didn't belong to her, she had grown fickle—her personality as unsteady as light on water.

Harriet had no idea how to undo the damage that had been done, but she had to try. *How have I let this happen? How could I not have seen this sooner?* The truth was, she had seen it—but she'd made excuses. She blamed it on growing up, becoming a young adult, their unconventional situation, even Arabella's grief.

She hoped the little girl she'd raised was still in there. Underneath all the layers of refinement, all of Arabella's conditioning, the real Lillian would be waiting with arms open wide. She had to be.

Harriet went straight to the drawing room, took the decanter from the cabinet, and poured a large glass of whiskey. She wasn't used to drinking strong spirits, so the amber liquid took her breath. Draining the glass, she slammed it down on the counter and wiped her mouth on the back of her hand.

"Jesus fucking Christ!"

The words shocked even her. She'd never said anything like that in her life. Aggie would have tanned her hide for it —but it summed things up nicely. Straightening up, she carried on to her room—only to find that Lillian had beaten her to it.

~

LILLIAN SMILED BROADLY at her as she walked into the room.

Oh God I'm not ready for this conversation. I need to gather myself. Harriet smiled back with some difficulty. She could still feel the burn of whiskey at the back of her throat. *Calm. I must stay calm.* She took a small publication from her desk and sat beside Lillian.

It was open at a page that showed two identical pictures, side by side. Harriet covered one of the pictures and showed Lillian the other. "Tell me what you see."

Lillian leaned in to examine the first picture. "A bird."

"Are you certain?"

Lillian nodded. "Yes."

Harriet uncovered the other picture. "Now look at this horse. Do you see it?"

"Yes."

"You're certain it's a horse?"

Lillian nodded again, looking at Harriet as though she'd lost her sanity.

"Now look at them side by side."

Lillian paused, her brow furrowed. "They're the same."

"Exactly," Harriet said. "But you saw what I told you to see. That's how easy it is to be led."

Lillian rolled her eyes. "Must everything be a lesson?"

"I'm trying to illustrate a point. You allowed yourself to develop a prejudice that wasn't there before. It altered your perception of what you knew to be true."

Lillian stared at her with a blank expression.

"This is what Arabella has done to you, sweetheart. She has told you what you should like and who you ought to be, and now you cannot see anything else because of it."

Lillian sprang to her feet. "What does any of this have to do with Arabella? It's you who doesn't want me to go to the ball."

"And I heard what she said to you just now in your room. Do you—"

"You were spying on us?" Lillian interrupted, looking down at her mother.

Harriet stayed seated and kept her voice very low. "No Lillian, I came to speak to you, and I heard your conversation when I reached your door."

They eyed each other.

"Do you think it was an appropriate conversation for Arabella to have with you? Do you think it was proper for her to suggest such deceit? To lie to your own mother?"

Lillian started to pace the room. "I don't understand what you have against Arabella. What has she ever done to you?"

"I have nothing against Arabella, except that she has overstepped the mark. It is not her place to decide what you are allowed or not allowed to do." She was barely in control of the rage simmering under the surface.

"I don't understand what the issue is. Why don't you want me to go to the ball? You brought me here. You've shown me a world where I can only press my face against the glass. At least Arabella is willing to let me enter it."

Harriet stood. "By denying who you are? And to what end, Lillian? How long do you think this deceit can last? Are you so ashamed of who you are that you would pack up your entire history and hide it away to please these people?"

"Ashamed of who I am? Who am I Mother? Please—enlighten me." Her voice cracked. "This education—this upbringing—has left me neither one thing nor the other. What has it achieved but fostered a yearning for unattainable things? Nurtured principles that have no place in the working class." Hot, angry tears streamed down her cheeks.

"I have only done what I thought best for you, Lillian. To give you a better chance in this world than most. I've told you before, I wanted to give you freedom."

"Oh, so you've liberated me, is that what you think? Because I am not liberated, Mother!" There was a menace to her tone that set Harriet's nerves on edge. She continued to pace the room, stalking her mother like a hungry wolf. "You have confined me in ways you cannot possibly imagine. The working class rejects me for my privilege, and society rejects me for my disadvantage."

Anxiety sharpened Harriet's temper. Her patience was wearing thin. "How can you be so ungrateful? You've led a charmed life young lady. I have given you everything you desired."

"Indeed, you have, but you've lived an unsatisfactory life, with low people. You have no ambition Mother—you lack the courage of your convictions. You stand at the edge of your little boundaries, looking out into a great new world that you dare not enter."

Harriet clenched and flexed her fingers.

"You will never be anything more than household staff. Well, I want more than you have to offer." Lillian spat the vile words, snapping the last thread that held Harriet together.

Her hand moved before she even realised, and the slap landed smartly across Lillian's cheek. She stared as the white imprint of her fingers turned red, horror dawning across her own face. They stood in silence, shoulders rising and falling with the effort of breathing.

Lillian's hand rose slowly to her face, touching it as though she couldn't believe what had happened until she felt the burn with her own hand.

Harriet stepped forward, but she backed away. "Lillian... there are many people like us," she said, voice shaking. "Decent people who are privy to life's luxuries, but must work for what they have. They don't belong to either world—but they make their own."

"Then where are they? Where are my people? You've shown me none." Her voice was quiet now, laced with hurt.

"Then let us go home to find our place." Harriet looked at her daughter, trembling with unspent emotion, and silently pleaded for her to understand the love she felt. "I'll tell Arabella we won't be attending the opera this evening. Pack your things. We'll leave tomorrow morning. It's time we went home."

Lillian ran out of the room and a door slammed somewhere down the hall. Harriet heard the muffled sound of crying, and Arabella's voice, low and soothing. She'd gone to Arabella for comfort. That stung more than she'd expected.

"Oh God, what have I done?" Harriet raised her eyes to the ceiling, pinching the bridge of her nose to staunch the tears. *I shouldn't have lost my temper.* She pulled her trunk from under the bed and tore everything from the closet. Stuffing dresses and undergarments into the case, not bothering to fold them. She left it half done, paced the room like a caged animal and breathed deep, noisy breaths. *I can't stay in this room. I need to get out before it suffocates me.*

She walked part way down the hall before breaking into a run and didn't stop until she reached the garden. Outside, she could breathe even though her head still reeled. *I don't understand. Theodora so desperately wanted out of this world and here is Lillian, desperately trying to enter it. Have I failed them both? Have I done this? I brought her here—showed her this. I never thought for a moment that she'd want any of it.*

She steadied herself with two hands on the fence and rested her forehead on a wooden rail. *I need to go home. Everything will be better when we get home. I know it will. She doesn't know what she's saying. It's Arabella; she's the bad apple here. Delphine never liked her. Neither did Lady Montgomery. They warned me. I should have listened. God, why didn't I listen?*

Her heart hammered in her chest with the effort of holding herself together. She took a steadying breath and reached deep into herself for the composure she'd always been capable of. That iron rod of sensibility she'd used to beat down every emotion daring to raise its head. She spoke aloud to herself. "Alright, Hattie, pull yourself together. Let's go home."

A familiar noise pricked her ears. It was coming from the front of the house. Iron wheels crunching over granite setts. Someone arriving at the house? A visitor? They weren't expecting anyone. Harriet glanced at her watch. They were supposed to set off for the theatre soon. *I'd better tell Arabella we won't be joining her.*

She made her way through the house to the parlour, where she could see through the front window, who was arriving. There was a carriage outside, but it bore no crest, and the footmen were in plain livery. *It must be a hired cab.*

As she waited to see who got out, two women descended the front steps of the house to get in. *Wait—is that—Lillian? Where are they going?* She raced to the front door in time to see the carriage pull away from the kerb. She could see the back of their heads through the carriage window behind. Lillian and Arabella.

Rage swelled in her like the tide. It tore through her carefully constructed barriers—the lies she'd told herself, the excuses she'd made for Lillian's actions.

She started running, with a force she wasn't aware she possessed, propelled by anger and disappointment. She ran past trees and parks, carriages and buildings, hardly aware of her surroundings. Focussed solely on the destination. She had to get to the opera house before them—had to take her home—to Delphine and their own people. Away from this glittering mirage of a world with all its serpent inhabitants.

She clawed at the top button of her blouse, ripping it open to breathe more freely, and held up her skirts in bundles of crumpled satin. Her hair was coming loose, whipping in the wind, and salty tears stung her face, but she carried on. There was no sense in following the carriage, she'd never keep up. She needed a shorter route but was uncertain of the way. She ran for what felt like an age before anything looked familiar.

As she turned the last corner into the square, the Davenport carriage was approaching the steps of the opera house. She crossed the square at speed and came to an abrupt stop in front of the two black horses. They were startled by her sudden approach and backed up in alarm, pawing at the ground.

"Woah there," the driver said, looking Harriet over with a critical eye.

She heaved and coughed, trying to catch her breath.

"What's the matter man? What's amiss out there?" came Arabella's voice from inside the carriage.

"Beg pardon ma'am. There's a mad woman out here, scaring the horses," he said, not taking his eyes from Harriet.

She became suddenly aware of her wild appearance. Panting heavily, her face slick with perspiration, damp strands of hair stuck to her forehead and cheeks. She could taste the salty beads blooming on her upper lip, and sweat trickled down her back. *A mad woman. Is that what they see?* She tried to fasten her blouse with shaking fingers and smoothed back the hair from her face.

Before Arabella had a chance to speak again, Harriet strode towards the carriage door. Reaching for the handle, she wrenched open the door and Arabella recoiled like a frightened animal.

Lillian's eyes opened wide as she took in her mother's appearance.

"Lillian. Get out." Her breath not fully recovered, the words came out in short, clipped bursts. The effect was menacing, and she saw fear flash in Arabella's eyes.

Lillian pressed herself further into the corner.

Harriet felt a pair of rough hands clasp her upper arms, and a piercing whistle screamed somewhere close.

"Now, miss," said a gruff voice in her ear. "Just come away and leave these good ladies to go about their business. We don't want any trouble here."

Harriet tried to shrug him off, but the coachman held fast to her. She struggled against him, and then a second pair of hands were upon her—a policeman who had been close by.

"Please Sir, if you'd be so good as to let go of me and listen," Harriet said, trying to maintain some semblance of dignity.

The constable stared at her, unmoved.

"She has my daughter. This woman has taken my daughter." She was growing less composed by the second.

Lillian stared wide eyed from the corner of the carriage.

"Is there any truth in what this woman claims, Madam?" The constable said, directing the question to Arabella.

She shook her head as though she'd been struck dumb. Whether in fear or calculation—Harriet couldn't tell.

"Didn't think so." He started to pull Harriet away from the carriage.

"Wait… ask my daughter. Ask the girl, sir. Lillian, tell him." She looked at Lillian in desperation. *This cannot be happening.* "Lillian, please. I'm your mother—for the love of God, tell him!"

The constable rolled his eyes. "I don't get paid enough for this sort of carry-on. Look Miss, is this woman your mother or not?"

Lillian paused.

Everyone waited.

Her back stiffened. She sat taller and met Harriet's eye without blinking.

Harriet knew that look. Defiance. Determination. She held her breath as Lillian's lips parted.

"No."

A LIFE ALTERED

Reality seemed to tilt. The world toppled of its axis and skittered to a halt. Nothing existed except that word.

No.

So small. So powerful. It fell from her lips like the dropping of an axe, severing the invisible ties that bound them together as mother and child. The pain struck like a bolt of lightning. A brilliant and brutal cracking open of her soul. It was, to the outside world, nothing more significant than the snuffing out of a candle. Imperceptible to all but Harriet—the stricken receptacle of its mighty force.

Lillian's expression faltered as the two men took hold of her mother again.

Arabella handed a purse to the constable. "Make sure she leaves London." And then the carriage door slammed shut. It was the last thing she saw. Her brain engaged in a final momentary struggle against the truth and gave up. Blackness swamped her vision, and the world shrunk and fell away.

When she opened her eyes she was being half carried, half

dragged by the coachman and the constable. They dumped her on the pavement across the square, and then the coachman disappeared.

She stared at the constable in bewilderment, Arabella's words ringing in her ears. She leant to one side to look past his legs, but the carriage was gone. There was no sign of Arabella or Lillian anywhere. They were probably inside the theatre already. She had no prospect of getting in there now. Not whilst this brute stood over her.

The constable held up the purse Arabella had passed him and cupped his hand underneath it, feeling the weight of the coins. "I don't think you'll be needing this," he said. He tipped out the contents, put them into his pocket and threw the empty pouch at her. "I'll escort you a little way out of the centre, Miss, then you can be off. Make sure you leave this city by tonight. Don't care how you do it, but be gone by sunrise." He nudged her with his boot. "Oi, are you listening?" He yanked her up by the arm. "I said, are you listening? That nice lady paid a lot of money to see you leave this city, and I like to provide a good service." He patted his pocket and winked at her.

Harriet nodded. *You brute.*

He started up again. "Make no mistake. If I see you in this city after tonight..." He leaned in, his breath hot and sour. "... I'll personally see to it that you're carted off to Bedlam. Do you understand me?"

Harriet winced at the thought and allowed herself to be frogmarched through the streets without resistance. She heard his bristly whiskers scraping against the chin strap on his hat. His breathing was laboured as though walking were a struggle, and he wiped his sweating red face every few minutes.

As they walked further away from the city's affluent

centre, smart, clean pavements gave way to cobbles, then to wooden slabs, and finally a dusty track. Buildings became darker and closer together; colour drained away with every step until everything was mud brown and grey. The air grew thick and heavy with damp as night drew in.

After walking about a mile, they came to a spot where the landscape was bleak. Everything was blackened with ashes and soot, and a constant stream of sludgy brown fluid ran along the road. The air here was rank and made her eyes run. She covered her nose with her sleeve and tried not to vomit at the offensive smell.

The constable gave her some instructions as to how she could get to the mail cart, but she didn't listen, only stared at him. What was the point of listening? He'd taken the money she could have used to get out. He left her then, and she wandered without aim through the dirty streets.

Moving slowly, her feet shuffled without direction. Her heart pounded, a drum in her chest, and she heard nothing but the dull roar of blood rushing in her ears. She concentrated only on remembering to breathe.

In.

And out.

She breathed, and she walked. That was the limit of her abilities.

Her face was marred with dust and sweat, and her velvet slippers had worn clean through.

She could tell from the sting that her feet were bleeding, but she didn't care. She might have walked to the end of the world without stopping, commanding her legs to keep moving forward. Away from this city—this awful reality that her mind refused to accept. But her body began to rebel. Her legs trembled beneath her, and her breath came in short, ragged bursts.

She did not recall making the decision to rest, but her body led her to an alley where she slumped down onto a wooden crate, leaned against the wall. Her eyes closed against the dim light.

A lamp-lighter asked her if she was alright and she nodded slowly. Each time she opened her eyes, the shadows had lengthened, and the sky had grown blacker. No sunset, she thought. No red or violet skies here, just dark. She knew she had to keep going—to make her way out of this God-awful place.

Who knew how many policemen Arabella had out on the streets looking for her. After what just happened, she couldn't say what lengths Arabella would go to in order to get rid of her. If they took her to Bedlam, she would never get out. The safest option was to make it home to Delphine, and there they could make a plan together.

There was a movement in her peripheral vision. A large portion of shadow peeled itself away from the black mass, taking on shape and form as it moved closer. A man, a ribbon of grey smoke encircling his head. The red tip of a cigar glowed as he brought it to his mouth, and a bottle hung casually from his other hand.

He approached in a zigzag motion, walking with some difficulty. Intoxicated, she thought. He was saying something, but to whom she could not tell. She sensed in some distant and murky part of her mind that she ought to be afraid, but she felt nothing. Until he came closer, and the darkness dissolved from his face. Realisation sliced through her.

Caiaphas.

Even in his drunken state, Caiaphas recognised her instantly. She saw the gleam of pleasure pass through his cruel eyes—the lascivious smile slide over his lips. He came very close and looked around him, checking they were alone in the dark place.

Harriet tensed.

His gaze lingered over her breasts, and she knew with sudden and absolute clarity what he was going to do. He smashed the bottle against the wall, littering the floor with splinters of glass. Whiskey fumes filled the air.

With the crate behind her knees, Harriet had nowhere to move. She braced herself, anticipating the blow. Too late to escape.

He stepped back and hit her with a dramatic swing of his arm. The back of his hand connected with her face with a mighty thwack and threw her sideways. She fell against a barrel but managed to scramble upright as he came towards her again.

"Stand still you stuck up little whore."

Harriet kicked furiously at him, but he stood on her tiny feet, pinning them down and rendering her defence useless. She screamed and rained down frantic blows about his head, but she couldn't hurt him. "No—don't touch me—help! Help!" she screamed.

He fumbled to pull up her skirts and ripped away her under linen.

She tried to scream again, but he covered her mouth with one large hand. She bit down, but he only pushed his hand further into her mouth, barely leaving her room to breathe.

He released her left foot and wrenched up her leg by the knee.

She felt the rush of cool air against her sensitive flesh and the brush of his hand against her thigh. She shuddered. Cold crept through her, radiating from every place he touched, like ice spreading over her body. The pain was intense, her every sensation alive with keen sharpness.

He put his mouth to her ear. "I'm going to make sure you never forget me." Not as drunk as he had appeared. He steadied himself with a hand on the wall beside her head. "You'll never wash me off no matter how hard you scrub." He made a horrid sound, like the cackle of a witch. His fetid breath, soured with tobacco and whiskey, expelled from his lungs in great guffaws with every thrust of his hips.

She tried to turn away, but he wouldn't let her.

He gripped her jaw, so that she faced him.

She squeezed her eyes shut.

"You'll search for my face in every crowd. You'll dream of me in your bed at night. Every sound will be my foot on the stairs, my hand on the lock. And when you've driven yourself half mad thinking of me, they'll drag you off in a white jacket, to die screaming my name."

The metallic tang of iron filled her mouth. She was bleeding, or perhaps it was his blood. She couldn't tell.

His boots scraped and scuffled as he struggled to find purchase in the dusty ground. Then a ghastly guttural sound tore from him as his body shuddered its release.

It was over, and she felt him slacken against her, trying to recover his breath.

He nuzzled his face into her neck, and his mouth stretched into a smile.

Bile rose in her throat.

He removed his hand from her mouth, sliding it to her neck and squeezed, while smiling.

She tried prize his hands away, but he was too strong.

"I told you not to fight me, bitch." He spat on the ground,

then leaned forward and dragged his tongue across her mouth.

She was sweating and her vision started to blacken at the edges but he released her then. She slumped, exhausted against the barrel, her head thrown back at a painful angle. Tears ran down the sides of her face and filled her ears. Something caught her attention. A bright flash of movement.

The neck of the broken whiskey bottle—set in motion by the scuffle—rolled gently toward her. Its jagged edges gleamed in the light from the gas lamp. She strained her outstretched fingers until her hand tightened around it. She glanced at Caiaphas.

He struck a match and brought it to the cigar held in his teeth.

Everything slowed, and what followed seemed to happen in one long, drawn-out second.

She lifted the bottle and struggled to her feet.

He glanced sideways, shaking out the flame from the match.

Harriet raised the bottle above her head.

His eyes widened.

She brought it down hard, plunging the jagged edge into his neck.

Someone called out, but it was not Caiaphas.

Hot blood spurted from him and gushed over Harriet's hand. He clutched his neck, blood running between his fingers, down his arms and dripping off his elbows.

Harriet watched, utterly motionless and stricken with horror. She heard him gurgling, choking on his own blood. Her hand still grasped the neck of the bottle, fingers like stone.

"Harriet?" The voice called again somewhere in the dark. "Harriet, is that you?"

She did not move to see who called her, but started as the broken bottle fell from her hand with a clatter. She stared at the sticky red liquid coating her hands, turning them over in disbelief. She saw him then, coming further into the alley. "Charlie?"

"Are you hurt?"

Relief flooded her at the sight of his familiar face, but she couldn't recover herself enough to meet his urgency. She stood vacant and dumb.

"Christ—Harriet. What happened?" Charlie looked from Harriet's blood-covered hands to Caiaphas, slumped on the floor. "We need to leave. We need to move him before somebody comes." He tried to urge her into action, but she didn't understand.

"Why are you here?"

"There's no time for that now. We need to go!" The alarm in Charlie's voice did little to wake her from her stupor.

"The blood," she said, "we need to stop the blood. He needs a doctor." She turned to exit the alley to shout for help, but Charlie yanked her back by the arm.

"No Harriet. Look at him. We can't save him."

Caiaphas was hunched over on the ground, his life flowing rapidly down his arms.

"He's lost too much blood already Harriet. He'll be dead by the time we get help. We have to get rid of his body before somebody sees us. The police will be here before long."

Harriet stared at him in horror. "I must tell them what happened."

"Jesus Christ Harriet, look at us! You haven't even got shoes on your feet! You're filthy and your clothes are torn. He's a gentleman. They'll have us locked up before you can open your mouth, let alone explain what happened. Look at him Harriet!" He shook her by the shoulders. "Do you think they'll believe this man was the one in the wrong?" He turned her to face Caiaphas who was no longer struggling. "Do you want to swing from a rope for this scum? Because that's what will happen if we don't move now!"

She shook her head, her eyes wide with fear.

Charlie bent down, hooked his arms under the lifeless body and began dragging him backwards.

Harriet watched in bewilderment as two channels appeared in the dirt where his boots dragged along, a dark red smudge blooming in his wake.

"Cover the blood. Slit open one of them there sand bags and scatter it about a bit." Charlie said.

Still, she didn't move.

He dropped the body and slit open a sandbag with his pocket knife, pushed it into her hands and told her again, "For God's sake, hurry. We haven't got a lot of time. I'll drag him to the river. Now follow me and cover the blood."

This time she was stirred to her senses, her wits sharpened by fear. She poured the sand over the scene, filling the channels and covering the stain as Charlie dragged him down the alleyway.

He reached the end of the passage with Harriet close behind and swept his gaze across the intersecting pathway. There was no-one about. He stepped up to the railings and hoisted Caiaphas onto his shoulder, then leaned forward and, with Harriet's help, heaved him over the railing and into the water.

There was a loud splash as he broke the surface, and Harriet looked about, wondering if anyone had heard. She leaned over to look in the river and could just make out his form in the weak light. He bobbed about in the current and his jacket ballooned with air. Then he rolled gently over, white face turned upward, staring at her with unseeing eyes.

They both held their breath until slowly, he began to sink. The black depths of the Thames swallowed him up, closing over him to lie at the bottom of the river with the rest of its countless secrets.

Charlie took a rag from his pocket and wiped the railings clean of blood then he threw that into the river too. Stripped now of convention or any code of practice, he grabbed Harriet by the hand and interlocked their fingers.

Harriet stared at the strange and unfamiliar joining.

He squeezed hard. "We've gotta run now, alright?" He said. "Don't let go; we've got a fair way to go from here. Can you do that?"

Harriet nodded, still speechless, and with her free hand, gathered her skirts into a great bundle. For the second time that day, she ran as though her life depended on it.

ESCAPE

Harriet ran like she'd never run before—her ravaged body fuelled by adrenaline alone. They ran through narrow streets and alleys, along pathways and under bridges, always keeping to the darkness. She could barely see two feet in front of her, but she trusted Charlie and took some comfort from the tight grip he held on her hand. They had more or less followed the curve of the river and when they emerged from the last alleyway, they were back at its banks, albeit a lot further upstream.

There was a break in the iron railings where they disappeared down the banking side and she could just about make out the top of a flight of steps. They descended with caution. Charlie held a finger to his lips, so she muted the question hovering on hers, wondering in silence where they were going.

They stepped down onto a patch of gravelly stones. She could hear their breathing, which seemed very loud in the dark. The soft sloshing of water against the stones told her they were close to the river's edge. Occasionally she heard a scuttling of tiny feet and a faint shrieking as rats ran along the riverbank. She found it near impossible not to scream out. How horrid it was to hear the noises of moving things and not be able to see them.

Charlie dropped her hand and cupped both his to his mouth. He made a sound like a birds call. She didn't know what sort of bird he mimicked but it was certainly out of place in this filthy city in the middle of the night. When he had done it a couple of times, he fumbled at her side to grasp her hand again. "Almost there now" was all he said.

She was still no wiser as to where 'there' might be and decided at this point, she no longer cared. All she wanted was to stop and fall apart somewhere in relative safety.

Then there came a new sound, like the slither of something moving through water. A gentle lapping of something cutting through the current. Harriet strained her eyes to see what it was. Black shadows undulated, rolling and swelling as her eyes tried to adjust to the darkness. It pulsated around her.

For a brief moment, the moon peeped out from behind the clouds, and the view reassembled itself into familiar forms. It revealed the crude shape of a small boat, and she saw the rise and dip of oars, scattering drops of moonlight on the surface of the river. A solitary figure sat in the boat, and as it approached, she saw a crooked top hat and the glint of metal where his waist would be.

Is that a knife? Her grip tightened on Charlie's hand.

The boatman's voice was thin and sharp. It sliced through the night, splitting the air when he spoke. "You said one passenger. The deal was for one, not two."

The deal! What deal? How could he know we would be here? What on earth is he talking about?

Charlie answered him with a gold coin from his pocket. He flicked it into the boat with his finger and thumb, and the man caught it deftly in mid-air. Charlie continued. "Come on, I'll carry you to the boat," he said, and bent to pick her up. He scooped her up with one arm under her knees and the other around her back. It barely seemed to cause him any effort at all. He waded out up to his knees in the black, filthy water and placed her gently into the boat.

She shot a glance at the boatman. *Oh God he's sending me with him. He's leaving me, oh God no.* She clung to Charlie's coat-sleeves. "Don't leave me," she blurted out, panic rising in her throat.

"Shhh," he said. "Settle now, I'm coming with you. Let go so I can get into the boat." His voice was soft and calmed her.

She let go with trembling fingers, but didn't move her hands far from him in case she needed to make a sudden grab.

He climbed over the side, spraying her with the foul water as he flung his legs into the boat. Once he was in and the boat steadied, he took both her hands in his and nodded to the boatman.

The man took up his oars and began to row them away from the banking and upstream through a thick yellow, brown fog. She tried not to look at him but found it difficult. He had the kind of face that would imprint itself on your memory in ghastly detail. His features were only partly illuminated in the pale light, making his eyes nothing but sunken black hollows. His skin was pale as stone and tinged with green. He looked waxy, cadaverous, and his dark hair hung in limp, greasy tendrils from underneath his crooked hat. Each time he leaned forward to row the boat, his face loomed towards her, and she smelled his scent, like spoiled milk and wet dog.

She shrank away from him and pressed herself as far back as she could in the small boat.

They travelled a half hour upstream, and the man

deposited them on the opposite bank of the river. They walked a way further- much slower now- to a small plot of wasteland on the outskirts of Shoreditch.

She asked him now how he came to be so far from home and how he had chanced to come upon her in such extraordinary circumstances.

"I was following him," Charlie said.

"Who, Caiaphas?"

"Yes." He looked down at the ground as he walked. "I've been following him for days, but tonight was the first time he left the group he was with. He gave me the slip a few hundred yards before I got to you." There was a hurt in his voice she couldn't fathom.

She didn't respond, but waited to see how much he was willing to divulge.

"He did something terrible to my sister, and she killed herself. I wanted to make sure he never did it to anyone else."

Her heart thudded. *His sister! It had been Caiaphas. The gentleman who destroyed Charlie's life was Caiaphas. No wonder he followed him.* "Were you going to kill him?"

He paused for a long time. "Yes I was."

Harriet saw him glance her way from the corner of her eye. "Then I'm glad he's dead."

He looked sidelong at her shoulder and Harriet realised that not only was her sleeve torn, but a great piece of her bodice hung down in a flap at her waist. There was no flesh showing but she tried to hold the piece in place all the same.

He cleared his throat and made a stumbling start at speech, before clearing it again. "There's something I must ask. And I'm sorry I have to ask it, but I must know, for my own peace of mind." He looked at Harriet with pleading eyes but she had no idea what he wanted to know. "Did…I mean…did he…did

I.." He stopped walking and blew out a long breath. "Did I reach you in time?"

Harriet was no wiser as to what he meant.

"Was I…too late? Did he…"

Oh! He wanted to know what Caiaphas had done to her.

Harriet looked away as tears sprang to her eyes. She didn't want to make him feel any worse, but she hadn't the energy to keep up such a lie. "It doesn't matter," she said. "He's gone now and he will never touch another woman again."

Charlie groaned and held his face in his hands.

She knew that he was crying from the shaking of his shoulders. She'd never seen a man like him cry before.

His whisper was barely audible but he repeated it over and over. "I'm sorry, I'm sorry."

"It's alright, Charlie, I'm alright." She was anything but alright, but she didn't know what else to say. She didn't want him to carry the weight of that too.

~

WHEN THEY REACHED CAMP, she saw tents pitched here and there across the site, and three bow-topped wagons like the one she had seen in Skerton the night Charlie bought her mother's jewellery. She couldn't help but think how wary she'd been of him. How odd that she was here now, both of them bound together by this monstrous act. And he—so concerned for her welfare, when she had cared so little about him.

He took her to a wagon and led her inside to his wife. He communicated with her in words Harriet could not understand. She knew what he'd said all the same. She saw the horror on the young woman's face as he told her, and the kindness bloom in her eyes when she met Harriet's.

He told her what Caiaphas had done.

The young woman left them momentarily to fetch another, older by far than Charlie's wife. Harriet didn't recognise her at first—her accent was coarse, unmistakably cockney. But when she looked closer, she realised it was the fortune teller who had read her palm at the fair all those years ago.

"Hello Madam," the woman said.

"Harriet, please. Just Harriet." Harriet held herself tightly and rubbed her arms.

"Very well, and you can call me Tilly. I'm going to look after you tonight and see that you get some rest. You'll be leaving with Charlie tomorrow, alright?"

Harriet nodded.

The young woman came back with a bowl and cloth for Harriet and closed the curtains across the opening of the wagon, leaving her inside with Tilly.

"Now then Harriet. What d'you say we get you out of them dirty things and get you all cleaned up, eh?"

Harriet's hands flew to the neck of her blouse, clutching it together in terror.

"It's alright darlin' I won't hurt ya. You can trust me. I've done this before and believe me, you'll feel better." She looked at Harriet with wise eyes.

"I can't" Harriet shook her head.

"If you don't wash him off you now, you'll feel him there forever." She moved very slowly and carefully, speaking to Harriet all the while, as though she were a wild thing. A skittish horse that might be spooked and gallop away. Her voice was careful and steady. "I had a daughter myself, you know. She was just like you, so beautiful, so fragile."

Harriet shuddered as Tilly peeled off her blood soaked blouse and draped a blanket about her shoulders.

"There, you keep that pulled tight about you for now." She

knelt and unlaced Harriet's boots, pulling them off and setting them aside. She hesitated for a moment, to tell Harriet what she would do next before touching her. "I'm going to take down your stockings now. Look at me."

Harriet's chin wobbled and she felt her thighs tense instinctively but she held Tilly's gaze.

"That's it, good girl. You keep looking at me. We're almost done.

Harriet flinched at her touch.

"It's alright it's only me. You keep looking at me so you know who's touching you. That's it, good girl."

Both stockings were off and Harriet was breathing heavily.

"Now then we need to take your dress off so as we can get to your underthings alright?" She went on in this manner, soothing and explaining until Harriet was all but naked except for her cotton shift and the wool blanket around her shoulders. Her torn undergarments were rolled up and sent outside to the fire.

Harriet allowed Tilly to wash her face and neck with the warm water. She rubbed at the skin with gentle, practiced hands until Harriet's hands, face and neck were all clean. She bent to soak the cloth again and handed it to Harriet. "Your turn now. I'm going to stand outside to give you some privacy. Now you wash him off, my darling. You wash him off good and proper and be rid of the filthy bastard."

Harriet took the cloth and squatted over the bowl to wash between her legs. Tears ran freely down her face and she stifled the urge to blubber and wail like a newborn. When she finished, she called for Tilly, who brought her some fresh clothes.

Tilly handed her a pair of bloomers. "Put these on my love, you'll feel better covered up."

She put them on and wrapped herself up tight in the blanket as though it might protect her from anything.

Tilly brought her a crust of bread and some bacon that Charlie had cooked on the fire for her. She didn't feel like eating, but when she smelled the food, her stomach growled in protest, so she ate what they brought her. Then Charlie gave her a cup of strong wine and bid her drink it before she slept. She did as she was told and climbed onto the raised bed with Tilly, where she curled up and wept.

The sky wept with her, washing the slate clean for the coming of the new day. She could hear the gentle patter on the canvas roof and it reminded her of home. Tilly held her all night. She did not speak, nor did she try to stay Harriet's tears —only held her, as a mother might. As Aggie would.

HOMEWARD BOUND

The next morning, Tilly sat Harriet down to speak with her. "Now, pet, it's important you listen to me and you answer me best as you can, alright?"

Harriet nodded.

Tilly softened her voice. "I know it's hard to speak of, but I've seen what happens to girls who wait too long. I need to know if he took what he came for."

Harriet didn't answer.

Tilly tried again. "I need to know if he finished, my love. Did he spill his seed?"

A flush crept up Harriet's neck, a mixture of shame and something else, something darker. "I—I think so," she whispered. "I don't know."

Tilly reached out and touched her knee gently. "That's all right, sweetheart. That's all right. I only ask so we can do something before it's too late. There's women who can help if you go soon enough."

Harriet frowned. "I don't understand," she said.

"While there's still time to turn the tide, if the seed hasn't yet taken root yet, there's herbs and tonics," Tilly said. "And later, other things."

"You mean to—" she dropped her voice, "to undo it?"

Tilly looked at her as if she were a small child. "Nothing can undo it, pet, but it might stop anything from settling, if it hasn't already. It won't undo the wrong, but it might spare you the rest of it."

Harriet's eyes welled, but she didn't let the tears fall. "But isn't it a sin?"

Tilly's expression hardened. "What he did was a sin. What happens now… that's survival."

Harriet nodded, slow and uncertain. "I don't know, Tilly. Is there someone here who could—?"

Tilly stood. "There's a wise woman—a midwife—a few streets over. She works quiet and clean, and she don't ask questions. You think on it, but don't take too long."

Harriet did think, and after some deliberation, decided she would visit the midwife after all. She must do what she could to limit the damage of this diabolical situation.

Tilly took her to a street nearby where a row of ramshackle houses leaned against each other. "We need to go around the back," she said. "She won't like folks seeing us at the front door."

The alley behind the tannery reeked of old hides and lye. Harriet stepped over a puddle that glistened like oil and tried not to gag. They walked up to a low door in a crumbling brick wall and knocked twice. A slat slid open, and two pale eyes peered through.

"Who sent you?"

Tilly moved so she could be seen through the gap.

The woman recognised her and asked, "Who is she?" throwing a quick glance toward Harriet.

"She's mine. I vouch for her."

There was a pause, then the door creaked inward. The room was dim, lit by a single oil lamp whose wick hissed with damp. The bundles of dried herbs hanging from the rafters did nothing to mask the smell of old blood. Harriet had thought the smell outside was bad, but it was nothing compared to this. It made her eyes water.

The walls were lined with rickety shelves laden with tiny glass bottles of liquid. Some were black, some green, some a deep burgundy red. They looked like poison. Perhaps they were.

Tilly spoke in hushed tones to the woman and handed her a coin. The midwife took down a bottle from the shelf. She turned it over and held the dark liquid up to the light. It still looked black.

"You sure?" She said to Harriet. "Once taken, it don't untake."

Harriet nodded, her throat too tight to speak.

The woman handed her the bottle with yellow-stained fingers. "Take half before sleep and the other half in the morning. There'll be cramping, maybe worse. But if it's early… it'll pass. And if your time still don't come," she added, fixing Harriet with her small, sharp eyes, "don't wait. There's other things can be done later on."

Harriet shuddered and they left the house, a half-formed prayer already clenched in her chest. She felt as though she'd just stepped inside a story book. Nothing felt real in this strange and mysterious place.

On the way home, she asked Tilly something which had been nagging at her. "Do you remember me, Tilly?"

Tilly sighed as though she'd known the question was coming. "Yes, my dear, I do."

"I remember what you said to me that day at the fair."

"As do I." She nodded.

These people give nothing away, do they? Getting a conversation out of them is like extracting teeth! Harriet wasn't entirely sure of what she'd expected or what she wanted to know. Perhaps she wanted to ask if she'd made it up? If her gift was genuine? She relaxed her hands and rubbed at her white knuckles, suddenly aware that she'd been clenching her fists. "Why did you say those things to me?"

"Because it's what I saw." She showed no emotion, no eye contact or attempt to persuade her, just a simple statement of fact. She didn't care whether Harriet believed her.

"So you really do see things that are yet to pass? It's not just an act?"

"I really do."

"Well, I suppose you were right about Lillian. She has caused me great pain."

Tilly nodded again, but said nothing.

Harriet thrust her palm out to her, bringing them both to an abrupt halt. "Please look again. Can you see anything else? Do you know if she comes back to me?" Desperation laced her voice.

Tilly pushed Harriet's hand gently back to her side. "I told you then the palm was for show. What I see is shown to me. I cannot ask for information; it doesn't work like that."

Harriet felt embarrassed for asking such a silly question, but she still wasn't satisfied. "You suggested I would bear another child." She looked at the potion in her hand. "Can what you see be changed?"

"We'll see. Drink the tonic, lass, and you'll know by the turn of the next moon."

Harriet pulled the cork plug from the bottle and drank half the bitter liquid. It burned her throat and made her cough. "We will see."

KINGSLAND BASIN SMELLED of damp rope, smoke, and coal dust. In the fading light, Harriet saw a coal barge sitting low in the water, its hold piled with black lumps glinting like wet glass. A thickset horse pawed at the ground on the towpath, eager to get going. There was a small boy on its back, no more than ten years old, with a cap pulled low over his coal-streaked brow.

Charlie, sure-footed and grease-smudged, looked as familiar on the water as he was with the horses. "Keep low," he muttered, helping her onto the barge. "Most coal's headed west tonight, so they won't look twice so long as we're quiet and we stay low." He guided her into a narrow space between two crates and the side planks and squeezed in beside her.

The bargee, a rough looking squat man, pulled a tarp over the crates and secured it along the outer edge of the barge. The tarp roof overhead left them in near complete blackness. The only thing Harriet could make out was the cigarette dangling from the man's lips, glowing briefly in the dark.

The barge pushed off without ceremony: a soft creak of wood, a groan of ropes, and the splash of the pole in the canal bed. She tried not to think about the danger they were in. It had all seemed a little surreal until now, in the dark and the stillness. The barge creaked and shifted beneath them, and the tarp pressed down on her, cold and damp. She pulled her shawl tight around her and shivered. Her fingers were already slick with black dust. She could feel it lining her lungs, and taste it, bitter on her tongue.

Outside, the sharp clip of the horse's hooves echoed along the towpath. Every snap of a twig, distant bark or splash of water, sent Harriet's heart hammering. She closed her eyes and imagined the city's lanterns fading behind them, swallowed by the dark.

The slow journey westward felt endless as the Regent's Canal stretched out before them. Silent but alive with unseen watchers: rats, smugglers, ghosts. Eventually, the slap of water against the hull and the gentle rocking motion soothed her. The grinding and creaking of the tiller in its socket and even the gruff voice of the barge driver murmuring orders from the stern became comforting.

She must have drifted off because Charlie woke her some time later at Islington Tunnel. The horse had to be unhitched, and Charlie climbed on top of the barge to help the driver with the legging. As he lifted the tarp, she caught a brief glimpse of a sooty fog in the moonlight before they disappeared into the tunnel for over half a mile of pitch-black silence.

Days blurred into one another as the barge slipped steadily westward through endless stretches of water and lock gates. The potion barely had any effect, other than causing a mild stomach ache. Harriet could only hope it had worked. She thought little about what she'd endured the last few days. She couldn't. Falling apart wasn't an option for her right now, at least not whilst they were still running.

When they reached Little Venice junction, they joined the Grand Union Canal and headed northwest to Birmingham. They passed through without any trouble and met with another group of gypsies to travel the rest of the journey by road. Charlie said they were distant relations of his family. It seemed to Harriet that all gypsies were related to each other in some way or another. Travelling around afforded them far-reaching connections in all corners of the land.

THE WOMEN in their group did not speak much to Harriet. They were polite but did not take her into their confidence or show her kindness the way Tilly had done. When they did speak to her, their conversations were measured, wary, their eyes searching and mistrusting.

Charlie tried to make her feel like she belonged, but she did not. She was an impostor. Worse than that, she was a criminal: a killer who would bring them no end of trouble should anyone find out what she'd done, and that they'd harboured her. Yet still, they had welcomed her despite this. Despite their fear and mistrust, they sheltered and fed her and offered her their protection—a stranger in their world.

It was a strange world, the one she inhabited now: built every night and torn down every morning. Each man, woman and child had grown into their own duties. Even inanimate objects seemed to migrate unaided toward their rightful place. Pots, pans, blankets, tent poles, canvas, all packed with great efficiency without the utterance of a single command.

Their physical world may be dismantled, but the invisible bond that kept it all together held fast. It was a community so tightly bound that they lived and breathed and moved as one. A child of one was a child of all: an insult to one, an insult to all. And from the bonds in this small world, rules and laws had grown. Unspoken, but acknowledged all the same. Rights were respected, wisdom accrued and shared, sins—some forgivable—some unforgivable were punished, justice served, stripped to the waist with knuckles bared and hands shaken afterwards.

Many of man's laws were broken, but God's laws were always obeyed. It was a government of their own making, a government borne of kinship and mutual respect, founded on principle and trust, and it worked for them. They had customs, rituals, superstitions—some common—some bizarre. A silver coin placed in a newborn baby's hand for luck, a bird flies into a living space and foretells of imminent death, a death in a wagon and the wagon must be burned.

They shared bread and wealth as they shared grief and happiness, and they looked after each other. Their loyalty was unshakable. They may fight amongst themselves, but no one from outside would lay a hand to one of them without experiencing the wrath of all.

Harriet looked at Charlie through the smoky air of the campfire and thought about Delphine. Her heart ached for home. There was so much she had to thank Charlie for, and she knew so little of him, this strange and mysterious man who had helped her for no benefit to himself. She couldn't say with any certainty that she would have been so charitable had the situation been reversed, and the thought humbled her.

He looked up at her and smiled, holding his palms out against the flames to warm them. "You alright?"

Harriet managed a tight smile. "I'm fine, thank you."

"You're a strong woman, Harriet Blackthorn. I can see why Delphine thinks so much of you.

She felt herself blush at the unexpected compliment and changed the subject. "How far have we left to travel?"

Perhaps he noticed her discomfort because he smiled and reached for her shoulder, squeezing it with fatherly affection. "Another fortnight at most. Sooner, if the weather holds. You'll be home soon, don't fret, lass."

Harriet smiled her first genuine smile since she left London. The pace had been slow as wagon wheels lumbered along rough roads, each mile a battle against mud and aching muscles, but the thought of safety pushed them onward, the promise of home beckoning just beyond the horizon.

Harriet watched one day bleed into the next; pale misty dawns followed by endless rain and grey nights. She waited for some sign that the potion had worked, waited for the blood to come, but it did not. She thought perhaps it was the stress of everything she'd been through. Aggie always said stress did that to a woman. Yes, she assured herself that her courses would come soon enough, when she was safe at home with Delphine. There was little she could do about it now anyway. It was in God's hands.

TOO SOON

Four weeks had passed. Four weeks of fear, cold, and uncertainty. When they got closer to home, Charlie sent word ahead to Delphine that they were coming. He told her only that he was bringing Harriet home and that all would be explained when they arrived. At least that's what he told Harriet; she didn't see the letter herself.

The day they arrived home, Delphine was standing on the steps of Greenacre with a smile that did nothing to mask her concern. Harriet ran into her arms and fell to her knees as the emotion she'd held at bay all this time broke loose. The rush of grief was so intense that it left her unable to function. Charlie swept her up in his arms and carried her into the house.

She slept for some time, and when she awoke, Delphine was sitting by her bed. She tried to sit. "Charlie? Where's Charlie?" There was an edge of panic in her voice.

Delphine guided her back down onto the pillows, smoothing her hair back from her forehead. "He's gone to make camp."

She tried to sit again. "But I didn't get... I need to say...."

Delphine smiled. "Shhhh now it's alright. Charlie will be back."

Harriet slumped back onto the pillows and tried to bring some order to her thoughts. "I didn't get the chance to thank him." She wasn't sure she even could. Where would one begin to show thanks for such a colossal act of bravery, kindness and generosity? To add to that, she discovered that whilst she'd slept, he had spared her the re-living of her sordid ordeal by telling Delphine everything. For that, she was truly thankful.

She spoke little about what happened. As much as she wanted to take comfort in Delphine, she couldn't—couldn't bring herself to say it out loud. It would make it all too real. It meant admitting to herself that Lillian was gone, admitting that Caiaphas had won in the end. He had taken from her something she could not articulate but knew she could not replace.

Delphine did not ask her anything and seemed content to wait until Harriet was ready. The expression she wore was of quiet concern, her brow becoming more furrowed with each day that passed.

Harriet wanted to alleviate some of the pressure building inside her, wanted to ask for help. She wanted to cry and sob and tell Delphine all the hurt she felt but she didn't know how. She was so afraid of breaking down the walls that held her together, she just couldn't risk it. What if she couldn't put herself back together once she'd fallen apart?

Two weeks after arriving home, that decision was made for her. Harriet awoke one morning, sweating and weak, with a sickness she knew all too well. She got up from the bed as a wave of nausea crashed over her. Barely making it to the washstand, she lunged for the basin and retched until her ribs ached, hands trembling against the cold porcelain. When the first wave passed, she sank to her knees, dizzy and breathless. Hair clung to her damp forehead, and the taste of bile was sharp on her tongue.

She glanced toward the window where the early June light stole in through the curtains. She needed fresh air, but she couldn't pull herself to her feet to open the window. The thought of Caiaphas pushed at her, uninvited, unwelcome. *No! Please, no!* She began to cry as her brain tried to refuse what her body was telling her. "No," she sobbed. But it came again, stronger this time, and she doubled over, pressing a hand to her belly as she retched. "Delphine," she whispered, her voice hoarse. And then more urgently, "Delphine!"

Footsteps thundered up the staircase, and the door flung open wide. Delphine stopped short at the sight of her on the floor.

Harriet looked up at her, wide-eyed and pale, and in that moment they knew.

As Harriet's belly grew, so too did the walls around her. She sealed herself off from the world and hid away in her room. At first, she hated the thing inside her. The thing that belonged to him, that would continue his terrible bloodline and forever bind her to him. The thing that would shame her as an unmarried mother. What would Lillian think? Would it ruin their chances of ever being re-united?

But gradually, as she felt the tiny life stir inside her, she felt less and less malice toward it. After all, no child asks to be conceived. The child was innocent, wasn't it? Should a child receive punishment for the sins of its father? Many believed they should but not Harriet. Could she love it though? That was another thing entirely.

Delphine continued to coax and entice her out of her room whenever she could. She brought a doctor to see Harriet every few weeks to make sure she was healthy. She even employed a midwife who resided in the adjoining rooms to Harriet's, just in case anything should happen.

Harriet sensed a feeling of excitement building in her friend. There was a gleam in her eyes whenever the impending arrival was mentioned. Harriet thought of the tiny headstone in the garden and felt ashamed. Delphine would most likely never have the opportunity again to have a child of her own. Perhaps she would help Harriet raise this one.

By the time Harriet's belly was full and rounded, she had accepted her fate and awaited the baby's arrival not with excitement but determination. She would do her best to raise an honest and God fearing child despite the blood it carried, and she would love it to the best of her ability.

This revelation permitted Delphine to show the extent of her true feelings. She radiated happiness and warmth in a way Harriet had never seen her. She knitted and sewed and embroidered from morning till night, chatting about names and cribs, nursery furniture and linens and anything else she could think of that was baby related.

Harriet imagined how Delphine would have been as a mother and knew she would be a spectacular aunt.

~

As they waited patiently for January to come, Delphine appealed to her contacts in London for any information they could find on Lillian and her whereabouts. There were many people who would know something, but few who could be trusted and loyal enough to report what they knew. Even then, no-one had seen the Davenports recently.

Harriet considered appealing to Lady Montgomery but doubted very much that the letter would even reach her.

Arabella would no doubt be expecting her to try contacting them, and intercepting both Lady Montgomery's and Lillian's mail. She tried anyway, but received no response.

In late November, they sent for the doctor to check Harriet as she hadn't felt the baby move for some hours. Harriet didn't like him much. He didn't seem to like her much either and made frequent reference to where the father of this child might be. His Christian uprightness seemed to bolster his conviction that her misfortune was deserved and his conscience was thoroughly unmoved. He even brought her a bible on one of his visits.

Dr. Beech entered the room and looked at Harriet with thinly veiled distaste, removing his gloves one finger at a time. "Miss Blackthorn," he said, with the kind of formality that suggested judgment.

"It's Mrs Blackthorn," she corrected.

He cleared his throat and raised an eyebrow. "Indeed." He opened his bag, preparing himself with a quiet disapproval that filled the room, and took out a pinard horn. He pressed it to her stomach in silence, his ear to the wooden funnel. The only sounds were the ticking of the mantel clock and Harriet's unsteady breaths. He moved the horn, listening for longer this time, but said nothing. Finally, he straightened. "The heartbeat is slower than I'd like," he said. "You need bed rest. No exertion. And you must keep warm."

Harriet nodded, her face drawn and shining with sweat.

"I should caution you that your situation is... delicate. Outcomes are not always favourable in such cases," he added, already repacking his bag.

Delphine stepped forward. "But Doctor, she's already warm. Look at her. She's almost feverish."

"Madam, do you presume to advise me on how to conduct my profession?"

Delphine visibly stiffened. "I *presume,* Sir, to expect the standard of care I have paid you for." Her chest heaved under the strain of her fury.

"I'll return in two days."

"If anything changes tonight I will send for you." Delphine said, trying to stay calm.

"I'm out of town tonight. I have a lady to attend to." He left without another word.

Harriet lay back against the pillows, her hand resting over the place where the baby had once kicked. It was still. Too still.

Delphine moved to her side, brushing damp hair from her face. "He doesn't know everything."

Harriet only stared at the ceiling, her eyes glassy with the kind of fear that had no name yet. She was filled with a sudden and urgent love for this child. She turned to Delphine, eyes brimming and her heart full of shame. "I didn't love it until now," she said desperately. "Oh God, am I too late? I do love it, I do! Oh, please let it be alright!"

And then as though fate issued her cruel reply, the first pains struck her. It started low in her abdomen and raced across her belly like fire, tightening and squeezing until she could scarcely breathe. It continued on through the night and the midwife attended her, but nothing could be done to stop it once it started.

At three o'clock in the morning, Harriet delivered what should have been a healthy baby boy.

He did not cry.

A silence came out of the darkness. Not a peaceful silence, but the haunting kind that made her ears strain for a sound that would never come. Hollow and heavy, it crept in from every corner of the night, stealing sound from all that it fell upon.

Harriet's breath came fast and shallow, her eyes wide and searching. Then she heard the faint, useless rustle of linen as the midwife wrapped the still body.

Delphine knelt at her side, sweat darkening the collar of her cotton shift. Her hands were steady even as her face betrayed the truth.

"What...?" Harriet began, the words sticking in her throat.

Delphine looked to the midwife, whose lips pressed into a firm line as she gently held the bundle out to Harriet.

Harriet reached out, her arms trembling, but Delphine caught her hand.

"No," she whispered, voice breaking. "No, Harriet, don't—"

"Let her," the midwife cut in. "She must. It's part of the letting go. It's better to hold him," she said, turning back to Harriet.

Harriet pulled her hand free and sat up, gasping with the effort. She took the small, swaddled bundle into her arms and pulled back the cloth from his face. A gleam of moonlight fell upon the alabaster skin of his lifeless body. His little face was no bigger than an apple, his features a pearly grey, almost translucent. His mouth drew up into a tiny rosebud pout. He looked like Lillian.

"A little boy," she murmured. "Hello little one. I'm afraid you're here too soon, sweetheart. Just too soon." She stroked his cheek, marvelling at his softness, then lifted him to nuzzle into the space between her face and neck. She rocked him gently, crooning and whispering to him through her tears. "I'm sorry, my love. I'm so very sorry." She told him over and over how much she loved him. "Do you think he knows?" She asked Delphine.

Delphine reached out to touch a miniature hand and pressed her lips to it as she stroked Harriet's head. "Of course he does. He's known all along."

Harriet nodded, pacified for the moment. After a few minutes more, she noticed he felt cool to the touch. "I need a blanket," she blurted out. "Get me a blanket. He's too cold!"

A look of panic passed between Delphine and the midwife and Delphine stood up. "You need to pass him to me now, Hattie, so the midwife can tend to you. I'm afraid you're not finished yet, my darling. You've still the cleansing to come."

Harriet's head snapped up, and she looked at Delphine with the eyes of a hunted animal. All sense had vanished, and only the primal instinct of a mother remained.

Delphine continued with caution. "Hattie? It's time to let go now, sweetheart. Give him to me and we can get you cleaned up, alright?"

Harriet wasn't convinced. She wasn't ready to give him up yet. Somewhere in the recesses of her mind, she knew she had to. She knew he was not alive, would never be alive, but she couldn't command her fingers to let go of him. She looked at Delphine, who was holding out her hands to take him.

"I'll take care of him, don't you worry. Come now, won't you let Auntie Delphine hold him?"

She still couldn't willingly relinquish her hold on him. She looked pleadingly at Delphine, who seemed to understand, and laced her hands through Harriet's arms to take hold of the baby. Harriet loosened her grip, but then lurched forward again. "Wait!" Her hands tightened around him for just a second. "Wait," she whispered. "His name is Charlie." Then she let go of her son and withdrew into herself.

THE SEA

Morning stole into the room like an unwelcome guest. The sky was silver with frost and weak, winter light filtered in through the windows. A fire burned vigorously in the grate, casting orange light across the floorboards. Someone must have tended to it during the night.

Harriet lay motionless beneath the blankets. Not sleeping but not entirely present. Her arms folded around her knees as though trying to hold herself together from the inside out.

The stillness in the room was so heavy, sacred almost, that Delphine was hesitant to break it, but the day had demands. There were things that must be done. "Hattie," she said softly, "are you awake?"

Harriet didn't respond.

Delphine crossed the room quietly and came to sit beside her on the bed. "Hattie," she said gently. "I need to speak to you about Charlie. We've bathed him and dressed him. But... well, we can't keep him here, Hattie. It's time to lay him to rest now."

Harriet still didn't respond.

"I was thinking. You remember the garden where my daughter rests? I thought perhaps it might be nice for Charlie to rest there with her. Would you like that?"

Harriet turned her head slowly. She willed her mouth to speak, but no sound emerged. She just nodded.

"I will ask Henri to prepare the ground, and I'll perform the service myself. You don't have to be there if it's too much. We can—"

"No," Harriet said sharply. "I want to."

Delphine gave a small nod. "Of course." She got up to leave, but Harriet called her back.

"I want to see him."

"Hattie, I don't thin—"

"I want to see him." Harriet cut her off and threw back the bedclothes to follow her. She looked down and saw the evidence of her loss blooming dark and red-brown across the linen of her gown.

Delphine crossed the room and was beside her in a split second. "Let's get you bathed and into a clean nightdress and then I'll take you to see Charlie, alright?

Harriet allowed herself to be washed and clothed. She closed her eyes as Delphine brushed her hair and wondered idly if Aggie was with her boy. The thought offered her some small comfort but not enough.

Delphine brought her a pair of slippers, wrapped a heavy woollen shawl around her shoulders and guided her to her feet. "Are you certain?" she asked her.

Harriet knew what she was asking, and yes, she was certain. She wanted to see him one last time. She entered the room with Delphine at her elbow, and her knees almost buckled at the sight. A polished wooden box, the size of a large jewellery case, was set upon the table. On its lid, carved lettering which read simply "Charlie." She pointed at the box with a trembling hand. "He's in there?" she whispered. "My baby...My boy's in there?"

Delphine kept a tight grip on her waist and elbow and guided her toward the table. She lifted the lid and gently leaned it back on its hinges. "Henri made it for him. You see, he's all snuggled in his new shawl." She lifted the delicate, lacy edge to show Harriet the shawl she had knitted for him.

Harriet stared. "He won't be cold anymore."

"That's right," Delphine said. "He won't be cold anymore."

But he was cold. Harriet knew that he was cold. She knew that if she touched those tiny fingers, or the smooth cheek, they would be cold as marble. She wanted so badly to hold him one more time, but she couldn't bear to feel that icy touch. Soft and warm, that's how she wanted to remember him. Wanted to convince herself that the shawl would hold his warmth forever.

"When you're ready, Henri is waiting for us outside."

Harriet nodded. "I want to carry him myself."

Delphine looked uncertain, but she agreed.

Harriet couldn't close the lid. It felt like turning her back on him. She had to leave the room whilst Delphine did it.

Delphine brought the box out to her, and she took it, managing to keep her hands steady. She thought about John and his quiet dignity when Aggie died and summoned all her strength to get through the next hour. She'd been afforded no chance to do anything for him in life, so carrying him now felt like the last and only thing she could do.

They stepped outside into the freezing air, and Delphine wrapped a large blanket around Harriet, but she barely registered the difference in temperature. Members of staff from the house and stables lined the pathway, heads bowed and caps in their hands. She could hear their muffled sobs, but she fixed her eyes straight ahead on the half-hidden gate to the garden. There stood Charlie Shaw, her son's namesake, his eyes full of tears, his face pale and unreadable.

The grave was small. Just wide enough for the tiny box. The air around them smelled of cold earth and damp moss, and the ground was hard under her slippers. Charlie took the box from her and lowered it gently into the grave. The footman stood back, his spade resting quietly beside him. Delphine read a sermon from a book and said a short prayer. Harriet didn't hear any of it. She just stared at the hole in the frozen earth.

"Hattie?"

Harriet looked up.

"Hattie, it's done. Let's go inside now. It's best not to watch this part."

As Delphine led her away, the first shovel of earth struck the lid with a sound that echoed in Harriet's bones. She flinched. The second thud came, and something inside her gave way.

"No! Stop!" She lurched forward, falling to her knees beside the grave, clawing at the loose soil with her bare hands. "Don't cover him. He can't breathe! You're covering his mouth!" Her fingers scraped at the dirt, pulling it away, weeping and gasping in the same breath. "Please! Don't cover him up! Don't!"

Charlie was at her side in an instant, arms around her, holding her back and pinning her against him as she fought and beat frantically at his chest. From somewhere deep inside her broke a cry of anguish and desolation, the likes of which should never fall upon human ears. It was a sickening and terrible sound, like a soul being torn in two or an angel being shorn of its wings.

Delphine shuddered.

Harriet had spent her entire life as ringmaster to her emotions. Always in control, every emotion trained and harnessed to perform in strict obedience to her command, but this was different. This grief was too wild to harness. It altered the rules of ordinary behaviour. It operated under it's own command, raging inside her like an angry sea until she became unmoored by the loss and completely set adrift from reality.

She sobbed until she fell asleep, then awoke again with earth still caked beneath her fingernails, just as frantic as she was before. "We didn't open the window," she screamed. "Aggie said we must open a window or it will be trapped!"

Delphine looked confused. "What will be trapped?"

"The soul," Charlie said, and walked toward the window to open it. But Harriet was already running from one window to another, throwing up the sashes like a madwoman. He grabbed her wrists and shouted at her. "Stop Hattie! Stop! The windows are open. The windows were already opened yesterday. His soul is not trapped here. Do you hear me? He's gone!"

She sagged against him, and he held her again whilst she cried. The doctor came back then and put her to bed. He pricked her arm with something sharp, and she saw him draw back the syringe. She felt strange, then the edges of her grief blurred, and everything melted away.

THE DOUBLE BLOW of grief and loss that Harriet had sustained destroyed her faculty for reason. The world around her no longer made sense. She spent most of her time sleeping, for in sleep, the child was pink and fleshy in her arms, warm under her lips.

There was but one fleeting moment each morning: a breath of innocence between sleeping and waking, where she simply awoke to a new day, unburdened. Then reality fell like a blade, and she had to learn the dreadful truth all over again. Her first and only thought: My baby is dead. Lillian is gone.

It was a pain so oppressive that every intake of breath caused her agony. Tears did not offer sufficient release. Sometimes the only outlet was to cry out in her anguish. What started out as a low groan would end in a loud and visceral roar.

Delphine often found her this way: on hands and knees, tangled in sheets and pounding the floorboards with her fists until they bruised and bled. She'd hold her until the screaming became sobbing and then put her back to bed.

For a time, she didn't leave her bed, constructing for herself a refuge from the miseries of life. She existed in her own private world: a little pocket of time which stood still, while she blindly sifted through the past. Sometimes she drew strength from the memories; they sustained her. At other times, they sucked the very life from her like leeches. She grieved the loss of someone who had never lived, and someone who lived still. Of the two, she could not distinguish which was the more potent.

On days when she managed to leave her bed, Delphine would bring tea to her room. Harriet would sit by the window, staring out with blank eyes, while Delphine sat beside her. She never urged her to speak, just sat with her, the silence companionable, unintrusive. Harriet never drank the tea, only turned the teacup in her hands, over and over.

One thing Delphine insisted upon was that she ate. Harriet

obeyed, but food had lost its taste. She chewed because she had to, swallowing as if the weight of it might keep her tethered to the world. Some days, she would sit on her bed and watch the shadows stretch across the floor, never quite sure when morning became afternoon, or when eventually the sky had turned dark again.

Harriet's grief, in time, began to change. A strange quiet settled over her. She stopped dreaming of Charlie. Stopped waking with the jolt of memory. The pain lost its edges and smoothed into something blank and endless. Her inner self had been utterly obliterated. Everything she knew, everything she believed in, all that made her who she was, had gone. Nothingness was all that remained. A void so great that it robbed eternity of its vastness. The gnawing emptiness tried desperately to fill itself up, but no matter how far she went, she couldn't outrun it. However loud she screamed, she couldn't drown it out.

The magnitude of such a loss was immeasurable. It became the touchstone by which she calibrated all other feelings. In its shadow, any other feeling was nothing at all. And nothing was so much worse than pain. Seeking something hideous, she searched for something big enough to block it out, swallow it up. She began to hunt feelings in unnatural circumstances, sought thrills in the dangerous and found a morbid beauty in tragedy. Harriet wanted to lay waste to the entire world, watch it burn to nothing but powdery ash and stand in the absolute desolation. Then she might feel something.

She could not cry. She could not laugh. Most days, she forgot to eat until Delphine told her to. Other days, she walked for hours without remembering where she'd gone or why.

Delphine watched her with growing concern, but Harriet met her kindness with indifference.

She thought about dying, about how it would feel on the other side. Would death offer up the oblivion she was looking for? Would Lillian be sorry when it was too late? Might she employ her heart to better use under the stimulus of remorse? She had no intention of dying as such. She only wanted to feel something sharp enough to cut through the numbness. Eventually, she did.

It was a bitter January morning when she walked out into the sea. The sky was brighter than it ought to have been. The sun had no business shining when her children were gone. It should have been dark. The world had stopped turning, had it not? The sky should be frozen in eternal midnight.

The tide was coming in, white with cold fury and lapping at the shore in waves. Harriet slipped off her shoes and wriggled her toes to feel the sand yield under her bare feet. The water spoke to her in a fierce whisper, hissing as it clawed its way onto the beach. She watched it pool around her, then pull back as though it had changed its mind.

She closed her eyes and breathed in deeply, smelling the salt in the air and remembering: a picnic at the seaside; Lillian small and excited; Delphine laughing; iron railings with paint peeling and red salt-pitted iron underneath. The details were so mercilessly impressed upon her; she hoped this exquisite form of torture might relieve the dead numbness of her heart, but the memory did nothing to stir her emotions.

She looked down at the water surrounding her now and tugging at her skirts. The sea opened its arms wide and welcomed her in. She stepped forward with the slow, deliberate motion of someone wading into memory. She held up a hand and stared at it, turning it over as though she could see all the tragedy flowing through the veins under her skin. *Strange. My wounds are so many, yet I feel no pain.*

A strange noise called to her in the distance, and she

strained to hear it above the crash of waves. *It's coming from out there on the horizon.* She cocked her head to one side and listened harder. It sounded like a baby crying. She walked forward, the water up to her knees. "Charlie? Is that you, baby?"

Her mind began to drift, consciousness separating from flesh. She waded out further still, calling his name and then Lillian's. *Perhaps the waves will wash away all the terrible things I know.* Her fingertips trailed the surface of the water, and she felt the cold climbing up her thighs.

The sensation sliced open a memory like a ripe peach. Caiaphas: his clammy hands forcing their way under her skirts. A bolt of fear shot through her, and she looked about her as if noticing where she was for the first time. She took two steps backwards and felt the full weight of her dress. The water pulled at her as though it wanted her back. A wave swelled and soaked her to the waist. She stumbled back again, retreating, but the current was strong.

"HARRIET!" The voice was urgent: furious but terrified.

"Hattie!" Another, quieter but just as insistent.

She turned around to see who called her name. There were two people. Running. *Where are they going?*

"Hattie, come back!" The man was running, wading into the water.

I know him. He looks like Charlie—why is he running?

The water pushed her toward the shore, and she lost her footing, but before she could right herself, it dragged her backwards again, down and into its cold embrace. She felt the waves close over her head and gave herself up to them.

A pair of strong arms wrapped around her, pulling her to the surface. Charlie fought and heaved to pull her from the sea's grasp until it churned them out and they tumbled into the shallows, soaked and breathless. He got to his feet as

Delphine came splashing into the white foam. He hauled Harriet's shivering body onto the sand and then collapsed beside her.

Delphine's fear and concern darkened into fury. "What the hell were you thinking, Hattie? Out there in the water! You could have been killed! Charlie might have been killed! We've been searching for you for hours."

Harriet hung her head, awakened from her stupor by this stark reality. Delphine was right. He could have lost his own life trying to save her, and then how would she have felt? Much worse than she did now. She knew deep down that she and Charlie were the two most important people in the world to Delphine. What torment must she have felt in risking the life of one to save the other?

Charlie lifted her to her feet as Delphine began another torrent of words, but he shook his head, and the admonishment died on her lips.

"I'm sorry," Harriet said, her voice strangled. "I didn't mean to. I just...I needed..." She didn't know how to finish the sentence.

Delphine's eyes brimmed with tears. "I know," she whispered. She grasped Harriet behind her neck and pressed their foreheads together, squeezing her eyes shut. "I thought I'd lost you too."

Then Harriet realised something that she hadn't before; she wasn't the only one in pain. She had greedily owned all the grief for herself, believing she was the only one suffering.

"It won't always feel this way. It will get better with time," Delphine said.

"I don't see how."

"I know you don't, but it will."

Harriet struggled to speak through her sobbing. "But I'll never love him any less. I don't love Lillian less now than I did when she was born. Love doesn't diminish with the passing of time."

"Of course not darling. I don't mean that your love will change, but your grief will. Your grief will lessen."

Harriet looked at her, disbelieving. "But I cannot bear it."

"Yes, you can. And you shall."

THE RUDEST MAN IN HATFIELD

The days that followed passed like a procession of ghosts. Harriet moved through them as though she were asleep, drifting in and out of reality. But something had shifted. The sea had not swallowed her. She had emerged. Battered, but breathing. She began dressing again. She washed and ate without being told to. Slowly at first, just small changes, but eventually, she emerged from her room.

In time, she ventured outside under the watchful eye of Delphine. Some days, she would weep for Lillian and some days she wept for Charlie. She found a lace glove of Lillian's and tucked it away in case she came back for it. A notebook too, full of her childish musings and little girls' dreams. Sometimes she went to call her for supper, only for her breath to catch in her throat. She woke one morning to discover that she couldn't recall the baby's face.

Delphine had found her stricken with panic and spent hours soothing her, describing what he looked like. Everywhere she turned, there were little reminders of absence and loss, but each day Harriet became stronger.

The days that really made her strong though, were the days she thought of Caiaphas, and the ruin he'd shrouded her in. On those days, she raged against the world and everything in it. She ransacked her room; shouted into the empty dawn and screamed her fury at God, berating him for what he had allowed. But those were the moments that reminded her she was still alive and how much fight she had left in her.

She wrote to Lillian every week, as though nothing had happened. She hoped that news from home would make her miss her mother, somehow rouse her from Arabella's spell. No replies came, but she kept on writing. It helped her.

The first whisper of Lillian reached them in April. Harriet was in the garden, her shawl pulled tight against the wind, when Delphine emerged from the house with a letter in her hand and an expression that Harriet couldn't read.

"It's news from London," she said and weighed Harriet's response before she continued.

"Lillian?"

"Yes. Apparently, the Davenports have returned to Hertfordshire but are due to leave for Paris soon."

"They're at Elmridge?"

Delphine nodded.

"What should I do?"

"That is your decision to make, but whatever you decide to do, we will do it together."

Harriet turned her face away, swallowing down the lump in her throat. "I don't know." Her voice was barely a whisper. Even the thought of seeing Elmridge Park again—a place she had called home for so long—filled her with trepidation. *What if she doesn't want to see me? What if she denies me again?* "What does it say of her? Is she well?"

Delphine scanned the page and shook her head. "It doesn't

say, but one would assume she must be if they are travelling to Paris."

"What about Arabella?" Even saying the name made her feel sick.

"What about her?"

"Well the last time I saw her she had me thrown out of London. What if she finds out I'm back? She's dangerous."

Delphine took Harriet's chin in her hand and looked her square in the eyes. "Arabella holds no power over you. Remember that."

Harriet nodded, but she could not muster Delphine's conviction. Her hands shook. "I want to go. To Hertfordshire I mean. I have to try, whatever happens."

"Very well. We'll leave at the end of the week. I'll have Henri go ahead and arrange lodgings in Hatfield again. We'd better start packing." She turned and headed back toward the house.

"Delphine?"

"Yes?"

"Do you think she'll know? About Charlie?"

Delphine's face softened into a sad smile. "I think it's a possibility you need to prepare yourself for. If Arabella found out you had a child, then she will certainly have told Lillian. She'd use anything she could against you."

"Do you think I'm a bad person Delphine?"

"What on earth are you talking about? You know perfectly well how much I love you."

"But I killed a man. Sometimes I think that maybe God has punished me for what I did. My sense of moral superiority was certain and unwavering. I knew the difference between right and wrong. I knew that good people did good things and bad people did bad things and there was no excuse for sin. I thought the world a very black and white place. Until it wasn't."

"Oh Hattie. Life has never been black and white. It's lived in the dirty grey bits in between. The world is full of murky, shadowy things, and people are complicated."

"It feels like a stain on my soul that will never come out. Like people can see it when they look at me."

"That man was an abomination. He took what he wanted from Charlie's sister and cost her her life. Cost Charlie and I a lifetime of happiness together. He took what he wanted from you and countless others. He deserved a far worse death than you gave him." Delphine was breathing hard when she finished, an angry flush creeping up her neck.

"It's not just that," Harriet said.

"Then what is it?"

Harriet fidgeted, eager to unburden herself, but uneasy with sharing her most private thoughts.

Delphine seemed to sense it and encouraged her. "Tell me what bothers you so."

For a moment, the silence stretched like taut thread.

"I'm ashamed." She lowered her head and looked away. "It's unnatural. The idea that a child can reject its mother is so abhorrent, the shame feels like a yoke around my neck." She placed a hand to her throat as if feeling it there. "And Charlie. Another child so desperate to shrug me off as his mother, he rejected me at the cost of his own life." She looked up at Delphine. "Do you think it's because I took the potion to stop him from coming? Is it my fault?"

Delphine drew a sharp breath. "Oh, Hattie, you cannot truly think that!"

Harriet crumpled at the release of her torment. "I didn't want him at the start. I hated the very idea of him! I should have loved him sooner, Delphine. It's my fault. It's all my fault!"

Delphine pulled her into an embrace and held her as if she could squeeze the guilt from her bones. "It's not your fault, Hattie. None of this is. You are not being punished. You're a good person and a wonderful mother; you must believe that."

Harriet wept then. Not the wild, keening grief of earlier days, but something quieter, more exhausted. She let the words settle inside her, unsure if she believed them, but grateful all the same. She may have been afraid, but her decision was firm. She was ready. Back to Hertfordshire. Back to Elmridge and whatever waited for her there.

THE JOURNEY to Hatfield was a blur of hedgerows and grey skies pressing low over flat fields. Harriet sat in near silence, watching villages passing down the lines, her thoughts spiralling between anticipation and dread. When they arrived at the station, she stepped down onto the platform with her heart thudding in her chest. It was all at once both foreign and familiar.

Their lodgings were in the town centre. She'd expected to stay in the rented rooms where Delphine had stayed the last time she visited them. The cab, however, had come to a halt outside a modest shopfront with two bow windows displaying a selection of elegant hats.

"Our rooms are upstairs, above the milliners," Delphine said, climbing down from the cab and smiling up at the top floors.

Harriet's eyes darted up and down the street before she put her face to the curved glass to peer inside. "Is there a side door, or do we go in through the shop?"

Delphine just smiled and knocked on the front door.

"I think it's closed Delphine. I can't see anyone inside." Then she saw a stir of movement in the dim interior.

"Here he is." Delphine stood back as Henri opened the shop door

"Afternoon Henri. Is everything ready?"

"Oui Madame." He moved aside to let them in.

Inside, bolts of fabric, baskets of haberdashery and hat stands lined the walls. The air smelled of dust and old leather and everything looked as though it had stood still for a long time.

Harriet turned to Delphine, frowning. "Was the lease for the shop as well?"

"Oh, it wasn't to let, it was for sale."

Harriet stared at her, openmouthed. "You mean to say you bought it? This is yours?"

Delphine gave her a sly smile and shrugged. "Ours. Henri arranged everything the last few days. It seemed like a sensible plan, just in case... Well. Just in case we're here for a while."

"Why didn't you tell me?"

"Because you would have said no."

Harriet laughed and shook her head. *She will never cease to amaze me.*

That afternoon, as Delphine made plans to furnish the apartment, the air inside felt close and unfamiliar, thick with the scent of old polish and fresh paint. Harriet, unable to settle, paced like a caged animal. She volunteered to fetch bread and tea from the grocer's. She needed to be outside.

As she stepped out onto the street, she paused for a moment with her back against the door. She closed her eyes and inhaled deep, steadying breaths. *What if she's out there? What if I see her? Oh God, what if I see her in the street? No, she won't be here. Arabella never came into town herself, so Lillian won't either. She sent servants to run her errands. She sent me.*

The thought of coming face to face with Lillian after almost a year, filled her with dread and longing in equal measure, but if she didn't face this now, on the first day, she would never leave the apartment.

It was unusually busy for a late afternoon. The cobblestones were slick with recent rain, but the sky had cleared, and it was mild enough to go out without her cloak. Harriet ambled along the busy street, lost in the past. Familiar sights and sounds assailed her from all sides, stirring up unwelcome memories. It seemed her life had become split into two halves: before that day and after that day. But even the memories of happier times were now all tinged with sadness.

She was so tangled in her thoughts that she barely noticed where she was stepping until a sudden blast of hooves and the harsh clang of a carriage bell shattered the quiet.

"Look out!"

Before she could move, a firm arm grasped her by the waist and yanked her backward with alarming force. She stumbled but stayed upright, heart pounding.

The carriage thundered past just inches from where she'd stood.

She pivoted to face her rescuer. A tall man with a fierce expression.

"You'd do well to watch where you're going. You could have been killed," he said, his voice edged with restrained anger.

Harriet flushed crimson. "I…I was distracted. I'm terribly sorry." She noticed then that he had injured his hand. "You're hurt," she said.

He flexed it, grimacing. "The carriage handle hit me as I

pulled you back." He grimaced again, bruising already beginning to bloom across the back of his knuckles and wrist.

She reached out for his hand to inspect it—a mother's habit—but he snatched it back. "Please, Madam, you've caused me enough pain for one day." His tone was sharp, almost bitter. "What on earth were you doing wandering about in the road? Have you never been outside before?"

Harriet swallowed hard and then snapped. "I'm terribly sorry that you've sustained an injury on my behalf, Sir, but there really is no need to be so rude. Perhaps since it has caused you so much trouble, you'd have been better off not bothering. Please, I implore you, if you ever see me again in such peril, consider just letting me die." *That felt good.*

He studied her for a moment, taken aback by her outburst, then his expression softened. "Are you hurt?"

"No."

"Very good, then I'll say good day to you." He made a small bow, and before she could say anything else, he turned and strode away, his footsteps echoing against the wet stones.

Harriet was shaking. *How rude! Of all the arrogant, conceited, puffed-up peacocks to have saved me!* She couldn't wait to get back to Delphine and tell her what had just happened. In her flustered state, she forgot how nervous she'd felt and shifted to rage, punishing the pavement with her angry walk.

She collected the rest of her shopping and marched back home in half the time it would have taken anyone else. "Delphine!" she called, heading straight upstairs to their apartment. "You won't believe what just happened." She didn't even make it to the top of the stairs before launching into her tale. "I have just encountered the rudest, most arrogant man in Hatfi—" She halted mid-sentence as she burst into the room and saw Delphine instructing a tradesman who appeared to be measuring the opposite wall. "Oh, I'm sorry, I didn't realise we had company."

Delphine crossed the room to meet her and took her by the elbow toward him. "Hattie, come and meet our neighbour. Mr Bennett is a cabinetmaker. He's going to build the bookshelves we wanted along this wall."

Mr Bennett, who was on his knees, scribbled some markings on the lower part of the wall and stood to greet Harriet. He turned around and extended his hand. "Elijah Bennett."

Harriet's eyes widened. Her mouth opened and then closed without speaking. Staring back at her was the very same arrogant, conceited, puffed up peacock who had just saved her in the street. She extended her own hand and felt heat rising up her neck and into her cheeks

"Harriet Blackthorn. Forgive my rudeness, Mr Bennett. I was eager to tell my friend about my outing." She wasn't sure how much he'd heard or if he would even realise she was talking about him. She felt the prickle of sweat breaking out across her brow.

"No apology necessary, Mrs Blackthorn. I can certainly understand your outrage at having met the rudest, most arrogant man in Hatfield." He raised his eyebrows and smiled at her, not kind but mocking. He looked at her as though he had a secret.

As soon as the door clicked shut behind Mr Bennett, Harriet let out a strangled sound somewhere between a gasp and a growl and told Delphine what had happened in the street. "Of all the people in Hatfield to live next door to, it had to be him!"

Delphine said nothing, but her lips twitched at the corners.

Harriet threw her arms into the air. "He all but crushed my ribs and then scolded me as though I were some wayward child chasing after a hoop! I've never been so humiliated!" She began pacing in short, sharp strides. "He practically snatched his hand away from me as if I were carrying the plague. And now I find he's our neighbour? And building shelves no less, which means he'll be in and out of this apartment for weeks!"

Delphine watched her with infuriating calm. "Well, Hattie, I don't think I've ever seen a man affect you like this."

"Oh don't you look at me like that."

Delphine lifted her hands and shrugged, protesting her innocence. "Like what? I have no idea what you mean. I'm simply saying that Mr Bennett has made quite the impression on you, that is all."

Harriet stopped pacing and narrowed her eyes. "He's arrogant and smug. He knew I was talking about him and he smirked."

"You noticed his smirk?"

Harriet scowled.

"Can't you find it in you to give him another chance since he's our neighbour? It might be very awkward if you're on bad terms." She was almost grinning.

"I just did, and his conduct did nothing to raise him in my estimation." She fell silent for a moment, then muttered, "I hope he bruises all the way up to the elbow."

NEIGHBOURS

Harriet woke the next morning, still cross. She'd dreamt about Mr Bennett. His voice sharp, low, insufferably sure of itself. "Please, Madam, you've caused me enough pain for one day." *Who says such things? Who even thinks such things?* It was bad enough having to deal with him during the waking hours, but it infuriated her that he'd infiltrated her sleep.

Delphine irritated her further with her indifference toward the whole situation. She chuckled, shaking her head. "Honestly, I don't understand why you're so bothered by him. He's not here to torment you."

Harriet scowled and took a sip of her tea. She didn't know why he bothered her either, but she'd grown used to Delphine always being outraged on her behalf. This time she wasn't, and Harriet was forced to consider that maybe she was overreacting just a little.

"We really ought to take Mr Bennett his deposit so he can begin right away on our bookshelves," Delphine said, looking sidelong at Harriet. "I'd do it myself, but I'm frightfully busy today."

"Are you really going to be so transparent in your attempt at manipulation?"

Delphine flashed her a wide grin.

As they finished breakfast, Harriet sighed and met Delphine's steady gaze. "Very well, since you're not going to let this drop. I will take the deposit. I suppose we could start over, for all our sakes."

Delphine smiled. She'd won again.

~

AN ORNATE WOODEN sign above the shop introduced their neighbour as "Elijah Bennet-Cabinet Maker." Harriet stepped inside, the tinkle of a brass doorbell announcing her arrival. The smell of wood filled the air, warm and earthy, wholesome even. She liked it. It was comforting. There was a small counter at the front of the shop, and two or three pieces of highly polished furniture. Beyond that, through an open arch, she could see a larger space, a workroom with benches and tables and walls lined with tools.

Mr Bennet appeared in the archway with a broad smile that died on his lips when he saw her.

"Good morning, Mr Bennett." She tried her best to be bright and cheery, even though she didn't feel it.

He crossed his arms and nodded. "Mrs Blackthorn."

She had hoped he might lead the conversation, or at least say something else, but he just stood there, looking at her. She wasn't at all sure what to say next.

"Can I help you with something, Mrs Blackthorn?" He raised an eyebrow, and she thought she saw the flicker of a smirk, but it vanished before she could be certain.

"I…Well, I thought…that is to say…" She cleared her throat. "I've brought your deposit." She paused for a beat, then shoved it across the counter at him as though it were burning her fingers.

He considered her for longer than was polite. "Is there anything else?"

"Yes…I…" *Oh, for goodness' sake, Hattie, come on!* "It was a rather unfortunate introduction we had yesterday, and since it seems we are to be neighbours, I thought we might start afresh."

"I see. Well, go ahead, Mrs Blackthorn. I'm ready?" He straightened and brought his large hands together neatly in front of him.

Harriet's brows drew together in confusion. "Ready? For what?"

"My apology, of course."

She'd started with the thinnest veneer of patience, and his smug expression tipped her over the edge. Harriet clenched her fists at her sides. "I came here in the spirit of friendship to offer a fresh start, but if that doesn't interest you, Mr Bennett, I will trouble you no longer."

"That's very thoughtful of you, Madam, but I have no time for friends."

"I'm not asking to be your fr—" She stopped, realising too late that he was teasing her. "I can see that you're busy Mr Bennett, so I shall leave you to your day." She spun on her heel to exit.

"Wait," he said. "I was teasing. Forgive me. I'm afraid my solitary lifestyle has rendered me less courtly than I ought to be in the presence of a lady." He bowed, and she couldn't tell if he was mocking her or being genuine. "Come in, let me show you my work." Not a request, but an instruction. He turned and walked back into his workroom, leaving her standing there.

She felt oddly compelled to follow him.

He showed her the various pieces of furniture he was working on, and she admired them all with clinical politeness. They discussed options for the type of wood and different finishes for the bookcase, but Harriet didn't really care one way or the other. Her attention strayed to a small wooden box on the centre work table. An intricate fretwork of vines and leaves adorned the lid, all carved in minute detail. There were a variety of figures depicted among the vines: birds, a heart, a cross, a tree, and what appeared to be the beginnings of a winged cherub.

"Did you carve this?" She asked, feeling the surface of the fretwork with a featherlight touch.

"Yes." He swiped the box from the table and placed it high on a shelf. "It's nothing, just a piece I work on in my spare time. It helps me to relax.

"It's beautiful." Harriet's gaze fell to his large hands, then back to the box, not quite believing they could make something so delicate. "I've never seen anything like it. What inspires your designs, Mr Bennett?"

"Nothing particular. I just carve whatever comes to mind at the time. Whatever I happen to be thinking about."

"So it's a sort of visual representation of your thoughts." She said, more to herself than to Elijah. The notion intrigued her more than she was comfortable with.

He didn't answer, just cleared his throat and moved away from the box.

There was a bookshelf across the room, and Harriet wandered over to it, expecting to find a compilation of manuals with wood carving techniques, maybe a book or two of a botanical nature. Arboriculture perhaps and the qualities of certain woods, that being the principal material in his profession, but what she found was nothing of the sort.

Shakespeare, she noticed first, then Plato, Socrates and Homer, all nestled together with Dickens and Darwin. Such great men huddled on this small shelf, jostling each other for the most prominent position. At the other end of the shelf were a Bible and a cookbook, outcasts from the rest, with nothing in common. All of them were covered with a light film of sawdust.

"You read?" She said, turning to look at him, surprise evident on her face.

"Yes, Madam, I can read." The edge of sarcasm in his tone was not lost on her, and she bitterly regretted the phrasing of the question.

"Oh no, I didn't mean…What I meant was you read for pleasure. I wasn't questioning your ability to read. It's just that your library was not what I expected." *Oh dear, I'm making a mess of this. What is wrong with me?*

"And what were you expecting?"

"Well, manuals and books of your trade, I suppose, but that was very presumptuous of me, and now it appears that I've caused you offence, and that was not my intention. Please forgive me. This is not how I wished for us to restart." She couldn't recall ever feeling so ruffled or ill at ease in anyone's presence.

He, on the other hand, leaned against the bench with his arms folded across his chest in lazy repose, that same unreadable expression on his face. "Tell me Mrs Blackthorn, what does such a library say about a man, in your opinion?

"Oh, I'm not qualified to form such opinions Mr Bennett. I'm afraid I might cause you further offence."

"I can assure you no offence has been taken. Please, I'm

intrigued to know your opinion." He was pushing her to engage in this verbal warfare.

She felt her throat tighten and swallowed hard. For a fleeting moment, she imagined telling him exactly what she thought of him and wondered how he'd take it. What expression would his arrogant features assume? "Well, since you insist on hearing it. I would assume the owner of such titles was somewhat at odds with himself." She paused to assess his reaction, but there was none.

She trailed her fingers along the spines of the books. "A Christian man, but conflicted. Torn between science and religion. A contradictory nature, philosophical yet theological, perhaps even romantic." She paused again and risked a glance at him, regretting it instantly as a flush warmed her cheeks. "Someone who has suffered perhaps and searches for peace." She finished with conviction, not quite believing she'd said all that aloud, but she stood her ground, daring him to contradict her. "How did I do?"

"To what do you owe this wonderful gift of perception? Are you a fortune teller then, or a witch?"

"If I were either, I might have saved myself a lot of trouble these past few years."

He stared at her openly, unapologetic in his boldness.

Harriet fiddled with her gloves, afraid she'd given something away. "I must go now. I've taken up quite enough of your time."

He bowed his head. "Then I'll bid you good day, Madam."

Something about the way he said it irked her. He made it sound cold, distant. She didn't like being called 'Madam'. At least not by him.

"Harriet, please," she corrected him, offering him a false smile.

"If that suits you Madam. Modes of address are a matter of indifference to me." He made a gesture with his hand to indicate the unimportance of her name.

That was it. It was the indifference—the nonchalance—that irritated her beyond reason, although why it should, was as much a mystery to her as it would have been to him. *The audacity of this man is incredible!* She wanted to claw the words back into her mouth, but it was too late. She'd given him permission to address her as a friend, and she could have bitten off her own tongue.

"Good day, Harriet."

She gave a curt nod. "Elijah." He hadn't returned the invitation to use his first name, but she used it anyway, hoping to regain some of her power. It didn't work. The name felt foreign and altogether too intimate.

HARRIET STEPPED out into the street, blinking against the sudden brightness. The cool air hit her flushed cheeks like a slap, and she let out a breath as if she'd been holding it the entire time she was inside. *Well, that was a disaster!* His name still lingered, intimate and awkward, like she'd crossed a line she hadn't meant to. And he, with his maddening and unreadable expression, had let her flounder without offering the smallest lifeline.

Living next door robbed her of the furious walk home she sorely needed. She let the door slam behind her and stormed upstairs to her room, thankful that Delphine was out. The last thing she needed were her witty remarks and arching eyebrows. It almost felt like the pair of them were conspiring to irritate her. *He's just a cabinetmaker, nothing more. Just an ill-*

tempered neighbour with too much pride and not nearly enough manners. She had no intention of allowing him any more space in her mind than was strictly necessary.

The sooner those bookshelves were finished, the better. She'd just have to make sure she was out while he worked.

WIT AND WISDOM

Harriet told herself she'd be rid of Elijah once the bookshelves were finished. She imagined the relief of quiet evenings and empty rooms, free of his enormous presence and those sharp, wolfish eyes. She busied herself with daily errands and avoided the apartment whenever she heard his hammering or the scrape of his plane.

But Delphine had other ideas. Each day, she found new tasks for Elijah. A loose floorboard, a cracked window frame, even a new dining table. Her bright eyes sparkled as she insisted Elijah's skill must not go to waste.

Harriet's protests were met with only a knowing smile.

News reached them quickly that Lillian had already left for Paris and would not return until the end of the season. The quiet ache of absence settled anew in Harriet's heart but she was determined not to be undone by it. She decided the shop downstairs would re-open. "We're going to make hats," she announced in the midst of Elijah's hammering and sawing.

"Oh are we? And do we know anything about millinery?" Delphine asked, looking genuinely astounded.

"Well, it can't be so difficult, can it? There are some manuals downstairs. I've seen them amongst the haberdashery. I can learn anything from a book if I put my mind to it."

Elijah scoffed behind her, and she bit back the urge to throw something at him.

Delphine smiled, slow, purposeful, as though a wonderful and terrible idea had just occurred to her. "Elijah?" She said. "We will be requiring your services for the refitting of the shop if you're available."

"Absolutely."

Damn you both!

Harriet had no option but to accept his growing presence. She watched him work, annoyed but undeniably impressed, as the space transformed around her. Their exchanges remained prickly, and they battled daily over one thing or another. When he wasn't vexing her, he perplexed her. He was a difficult man to read, so changeable was he in his nature. He would say nothing for long periods, then become suddenly incredibly eloquent.

When the shop fittings were finished, Harriet breathed a sigh of relief, welcoming a break from the battleground. She paid him what he was owed and closed the door behind him with a resounding "Thank goodness!" But the relief was short-lived. She went upstairs to find Delphine laying the table for supper. Three places were set at the new dining table. "Is Henri joining us this evening?" She asked.

Delphine held up a crystal goblet to the light and rubbed at a fingerprint. "No, I asked Elijah to join us this evening. He's worked so hard." She carried on checking the glasses as if nothing were amiss.

Harriet's temper flared immediately. "Yes, we paid him to work hard. That's what tradesmen do. They work and they're paid. You don't invite them to supper."

"Harriet!" The look on Delphine's face told her she'd misunderstood. "Oh, I didn't mean it like that. I don't care if he's a tradesman or a prince, you know that. I just meant it's not a courtesy that's required just because he's worked for us."

"No. It's a courtesy I wish to extend because he's our neighbour and I like him. He's a good man Harriet if you could only open your eyes enough to see it."

Harriet did not change for supper but fixed her hair twice whilst Delphine was busy. At eight o'clock, she heard a smart rapping on the door downstairs and straightened her dress before going to open it.

Elijah's ample frame filled the narrow space as he looked down at her. "Evening, Harriet."

She looked at him in silence before realising it was her turn to speak. "Good evening, Elijah, do come in." She stood to one side and motioned for him to enter.

"Thank you." There was an edge of uncertainty in his voice that she hadn't heard before. "I brought these." He thrust a posy of wildflowers at her. "From the meadows."

Harriet took the humble offering and lifted it to her nose. Oxeye daisies with simple white petals and cornflowers, the colour of summer skies. Warmth bloomed in her chest.

"My grandfather taught me the meaning of all the flowers when I was a boy, but I'm afraid I've forgotten them now." He held his cap in his hands and looked down as though he'd somehow disappointed her by forgetting.

Harriet smiled. "My nurse taught me the same when I was a child." She lifted the head of a daisy to show him. "Daisies mean innocence and new beginnings; and cornflowers are a symbol of devotion." The last word felt uncomfortable on her tongue, and she regretted saying it.

"Well, it seems your memory is holding up better than mine," he said.

"Careful, Elijah, that was dangerously close to being a compliment." She needed to get the conversation back onto a more familiar footing. Being nice to each other was unsettling.

All throughout supper, whilst Harriet struggled to steer the conversation toward safe topics, Delphine, of course, spoke freely of anything she wished. "You must tell us, Elijah, why a man of your talents is hiding down here in the countryside when you could be charging ten times the price in London?"

"Oh, London's not for me anymore." He swirled the whiskey around in his glass.

"Nonsense! I think London would suit you very well. A handsome young man like you would do well with the ladies." Delphine spoke to him the way one would tease a nephew, as though she were trying to embarrass him.

"I've no interest in the ladies of London, either." He looked at Harriet, who turned quickly away.

"Well, if not the ladies of London, then where? Among which ladies will you find your true love?"

Harriet gasped. *Good Lord, what on earth is she doing? Why must she ask such impertinent questions?* "Delphine, behave yourself. You're embarrassing our guest." Harriet turned to Elijah with an apologetic smile and found he was still watching her. She swallowed and twisted the linen napkin in her lap, fingers tight.

"I'm not embarrassed, Harriet. I'm just not interested in love. It isn't real."

Delphine made a noise of disapproval and almost choked on her wine, but Harriet didn't respond. She was busy turning the phrase over in her mind. Did he really believe there was no such thing as true love? And when had *she* come to believe that there was?

Delphine's eyes sparkled with mischief. "Then I'm afraid you're in quite the wrong company, Elijah. I'm an incurable romantic."

"Incurable? I think not. Experience enough pain and betrayal and even the most obstinate of romantics will cast off such claims." He leaned forward and refilled his glass from the decanter. "And what of you, Harriet? Do you think love can endure in the face of disappointment? Are you a hopeless romantic?" He asked her as if it were a challenge.

"You wish to understand the geography of my heart, Mr Bennett?"

His eyebrow rose at the sudden use of his surname.

"Should you presume to undertake such a task, you will find the landscape bleak and barren." She raised her chin and waited for his response. There was little chance of her admitting anything about her heart to *him.*

"You lie." His voice was low, unhurried. She felt the intensity of his stare, and blood rose to her cheeks.

Delphine cleared her throat, breaking the spell. She began with dogged determination to engage him in more chatter. "Harriet tells me you're something of a reader, Elijah. What do you make of Tennyson's work?"

Harriet shot her a sharp look. She had only mentioned in passing, their awkward conversation about the books in his workshop. Now he was going to think she'd been discussing him with Delphine. "I can't imagine Elijah would waste much time on poetry if he doesn't believe in love," she said, hoping the conversation would move on swiftly.

"I prefer Browning," he said simply. "There's an honesty to

his work. The man means what he says. But I don't read much poetry."

"Then what do you like to read?"

"Philosophy mostly. Plato, Homer, Marcus Aurelius and such."

"Really? Ooh, do you hear that, Hattie? We have a real-life philosopher on our hands. Do you find it useful?"

"Useful?" He looked amused. "Well, that's a strange question, but yes, I suppose I do."

Delphine took a sip of her wine. "Alright then, tell me a useful quote. Something that you live by."

He didn't hesitate. "I've always liked Marcus Aurelius. '*Waste no more time arguing what a good man should be. Be one.*' But I'll admit, it's easier said than done."

"And are you a good man?" Harriet said before she could stop herself.

He cocked his head to one side and studied her. "I try my best. Although I can't imagine you would suffer yourself to be persuaded of that." He took another sip of his drink, then licked his lips. "It's not really about being useful though. That's not why I read. The written word has always fascinated me. You see reading as a transaction," he said, looking at Delphine. "A simple transferring of facts from paper to person. But for me, it's different. It's one person reaching out to another, across unimaginable distances and immeasurable time, and speaking to that person as if they were standing right next to each other." His eyes glittered with enthusiasm.

It was the most passionate Harriet had seen him, and she'd seen him angry.

"When you read something like the works of Aristotle, you're in the mind of another person who lived a thousand years ago. Imagine speaking directly to the heart of someone a thousand years from now, our words having lost none of their urgency or their power in the journey. Don't you find that incredible?"

Delphine squeezed her hands together and grinned, just the way Lillian used to.

The memory struck Harriet like a blow: Lillian, eyes bright, hands clasped together, and blonde ringlets bouncing about her shoulders. It was an acute and specific pain. One that she could not easily articulate. She only knew that it ached in places she had no name for.

"Hattie?" Delphine was watching her with concern.

Harriet blinked, the room rushing back in.

"Hattie, are you unwell? You're as white as a sheet."

Keep yourself together. Not in front of him. She took a deep and steadying breath. "Yes, I'm fine, just a little tired is all." She mustered her best attempt at a smile, but it didn't appear to fool the others.

Elijah reached across the table and touched her arm. "Are you sure you're alright? You don't look well." A deep furrow creased his brow. He almost looked worried, but Harriet knew better than to think that.

She pulled her arm away. "I'm fine, really." *Please stop asking me. Can we just move on?*

"Well, ladies, I'm a little tired myself. I shall leave you to get some rest." Elijah stood up, smoothed his waistcoat and made a curt bow to them. "I'd be delighted to return the favour if you'd care to join me on Friday for dinner?"

He didn't look tired at all, and Harriet suspected he was uncomfortable. Perhaps he sensed she was upset and wanted to make his escape before getting trapped with a hysterical woman.

"I'm afraid I already have plans on Friday, but Harriet is free, aren't you, Harriet?" Delphine said.

"Am I?" *And what is she suddenly doing on Friday?*

"Yes, of course you are, silly."

How do I get out of this? "That's a lovely offer, Elijah, but I must decline. I cannot dine alone with you—it wouldn't be proper. A lady must protect her reputation you know." She tried to sound coy and playful, but the statement missed the mark and landed awkwardly."

"Your reputation is of little consequence to me, Harriet. It is your character that interests me. A reputation is nothing more than an evaluation made by other people, but as you wish." He bowed again and descended the stairs.

Harriet watched until the top of his head disappeared from view and the door below clicked shut. Her thoughts were all muddied, like silt in a stream. She couldn't see any of them clearly.

WHO ARE YOU, ELIJAH BENNETT?

Harriet woke with a sore throat and the uncomfortable awareness that she had dreamt of Elijah Bennett again. She couldn't remember any of it—only the sense of him lingering at the edges of her thoughts. It caused her to go about her morning routine with more force than was strictly necessary, slamming doors and yanking her corset laces until she saw stars.

Delphine noticed, of course, but said nothing. Her smug smile and silent sips of tea were enough to set Harriet's jaw tighter.

The supper had gone better than she expected—even if it was a battleground of wit and will. Words had flown like arrows, cutting and weaving as each held their ground, but beneath the clash, a fragile understanding had formed. One might even say, respect.

That being said, he still bothered her immensely. She wasn't sure why exactly. Perhaps it was because he'd surprised her with that Marcus Aurelius quote. Or maybe because he didn't fit the description she'd told herself about him. She couldn't work out who he was. There were so many different sides.

As the day wore on, she found herself unable to focus on any one task. She flitted from one room to another, restless and wandering. She lingered at a worktable in the back room of the shop, turning over an old hat block. Its stand had split and wobbled slightly on the wood dowel mounted beneath it. It still worked, but she took a hammer to the joint and broke the piece away.

Delphine appeared in the doorway. "Having fun?"

"Aah!" Harriet jumped. "What are you doing creeping about down here. You scared me half to death!"

"Are you having some manner of disagreement with the hat block?"

"It's loose," Harriet said stiffly, not meeting her eye. "It needs fixing."

"How convenient."

Harriet did not dignify that with a reply. Instead, she waited for Delphine to go out, then took her broken hat block next door.

Inside, the scent of sawdust and varnish filled the air. Elijah was at his workbench, sleeves rolled up, chiselling a delicate pattern into a headboard.

She watched him work with the knife, peeling away ribbons of curling wood to reveal shapes unearthed like beautiful secrets.

He didn't look up immediately. "Didn't expect you to visit so soon, Harriet. Shop's still standing, I presume?"

She bristled. "I require a repair." She set the hat block on the countertop. Can you manage that?"

He finally looked at her then, and something she couldn't

identify crossed his face. "I'll take a look. If it's salvageable, I'll fix it. If not, I can chop it up for firewood." He brushed wood shavings from his hands and reached for the block, frowning in concentration. "This was well-made once. Shame it's been neglected." He turned the base over and examined the dent she'd made with the hammer. "What happened to it?"

Harriet crossed her arms. "I don't know. I found it that way. Can you fix it or not?"

"I can fix most things, Harriet." He glanced up at her. "Even the ones people give up on."

His words struck a chord, echoing her own life. He said it, like he was talking about more than just furniture. He smiled as though he already knew something she hadn't admitted to herself yet. "Come through and I'll mend it while you wait." He paused in the archway. "Don't worry. You can leave your reputation outside."

Harriet didn't know whether to be angry or to laugh out loud, but she followed him inside.

He set to work on the hat block, sawing and sanding as Harriet watched. Now and then he paused and explained to her what he was doing and why. How he cut the wood against the grain, sanded in one direction and planed in another.

She listened to him, eyes wide and attentive, soaking up the new information like a sponge.

"There you go," he said, placing the finished block in front of her. "Good as new."

She picked it up and ran her fingers over the smooth surface of the new wood, still warm from the sanding. "Thank you. It's perfect." She lifted the purse tied at her waist and opened it to pay. "What do I owe you?"

Elijah covered her hand with his and shook his head. "Put that away."

"But I—"

"Put it away." He was firm this time. Not unkind, but it was a command nonetheless.

He was so at ease when he demanded, Harriet had an inkling he was used to getting his own way. She was not naturally disposed to subservience, but felt an inexplicable desire to obey him. It shook her.

"Will you have some tea?" He made toward the staircase that led to his apartment.

Harriet moved, then stopped. "I…I don't…"

His eyes narrowed. "What is it Harriet? What are you so afraid of?"

She looked from Elijah to the stairs and back again. "I'm not afraid." But even she could hear the fear in her voice.

"Then I must assume you don't like my company." He started walking toward her, his head cocked to one side. "I know I provoke your temper, but tell me, what is it about me that infuriates you so much?"

She didn't know. She wasn't even sure she was angry anymore. Her mouth opened and closed, words caught somewhere between pride and uncertainty.

"Just as I thought."

What does he mean by that?

"You lack the courage to say it."

"I don't take kindly to being insulted." She swiped her hat block from the counter and took a step toward the door.

Elijah sidestepped and barred the way. "On the contrary, Harriet, I'd say you bear insult remarkably well."

Her hands shook. "How dare you! You question my disliking you when you were the one to set the tone from the beginning. You made your disdain for me crystal clear. I was left with no doubt of your opinion of me."

"You irritate me, and I'm not afraid to tell you, Harriet.

You're not a woman to crumble because you didn't hear what you wanted."

She was breathing hard. "And what do you know of me?"

"I know you don't care one whit about the societal expectations you hide behind. You won't free yourself, even though you could." His eyes were wild, and tension flickered in his jaw. "I know you're not fazed by my ill temper and rough manners, and I know you can hold your own in a debate better than any man I've met. You're a powerful woman, Harriet, and it angers me that you allow yourself to be hemmed in by such nonsense."

It was true—all of it. She was absolutely afraid to be herself. What could she say? She clenched her fists. "Fine. I'll have tea."

They stared at each other in silence, weighing their next move.

"Not so fast," Elijah said, holding up a hand. "I want to know."

"To know what?"

"I want to know why you dislike me."

Oh, God! "I don't."

"Don't lie to me. You lied last night, and I can see straight through you."

She raised her chin in defiance. "What did I lie about?"

He looked down at her chest, then leaned in close to her ear. "You said your heart was bleak and barren, but I can see it is not."

Her breath came in short, shallow gasps. "You don't take pains to be agreeable. You're ill-tempered and stubborn, passionate to the point of irrationality, and you always think your view is the right one. There. Now you have it."

He smiled. "Now we're getting somewhere."

"And what about you? You've made it very clear you're not

afraid to flout social conventions and you despise class divisions. Why is that, Elijah? What do you hate so much about class?"

He gritted his teeth. "I have my reasons."

"Now who's lying? You're hiding something. It's taken more than the books in your workshop to cultivate the passions and intellect of such a complex personality. You can't expect me to believe you're a humble carpenter." Her eyes narrowed. "Who are you, Elijah Bennett?"

He withdrew so quickly she felt the absence of him stir the surrounding air. "You want to know my secrets?"

Harriet nodded.

"Very well. I will answer one question for every question you answer of mine."

"Deal."

~

HARRIET HELD his gaze for a long moment. She wasn't sure who would break first. Then he turned without a word and started up the stairs, the scent of sawdust swirling in his wake. She hesitated only for a heartbeat, then followed.

The room was simple, but homely. Afternoon light spilled across the polished floorboards and danced over shelves of books that lined the walls, floor to ceiling. *He really does like to read.* Harriet stood just inside the doorway, her anger dying and suddenly aware of the quiet.

"This isn't a trap, Harriet," Elijah said without looking at her. He reached for the kettle and began preparing the tea with practised movements. "It's just tea."

"Tea and questions," she said, stepping further in. She sat on the edge of a small settee, still holding the hat block in her lap like a shield.

He handed her a cup, and the warmth of it seeped into her hands. "So," he said, settling across from her, a faint smile playing at his mouth. "Who goes first?"

Harriet's mind blanked. What did she want to know? She cleared her throat. "Where were you born?"

He chuckled. "Really? That's what you want to know?"

"No, not really." She laughed and looked down at her hands. "Why do you dislike society so much?"

He set down his cup on the table between them and stretched out his arms across the back of his couch, one ankle resting on the other knee. "My father was a gentleman." He ran a hand through his hair and blew out a long breath. "My mother was a maid. I'm a bastard son, raised by the nursemaid and governess in my father's house."

That was not what I expected. Harriet swallowed. "I see."

"Do you?" His expression was soft, but his eyes were wolfish, sharp. "My mother died giving birth to me. My stepmother hated the sight of me, and my sisters never accepted me either."

"I'm sorry."

He shot her a sharp look. "I'm not looking for your sympathy."

"I meant I'm sorry I questioned you." *Don't lose your nerve.* "How many sisters did you have?"

"Four. Three before me and one after. I lived in luxury, had the best education, but I was never part of the family. My father couldn't show me affection openly."

She'd known he had good breeding. It showed in the set of his jaw, the way he carried himself, his arrogant expression and haughty manner, but why then was he here? "So, where did you learn your trade?"

"My grandfather. I spent a lot of time with him."

"What happened? Do you still see your father?"

"He died when I was twelve. The estate was entailed, but there was no other male heir. An illegitimate child doesn't count when it comes to entailment, so it ends and a will must be made. My stepmother had insisted a will be drawn up to ensure I wouldn't inherit anything. My father complied with her wishes, but in an act of defiance, he left the estate to me." He laughed bitterly. "She threw me out of the house before my father was cold.

"Oh, Elijah, that's awful. What a dreadful thing to do to a child! I can't imagine what you must have gone through."

"Apart from losing my father, the rest didn't bother me. I didn't want it. I never belonged there anyway. When I came of age, I tried to give it back to her, but she was too proud to take it."

"She doesn't live there anymore?"

"No, it's stood empty for years."

"Then why don't you live there?"

His eyes flicked to her. "Would you?" He let that sit for a beat before continuing. "I don't want to be like them. I hate everything it stands for. If it weren't for class boundaries, my father could have married my mother to begin with. He loved her from the start. Just not enough to break the rules."

Harriet said nothing for a moment. The words struck something deep and uncomfortable in her chest. She wanted to say she understood, but didn't dare. Those same rules had shaped her life—bent her, broken her—but she'd spent so long trying to survive within them, she wasn't sure she could ever truly break free.

"I don't know what I would have done," she said finally. Her voice was quiet. "But I don't think I'd have had your courage."

Elijah took a drink of his tea. "It wasn't without its challenges."

She wondered what that meant, but he offered nothing more. She looked down at the hat block still perched in her lap. Her hands loosened around it, and she set it down on the floor. It seemed foolish now. "Did you never marry?" she asked.

He smiled, and something wicked flashed in his dark, intelligent eyes. A promise of something she couldn't name yet. He shook his head. "My turn."

Harriet winced, hoping he wouldn't ask anything too personal. She wasn't ready to show the inside of her wounds yet.

He stood and crossed the room to an oak sideboard and poured a generous measure of amber liquor into two glasses. He brought them back to the table and held one out to her. "You need more than tea for this one."

Harriet gulped. "I couldn't possibly drink that," she said, eyeing the glass. "It's far too strong for a lady."

"Who told you that?"

She didn't know, but she remembered the last time she'd tasted it.

"Drink it. I assure you, you're stronger."

She accepted the glass and drank it in one go. The fumes alone made her eyes sting, but she was determined not to show weakness. Fire surged down her throat and up behind her nose, making her blink hard against the urge to cough. She drew a long breath, then squared her shoulders and met his gaze. "Alright," she said, voice hoarse but resolute. "I'm ready. Shoot."

Elijah leaned forward, resting his forearms on his knees, his voice so low she felt the rumble of it in her chest. "Who broke your heart?"

Harriet's fingers tightened around the glass. *Lillian.* She looked at him, expecting to see a smirk, but there was no smugness in his expression—no satisfaction in making her flinch. Just genuine curiosity.

She willed her voice not to crack. "No one person in particular." She couldn't tell him. "Life did, I suppose. In pieces. Bit by bit."

Elijah didn't speak or look away.

She liked that. He was strong enough to sit with pain and not move to fix it. She offered a crooked smile. "If you're hoping for a Greek tragedy, I'm afraid you'll be disappointed. There was no romantic betrayal or ill-fated lovers. Just…" She shrugged. "Hope turning to ash. A string of good intentions gone wrong."

His voice was almost a whisper. "I think that's worse."

Harriet blinked, surprised by the ache in his words. Then she nodded. "Yes. I think it is."

They sat in silence, the weight of their confessions between them, neither quite ready to move. After a moment, Harriet said quietly, "I think that's enough for one night."

"I think you're right."

She rose, smoothing her skirts with a shaky hand.

"I'll see you out," he said, walking ahead of her. When he reached the staircase, he turned back and offered his hand.

She hesitated but then took it, glad of his steadying grip.

He walked her to the front door and opened it, and it felt like all the magic rushed out into the street.

"Goodnight, Harriet," he said, his expression suddenly serious and sombre.

"Goodnight, Elijah."

She stepped out into the evening air, the scent of sawdust still clinging to her. The street was quiet, caught in the hush that came just before night fell. The hat block tucked beneath her arm felt heavier than it should have.

She entered her own shop and set it down; the evening

replaying in her mind. 'Who broke your heart?' She'd told him a version of the truth, or as close to it as she dared. And she'd been surprised at his honesty when he answered her questions. She'd expected him to be evasive—clever with his answers, to avoid letting her in. Something had shifted between them. Not much, but enough to unbalance her.

LOVE ME, I DARE YOU

Harriet and Elijah's evenings together became the anchor in her restless days. Elijah often shared supper with her and Delphine, and the three enjoyed many a quiet evening in each other's company. Delphine stopped teasing her with loaded comments about him—but continued to study them with interest. Harriet could feel her watchful eye.

She began visiting Elijah's workshop with paltry excuses—a broken chair, a loose table leg. Each time, he agreed to help her on one condition: that she answered a question. It became a game of sorts. A game, Harriet told herself, she had no choice but to play if she wanted things mending. The obligation to answer his questions took away the weight of opening up.

He kept them light-hearted mostly: what was her father's name, where had she lived, whom did she marry? But inevitably, the question of children came—and she had to decide if she was ready to share that grief. She was.

He listened quietly, giving her pain room to breathe. He

never rushed her or tried to stay her tears, but remained a grounding presence she could cling to.

Something in her awoke—fluttering and weak—like hope that had been left to die until now.

Each time she told him something, he gave her a piece of himself in return. She learned he had known tragedy too—a wife gone mad with grief after a miscarriage. She'd stolen a baby and been locked away in an asylum.

Harriet knew now why his heart had closed. But the grief had not ended there. The poor woman had escaped, but her body was found in a country lane almost a year later.

She asked him once if he missed her, and was surprised by his answer.

"She was never happy with me."

Harriet felt a stab of annoyance. Why wouldn't someone be happy with him? She was sure he'd make a perfectly good husband.

"She knew about the estate at Bakewell. All she ever talked about was living at Foxleigh Park. She just couldn't settle for what we had here, knowing there was something more elsewhere. She never understood why I didn't want it. She thought I was a coward." He smiled tightly. "I found out later —after she'd died—that she'd been mistress to a number of wealthy gentlemen whilst we were married."

Ah, another nail in the coffin for the gentry! His distaste for the upper class made even more sense now. And as for calling him a coward? Elijah Bennett had a number of things to his discredit, but cowardice wasn't one of them.

"I was never enough for her," he said. "I'm sure they all had a good laugh about the wealthy carpenter who lived like a pauper."

And there it was: the chink in his armour. The quiet thing he believed about himself, the thing that haunted him still.

Harriet felt the urge to reach out and touch his cheek, to comfort him, just for a moment, but she stopped herself and rubbed at her neck instead. "Do you think….that it's changed you?" It was something she'd begun to ask herself, wondering how she might be if her life had taken a different path.

He frowned and ran a hand over his beard. "It changed me for a time. I was very different a few years ago. But now, it's difficult to say. Would I have been just as I am, regardless? I really don't know."

"In what way were you different?"

He looked at her as if weighing up how she might react. "Well, I was younger then, more impulsive, and very much guided by the senses. So when happiness was denied me I abandoned principle in the pursuit of pleasure."

Harriet's brows knit. *What does he mean?*

"I fell prey to frequent and violent temptations." When she still looked confused, he elaborated. "With women."

Harriet flushed and pulled at her collar. Her blouse felt suddenly too tight.

"That's when I spent time in London, in a never-ending cycle of indulgence followed by repentance. I knew what I was doing was wrong, but I was angry with God. I just wanted to feel something other than pain." He shrugged. "Want, desire, appetite: those are the things that let you know you're still alive."

So he'd needed to feel alive just as she had when she walked into the sea. They'd suffered such similar pain but coped with it so differently. *How easy it is, she thought, for men to temper their grief.*

Elijah crossed to the hearth and stoked the fire. It was September now and cold enough to need it in the evenings. When he turned back, his gaze caught hers. Something passed between them: fragile, flickering, and impossible to name.

She tried not to be the first to look away, but his gaze was too intense and she wilted under it.

"I have another question for you," he said, not taking his eyes from hers.

"Go ahead." She folded her hands neatly in her lap and fidgeted absently with her wedding ring.

"Did you love him?"

It took her a moment to realise he was talking about her husband, so seldom did she think of him. "No, I don't think I did."

"You don't think?" He looked surprised but pleased by her answer.

"Well, I've seen other people who love each other in the romantic sense, and it looks nothing like what Arthur and I shared." She thought of Delphine and how she loved Charlie with such unrelenting madness.

"Have you never been in love then?"

"No, I don't suppose I have. Have you?"

"I have." He took a drink. "But it wasn't returned."

"Your wife?"

Elijah nodded.

Emboldened by the bud of jealousy forming in her chest, Harriet pushed for more. "Is that why you said you don't believe in love?"

One side of his mouth drew up in a sad half smile. "Yes."

"How sad." It didn't come out the way she meant. Too sharp, sarcastic even.

"Well, you don't either," he shot back.

"I didn't say that. I said that my heart was bleak and barren, and it's the truth. I'm so broken there's nothing left inside."

His face grew serious. "You speak of love as though it were finite: a commodity that you might run out of if you give away too much."

"And you speak as though your emotions are a decision. You can't just decide not to love anymore! Especially not when you already know what it is to love."

"You're right, I can't. Anymore than you can." His expression lit the fuse of her anger.

"I didn't say I'd decided not to love. I said I didn't think I could."

"Then try." He levelled her with a gaze that caught her breath. "Love me. I dare you." A gleam of pleasure flickered in his eyes, and the unmistakable insinuation of desire. Unmasked and without restraint.

Harriet couldn't speak. Not because she didn't want to, but because some part of her had already begun to want too much.

~

HARRIET CLOSED the shop door and pressed her back to it, the sound of the latch clicking into place louder than it should have been. She couldn't have stayed any longer.

"Love me. I dare you," he'd said.

They existed in a space somewhere between attraction and fulfilment. Her thoughts lingered between the remembrance of the last visit and the anticipation of the next until she found herself in a near-constant state of agitation. Her heart hammered in her chest. She'd made her excuses and left as quickly as she could, but her pulse was still skittish and irregular, even now in this safe place.

Upstairs, the fire burned low, and orange light flooded the sitting room. Delphine sat by the fireplace, looking like a pixie suspended in amber. She looked up from her sewing, eyes narrowing as she took in Harriet's anguished appearance. "Well," she said, drawing the word out like a ribbon. "Either you've seen a ghost—or Elijah has finally told you how you feel."

Harriet blinked. "How I feel? You mean how he feels?"

"No Hattie. How *you* feel. Everyone else can see it but you. I'm merely suggesting that he's pointed it out to you."

Harriet shook her head. "I'm not in the mood," she muttered, flopping into the opposite chair.

"No?" Delphine set her stitching aside. "Well, that's too bad because I've had just about enough of watching you moping about like a woman haunted."

Harriet sank further into the chair and stared at the flames. When Delphine didn't say anything else, she prompted her. "Go on then. I may as well get it over with." She knew it was coming sooner or later.

"Admit it first. Out loud. To yourself."

"Admit what?" She knew what Delphine wanted, but she resisted—more out of habit than anything else.

"You're in love with him."

"What?"

Delphine tilted her head. "You heard me."

Harriet blew out a long and exasperated breath. "I don't know what I feel."

Delphine raised one brow. "No? I know you, Hattie. I know the sound of your silence when you're grieving, and this is not it. You're different. And I've never seen you look at anyone the way you look at him."

Harriet stared into the fire. "It's not that simple."

"It never is."

There was a long pause. Then Harriet remembered who she was talking to. Her best friend, sister, her saviour. She'd shared the most horrific days of her life with Delphine. Why on earth was she resisting this confession?

She looked at her, eyes wide. "I don't like it. If this is being in love, I don't want it. I can't eat. I can't sleep. My stomach is knotted. I'm replaying conversations, looking for hidden meaning in words. I'm not even in control of my own body for goodness' sake! Sometimes I feel like he's controlling my temperature, my pulse *and* my ability to breathe! It's dreadful!"

Delphine's eyes creased at the corners in a playful laugh. "That's because you're resisting it, Hattie. You're fighting so hard not to feel it, you're going to make yourself ill."

"It frightens me, Delphine. It feels...too fragile. Like if I reach for it, it'll vanish."

Delphine sat forward and took Harriet's hands in hers. "Nothing worth having comes without risk. People come in and out of our lives at God's will—not ours. You know that as well as I do. All we can do is make the most of them whilst they are with us. There are so many beautiful things in life, but the beauty is not in their lasting. They are beautiful because they end. That's what makes them so precious."

"But how can I be certain of his feelings? I've been so taken in by people in the past that I no longer trust my own judgement. It's cost me dearly." Harriet shook her head slowly.

"Come now Hattie, you cannot doubt his feelings. I refuse to believe you are so blind."

They sat in silence, the weight of the words settling between them.

"You cannot allow your past to condition your future. You must live, and you deserve to be happy."

"But what if...," she whispered. "What if...Lillian never forgives me?" Fat, glossy tears rolled down her cheeks as she unearthed the last reason for her resistance.

"Oh, Hattie! Is that what's keeping you from living your life?" She knelt in front of Harriet and held her face. "You have committed your happiness entirely into her charge. And as much as it pains me to tell you, she is unsympathetic to your state. She is continuing with her life regardless of you. In fact, I was waiting for you to come home so I could tell you. I've heard news of her this evening."

Harriet's head snapped up. "You have?"

"Yes, they're returning next month." She paused. "And she's engaged."

Harriet felt the air rush out of her lungs. "To whom?" She asked.

"Lord William Alfred Byron."

Silence stretched between them. Harriet wrapped her arms across her stomach, trying to stop the ache. "I don't know him," she said, voice cracking.

"I do."

"And?"

Delphine rose and seated herself on the chair arm. She cradled Harriet's head against her. "He's respectable, and from a good family."

"I don't care about that," Harriet interrupted. "Is he kind? Does he value integrity, honesty? Will he treat her well?"

"I cannot tell you much, but I do know the reason you probably haven't heard of him is that he keeps a low profile. He doesn't flirt or gamble, and he's known to show kindness and courage. I think you would like him. Surely that must be a comfort to you?"

Harriet nodded. "Do you ever wonder what life would be like if you'd made just one different choice? I mean the little choices we make: the seemingly insignificant ones. It's the trivial decisions that create the most impact. One minuscule change, a moment's deviation from a plan, a turn in another direction. The tip of a shoe over the edge of your path can send you careening into another future altogether. Your fate irrevocably altered."

She looked up at Delphine. "What if I hadn't chased the

carriage, if I hadn't lost my temper, or chosen that day to speak to her? What if I hadn't said we were going home, or that she couldn't be presented at court? Would it have been different? So many minuscule things that could have caused a million different outcomes."

"Hattie, you can't think like that. You'll drive yourself insane."

"But don't you think it's strange? The big decisions that require strenuous thought and weighing of pros and cons. The ones we expect to initiate great consequence rarely live up to the expectation. They cause barely a ripple on the surface of our lives."

Delphine didn't say anything, just held her and let her continue to pour it out.

"I still don't understand it, Delphine. How can a lifetime's love and care be cancelled out in the blink of an eye? Scratched out of existence."

The template of motherhood had been forged long ago, and Harriet knew no other way of living. Who was she if not a mother? And how could she trust love when she'd been so wrong about Lillian's? In her absolute certainty of Lillian's love, never could she have conceived that such a thing could happen. Where was all that love supposed to go with no one to give it to?

ELMRIDGE PARK

Elijah left it a few days before he knocked at the door. Perhaps he was waiting for Harriet to come to him, or maybe he was just giving her time to think. He didn't come in right away, just waited in the doorway like he was unsure if he should. "I haven't seen you lately," he said. "I thought I'd ask if you needed anything fixing? You must have broken something by now."

She laughed nervously. Did he know she'd been doing it on purpose? She hoped not. "Nothing's broken," she said. But she stepped aside and let him in.

He moved quietly to the foot of the stairs and waited. The silence between them was thick and humming.

"Let's sit down here tonight," she said. "It's too still up there." Delphine was out visiting a friend, and the apartment felt too big and empty. She preferred the comfort of the shop with its myriad distractions.

Elijah set his cap on the workbench and pulled out two chairs. He seemed cautious, like he were afraid of what she might say. The echo of their last conversation lingered in the room like wood-smoke. Love me. I dare you. "You're quiet. Is there something wrong? Are you well?"

Harriet laughed without humour. "That's two questions. It would cost you two repairs."

Elijah let out a breath he seemed to have been holding and smiled, running a hand through his hair.

Harriet sighed. "You know, I used to relish silence. The restorative power of quiet reflection. Now I can't stand it. It makes the thoughts inside my head seem so much louder."

"Tell me."

"I heard some news about Lillian."

He didn't say anything, so she carried on.

"She's coming back. And she's engaged."

He exhaled, slow and long, then ran a hand across his jaw. "How do you feel?"

"I don't know." She shrugged and fiddled with a worn handkerchief. "Like I've forgotten how to breathe."

Elijah braced his hands on either side of her chair and slid it toward him. She found herself between his knees. Not touching, but close enough to feel the warmth of him.

"When you see her, she might not be the person you remember," he said softly.

"I know." Harriet's eyes stayed fixed on her hands. "What if she won't see me?"

"I think you need to prepare yourself for that. There's a good chance she won't want to. But that doesn't mean you shouldn't try." He reached out and wiped a tear away with his thumb. "Is Delphine going with you when you see her?"

"No, I want to see her by myself."

Elijah frowned. "I don't like the idea of you being alone when you're upset."

"It's what I want. I need to."

"Very well. But if you change your mind, I'll gladly take

you." He tilted up her chin to look at her and smiled. "I can see the torment in your eyes. I wish I had more than useless words to soothe the ache for you."

She wished she could say something brave. Tell him that his words weren't useless; that he spoke the language of her pain. But no words came. Her throat was so tight she thought it might close up.

~

ELIJAH FOUND out that the 'SS Victoria' was due to dock in Dover on September 26th. That gave Harriet a rough idea of when to expect Lillian back in Hatfield. Depending on whether they stayed the night in Dover or caught the train straight away, she should be back by the twenty-ninth.

She watched the street for days. Their shop was on the main street in the village, so everyone who came and went had to pass it. On Wednesday, she stood in the window the whole day.

Delphine tried to get her to come away, but she wouldn't.

"But it's the twenty-ninth," Harriet said. "And she should be back today." Besides, it was market day, and the street was busy. On a normal day, you'd hear the odd carriage coming up the street, but on market day there were carriages and carts everywhere. She couldn't afford to miss her.

But no carriage passed. The following week she had almost stopped waiting. But not quite. She went to the evening service at St Etheldreda's, but she found no comfort between its ancient stone walls. It was dusk as she walked home, and Delphine would be angry that she'd gone out alone in the evening. So would Elijah. They worried too much.

She heard the distant clip-clop of hoofs echoing through the streets and the grinding of iron on cobblestones as it came closer. She turned to look and saw a flash of black and red. The gleaming exterior of a landau with its familiar red wheels and there on the door, the Davenport family crest.

She's here.

That carriage. The very same carriage that had rolled away outside the opera eighteen months ago. The final click of the door closing rang out in her head like gunfire. *She's in there! My little girl!* She tried to keep walking, desperate to be out of the street, but her body rebelled against the command. Paralysed by memory, she stood still, one hand on the wall to steady herself, and one at her stomach to hold herself together. She willed her lungs to breathe, taking in great gulps of air and blowing them out through trembling lips. Her eyes stung with unshed tears, and her throat burned.

Please, she thought. *Not here, in the street. Don't fall apart in the street.* She stumbled along the pavement, feeling her way along the buildings, her vision blurred. She needed to get to Elijah.

When she reached the shop, she burst in, leaving the door wide open behind her. "Elijah!" Her voice cracked, unable to hold it in any longer. "Elijah!"

He rushed in from the workroom and froze when he saw her. "What is it?"

She couldn't answer for the sobs escaping her throat.

He rounded the counter and pulled her to him. "What happened?"

"Sh..sh…she's back," she managed between gasps. "I saw… the carriage."

He wrapped his arms tight around her, his chin resting on her head as she wailed into his chest.

She'd held herself together in the street. Just. But now, here in Elijah's arms, she finally let go. Here was the comfort she'd craved all this time. The balm to her lifelong wound.

THE FOLLOWING MORNING, she dressed with more care than usual. She twisted her hair into a smooth coil at the nape of her neck and pinned it so tightly it pulled at her scalp. There mustn't be a hair out of place. Today, she would call on Lillian for the first time. Her dress was sober but elegant. A deep blue taffeta with the cuffs turned just so, as if the right appearance might somehow ease her way through the door.

Delphine came to her in her room. "I have something for you, but you must close your eyes." She moved behind her and threaded something around Harriet's neck. A soft clink, the snap of a clasp behind her, and then Delphine turned her toward the mirror. "There," she said, hands resting on Harriet's shoulders. "That gives it just the right touch."

Harriet opened her eyes. Her mother's pendant hung like a droplet of midnight just below her collarbone. The mirror bright surface caught every flicker of light, glowing with a depth that seemed otherworldly. The rich blue echoed her dress beautifully. She touched it in disbelief, stroking the cool, creamy pearls.

Delphine smiled, delighted.

"Delphine…how? Where did—I don't understand."

She leaned in, mischief glistening in her eyes, and whispered, "Charlie."

"When?"

"He gave it to me when he brought you back from London. He said I would know when it was the right time to give it to you."

Harriet turned to face her. "Why would he do that? He paid so much money for those jewels."

"I told him they were your mother's. He watched your reaction when you laid them on the table that night. He said the way you looked at it, the way you touched it—so gently—he knew it meant something more to you. And such things," she added softly, "should never be parted from their owners."

"But I never told you they were my mother's," Harriet said, confused.

Delphine laughed. "Hattie, darling, I love you, but you'd make a terrible liar. I never believed you for a second."

Dear Charlie. He noticed everything. He possessed a keenness, a constant state of alertness, a sort of inborn knowledge which was perhaps his natural inheritance as a gypsy. She owed him more than she could say.

"Now, your mother is with you today, whatever happens."

Harriet nodded. She didn't need to speak. It was all there in her eyes.

~

THE WALK to the Davenport house felt longer than usual, even though her feet knew every turn. It was a fine autumn morning. Gold-edged leaves littered the road, and the sun was sharp and clear. When she reached the entrance to Elmridge Park, her heart gave a single, painful thud. She hesitated. Then, pushing forward, she walked the winding driveway and up to the door. She knocked twice, her chin held high.

A butler answered. She recognised him from before—a little older, with greying sideburns and an expression carved from stone. His eyes widened in recognition.

"I'd like to speak with Miss Blackthorn," she said, forcing steadiness into her voice.

He didn't meet her eye. "Miss Davenport is indisposed."

"I don't want Mrs Davenport. I want Miss Blackthorn," she corrected.

He looked down his nose, reminding her of Hortense. "As I said, Madam, Miss Davenport is not available."

Miss Davenport? There is no Miss Davenport. Not with Theodora locked away. Is that what Lillian is calling herself now? Had she even renounced her name? "Damn you, Edward, I want to speak with Lillian. My daughter!"

"I'm afraid that won't be possible." He hadn't shown so much as a flicker of empathy. He started to close the door.

"Wait! Wait," she said, panic lacing her voice. "I'll leave a message. Can you take a note to her?"

He shook his head. "I'm afraid I can't help you." The door closed with a resounding thud.

Harriet stood on the step, hands trembling in her calfskin gloves. *Fine. I'll try the servants.* Hopefully, there would be someone there she was familiar with. She went to the side entrance, where the kitchens led onto a small herb garden. She heard the familiar clang of copper pans and Betty's shrill bark issuing commands.

A moment later, Betty waddled out and seated herself on a low wall to light her pipe. She looked up when Harriet approached, and her face drained of colour. "What the blazes are you doing 'ere?"

"Well, it's good to see you too, Betty." They both laughed, but Betty recovered herself quickly.

"You can't be here lass. She'll have the peelers here if she sees you."

"But, Betty, she has my daughter. What am I supposed to do?"

The old woman's red face softened in sympathy. "She's not your daughter anymore, pet. The girl you raised is gone."

"I can't…I can't just walk away. She's my flesh and blood! I carried her, brought her into the world. I raised her!" She felt her composure slipping away and tried desperately to keep it, but she wasn't going to fall to pieces. No, this time, what she felt was raw and powerful, and it simmered just beneath the surface.

"I can't help you, love. I'm sorry."

"Can you at least tell me if she's well? Please, Betty, you cannot be so cruel."

There was a long pause whilst Betty considered this. She drew on her pipe and blew out a stream of smoke from the corner of her mouth. "I'll tell you what I can do for you. I'll keep you abreast of things. If I get to know something, so will you."

Harriet went to speak, but Betty held up her hand to silence her.

"But you mustn't come back 'ere. I don't care what you do at the front door, but don't come back to my kitchen. I don't want anything coming back to me. D'you hear? I can't afford to lose this."

"But how will you get word to me?"

"You let me worry about that. You'll get it one way or another. Just don't come looking for me."

"Very well. Thank you, Betty."

She puffed on her pipe again and dismissed Harriet with a wave of her hand. "Go on now, be off with you before anybody else sees you."

Harriet returned the following week, and a few times after that. Sometimes the butler didn't even open the door. Sometimes it was the maid, offering only a tight-lipped, "I'm sorry, Madam." Each time, she told herself this would be the day. But it never was.

NO MORE SECRETS

By January, Harriet had stopped going to Elmridge and writing to Lillian. No replies had ever come, but then the letters might never have reached her. Perhaps Lillian didn't know she'd been calling. Harriet began to wonder if she might even be missing her this very moment, but it wasn't long before that illusion was shattered.

It was Saturday, and the village was bustling. Market stalls overflowed with autumn produce—apples, leeks, turnips, and great piles of potatoes still clotted with earth. Children darted between carts, and shawled women bartered over ribbons and cheese.

Harriet was walking home from the printers, head bowed against the afternoon chill, a sheaf of order slips clutched under one arm. She heard the tinkle of a bell as she passed the dressmakers, and a peal of laughter from two young women. Then she heard a voice she recognised. Goosebumps prickled her skin, and her scalp tingled. She turned instinctively toward the sound.

There across the street, from the doorway of Maison Elise,

Lillian stepped out. She was taller than Harriet remembered. Her gown was expensive; her hair swept up in a fashion that seemed too old for her years. Then she turned and their eyes met. Recognition flickered.

Harriet took a single step forward.

Lillian's gaze cooled and her eyes narrowed before turning away and linking arms with the young girl beside her. She laughed as though nothing had happened.

"Lillian," Harriet called, her voice strangled. "Lillian, wait —" She lifted her skirts and elbowed through the crowd, jostling past shoppers and traders. The street blurred, and only Lillian was in focus. "Lillian, wait please! I just want to speak with you."

Lillian leaned in and whispered something to the other girl, who nodded and walked ahead. Then she turned on Harriet. "Don't ever approach me like that in public again." Her voice was acid sharp. "I have nothing to say to you." Her eyes were empty, cold.

"I am your mother Lillian," Harriet said, pleading. "This is not right." Lillian's lips curved into a cold smile. Arabella's smile. "You are no mother of mine." She watched the effect of her words as their poison spread. Then she turned and walked away, calling back over her shoulder, "And don't keep coming to the house. I don't want you there."

Harriet stood in the middle of the street, wind tugging at her shawl, people brushing past her on either side. *What monster is this? Who is this stranger who looks so much like my Lillian?*

She didn't go home right away. She wandered. Past the bakery, now shuttered for the day. Past Elijah's shop, but she didn't go in. Not yet. The pain was too fresh. She walked until her feet ached and her thoughts began to slow. Eventually, she found herself on the edge of the common, where the winter grasses bent in the wind and the sky was turning the colour of steel. The cold bit at her cheeks, but for the first time in weeks, her breathing came evenly.

The truth rose unbidden. Unwelcome, but irrefutable. *She is not mine.* The girl she had raised—had loved so fiercely it bordered on madness—was gone. She had to let go. Her gaze drifted over the trees, bare-limbed and unapologetic in their nakedness. A familiar figure moved towards her.

Delphine sat down on the bench next to her. "Elijah has been looking for you. He wanted to speak to you."

"How did you know I was here?"

"I saw you march past the window. You didn't look right."

Harriet stared straight ahead. "I saw her, Delphine. In the street."

"Did she see you?"

"She saw me, and she turned away." Her voice sounded far away. "I've never known such cruelty."

"I'm sorry."

"I expected something inside me to fracture—a violent shatter of despair—but there was nothing so visceral. It felt more like the snapping of a thread."

"You're right not to despair. Do not lose hope. She is young and impulsive, and there's time yet for her to change."

"Hope?" Harriet gave a bitter laugh. "Do not speak to me of hope. Just when I think all is lost and happiness is forever forsaken—that I might know some peace in its acceptance—hope rears its head. A great and mocking thing to raise me up so I might be thrown down again, my soul broken and battered anew. Hope is no saviour." She touched the pendant at her throat. "Peace is what I want, Delphine, peace and calm. The sort of calmness that can only be present in the utter absence of all hope. That is my wish."

~

IT WAS dusk by the time she entered Elijah's shop. She stood in the archway and watched him for some time as he worked, oblivious to her presence. The muscles in his broad back and shoulders strained spectacularly against his damp cotton shirt. Dark curls fell across his forehead as he moved back and forth planing the wood. He executed every movement with the utmost economy, precise and deliberate. There was an air of languid fluidity about him, a grace seldom seen in his sex.

He looked up suddenly and his eyes widened in surprise. "How long have you been standing there? You should have called out," he said, leaving his work and moving towards her.

She watched his hands as she spoke, not daring to meet his eye.

"I didn't want to startle you whilst you were working. Delphine said you came by to talk to me this afternoon."

"Yes I did but I don't want to talk about it down here. Join me for supper and we can talk about it then. Mrs Whetstone will be setting out my supper before she leaves. I'll tell her to lay another plate if that suits you?"

She hesitated before answering, unsure now whether it was wise to be alone with him in this state. "I can always come back tomorrow if it's not convenient. I don't want to put you to any trouble."

"No." He cut her off. "I'd rather do it now than wait. Once I've set my mind to a thing, I want it done. And I can't sleep another night with it swimming about my head."

What on earth is he thinking of doing?

He called up the stairs to Mrs Whetstone to make the necessary adjustments, then went to a large sink in the corner of the workroom. "I'll just wash off this sawdust," he said, "gets everywhere. Can you bring me the towel from the front desk?"

"Yes, of course," she said and went to fetch it. When she returned, she found he had removed his shirt and was lathering his whole upper body with foamy white soap. The way he moved fascinated her.

"Oh, my apologies," she said, turning away and shading her eyes. She wasn't sure if the privacy was for him or her as she willed the blood from her burning cheeks. She held out the towel at arm's length and she heard him chuckle.

"Can you pump the water for me? I can't get the soap from my hair."

She peeked sideways and saw him bend his head over the basin, his hands gripping the porcelain on either side. She felt for the handle and pressed down on the heavy lever, but it did not move.

"I think you might need both hands," he said, and she could hear the amusement in his voice.

She took the handle with both hands, still trying not to look, and pumped the water over his head until the soap was gone. She handed him the towel, and he dried his head and face before moving it down to his body.

She lowered her eyes again and she heard him laugh a second time.

"Surely I am not so offensive to look at that you have to avert your eyes from me. Are your delicate sensibilities so repulsed by the sight of a man's flesh?"

"Do not mock me, Elijah. It has nothing to do with repulsion. I am not in the habit of witnessing such bold displays of masculinity."

"I don't mock you, Hattie, I only play. Forgive me, I meant no harm in it." It was the first time he'd called her that. He looked down at her, and warmth bloomed in her chest.

"I saw her today, in the street," she said, unable to wait any longer.

"Lillian?"

She nodded.

"What happened?"

He listened patiently as she told him, then asked, "What are you going to do?"

She took a deep breath and blew it out slowly. "I'm going to live."

~

UPSTAIRS, the table was laid with a crisp white linen cloth, and set upon it were two china plates and pewter cutlery.

"I'm afraid it's only simple food. I wasn't expecting company tonight." He said, seeming embarrassed by his plain and hearty offering.

"It's perfect. It looks delicious." Harriet took her seat at the small table, acutely aware of her own body. It felt like a thing newly acquired, and she, ignorant of its function.

There was a small loaf of brown bread, a wedge of cheese and what looked like a pork pie.

They had barely started the meal when Elijah set down his fork and cleared his throat.

Harriet's pulse raced. She couldn't meet his eye and pushed a piece of pastry anxiously around her plate.

"Hattie," he said affectionately. "May I speak plainly to you without fear of offending you? For you must know that what I have to say is said with the best intentions."

She had to look at him now and the expression she saw in his face would have broken her heart were it not already in pieces. She knew what was coming. She knew it from the way he rolled her name around his mouth, tasting it on his lips.

Her courage abandoned her. "Please Elijah, let's not talk of anything too serious this evening."

"I have to."

The fire crackled in the hearth, throwing flickering light across the small parlour. Outside, the wind howled, rattling the shutters like it was trying to get inside.

"I can't continue with this friendship if I'm not honest with you. You must know, Hattie, what I feel for you?" Why everyone else can see it as if it were written plain across my face."

Harriet stiffened. She thought she knew—hoped even—that she hadn't misinterpreted his affection. But what if she had? What if she said it out loud right now, and she'd gotten the wrong impression? She would never recover from the embarrassment.

"Tell me," she said, her voice breathless and unsure.

"Hattie, since I met you, I've felt more alive than I'd ever thought possible and that's all down to you. I was angry and indifferent, but you saw past all that. Even though you carried your own grief. What I needed most was what you had least to give and yet you gave willingly."

She shivered and rubbed her arms.

"You're cold. Come stand by the fire." He took her hand and led her to the fireplace.

She wasn't cold but she was glad to be standing up. The conversation felt too big to have sitting down.

He looked at her, warm firelight dancing across his face. "Marry me Hattie. I cannot see a way forward for me in this world without you in it."

She turned away. "You don't know what you ask of me, Elijah. You don't know me at my worst. I am not the angel you think I am."

"Aren't you?" His voice was low, steady. He took a step

toward her, and she gripped the mantel, bracing herself. "You think you know me, but you don't."

"I know you sit in that shop of yours at night pretending you don't listen for my footsteps. I know you touch that locket around your neck when you think of things you won't say out loud. And I know—" He hesitated, tilting up her chin with his finger. "I know you feel something when you look at me."

Harriet swallowed hard. Every instinct screamed at her to speak, but the words wouldn't come.

"Tell me, Hattie. Tell me what it is that makes you impose this denial of happiness upon yourself. I'm sure it cannot be half as bad as you think it is." He waited for her to speak, his eyes searching hers for some clue to her thoughts.

"I can't," she said, breaking down. "I couldn't bear to see the disappointment in your eyes every time you looked at me."

He forced her to look at him. Clasping her face in his hands; he pleaded with her. "Isn't it worse not to tell me? Do you think it's fair to decide for me what my reaction will be? If you don't tell me, you'll never know my true self, nor I yours. All that's between us will be nothing more than counterfeit. I'd rather live a painful truth than a beautiful lie, wouldn't you?"

She knew he meant every word. She gave a small nod and turned away to gaze into the fire. She couldn't bear to look at him whilst she told him. "Just before we came here, Delphine and I. I gave birth to a baby boy. An illegitimate child." She winced as she said it, remembering how Elijah had called himself a bastard. "He was too early, pale and sickly, but he was beautiful to me. I loved him very much."

She looked at him then. It was important that he understood how much she loved little Charlie. She owed her baby that. "We buried him in Delphine's garden." She paused again, trying to gauge his reaction, but he gave nothing away. "Oh,

Elijah, spare me this," she wept. "Spare me this humiliation. If I'm to lose your good opinion, turn away from me now and let it be over." She covered her face with her hands.

He pulled her hands away and held them. "I am truly sorry for the loss you've suffered, but do you think you're the first woman who's searched for solace in the wrong place? So many tortured souls hope to find redemption in each other in a unity of flesh. There are worse sins in this world than for a woman to give herself freely to a man."

She cried anew at his unbounded kindness. "But I didn't. I did not give myself freely."

He stared at her, confusion furrowing his brow.

"What he took from me was quite against my will." She struggled against the sordid memory she had suppressed all this time.

A sharp flash of anger crossed his face as understanding set in. "Who" he said, menacingly calm. "Who did it?" He swallowed, and the tense muscles flexed in his jaw.

She had not seen this face before, fierce and protective. "He is dead."

His nostrils flared as he worked to control his anger. "I am sorry to hear that. I would have liked to kill him myself."

"There is worse to come," she said, eager to get it over with. "I did it. I killed him." The statement hung there, suspended between them. And then she told him the whole sorry escapade, leaving nothing out. When she was done, she felt oddly free. As if she had put down a great weight she had been carrying for years.

He brushed away her tears and tucked the loose strands of hair neatly behind her ears. "You are blameless. You are as sweet and dear to me as you could ever be and if that is all that has kept you from me, now it's over. There are no more secrets between us. Now accept me as your husband and let us be everything to each other. I'm a simple man, Hattie, and I offer you nothing but love and kindness. I've no interest in riches, but I can promise you, there's not a man alive that could love you as I do."

She spun away from him. "I cannot." Her breath was shallow. "I cannot. You say you have nothing to give except love, but I cannot give you even that. I have been so hollowed out by grief and loss that I've nothing left to give. And you deserve so much more than that."

"What are you so afraid of?" He watched her with that quiet patience that unsettled her so much.

Her lips trembled. "What if I love you and it's not enough? Everyone I've ever loved has left me in some way or another."

"I can't promise you that you'll never feel pain, Hattie. That isn't real life. But I know what you've felt. I know how it feels to watch the whole world carrying on with their lives as though nothing's happened while your reality is crumbling around you." He cupped her cheek. "There were times I wanted the heavens to falter, angels to cry out in anguish. I wanted the sky to crack open with thunder loud enough to loose the bolts of hell. But it doesn't, my love. All that is just beautiful poetry. The world carries on, another day, another week, and it hurts and it's terrible, but we must live, Hattie! You said it yourself this very night!"

She had, and she'd meant it.

"If we can find solace in each other, then should we not embrace that? Don't you want something to love now that everything else is gone?"

She did want something—someone to love. She wanted him. Only him. Her voice was barely a whisper. "I don't know how."

He moved behind her, his hands on her arms. He was

impossibly close, his words warm at her ear. "You don't have to know how, you just have to let it happen."

She drew in a sharp breath then exhaled shakily. "I told you once," she said, still facing the fire, "that I'd seen people in love, and it didn't look like what I had with Arthur."

"Yes." His voice was soft, sure.

She turned slowly to face him. "Tell me...is this what it should look like?"

He reached up, brushing her cheek with the back of his hand. "I'm not interested in what it looks like, Hattie." He lowered his voice, his eyes searching hers. "I want to know how it *feels* to you."

"I—I don't know."

Then, without another word, he kissed her. Not gently, but like a promise. He kissed her with a certainty that banished every ghost of doubt still clinging to her heart. It was a claiming. A declaration. A pouring out of all the words he hadn't said, all the nights she'd spent wishing, fearing, doubting—they lived in that one moment. It was grief and healing, ache and comfort, fear and forgiveness, all wrapped in a single shared breath.

Her hands found their way to his chest where his heart thundered beneath her palms. She felt the shape of her life changing—stretching to make room for this man and this moment—this love.

When he pulled back, only slightly, their foreheads touched, their breaths mingled in the silence. "Has it ever felt like that?" he asked softly.

"Never."

THE DEAD WALK AMONG US

Spring had arrived in full, painting the village in soft hues of green and gold. Apple blossoms fluttered in the breeze; children played barefoot along the lanes. For Harriet, it was the first time in years that the turning of the seasons had brought with it something other than sorrow. It held the taste of promise—like sugar in the air.

It was Sunday, and she stood at the shop door, gloves in hand, watching as Elijah approached up the street.

He had a pair of boots in one hand and wore a knowing smile—the kind he reserved only for her.

"Are they fixed?" she asked, tilting her head toward the boots.

"No, Joe said they were beyond saving—and no friend of his would be getting married without being properly shod." He held out the boots for her inspection. "He made me a brand new pair and wouldn't take a penny."

Harriet quirked a brow. "I'm surprised you let him get away with that."

Elijah laughed. "It wasn't for lack of trying. He wasn't

having it though." He ran a hand over his beard. "I said I'd make him a crib when the baby comes."

"That's a lovely idea. Come on, we'd better get Delphine or we'll be late for church."

Delphine had wept openly when they told her they were to be married—not from sadness, but from sheer joy. "Well, it's about time!" she'd said. "I can't tell you how glad I am. You've both earned some happiness."

Now that the date was set, the church bells would soon ring out a peal of joy in celebration. The three of them sat near the back of the church, Harriet and Elijah shoulder to shoulder in the pew, as Reverend Holloway rose to begin the first reading of the banns. The hush in the old nave felt sacred.

A door creaked behind them, and Harriet turned to see a parishioner coming in late. She had an odd look about her. Her hair was white—not with age—but so pale it could not be described as blonde. Her eyes were hollow and red rimmed and her dress, the colour of old bones, hung from her narrow frame. She looked… wild.

Her eyes met Harriet's and locked, unblinking, then she slid into a pew.

A chill rose along Harriet's spine. Her breath caught. She reached for Elijah's hand and felt his thumb trace a slow circle against her knuckles. She turned and smiled at him.

The vicar continued. "I publish the banns of marriage between Elijah James Bennett of this parish and Harriet Elizabeth Blackthorn, also of this parish. If any of you know cause or just impediment why these two persons should not be joined together in holy matrimony, ye are to declare it. This is for the first time of asking." His voice echoed through the rafters.

A beat of silence.

Harriet squeezed Elijah's hand and grinned.

"Very well—"

"Wait!" The voice came from behind. Crisp. Measured. And unmistakably cold.

Harriet felt her presence in the marrow of her bones, like something wicked had entered the church. Something brittle, vengeful. And it was watching them.

Heads turned.

"Elijah Bennett," the voice rang out again, "already has a wife."

A stunned murmur rippled through the congregation.

Harriet turned to Elijah. He was pale as ash, his mouth slightly parted, eyes fixed on the woman at the back of the church.

"Margaret?" The name left his lips like a breath he'd been holding for years.

The woman tilted her head and cackled. "So you *do* remember me?" Her pale skin was almost translucent, and a sheen of sweat clung to her brow, despite the chill in the nave. Her clothing was disordered, as though she'd slept in it for days. She took a single step forward—and then stopped. Her lips curled, and she cocked her head to one side. "You didn't think I'd stay buried, did you?"

Elijah stood. "How—? You were...dead. I saw your body."

"Not *my* body."

"But...your dress—your wedding ring. Who...who was she?"

Margaret shrugged. "Some unfortunate soul." She turned then and skipped away. Her footsteps echoed with unnatural clarity as she passed back through the doors. One slammed shut behind her with a force that vibrated through the pews like thunder.

Elijah didn't move. Harriet touched his arm, and he flinched—suddenly back in the room.

The vicar's voice trembled as he cleared his throat. "Perhaps...we should conclude the service there. Mr Bennett...a word if you please."

~

Reverend Holloway removed his spectacles and pinched the bridge of his nose.

"I'm sorry, Mr Bennett, but you must understand. I cannot under any circumstances proceed with the banns if your wife is still living. It would be contrary to both church and law."

Elijah's voice rang with disbelief. "But I saw her. I identified her body, Hattie. How could I not know my own wife?" His face was still drained of colour.

Harriet's mind raced. "You did say the body was found long after she escaped. It couldn't have been easy to tell."

He nodded, not really listening. "But the clothes," he said, "and Margaret's ring. How did she get them?"

"Margaret must have planted them herself," Harriet said.

"It's a little far-fetched to think a dead body was conveniently waiting there to be used as a scapegoat. Don't you think?"

"You said yourself she was mad. Is it possible that she might have killed her?" She watched the weight of this sink in.

Elijah ran his hands through his hair and sighed. "This can't be happening." He looked at the vicar. "I didn't know, Vicar—I swear it. I didn't know."

"I don't doubt your sincerity, Mr Bennett. But sincerity does not constitute a dissolution of marriage." He paused, glancing toward the closed door of the vestry. "If you wish to remarry, you'll need to obtain a divorce through the proper legal channels."

"How do I do that?" Elijah asked, hope edging into his voice.

"Well, since the Matrimonial Causes Act, I'm afraid divorce no longer falls within ecclesiastical jurisdiction. That's a matter for the civil courts now. The Court for Divorce and Matrimonial Causes, in London."

"And I could petition for divorce? On the grounds of adultery?"

"In theory, yes. A man may obtain a divorce based on adultery alone. But I must warn you, Mr Bennett—it's not a simple matter. You'll need evidence. Witnesses willing to swear under oath. Names. Details. But if you cannot provide the necessary proof, the law offers you no easy escape."

Elijah rubbed his chin. "That may be difficult. The men she took up with were of a certain standing. They would not willingly enter into such public scandal."

The vicar nodded slowly. "Then it may prove...problematic. Without corroboration, the court will likely reject the petition. And there's always the risk of a counter-petition."

"What do you mean?"

"She might well claim cruelty or desertion in her defence."

"Desertion?" Elijah raised his voice and then, checking himself, continued through gritted teeth. "I didn't desert her—she died! Or at least she pretended to. She's completely insane!"

The vicar leaned forward. "If she were considered insane, there could be room to argue she was unfit for conjugal life, but the law doesn't make that easy. You might still be expected to house and care for her or pay for her institutionalisation." He looked thoughtful for a moment. "I'm no law expert, but I do know this: if she insists on returning to your home, and no formal separation or divorce exists, you would be legally bound to let her back in. The doctrine of 'cohabitation as a marital duty' still applies, and you may be forced to resume cohabitation."

Elijah stood. "I will not be forced to live with that lunatic!"

"You'll have to tread very carefully, Mr Bennett. Refusal could make you liable in court and may prevent you from obtaining a divorce as it could then be argued that *you* deserted *her*. It is a very complicated matter. I would strongly advise you to seek counsel from a solicitor before you petition the courts."

He set his jaw. "What happens if they refuse?"

Reverend Holloway looked at him gravely.

"Then I'm afraid the Church cannot solemnise another union. She may not have been your wife in deed these many years, but in the eyes of the law—and God—she still is."

Elijah sank back into the chair. "So I'm still shackled to her. Despite everything."

"For now, yes. You have my sympathy, Mr Bennett." He rose to signal the conversation's end, but Elijah didn't move.

Harriet sat quietly, her gloved hands clasped tightly in her lap, white-knuckled and trembling.

Elijah turned to her. "Say something, Hattie. Please."

She lifted her head slowly and met his eyes. "What would you have me say?" Her voice was measured, but not unkind. "I've finally started rebuilding my life, and here I am again, sitting amongst the rubble."

His shoulders fell. "I'll find a way. I promise, Hattie. I won't let her take this from us."

She gave a small nod but said nothing more.

They walked back through the nave together in silence, the tap of Harriet's heels and the dull thud of Elijah's boots the only sound. The light outside struck bright and sharp after the cool dimness of the vestry.

Delphine was waiting by the lychgate, brows pinched with

worry. She hurried to meet them. "What happened?" she asked, searching their faces.

Elijah couldn't speak.

Harriet shook her head. "It's complicated," she said. "We'll explain everything once we're home."

Delphine hesitated, then slipped her arm through Harriet's and squeezed. "Whatever happens, we'll face it together."

~

THREE MONTHS PASSED. Elijah petitioned every court he could. He wrote letters, travelled back and forth to London and stood before magistrates. Harriet watched it all unfold from the shop window—each time he left with a glimmer of resolve, and each time he returned with his shoulders lower than before, his face pale and drawn.

And then Margaret came again. She appeared like a spectre. Her clothes were cleaner; her eyes no less haunting. She'd pinned wildflowers into her hair and addressed Harriet with a slow, mocking curtsy. "I've come home," she said, placing a cool white hand on Harriet's arm.

She shuddered.

Margaret grinned, and a row of blackened teeth glinted like knife-points. She was a terrifying mix of insanity and cunning, and she knew the law when it came to marriage. When she announced she would be staying, Elijah was duty-bound to take her in.

For three long weeks, she lived under his roof. She paced the floor at night, tapping on floorboards and whispering nonsense into the walls. Harriet even found her downstairs in the shop one morning, singing to herself and trying on half-finished hats.

Elijah wouldn't leave whilst she was there. She was

dangerous. Neither Harriet nor Delphine could sleep either. They took to embroidering late into the night, sewing by candlelight with nervous, crooked stitches.

One morning they awoke to find her gone, but there was no rush of relief. So unpredictable was she that she might have appeared again at any given moment. Harriet operated on high alert for weeks, half expecting her to re-emerge at any moment. She walked quickly in the street, avoiding alleyways and quiet lanes. She sought her face in crowded places and felt those cold eyes on her back as though she were still there. Watching.

When Elijah returned from his final trip, it was with a heavy heart. "They won't be moved on the matter," he said. His voice was flat, listless.

Harriet's heart thudded, each beat carrying dread.

He took her hand in his but didn't meet her eye. "I've tried everything, Hattie. The best they could offer me was to petition for judicial separation—on the grounds of her erratic behaviour." He paused, and she knew from his expression that something worse was coming. "It legally absolves me of cohabitation obligations, but I will still be married to her. Without witnesses or confession, they won't grant the divorce."

Her stomach dropped like a stone. She felt the familiar sting of her old wound—the fissure that ran along her heart, where twice before it had split open.

They were silent for a long time, lost in their own thoughts—Harriet quietly resigning herself to this new and unexpected fate. She had the overwhelming urge to retire from reality. How much was a person expected to endure in a single lifetime? She was certain she'd had more than her share of misfortune.

They moved through the coming days in a kind of daze,

neither fully present nor entirely removed. Elijah spent most of his time at the workshop, but little work was done. At night, she heard the creak of his floorboards long after the village had gone to sleep. Once or twice, she thought she heard him sobbing. When she went to see him, he barely spoke, staring into the fire, unmoving, like a man watching his last flickers of hope turn to ash.

One afternoon, she found him in the back garden, sanding a length of wood with an intensity that looked more like punishment than purpose. He'd asked her to come, and after days of near silence, she knew he must have something important to say.

"You've been avoiding me," she said softly.

His movements stilled, but he didn't look at her. "I've been trying to spare you."

"Spare me? I don't understand."

He leaned his elbows on the workbench and lowered his head into his hands. "I didn't want to ask you what I'm about to ask you, Hattie. But I'm a selfish man and I love you too much to let you go." He turned to her then, truly looked at her. His eyes were red-rimmed and hollowed by exhaustion. "I swore I wouldn't do this. That I'd never ask you for less than you deserve. But Hattie... I've run out of honour and options. Forgive me."

Her breath caught.

"Come away with me. Let us leave this place and make a life together, somewhere no one knows our names. I can't live without you, Hattie. I won't!"

She opened her mouth, but the words would not come.

He reached for her hand, and the weight of it—warm and calloused and pleading—sent a tremor through her whole body.

She stared at their joined hands for a moment and then

pulled hers slowly away. "You—you want me to be your... mistress?"

Elijah winced.

"Is that what you would ask of me? To live with you in sin as your dirty secret, whilst your wife still lives?"

He raked a hand through his hair. "I don't know what else to do, Hattie! We've played our last hand, and it didn't work. You call it sin, but where's the sin in loving someone as I love you?"

"Elijah, you have a wife!"

"A wife?" He shouted. "And where is my wife? My dear sweet wife, who has married God knows who or how many times. Who has deceived and tricked, mocked me, deserted me, even falsified her own death. Is this then the wife I must bear? Is this the happiness I've been allotted? Must I settle for this and never strive to seek better?"

"So you would have me live the rest of my life in disgrace?"

"You would not be a mistress to me, Hattie, you know that. You would be as much a wife to me as anyone could." He beat at his chest with a clenched fist. "In here—in my heart—I'm already your husband. Surrender yourself to me, bind your heart to mine, and we'll be as thoroughly married as two persons could be." His eyes held a desperate plea that tugged on the invisible cords binding her to him.

"Elijah, I—I can't live with another woman's husband. You don't understand what it's like for a woman. I would be shunned, ridiculed, spit at in the street."

"Please, Hattie, I can't bear it. She is not my wife in here." He placed a hand over his heart.

"But she is your wife in the eyes of the law." Her voice softened to a low murmur, and he pulled her in, crushing her against his chest.

"Would you relinquish me so readily, my love? To reconcile yourself to a law made by man, that you don't, at your heart's core, believe in." He trailed his fingers across her temple and down her cheek, and she pressed them to her lips.

"It is not man's law, Elijah. It is God's law."

"And what does God demand of this constitution? What does he require? A celebration? An exchange of vows? Faithfulness and fidelity? A promise that we will present to the rest of the world as man and wife? All these things I freely enter into. I pledge myself to you and you only until death us do part."

"I cannot." Harriet buried her face in the folds of his shirt, and her eyes filled with tears. She felt the furious beating of his heart against her ear. Like a caged bird, it flung itself frantically against his ribs.

"With whom have you made such a contract as to render you liable by our union?"

"Myself."

"Then who will you injure in its breach? You have no relation to disappoint by your actions, so who would you fail by living with me?"

"Only myself." Her own determination threatened to crush her. The pain was agonising, yet it was not for herself that she felt it. It was for him. She could not bear that he would endure such misery at her hand.

He held her by the arms to look at her fully. "Then this prison you occupy is of your own making, Hattie. And yourself the instrument of torture. You're free to follow your own heart if only you'd rid yourself of these shackles. For pity's sake, Harriet, do not abandon me!" He was wild now, his eyes blackened and his face drained of colour. His stony grip bruised the flesh of her arms in his impassioned attempt to cleave her to him.

She didn't know what else to say. There was another tense

silence, and then he seemed to sense his defeat. She felt the slipping away of his resolve in the slackening of his grip. His shoulders slumped and his head bowed, and then he let go, kissing the top of her head as he moved away.

The air was cooler where he no longer held her—like getting out of a warm bath in a freezing room. The distance felt too great already.

His face hardened. "If I am to be denied happiness with you, Hattie, then I shall seek it elsewhere. Not happiness, but pleasure. That is available to all men." His look pierced her to the core.

"Elijah, how can you speak of such things?" She knew on some level that it wasn't said in earnest. He wanted her to feel the sting of jealousy—a last desperate bid to change her mind. It was the cry of a wounded animal, but the words stung no less for that.

"Am I not a man?" he said. "Am I not of flesh and blood like you? Do I not want and need and yearn? Harriet, if this is the fate you resign me to, if this is truly the inclination of your heart, then go. Go! Leave me now whilst I still have a shred of dignity."

The resignation in his tone was more frightening to her than all the anger he could have raised. He turned his back and placed his hands against the fireplace, his head hanging between them.

She looked at him, her love, her friend, her saviour.

His shoulders began to shake as he sobbed.

"Elijah?" she said, reaching out a hand to touch his back.

"I said leave me." The anger had all gone; only despair remained. He looked as though the shadow of death was upon him.

THE WHITE HART

It had been weeks since Harriet saw Elijah.

He had not returned to the shop, nor sent word. Delphine said he may be staying with friends, trying to clear his head, but all Harriet could think was that he'd gone to punish her. He could be in London this very minute, enjoying what was 'available to all men,' as he'd put it. She didn't press for information. She wasn't sure she'd be able to bear what she found out. Some wounds needed space to breathe.

She threw herself into work instead. The shop was now open and fully stocked with fine hats for ladies and gentlemen for all occasions. One hurried morning blurred into another as a steady stream of customers came to buy her wares. It kept her busy, too busy to sink into those dark and lonely places inside her. And yet, Elijah was never far from her thoughts.

Then one morning, a young boy came in, no older than six or seven, a dirty face peeking from under his cap. He handed Harriet a crumpled piece of paper and ran away. Betty had made good on her promise to keep her informed. The note was difficult to decipher with Betty's crude spelling, but she got the message. Lillian Davenport was to be married. The ceremony would take place just two weeks hence, on the 3rd of August, right here at St Etheldreda's.

Even though she knew already of the engagement and had reconciled herself to the fact, it was still a blow to see it written. So much hurt was woven into those small, childish words.

Lillian Davenport was to be married—so she had relinquished her name. *I won't be there,* she thought. *I won't be there to dress her, to braid her hair, to kiss her forehead before she walks down the aisle.* She wanted to scream at the top of her lungs—tell everyone in the street, 'Her name is Blackthorn, not Davenport! She's mine! That's *my* daughter!' But she said nothing. Who would believe her anyway?

She tried to put it from her mind, but the knowledge itched beneath her skin. Where was Elijah? He would have soothed her—made it all feel more bearable.

"Wednesday 3rd of August," she said to Delphine that afternoon. "That's her wedding day...and I won't be there."

Delphine didn't say anything. She didn't need to. All Harriet needed was to be listened to and to be held.

When the day arrived, she rose early and moved about as if she were in a dream. She went to St Etheldreda's and took a seat high up in the gallery, far away from familiar eyes. She would have liked to watch Lillian arrive, but she couldn't risk being seen. Arabella would surely have her removed if she saw her. So she sat by a stone pillar, tucked away in shadow, hoping for a glimpse of her own baby girl.

Below, the guests assembled in rows, pew after pew full of suits and silks and pinned curls. Choirboys dressed in their white robes lined the stalls, bristling with the hum of excitement. The groom arrived in a crisp grey morning coat, a white rose pinned to his lapel and a top hat under his arm. He paced back and forth, setting down his gloves and then taking them up again.

His parents were next to arrive. Delphine had told her who they were—the Earl and Countess of Marlow. William was a viscount, heir apparent to the Earldom. They were everything Arabella would have wanted.

Harriet's stomach ached with longing, and her lungs felt like they were shrinking by the minute. Breathing became agony. None of it seemed real—sitting up there in the half-light, apart from everything, like a ghost. She began to wish she hadn't come, but it was too late now. She couldn't descend the narrow staircase and exit the church without being seen. There were too many people.

Just as she thought it was all going to be too much, she heard the soft shuffle of shoe leather on the flagstones behind her. Elijah appeared and took a seat beside her. He was wearing his new wedding boots. Without a word, he took her hand in his and squeezed it.

"What are you doing here?" She whispered.

He smiled and kissed the back of her hand, brushing his lips across her knuckles. "I couldn't let you do this alone."

"But how did you know?"

"I read it in the papers. I knew you'd come."

She allowed herself this small comfort, relaxing against him and leaning her head on his shoulder.

A hush swept over the congregation below, and the first bold notes of Wagner's Bridal Chorus echoed through the nave. Every eye turned toward the doors. The organ swelled, filling the vaulted ceiling with grandeur and promise. Every note vibrated through to Harriet's core. Her heart rose and fell in a single breath. She gripped Elijah's hand and waited for Lillian to emerge into view from underneath the gallery.

And then she was there. Resplendent in ivory silk and glittering with Arabella's diamonds. Harriet couldn't see her face, only the top of her head, but she could see William's. His face split into a beaming smile that seemed to light up everything around him. His eyes brimming with glee as Lillian made her way toward him on Mr Davenport's arm.

"What do you think he's like?" Harriet said, sounding far away. "I wish I could have met him. Just once."

Elijah didn't answer.

They sat that way in silence as the vows were spoken. Harriet couldn't watch. She closed her eyes and let the tears run freely down her cheeks until it was over. Then, when the happy couple turned to leave, Elijah squeezed her hand again.

"Look Hattie."

She leaned forward as far as she dared. Lillian looked radiant, happy. *Oh God, please let her be happy. Let him love her as I do.* They waited a long time for the church to empty, and then a little while longer for Harriet to compose herself.

When they finally stood to leave, she couldn't find it in her to let him go. "Elijah," she whispered, "take me away."

~

THE PLATFORM at Hatfield station hummed with the idle chatter of strangers and the distant hiss of steam, but Harriet heard none of it. She stood shoulder to shoulder with Elijah, his hand gripping hers. A train was due in ten minutes.

"Where do you want to go, Hattie?"

"Anywhere, I don't care. Just...anywhere but here."

Elijah nodded. "Alright." They boarded the first train that stopped. Its sign read *St Albans*. "Have you ever been?" he asked her as they settled into a carriage.

She shook her head. "Have you?"

He gave a faint smile. "Once. A long time ago. There's a beautiful park and some old Roman ruins. I'll show you, if you like."

She nodded and tightened her grip on his hand. Words felt like too much effort. The train rocked gently as it left the station behind. Harriet leaned against him and watched the countryside blur into green smudges, her reflection flickering across the glass. She breathed in deeply and inhaled his familiar scent—mature, golden, musky, like spices and jasmine. It made her smile.

In St Albans, they wandered the town without purpose. They climbed the hill to the cathedral, walked beneath the great arches and stood silently before the altar. The air was thick with broken promises, unspoken vows.

They browsed the old market square, admired trinkets they didn't need, and wandered through Verulanium Park, marvelling at Roman ruins and lazing by the river. It almost felt like peace, but with every hour that passed, the atmosphere grew heavier, conversation faded into silence and Harriet's grip tightened.

As day thickened into dusk, and the busy streets emptied of people, Elijah checked his pocket watch. "Hattie, it's time to go."

She clasped his arm, folded herself into him. "Not yet," she whispered.

"If we mean to catch the last train, we must go now."

Harriet looked toward the dusky horizon. "Don't take me home tonight...please."

Elijah stared at her. "I don't understand what you're asking, Hattie."

She wasn't sure what she was asking either. She only knew she wasn't ready to be parted from him. Not again. "I don't know. I—I just… can't bear to be alone tonight." She clutched at his shirt and pressed her forehead to his chest. "Please, Elijah…stay with me." The words fell from her lips like a prayer.

Elijah swallowed. "Hattie, you know what that would mean for you." His face was unreadable—cautious, shocked, happy? She couldn't tell. "You made it very clear this was not what you wanted."

She looked at him with all the courage she could summon to her aid. "Well, I want it now."

He still hadn't moved. "There's no going back from this. You cannot undo it."

She nodded. "I know."

~

THE WHITE HEART was a modest hotel near the train station. Bustling with travellers and busy enough to go un-noticed. Elijah held her hand as they climbed the front steps and approached the clerk. They checked in as Mr and Mrs Bennett and signed their names in the ledger.

The irony of that was not lost on her. *I ought to have been Mrs Bennett already. I should be signing my name in the church register, not a hotel ledger.* She heard a cackle from somewhere in the room beyond—sharp and shrill—and it reminded her of Margaret. An icy shudder ran through her.

The clerk passed Elijah a large brass key with a room number attached to it. He gave it to Harriet, who gazed at it as if it were a magical thing. That key wasn't just going to unlock a door, but her heart, body and soul. It was going to unlock a completely different life.

She suggested they eat dinner first, delaying the inevitable. Her courage faltered with every step, and a curious bout of shyness struck her, bewildering to both herself and Elijah.

A waiter seated them at a table in the restaurant, and Elijah ordered their meal. Clove-studded ham glazed with sweet sticky marmalade, and for Harriet, salmon dressed in butter and curls of lemon rind. Elijah cleared his plate, but Harriet could barely swallow. She lifted the fork to her mouth and nibbled at the edges, only to put it back on her plate a moment later. She twirled a salad leaf in the butter, then left that too.

He reached across the table and covered her hand with his. "Have you changed your mind Hattie?"

She looked up, surprised, as if she'd forgotten he was still there. "Oh...no, no—I'm...just thinking." The key felt heavy in her pocket.

"What are you thinking about?"

She blushed the colour of the wine. "I...er...I can't remember."

Elijah cocked his head and grinned. There was something wild in his gaze that she hadn't seen before—something feral and unguarded.

Her body lit with a snap of nerves, her pulse thundering in her ears. A tide of yearning swelled inside her, fierce and unspoken, battling the walls she'd built around her heart. Their eyes locked, and for a moment, the world held its breath between them. Then with deliberation, she withdrew the key from her pocket and slid it across the table.

No ceremony was necessary to highlight the magnitude of the moment—no words either could have said would alter its significance. He led her up the wide staircase, the warmth of his hand a tether in the dark, steady and sure.

Harriet exhaled, tension thick in her chest. She hadn't drawn an easy breath since they set foot in the hotel.

Inside the room seemed to pulse with the quiet hum of

possibility, shadows deepening around them. Time stretched and folded, each moment weighted with meaning.

He didn't stop to look around the room, light a lamp, or the candle on the nightstand. He just pulled her into the room and closed the door behind her.

She met his eyes, dark and searching, and felt the pull of the fragile thread that drew them together. Neither spoke but there was comfort in the silence between them — a soft surrender that needed no words.

He kissed her and she let herself lean into the ache of wanting. The kiss was a fragile promise held between two broken souls. He elicited a sound that vibrated through her, a low rumble of pleasure against her mouth.

Her entire consciousness, her every thought and feeling, every sensation possible all pooled into one place. Centred on that one delicious point of contact.

Then he broke away and rested his forehead against hers. "Harriet." He said her name like a plea, like a vow.

She stilled.

"Tell me to leave, and I will." The words hung in the air between them. A choice. The most important she'd ever make.

She knew if she told him to leave, he truly would. He had always given her that power. But she couldn't give him up now. Not when she'd come this far. "I can't," she said simply, her voice barely above a whisper.

He exhaled a shaky breath, like he had not dared to hope for that answer. Then, slowly, he reached for her, his fingers brushing the delicate skin at her neck, light as a whisper, sending a thrill that raced through her. He untied the lacings down her back with agonising slowness.

Harriet's breath hitched as a surge of longing stirred within her — raw and achingly beautiful. Her mind fought the shame of her body betraying her. Suspended in a moment of inward conflict, trembling on the edge, as the internal warfare between spirit and flesh waged. A violent conflict between reason and passion desperately trying to overcome the compulsion. But she could not.

Her dress abandoned her shoulders with a soft sigh, and the war was lost.

REGRETS

The room was still cloaked in shadows when Harriet stirred. The air was damp and heavy. For a moment she couldn't place herself. And then her heart pounded as the memory flooded back—his touch, his kiss, the way she had melted beneath him, had given in so completely. No hesitation. No regret.

Elijah's arm was draped over her waist, his breath soft against the back of her neck, the weight of him unfamiliar yet impossibly right. Her clothes were scattered, her petticoat draped over the chair, her gown crumpled on the floor. The sight of them made her stomach twist. *Oh God, what have I done?* This was reckless—foolish.

It was too much. She couldn't breathe. Not here in this room—in this bed—with Elijah still touching her. *I need to get out!* She swallowed hard and forced herself to move. Slowly, carefully, she lifted his arm from around her and slipped from the bed. Then, tiptoeing across the room, she made a frantic attempt to gather her clothes, ashamed by her nakedness.

Elijah shifted in his sleep, and she froze. If he woke, she would not be able to leave. She knew this with certainty. But she had to leave… didn't she? What would she even say to him when he woke? What promise had she made in doing this? She'd been so sure last night of what she wanted, but now, in the quiet of the dawn, the full weight of what she had done pressed down upon her and regret coiled tight in her chest.

She moved quickly, pulling her dress over her head, barely bothering to lace it properly. She forced her feet into her boots and clasped her cloak at her throat with trembling fingers. With daylight creeping over the horizon, she turned and took a last, lingering look at him—his face peaceful in sleep, dark curls spilling onto the pillow, the back of his neck coloured by the sun.

Go before you change your mind. She slipped through the door, her breath uneven, her body still aching from his touch. Her footsteps seemed unnaturally loud in the silence. No-one else stirred in the hotel. No clerk at the desk, no bellboy. She peeked at the clock on the way out. A quarter to six—too early to catch a train.

She decided to walk awhile to clear her head, but all she could think of was Elijah's confusion when he woke to find her gone—his disappointment, anger even. Would he forgive her? She hoped so. She hadn't meant to walk home, but she did: the whole seven miles.

Delphine was pacing the shop floor, her face drawn from lack of sleep. She rushed at Harriet when she came through the door and caught her in a fierce embrace. "Hattie! Where on earth have you been? I thought you were dead!"

Harriet saw the relief wash over her. "I'm sorry I've worried you."

"Worried? I've been going out of my mind!"

Harriet's lips trembled and her eyes filled. "Please, do not press me for an answer now. I'm unable to give it."

Delphine seemed somehow to know. She always did. She nodded, her smile tinged with sadness. "Oh Hattie." She wiped a tear from Harriet's cheek. "My poor darling. Come, let's get you upstairs."

Back in the comfort and safety of her home, she told Delphine everything. "What should I do, Delphine? I don't know how to do this."

"Only you can answer that, Hattie. I can't tell you what's in your heart, but is it what you want? Put aside all the difficulties for a moment. Is it what you truly want?"

"More than anything."

"Then you have your answer."

"What if he won't forgive me—for leaving I mean?"

"Of course he will. Just go to him. Explain how you feel. I can't understand why you didn't just speak to him this morning."

Harriet looked down at her clasped hands and sighed. "I panicked. I think…" she looked up at Delphine with watery eyes. "I…was afraid."

"Of what?"

"That he might be ashamed of me—that he would think me loose-moralled."

"Oh for goodness sake Harriet he loves you! What is it going to take for you to see that?"

Harriet nodded. "I've been such a fool."

"No, you haven't. You've just been through a lot. Now go, get yourself cleaned up and think about what you're going to say when he gets back."

Harriet waited all that day for Elijah to return, and the next. On the third day, there was a knock at the door. It was sharp, purposeful. Not the kind made by a neighbour or a customer.

Harriet glanced at Delphine, who was arranging ribbon spools in the window. She walked to the entrance.

A man stood in the doorway: tall, broad-shouldered, in a plain woollen suit. He removed his hat politely and placed his leather gloves into it. "Mrs Blackthorn?"

"Yes?"

"I'm Inspector Henley. I'd like to ask you a few questions, if I may. It concerns your neighbour, Mr Elijah Bennett."

Harriet's fingers curled around the edge of the counter. "What's happened? Is he…is he hurt?"

The Inspector paused, considering her, then looked around the shop. "Might we go somewhere less public?"

"Is he hurt?" she demanded. She felt sick.

"No Madam, he is not hurt. He's in custody."

"What? I don't understand. How is he—?"

The inspector gestured to the staircase. "Shall we?"

Delphine locked the door and followed them upstairs.

"There's been an investigation into the death of his wife, Margaret Bennett. Her body was discovered in St. Albans on Thursday morning last."

Both women gasped.

The room swayed, and Harriet gripped the back of a chair to steady herself. "She's dead?"

"Yes Madam. I'm afraid so."

"What happened? How?" Harriet asked, still trying to make sense of what she'd just heard.

He ignored her question and carried on. "I believe you and Mr Bennett were engaged to be married?"

Harriet could barely form the words. "Yes, that's right."

Inspector Henley raised a brow. "Were you aware that he was already married?"

Harriet shot him a glare. "Of course not! Neither of us were. She was supposed to be dead."

"Indeed. How inconsiderate of her."

"I *meant,* we both thought she was dead. Everyone thought she was dead and had for years!"

He made a note in his book. "Then I suppose it was a great inconvenience for yourself and Mr. Bennett to have her turn up alive and well?"

Harriet's eyes narrowed. "How dare you—"

"Hattie." Delphine placed a hand at her elbow and steered her to one side. "What my friend means to say is that she is appalled at what you insinuate Sir. She has a tender heart and of course she was disappointed not to be married, but she would never consider someone being alive and well an inconvenience."

"I see." He scribbled in his notepad again, his pencil scratching furiously at the paper. "Can you tell me your whereabouts on Wednesday the third of August Mrs Blackthorn?"

Harriet's blood stilled, her heart stuttered. *Oh God, she was there. That cackle I heard. It was her. She must have followed us. They think he did it. Or do they think I did it?*

"Mrs Blackthorn?"

She cleared her throat. "I went to St. Etheldreda's to see my daughter wed."

"Can anyone corroborate that?"

She just stared at him.

"Mrs Blackthorn, might I remind you that this is a murder case?"

"Mr. Bennett saw me."

"I see."

She couldn't tell from his expression if that was good or bad.

"Any one else?" He looked pointedly at her. "Is there anyone other than Mr. Bennett who could testify to your whereabouts?"

"No."

Inspector Henley set down his notepad and pinched the bridge of his nose. "Mrs Blackthorn, are you saying that you attended your daughter's wedding and not a single person saw you there?"

Everything she said either sounded ridiculous under his scrutiny, or incriminated them further. She drew a deep breath and sent up a silent prayer. "I was hiding. I sat high up in the gallery so I could watch undetected." Her voice wobbled, but she carried on. "Because I wasn't welcome."

He nodded and re-opened his book. He went on that way, asking her every minute detail of her routine that day. And then he asked the final damning question. "What did you do after that?"

"I went to St.Albans…with Mr. Bennett."

Inspector Henley snapped his book closed and stood abruptly. "Very good. Thank you for your co-operation, Mrs Blackthorn." He held out his hand and she stared at it.

"But what—? Wait…don't you need—?"

"I have everything I need thank you. You've been most helpful."

Helpful? How was any of that helpful?

Delphine made pointed eye contact with her, and shook her head ever so slightly. "Let me see you out Inspector." She turned him and led him to the staircase in one smooth movement.

Harriet was still rooted to the spot when Delphine thundered back up the stairs.

"We need to find out who Elijah's defence counsel is. The police aren't going to help you."

"I don't understand. Why didn't he want to know where we went in St. Albans? Or even when we came back?"

Delphine took her by the shoulders. "Listen to me, Hattie. He didn't ask because he didn't want to know—he didn't need to. All he needed was a witness to place Elijah in St. Albans, and now he has it. They'll charge him on your testimony alone."

Harriet covered her open mouth as though she could put the words back in. "Dear God no! Oh Delphine, what have I done? I should have lied. I—I…should have said…something else—anything else."

Delphine pushed her down into the chair. "Sit down." She poured a brandy and urged her to drink it.

"He'll be hanged for this. What do I do? How can I fix this?"

"First of all, this is *not* your fault. We must find out when this will go to trial and who will represent him." Delphine paced the room, her finger tapping her lips. "We'll go to the gaol at St. Albans and enquire there of the governor. Although he isn't known to be a sympathetic man. If he won't help, I will appeal to Mr Davenport. He would know."

Harriet's eyes widened. "Mr Davenport? As in Arabella's husband?"

"Well, he is the Justice of the Peace, Hattie."

Harriet ran a hand over her face. "He is not going to help us Delphine. If he knows I'm involved, it might make it worse for Elijah."

Delphine stopped pacing. "We don't have a choice."

The cold stone walls of the gaol loomed over Harriet as she approached, clutching the small parcel of food she had brought for Elijah. It had been a week since his arrest, and just as Delphine predicted; they had charged him the day they'd spoken to her. She'd also been right about Mr Davenport, who had given her all the information she asked for.

Elijah would stand trial for the murder of Margaret Bennett at the summer assizes in Hertford, just one week from now. It wasn't enough time to build a proper defence, but he had a good lawyer, whom Harriet was working alongside. She'd told him everything. When the defence called her as a witness, all she had to do was tell the truth. Just the truth. But that was no small thing.

The gallery would be filled with people. People she knew. Twelve men would sit on the jury, making judgements about her character. She would have to tell them all that she'd spent the night with a man she wasn't married to. Worse than that—a man already married to someone else. The life she'd hoped for would be over. She would be publicly scandalised—branded a harlot. A whore. Lillian would know, and any chance of reconciliation would be lost forever.

The iron gate groaned shut behind her as she made her way through the narrow courtyard. Wind tugged at the ribbons of her bonnet, and her fingers clutched around the paper-wrapped parcel as though it held the elixir of life. She approached the outer office where a constable sat, fingers laced together over his broad belly. "I'm here to see Elijah Bennett."

The constable's eyes narrowed. "Name?"

"Harriet Blackthorn."

He thumbed through a ledger, then closed it with a snap. "You're listed as a witness. You're not permitted to speak with the accused."

Harriet's heart dropped. "But I—"

"Rules, Madam." He raised his hand. "No contact between the accused and the witnesses before the trial."

A shadow passed across the doorway. Mr Davenport stepped in, still in his black coat, a sheaf of papers tucked beneath one arm. "Mrs Blackthorn," he said with a nod. "Is there a problem?"

"They won't let me see, Elijah," she said, struggling to keep her voice steady. "I—I brought him some food."

He studied her face a moment, then turned to the constable and said, "It's quite alright Mr Bates. I will attend to Mrs Blackthorn.

The constable gave a curt nod and stepped away.

Mr Davenport sighed. "I'm afraid you can't see him, Harriet. Not when you're a witness. But I will do what I can to aid you."

She met his eyes. They held nothing of Arabella's cold disdain—only weariness, and perhaps a trace of pity. She had always liked him better.

He held out his hand for the parcel. "Is there anything inside that I should be aware of?"

She looked at him quizzically. He wasn't going to open it? No, he trusted her, and she would not betray that. "Yes, there's a note inside."

He looked down at the brown paper parcel, and back at her, then he cleared his throat. "I...need to know what it says."

Harriet reached into the centre, where she'd tucked the note between the layers of paper, and drew it out. She offered it to him, but he didn't take hold of it. She saw the pain it caused him to ask. So she opened the scrap of paper herself and turned it to show him. Scrawled across the page in elegant handwriting, it read simply, "I love you more than life. Do not lose hope.—H."

Mr Davenport nodded and returned it to the package. "I'll see that he gets it."

She turned to go, her boots echoing on the stone. Then his voice stopped her.

"Harriet?"

She turned back.

"I'm... sorry."

She gave a small, grateful nod. "So am I."

~

HARRIET STEPPED out into the bright afternoon light, bonnet and gloves in her hand. The air was sultry, heavy with the scent of myrtle and lavender. The atmosphere was clogged with a damp and stifling heat that pressed against her chest. She needed to move. To breathe. She wasn't ready to go home yet, knowing that just beyond her own walls, Elijah's rooms were empty, but there was only one train back to Hatfield today, and she did not relish the idea of a seven-mile walk in such relentless heat.

When she arrived back in Hatfield, the high street was still busy with shoppers. Two women stood by the baker's awning, shielding their faces behind fans. They fell silent as Harriet passed. Then she heard one of them whisper.

"That's her." Then the other voice, louder. "They say he murdered his wife for her." The words struck like stones.

Harriet kept walking, her boots clicking too loudly against the cobblestones, her breath suddenly shallow. She ducked inside the first shop she came to, desperate to be away from prying eyes. She asked for a loaf of bread, even though they had plenty at home.

The shopkeeper hesitated. "Mrs Blackthorn," he said, nodding. Polite but stiff.

"Good morning," she said quietly.

He didn't answer. Just wrapped the bread in brown paper and slid it across the counter without meeting her eyes.

Harriet placed her money on the counter and turned to go, the bell above the door sounding like a funeral toll.

Outside, the street sounds carried on as though the world hadn't shifted. But it had. She felt the scrutiny of every eye, imagined her name on every tongue and convinced herself that people were crossing the street to avoid her. By this time next week, she would lose whatever remained of her reputation. She clutched the loaf and walked on, fingers cracking the crisp crust. When she handed it to Delphine, she looked at the mis-shaped loaf in horror and set it to one side.

"How was he?" She asked.

"I wasn't allowed to see him, but Mr Davenport took the food and my note to him."

Delphine draped a reassuring arm around her. "Well I'm sure he will be glad to hear from you, even if he couldn't see you."

Harriet sighed. "I can't bear to think of him rotting in that awful place, all the time thinking that I left and not knowing why."

"Did you explain in your note?"

"No. I was afraid it might fall into the wrong hands. I just said that I loved him."

"Well, there you go," Delphine said, "he knows the important part."

That night, Harriet lay awake, staring at the ceiling above her narrow bed. The walls of her room felt closer than ever, pressing in like a sentence already passed. She thought of Margaret—the chaos she'd brought, the destruction left in her wake—even in death she managed to tear their lives apart.

Dread closed its icy fingers around her. If Elijah was

convicted, she would have to live the rest of her life knowing she'd held happiness in her hands and let it fall. If he swung for this, she might as well place her neck in the noose with him. She really did love him more than life. Now she had to prove it.

THE TRIAL

The day before the trial, Harriet rose early and went into the sitting room. Nerves had roused her long before the sun, and sleep had not returned. Delphine was already there when she walked in, a shawl wrapped tight around her shoulders, a half-empty cup of tea cradled in her hands.

The clock had not yet struck seven. Delphine looked up and patted the space beside her on the settee.

Harriet sat slowly, folding her hands in her lap. "I can't sleep," she murmured.

"I didn't expect you to." Delphine took a sip of her tea, then set it down with care. "How are you feeling?"

She let out a laugh, brittle and dry. "Like Persephone walking into the underworld."

Delphine didn't smile. She reached out and rested a hand gently over Harriet's. "You're very brave, Hattie."

"No. I'm terrified."

"Brave doesn't mean unafraid." Delphine squeezed her

fingers. "It means being afraid and doing the right thing, anyway."

Harriet's throat burned. "What if I ruin everything? What if I get up there and all they see is a desperate woman with no decency, no dignity left? What if they don't believe me?"

"You know the truth," Delphine said calmly. "Elijah knows the truth. Anyone that matters to you already does."

Harriet looked down at their joined hands. "Not everyone."

Delphine knew who she meant. "Lillian has her own path to walk. You can't keep punishing yourself in the hopes that one day she'll notice."

Silence settled between them.

Finally, Delphine leaned back. "There is only one question you need to answer, Harriet. Not for them—for yourself."

Harriet glanced at her.

"Is he worth it?"

She gasped. "Delphine, how could you ask such a thing? Regardless of whether I loved him or not, a man's life is at stake!"

"That may be, but not all men are equal." She eyed her over the rim of her teacup. "So, is he worth it?"

"More than anything."

Delphine smiled. "Good. Oh—there's a letter for you on the table."

Harriet picked it up and turned it over. It was written in an unfamiliar hand, and the seal was blank. She opened it.

> *Dear Harriet,*
>
> *I write to you somewhat unexpectedly, having come across recent accounts in the newspapers detailing the difficult trials you have endured. I hope this letter finds you as well as can be. I have followed*

your story with great admiration and a heavy heart. I must commend your remarkable courage and resilience throughout these trying times.

It is with some relief that I can share news of Theodora. A little while ago, I was able to secure her release from the asylum. Her condition has markedly improved since then, and she is settled in a quiet home, where she continues to regain her strength with steady progress.

I know how much you cared for her, and so I've enclosed her address should you wish to visit her. I hope this may bring some comfort to you both and perhaps offer a new beginning where healing may continue. Though the past remains a complicated matter, I trust time may yet soften old wounds.

Please know you have my warmest thoughts and best wishes as you begin this new chapter.

Yours sincerely,

Clarissa Montgomery

Harriet sat down, her legs unsteady.

"What is it?" Delphine said. "Is something wrong?"

Harriet held it out to her. "It's Theodora—she's free." Her face cracked into a brilliant smile. It was the first good news she'd had in such a long time—a bright spot in the darkness.

That night, Delphine stayed by her side long after the candles burned out, but now alone in her bedroom, Harriet couldn't sleep. Even the knowledge of Theodora's release couldn't soothe her. She lay on her back; the covers tucked to her chin, eyes fixed on the dark beams above her. The air was thick with the scent of wax and dust, and her thoughts would not still.

Tomorrow, she would take the stand. She folded her hands over her chest as though preparing to be buried.

The prosecution would ask her questions. Personal questions. They would turn her acts of love into cold, clinical things. Was she with him that night? Where did they go? Had he left the room at any point? And she would have to tell them. Every shameful detail. That she had shared a bed with a married man, because she wanted him—longed for him—and had acted on that desire.

The fact that *her* desire had led them to this made it all the more shameful. Desire, she'd learned—like grief—operated without the regard for consequence. But there were consequences.

Her hands curled into fists at the thought of the gallery. Of eyes boring into her. Whispered words. Ruined. Fallen. Whore. Lillian, learning what she had done—if she hadn't already—and never looking at her the same way again. She swallowed hard and turned her face into the pillow. Was this punishment for Caiaphas? For his death? Had she not paid penance enough?

In the stillness, she thought of Elijah and the way he had held her that night, with a kind of desperate reverence, as though she were something sacred. He had whispered her name like a prayer, told her he loved her, and she had not returned the sentiment. At least not out loud. And now all he had was a crumpled scrap of paper as evidence of her love.

She exhaled shakily into the dark. Tomorrow, he would know for certain, perhaps not in words, but in the sacrifice she would make. It was the only way that mattered now.

RAIN HAD FALLEN in the early hours. The road to Hertford was slick with mud, the clouds swollen with the promise of more, but it brought no relief. Despite the slate sky, the heat persisted. Harriet and Delphine stood just inside the shop, waiting for the carriage.

She had chosen a plain dress of burgundy cotton. Nothing to distract, nothing to provoke comment. She pinned her hair low beneath her bonnet, and her mother's locket hung around her neck, cool against her skin. She'd tucked it inside her collar so it couldn't be seen. She had never felt more exposed. She fiddled with the ribbons on her bonnet, adjusted her bodice, and flitted about the shop, touching things—moving, re-organising already tidy shelves.

Delphine kept watching her but made no comment.

A carriage rolled to a stop outside, its wheels hissing on the wet stones. She stepped outside, and the driver leaned down, rain dripping from the brim of his hat. "The assize court, miss?"

"Yes, please." Harriet nodded, climbing in. Behind her, the shutters of Elijah's shop remained closed. She looked up at it now, her lips pressed thin, eyes shining. The door shut with a thud as Delphine climbed in. Neither spoke, only sat stiffly on the leather seat, hands clasped together.

The sound of Harriet's own heartbeat was deafening. This was it. No more imagining. No more rehearsing what she might say. No more waiting for the moment to come. It was here. The carriage rattled to a halt on Fore Street, and she peered out through the fogged window. Her breath caught at the sight of a small crowd lingering near the gates—hushed, watchful.

Shire Hall's great stone façade rose from the ground and towered mercilessly over her. It looked less like a court and more like a monument. A cold and ancient place where actions of the past become instruments of torture in the hands of destiny. Columns framed its triple-arched entrance, and a weathered clock loomed above, ticking steadily toward her fate.

The carriage door opened with a creak, and a young constable in a damp uniform offered his hand. Harriet hesitated for a breath, then gathered her skirts and stepped down onto the slick pavement. The hush of the street pressed in around her. She didn't look up at the crowd but kept her eyes steadily forward, Delphine at her elbow.

The constable nodded once and led them through the arched entrance. Inside, the air was cooler, stiller. It smelled of damp stone and wood polish. Their footsteps echoed across the tiled floor as they passed down a narrow corridor. Oil lamps hissed along the walls, casting long shadows that trembled with each step. They stopped outside a plain wooden door. The constable opened it without a word, and Harriet stepped into a small, bare room with a single bench along one wall.

"This is where you'll wait until you're called," he said. "The usher will come for you."

Delphine kissed her and wished her luck. Then the door closed, and Harriet was alone.

She sat stiffly on the narrow bench, her hands folded in her lap. She could hear the soft murmur of proceedings down the hall—distant voices rising and falling, the faint scrape of chairs, a cough, the shuffle of footsteps. Every sound made her pulse jump. She thought of Elijah standing in the dock alone. Of the twelve men who would decide his fate. Were they good men? Were they worthy of holding such power as to decide a man's fate? She wondered how many had stood in that dock wrongly accused. How many had been wrongly convicted and had died in the name of justice?

Then she thought of the eyes in the gallery—some familiar, some not, but all watching, all judging. She took long, deep breaths, closing her eyes and counting—in, two, three, four—out, two, three, four. *I can do this.*

There are many things a person may draw upon as sustenance for the mind. Grief is one of them. One of the most powerful of all emotions, second only to love. In fact, made possible only by the very existence of love. For what is grief but an inexhaustible wealth of love, robbed of its recipient? It was a thing Harriet had plenty of, and she drew upon its immense power to push her forward.

Her mind flickered back to her father, his calm, unyielding presence in the face of every storm. Steady and unshakable. He had given her that strength. Then Aggie—fierce, unrelenting in her loyalty and love. That fire, too, kindled a spark inside her chest. She felt the wildness of Theodora's untamed spirit. The defiant courage that refused to be silenced or bent by the rules of society—the rules of men. A reckless flame that burned brightly. And beneath it all, steady and enduring, was Delphine's love—the quiet warmth that held her firm. Her unwavering presence was a tether to safety and hope.

Her hand moved to the locket at her throat. She was not alone. She had never truly been alone.

The usher came then and called her to take the stand. His voice cut through the air like a whip. He led her back down the corridor to a pair of heavy oak doors. The murmur of voices drifted through the cracks, and she heard the click of a gavel, a call to order that echoed like a summons to her soul.

She lifted her hand and pressed her palm against the cool, solid wood, grounding herself in the moment. Out there in the stillness, time stretched thin—a fragile pause between what had been and what was yet to come.

She stood at the edge of a precipice, the ordinary life she'd clung to slipping away beneath her feet. All that remained was the dark drop ahead. She closed her eyes and took one last breath—deep, clear, resolute. Then she stepped forward.

~

THE GREAT OAK doors swung open with a groan, and Harriet stepped into the courtroom. Her skirts brushed the floor as she walked, the sound swallowed by the murmuring crowd packed into the public gallery above. Wooden benches creaked beneath the weight of curious townspeople. Whispers buzzed like hornets, rippling through the gallery.

She didn't look up. All she saw was Elijah—pale, proud, and defiant.

He stood in the dock, his hands clasped before him. He looked thinner than he had a week ago, his collar loose around his throat. His body tensed the moment she entered. His eyes, rimmed with fatigue, found hers and his lips parted. "No." The word was breathless, inaudible, but she saw it. He shook his head. A silent plea—don't.

But she kept walking, carrying herself with imperial dignity.

A hush spread like oil over water.

The usher led her to the witness stand, her spine rigid, but hands trembling at her sides. The silence was a living thing that pressed against her ribs and lodged itself in her throat. She felt the eyes on her—dozens, maybe more, but she carried on, each step an act of will.

She stepped up into the box and gripped the edge, her knuckles turning white. The floor beneath her seemed far away.

The clerk brought a bible and administered the oath, then asked her, "Please state your name for the record."

She cleared her throat. “Harriet Blackthorn.”

There was a pause, and whispers flickered through the gallery. Harriet drew herself up to her full height.

The prosecutor approached. He was younger than she expected, with a sharp chin and cold, intelligent eyes. “Mrs Blackthorn. Are you acquainted with the accused, Mr Bennett?”

“Yes.”

“How long have you known him?”

Harriet thought for a moment. “About a year and a half.”

“Thank you, and can you state for the court, what is the nature of your relationship with Mr Bennett?”

Her hands tightened around the wood. “We are—” she caught herself. “We were…engaged to be married.”

“And were you aware that Mr Bennett was already married?”

“Well, not at first—at least…not until—”

“Mrs Blackthorn, it is a simple enough question. Were you aware, at the time of your engagement, that Mr Bennett had a living wife?”

Panic rose in her throat. “No.”

“So Mr Bennett lied to you.” It wasn’t a question, but a statement.

“No, he didn’t know she was alive. No-one did.”

The prosecutor smiled with malice and pushed his spectacles further up the bridge of his nose. “I see. And when did you learn of her existence?”

“In April of this year. She came to the Church in Hatfield.”

“The church where you intended to marry.”

Harriet nodded. “That’s right.”

“Did the accused ever speak to you about his wife?”

“Yes.”

“In what terms?”

Harriet glanced at Elijah. He was staring at the floor now. "He said that she was dangerous, unstable, but he did not wish her any harm. He was simply... trapped."

"Trapped?" the prosecutor echoed.

"Yes, the court would not grant a divorce." Why did everything she say sound so damning?

The prosecutor stroked his chin. "So Margaret Bennett presented quite the problem for you and Mr Bennett?" He pointed to Elijah. "Here is a man, by your own admission, Mrs Blackthorn, trapped in a marriage until death. Do you think that might give a man motive?"

"Objection." It came from the defence. "Leading the witness."

The judge sustained it with a measured nod.

The prosecutor's mouth tightened, and he changed his line of questioning. "Where were you, Mrs Blackthorn, on the evening of the third of August?"

"I went to St Albans."

"Overnight?"

"Yes." She swallowed. "At The White Hart hotel."

"Were you alone?"

Here it comes. "No...I was with Mr Bennett."

Gasps shot round the room.

The judge rapped his gavel once. "Order!"

The prosecutor's tone sharpened. "But the hotel ledger shows that Mr Bennett stayed there with his wife. Their signatures are both clearly visible. Can you explain that, Mrs Blackthorn?"

"I signed that ledger. It was my signature."

The prosecutor paced a little. "So you stayed at the hotel under the name Mr and Mrs Bennett. Why?"

She hesitated—just a breath—but enough for the silence to tighten. "We were trying to avoid scandal," she said finally. "We didn't want anyone to know we weren't man and wife."

"So despite the knowledge that Mr Bennett was a married man, you chose to spend the night with him at The White Hart Hotel?"

Harriet closed her eyes, and a single tear slipped down her cheek. "Yes." She couldn't look at Elijah now.

"Did he leave the room at any time after you retired for the evening?"

She shook her head. "No."

"You're certain of that? Could he have slipped out whilst you slept?"

"I didn't sleep much," she said evenly. "I would have known if he'd left." Her face burned with shame.

There was a pause, then he said, "Nothing further."

She barely had time to catch her breath before the defence rose—calm, deliberate.

"Mrs Blackthorn, thank you. You say you stayed the whole night with Mr Bennett at The White Hart, and that it was you—and not Margaret Bennett—who signed the ledger."

"That's correct."

"Permission to approach the bench, Your Honour?"

The judge nodded. "Granted."

He handed a document to the judge. "Gentlemen, I have here a witness statement from the hotel clerk, identifying Mrs Blackthorn as the woman who arrived at the hotel with the accused. He states that he remembers her well because she was wearing a large sapphire on a string of pearls."

Harriet's hand moved unconsciously to her neck.

"Do you own such an ornament, Mrs Blackthorn?"

She drew the pendant out from under her collar, and the gallery inhaled in a collective breath.

"Thank you." He looked pointedly at the jury then back at

her. "Now, could you tell me please, when you left the hotel the following morning, were you alone?"

She took a breath. "Yes. I left early, while Mr Bennett was still asleep."

"At what time?"

"It was just after dawn, about six o'clock."

He looked at the jury again. "Two hours *after* Margaret's body was discovered. And why did you leave without Mr Bennett?"

She looked down. "Because I was ashamed," she said quietly. "I was afraid someone might see me—that they might know what I'd done. I panicked."

"And are you afraid now?"

She met Elijah's eyes. "Yes."

The defence lawyer stepped closer to the witness stand, his tone quiet, respectful. "Mrs Blackthorn, you've just told the court that you left the hotel early because you were afraid of what people might think. You are a widow, are you not?"

"I am."

He nodded, pausing for a moment. "And not a woman of considerable means or status?"

"No."

"You support yourself?"

"Yes. I run a small shop with my companion in Hatfield. A milliner's."

He nodded again. "And this... confession you've just made. That you knowingly spent the night with a married man, under a false name... what do you suppose that will cost you?"

There was a rustle of movement in the gallery—people shifting uncomfortably, some leaning forward, others whispering behind gloved hands.

Harriet's throat tightened. "Everything. My reputation, my friends, my family."

"And your livelihood?"

"Most likely that too. People don't take their trade to a fallen woman. I have already been called names in the street."

"What sort of names, Mrs Blackthorn?"

"Harlot. Whore."

The defence lawyer didn't flinch. "And yet you came here to stand in this court and tell us the truth. You sacrificed everything for Mr Bennett's sake." He turned, addressing the jury again. "Mrs Blackthorn has not tried to protect herself. She has nothing to gain from sharing her story with us. In fact, she could have refused to testify and said nothing. Mrs Blackthorn could have avoided scandal altogether, preserved her reputation and livelihood. But she did not."

He turned back to Harriet. "Why not?"

She looked at Elijah. "Because he didn't kill her," she said, her voice cracking. "And I cannot stand by and watch the man I love accused of something he didn't do."

A hush fell.

Her breath trembled in her chest, but there was no taking it back now.

The defence lawyer bowed his head slightly. "No further questions."

The usher led her off the stand and back through the echoing corridors. The heavy courtroom door closed behind her with a final, resonant thud. The murmurs of voices faded into a hollow silence. He showed her to another waiting room, much like the last: bare except for a single wooden bench and a small, grimy window that let in a slant of grey light.

The hours stretched thin and taut, every tick of the distant clock carving into her nerves. Her mind raced with thoughts of Elijah, his fate held in the hands of twelve strangers. Would they see the truth she had bared? Or would they condemn them both?

She wasn't sure how long had passed before Delphine entered. Delphine's face lit up with quiet relief, and without a word, she opened her arms.

Harriet folded into them, burying her face in Delphine's shawl. For a moment, she let herself be held—neither strong nor brave, only tired.

"The jury has retired to deliberate. We can only pray now that they make the right decision." They sat together on the narrow bench as the hours dragged by. They didn't speak much. Delphine simply held her hand.

Every muscle in Harriet's body was drawn taut as wire. She watched a single droplet of rain track its way down the cracked windowpane, slow as a funeral bell. She stood a while and paced, then sat again, drumming her fingers on the bench. The locket at her throat felt heavy, and she pressed her palm to it, willing herself to draw strength from the memories inside.

Through the small window, the sky darkened into dusk. "They're taking a long time," Harriet said.

"That's usual in a case like this, Hattie. We may not get a decision today." She glanced toward the window. "I imagine they will reconvene tomorrow. It's almost six o'clock now."

Harriet put her head in her hands.

Then came the sound of footsteps—measured, deliberate.

The door creaked open, and a solemn-faced usher stood on the threshold. "The jury has retired for the night. The court will reconvene at 9 o'clock tomorrow."

Harriet's knees gave a small buckle as she stood. She didn't remember leaving the court, only the chill of the evening air on her face, the grey light of dusk settling over the street.

They didn't go home but took lodgings in Hertford. Harriet could neither eat nor sit. She paced until Delphine caught her by the shoulders.

"There's nothing more to be done tonight, Hattie. We'll know soon enough."

Lying in the strange bed, Harriet stared at an unfamiliar ceiling, tracing the shifting shadows of lamplight. She tried to pray, but the words tangled in her chest. She thought of Elijah alone in the cold cell, waiting for dawn, waiting to learn whether he would live or die. Sleep never came.

THE PRICE OF FREEDOM

The city was still wrapped in a thin veil of mist when Harriet and Delphine made their way back to the courthouse. The air was damp, clinging to Harriet's hair and lashes, and every step toward the great stone building felt heavier than the last.

Inside, the corridors hummed with low conversation, the shuffle of boots and the rustle of papers. Her stomach twisted at the sight of the open courtroom door, the public gallery already filling with curious faces. Her heart thudded against her ribs, each beat louder than the last as she walked back to that small waiting room.

Delphine sat with her, fidgeting and fretting. Her face too, was pinched and drawn from lack of sleep. They watched the clock in silence, too tense for conversation.

At twenty-seven minutes past twelve, the usher's footsteps alerted them to his approach. They stood, hands clasped together as he entered the room.

"They're ready," he said.

Harriet's stomach lurched. She forced her feet forward, her breath short and shallow. "They've reached a verdict?"

"Yes, Madam."

They followed the usher back through the narrow corridor, their steps soundless on the worn stone. They didn't ask questions, didn't speak.

Harriet's mouth was dry. There was no room left for fear—only a taut, hollow stillness where it had once lived. She grasped Delphine's hand tighter as he led them through the same oak doors she'd passed through yesterday. It felt like she was walking to the gallows.

The courtroom was still. All eyes turned as she entered.

The usher seated them on a bench behind Mr Lockwood, the defence counsel. To their left, the jury filed in, one by one, like men returning from a battlefield—weathered but not victorious.

Harriet's gaze flicked to Elijah in the dock, a guard standing close behind him. He stood just as he had before, with hands clasped in front of him, jaw clenched. But his eyes found hers, and this time, there was no plea. No protest. Only a silent acknowledgement: whatever comes next, we meet it standing.

The judge re-entered the room and took his seat.

"All rise," the clerk said.

Judge Whitaker put on his spectacles and sorted a stack of papers before he began. "Be seated. This court is now in session." He turned then to the jury box. "Will the foreman of the jury please rise."

Twelve men shifted in their seats. One stood.

"Members of the jury, have you reached a verdict upon which you are all agreed?"

The foreman held a folded piece of paper trembling between his fingers. "We have, Your Lordship."

Harriet's chest rose and fell once, sharp and shallow. She dug her fingers into the flesh of her knees.

The clerk stepped forward. "On the indictment for the wilful murder of Margaret Bennett, do you find the defendant guilty or not guilty?"

She felt Delphine's grip tighten on her arm.

The pause seemed to last forever. Then—

"Not guilty."

The room did not erupt. There was no cheer, no outcry. Just a quiet, stunned exhale.

Not guilty! Is that what he said? Lord, please tell me I heard that correctly. She looked to Delphine for some sort of confirmation. *She's smiling.*

There was a rustle of movement. A scrape of wood.

Harriet's breath left her body all at once. She didn't move. Didn't speak. She sat perfectly still as the judge addressed the jury, thanked them, dismissed them. She hardly dared to believe it.

The sound of chairs scraping back, feet moving and voices murmuring, came and went like waves on a distant shore.

Elijah remained in the dock until the judge gave the formal order for his release.

"Mr Bennett, you are free to go. This court is adjourned."

The bailiff opened the dock and slowly, like a man waking from a dream, Elijah stepped down.

Harriet stood, her legs shaking.

Their eyes met.

She wanted to go to him. To run to him. But her feet stayed planted. The only thing that moved was the tear that slipped down her cheek. *He's free.* And so, perhaps, was she.

Delphine wrapped a steadying arm around her waist as though she might collapse.

She turned to her. "We won," she said breathlessly. "He's free, Delphine. He's actually free."

Delphine only nodded, unable to speak for crying.

And then his arms were around her. She folded into him as though she might never stand on her own again. He held her close, his breath ragged in her hair.

"Elijah," she breathed.

He pulled back enough to look at her. "You did that...for me," he whispered, his voice breaking. "I owe you my life."

"I only told the truth," she murmured. "I only did what anyone would have done."

"No Hattie. You told the truth even though it ruined you. There aren't many who would willingly make such sacrifices. "

The crowd was still shifting, still murmuring—but they no longer mattered.

Elijah rested his forehead against hers and smiled. "How am I ever going to repay such a debt?"

"Just love me," she said, "as I love you."

~

THE NEXT MORNING crept in soft and unannounced. The light that filtered through the curtains was pale and forgiving, casting no judgment, only warmth. Somewhere, a church bell struck six, the sound muffled by distance and dew.

Harriet stirred, sleep still clinging to her. Her eyes fluttered open to the hush of a world that was not yet awake. She lay curled on her side and still clothed, atop the bed. The blankets had twisted around her ankles in the night, and one stocking clung halfway up her calf. Her hair had slipped from its pins.

Everything was still. For a moment, she wasn't sure if it had all really happened—the trial, the courtroom, the verdict.

But then she felt it: the heaviness in her limbs, the soreness in her throat, the strange clarity in her chest that only came after grief or great relief. *He's free!*

She yawned and stretched out, the rickety frame creaking beneath her. Then she swung her legs off the bed with a lightness she hadn't felt in years. She pulled back the curtain to peer outside. Mist hovered over the rooftops like breath held in waiting.

Behind her, Delphine was still asleep in the armchair, her knees drawn up, one hand curled beneath her chin. She didn't wake her.

She rested her fingertips on the cool glass and let the silence soak into her bones. It asked nothing of her, only anchored her. There were no carriages outside yet. No bells, no boots in the street. Only the coo of a wood-pigeon and the distant clatter of a milk cart.

She didn't know what today would bring. What the papers would say, the townspeople, whether her name would survive, but she knew one thing. He was free. And that was all that mattered.

She pressed her palm to the locket at her throat, breathed in the stillness, and let herself hope—for the first time in forever—that something better might be waiting. And it was.

Later that morning, the shop bell jingled faintly, and she heard his boots on the floorboards. "Hattie?"

"We're up here," Delphine shouted, looking excitedly at Harriet.

Elijah came upstairs and stopped in the doorway of the sitting room. His hat was in his hands, hair damp from the mist, curls clinging to his brow. He looked different in the light—older somehow. Not aged, but stripped back. The kind of weary that came not just from sleepless nights, but from carrying the weight of a life he hadn't chosen.

For a moment, neither of them spoke.

Delphine rose from her chair and gently excused herself to put the kettle on.

He stepped forward and smiled faintly. "Morning," he said, his hat collapsing under his grip.

"Morning, Elijah." Harriet said.

"I feel like I ought to say something...clever. Or noble."

She chuckled.

He crossed the room slowly, like he might spook her if he moved too fast. "I wanted to thank you. But there aren't words big enough for what you did in that courtroom."

Harriet looked down. "I told the truth. That's all. We don't need to dwell on it now Elijah. It's over."

"No," he said gently. "You offered the world your shame, and they didn't hesitate to take it. You risked everything for me."

"And I'd do it again."

He stopped in front of her. "But I never wanted you to pay that price. I never expected it. Injustice is a difficult thing to bear, but not the worst. I would have borne in gladly for love."

"I didn't do it for a debt of honour, Elijah." She lifted her eyes to his. "I did it because it was right. And because I love you."

"I know that, but I want you to know how truly grateful I am. I want you to know that I understand what it cost you, Hattie."

She gave a small, tight laugh and tucked a strand behind her ear. "Oh well, you said yourself you weren't interested in my reputation, so I don't suppose it matters. Let's have some tea, shall we?" She went to move past him but he stopped her.

"No Hattie." He looked down at his cap. I'm not talking about your reputation. You're right, I don't care one whit about that. I'm talking about what it cost you with Lillian."

The words sat between them, fragile and flickering, like a candle flame. He reached for her then, with reverence, as though afraid she might vanish.

She let him pull her into his arms. Neither of them wept. There were no more tears left, only the thudding of hearts and the warm press of bodies that had yearned for far too long. When they finally parted, he brushed her cheek with the back of his knuckles. "So, Hattie, what happens now?"

She smiled. "You tell me. I've made quite enough decisions for this year."

He nodded, the ghost of a grin pulling at his lips. "Let's start with tea then, shall we?"

~

By the time September arrived, two 'For sale' signs hung in the windows of their shops. The milliners had seen a steep decline in patrons; the few who had entered the shop had only come to gawk or gossip. One morning they awoke to find Elijah scrubbing furiously at the window where the letters, WHOR had been scrawled in bright red paint. He'd just about removed the E but the message was still clear.

They stood at the window of Elijah's sitting room, the quiet murmur of Hatfield drifting through the cracked panes. The sun had broken through at last, casting light over the high street—but it brought no warmth to Harriet's chest.

"I saw Mrs Winthrop this morning. She crossed the road to avoid me," she said quietly.

Elijah's jaw tightened. "Let her rot."

Harriet didn't smile. "It's not just her. It's all of them. They stare at me like I'm something unclean. I want to walk in the market without whispers behind my back."

He turned to her fully, one hand sliding into hers. "Just a few more days, Hattie. Then we go home."

They were both finished with Hatfield. The only reason they hadn't left already was that their wedding was booked at St Albans Abbey in a week's time. They didn't want to go to St Etheldreda's. Not with all the locals still whispering about them.

"I've been thinking," Harriet said, "about when we get home. I don't want to open another shop."

Elijah frowned. "I wasn't expecting that you would. You don't have to keep yourself anymore Hattie, that's my job."

"But I want to do something," she said. "Not for money, but for meaning. I want to do something that matters—build something."

He tilted his head, the corners of his mouth twitching. "Like a bridge? A tower?"

She swatted him with the tea towel. "No, Elijah, not a building. Although I suppose I would need one."

He narrowed his eyes. "What on earth are you plotting now?"

She turned to him, alight with sudden purpose. "I was thinking, a place for girls like Theodora. And me. Somewhere to go when the world offers nothing. A charity—a foundation for young women—all women. A place to rest, recover, to begin again."

He watched her with reverence.

She began pacing, her voice quickening with every step. "It could be a maternity home, but not like those others, not cold and punishing. We could offer education, kindness...dignity." Her eyes glittered with excitement. "A woman shouldn't be cast out for her mistakes. We'd help them become mothers if they choose to be—or help them learn a trade if they don't. Or even both. It would be a place to reclaim themselves."

Elijah stepped forward, cupping her cheek. "You could use the estate for that. God knows it's large enough. But if you want to be in Lancaster..."

"I do. I want to be close to Delphine and to Charlie's grave." She paused, her mind somewhere far away for a moment. "And...Lillian knows where to find me there." It still lingered: the hope that one day regret might stir Lillian's heart enough to come looking.

"Then I'll sell it."

She looked at him, confused.

"The estate. I'll sell it. We can buy somewhere else."

She shook her head. "No, Elijah, I couldn't ask you to do that."

"You didn't. It's nothing but bricks and land. It means nothing to me. What you're talking about—that's legacy, and you're going to need capital to start something of that scale. It's yours."

Her throat tightened. "But it's your home, Elijah—your father's."

He tilted her chin up. "It was never mine, not really. I never belonged there. *You* are my home now."

She pressed her forehead to his. "And you are mine," she whispered.

HARRIET'S WAY

On September 7th 1870, Harriet stood in the tiny side room reserved for the bride at St Albans Abbey.

The morning broke clear and cool. A pale blue sky stretched wide above the abbey spire. Sunlight streamed through the stained glass windows, casting soft jewel tones across the ancient stone floor.

She smoothed the front of her dove-grey gown. It was simple, made of silk crepe with no embellishment save a lace collar that Delphine had stitched by hand. Her hair was pinned low in a soft coil at her nape, a few wisps already curling loose in the September air. No veil. No frills. No borrowed traditions that she didn't believe in.

Delphine stood behind her, fastening the clasp of her mother's pearl-and-sapphire pendant. "You look beautiful," she said.

Harriet met her eyes in the mirror. "I can't imagine what my life would have been without you, Delphine. I don't think I could have endured such damage."

She smiled. "Your strength is your own, Hattie. And

besides, damaged people are dangerous. They know they can survive."

"This won't change us, will it? You won't let us drift apart? Because I won't. We're sisters, you and I."

Delphine moved to face her. "When two people are broken at the same time, their pieces get a little muddled. When they finally become whole again, they are made up of pieces of each other. That means they can never drift apart."

The sound of the organ starting up sent a flutter to Harriet's stomach, but any fear she might have felt was long since used up.

Delphine reached for her hand. "Shall we?"

The nave of St Albans was grand, but not showy. A handful of parishioners sat scattered in the pews—but no invited guests. Just Elijah at the front, waiting with a quiet, steady strength that had carried them both through storm after storm. He turned as she entered.

Their eyes met, and he smiled and gave the smallest nod—*we made it.*

Her chest filled with something weightless and still—something like peace. She walked toward him on Delphine's arm, without any hesitation.

The vicar spoke with warmth and solemnity, but Harriet barely heard the words. All that mattered was the feel of Elijah's hands in hers, the rasp of his voice as he said, "I will." The last of her fear fell away, like a suit of armour she no longer needed.Then the vicar pronounced them man and wife and declared, "Those whom God hath joined together, let no man put asunder."

Afterward, they lingered on the abbey steps beneath the fading September sun, when there came a voice behind them.

"I suppose I shan't be able to call you Mrs B anymore."

They turned.

Theodora stood just behind them, a soft shawl wrapped around her shoulders. "But I am very happy for you," she added, eyes shining.

Harriet's mouth fell open, then curved into a smile. She wrapped Theodora in her arms, then stood back to look at her properly, touching her face and hair as though checking she was real.

She looked healthier than the last time she'd seen her. Her cheeks were a little hollow but rosy, and her raven locks were cut short. She looked older than her years, but recovered—on the outside, at least. Her eyes still held the weight of all she had lost. There's a sort of visible sadness that never really leaves when a person loses a child.

Harriet hesitated. "Oh, Theodora, are you well? Are you back home with your family? Oh, there is so much I must know."

Theodora giggled. "And you will, but not now, Mrs—Oh, I don't know your new name."

Harriet looked at Elijah and smiled. "Bennett," she said. "Mrs Bennett."

Theodora clapped her hands excitedly. "Then you are still my Mrs B."

"Always."

As they descended the steps, Harriet turned, casting a last look at the great arched doors behind them. She would never come to this place again. This was the past, and the place that had borne witness to its closing. She had only one thing left to do before she said goodbye to Hertfordshire.

"Have you got the letter?" she said, turning to Elijah.

He reached inside his coat and pulled out a piece of paper, folded into three and tied with a pale blue ribbon. "Are you sure about this?" he said, frowning. "I'm not sure it will change her mind."

"It isn't for her. It's for me—something I need to do…for myself."

He nodded.

They said goodbye to Delphine and Theodora and mounted a carriage to head for Lillian's new home. It rolled to a stop on Verulam Road.

Harriet stood on the pavement before an imposing townhouse. The door bore a new knocker of gleaming polished brass. She tried not to crease the pristine paper in her tightening hand and ran her fingers over the ink to trace the strange words. *The Viscountess, Lady Byron. So strange. It makes her seem so out of reach.*

A maid answered, blinking at the sight of a woman in a wedding dress, its hem brushing the dusty street.

Harriet offered the letter. "For Lady Byron. Please see that she receives it."

The maid nodded and bobbed a curtsy. "Yes, ma'am."

She'd agonised over what to write in that letter—had written it a dozen times, trying to perfect it. But in the end, she realised it didn't have to be perfect. It just had to be true.

It read thus:

> "*Dear Lillian,*
>
> *My own precious girl. I do not write to stir your conscience, or move you towards reconciliation. I only wish you to know how fiercely I have loved you all these years, beyond measure and doubt, beyond the limits of my endurance. Until my body has lain in ruin, ravaged by all that love.*
>
> *I have written and visited many times, only to be denied entry. I will honour your wishes and will not write to you again unless you invite it. I hope that life is everything you dreamed of. And if I failed you,*

know that it was not from indifference to your needs, but from a place of love and misunderstanding.

The light left me when you turned away, and I have wandered the darkness, searching for you ever since. My tears have all but drowned me, and my spirit is weary, but I continue to love you, although you remain blissfully unaware. Though my heart is heavy, it is, and will remain always yours.

But the time has come for me to set down the weight of your absence, and embrace the peace I deserve. I have re-married and am going home now, to Lancaster. Should you ever wish to, that is where you will find me, with open arms.

I will love you always.

Mother.

She walked back to the carriage, where Elijah waited for her, concern etched into the lines of his face.

"Are you alright?"

She nodded, looking back at the house. "Yes. I'm going to be just fine."

They left St Albans in the fading light, the abbey spire shrinking behind them as the carriage carried them home. Harriet watched the landscape shift through the window—stone cottages giving way to wide fields, quiet woods, and distant hills. A new life awaited them. As dusk fell, she reached for Elijah's hand, and he folded his fingers through hers without a word.

THE BENNETT FOUNDATION

When they first arrived back in Lancaster, they stayed with Delphine. It was going to take some time to find the right place to build their maternity home. They needed buildings and open space—plenty of it. It felt like a lifetime since Harriet had left Greenacre. She'd come home changed, lighter—renewed.

Theodora came with them too, eager to be involved in Harriet's vision. She breathed so much life and youthful excitement into their plans, it was hard to imagine she'd ever been any other way. Harriet asked if she'd seen her mother before they left. It hadn't seemed right to take her to Lancaster without trying to reconcile them. She knew Arabella didn't deserve such a courtesy from her, but Theodora did.

Theodora's reply had shocked her more than it ought to. She had gone home to see her mother, and Arabella had turned her away—her own child. She wanted nothing more to do with her.

Harriet wondered daily how Theodora found it within her to show such grace in the face of a rejection like that. But somehow, she did, and with each day that passed, a spark of her former self seemed to reignite.

They soon settled into their new roles in this makeshift family—Harriet and Elijah, Delphine, Theodora and even Charlie, who spent much of his time there.

One evening late in the autumn, Delphine called them all outside, where Charlie waited with a horse and cart. "I have something to show you," she said, a sly smile tugging at the corners of her mouth. She said very little on the ride, only that it was a surprise, and they would see soon enough, what it was.

They passed through narrow lanes, wild hedgerows, and quiet farmland, until Charlie finally stopped beside a sagging wooden gate. Beyond it, fields stretched wide under the pale gold sky. An old farmhouse stood sentinel among them. To the left, two massive stone barns—and behind them, a number of smaller buildings. Ivy crept up its walls, and the fences leaned slightly from years of neglect—but it was sturdy. Solid.

Delphine stepped down from the cart. "Come, have a look."

Elijah walked slowly, fingers trailing along the barn's side, eyes sweeping over the thick beams, the bones of the place.

Harriet followed, her boots sinking into the earth. She could see it already—see it becoming something else.

"It's part of Greenacre," Delphine said. "It hasn't been farmed for years. The land's just been waiting."

"Waiting?" Harriet asked.

Delphine looked at her and smiled. "For something worthy. I thought it would be perfect for the foundation."

"You want to sell it?" Elijah asked, turning to her.

She stiffened. "No, of course not! It's a gift." She paused. "Consider it a wedding gift."

Harriet's breath caught. She reached for Elijah's hand.

He glanced at her, then at Delphine. "We're grateful," he

said carefully, "but we can't accept something like this as a gift. It's too much."

"Oh, for goodness' sake!" Delphine threw her hands in the air and rolled her eyes. "You English people and your principles. Can a woman not bestow a gift on her family now?"

Elijah was unruffled by her. "You can," he said, "but not this." His voice was quiet but firm. "We either buy it, or we will find somewhere else."

"But it's perfect!" Delphine said, looking to Harriet for support.

Elijah smiled, completely immune to Delphine's powers of persuasion. "Yes, it is."

It wasn't a situation she was familiar with.

He folded his arms across his chest and waited for her to respond.

"Stubborn man," she said, narrowing her eyes. "Fine. I'll have the papers drawn up. Consider it sold—for a sum of my choosing." There was a flash of victory in her expression. She thought she'd won.

Elijah stepped forward and extended his hand. "For a price that we both agree upon."

"How about a price that won't insult either of us?" Her hand hovered halfway to accepting his.

"Done." They agreed to the sale with a handshake, like two businessmen. "You drive a hard bargain, Delphine."

She glanced at Charlie, leaning on the fence across the yard. "I was taught well."

A warm gust of wind stirred the tall grass. It hissed as Harriet walked through it to peer through a slatted window into the dusty barn. She imagined beds lining the walls, laughter, friendship, children playing. A safe place for the forgotten. A place for healing. For beginning. She turned back to Elijah. "What do you think?"

"I think," he said slowly, "we're going to need a great deal of paint."

She laughed.

He caught her hand. "We'll make it a home," he said, bringing her knuckles to his lips. "For them and for us." He looked at Charlie then. "Looks like Charlie and I have a lot to discuss."

She watched him walk over to Charlie, still not quite believing he was hers.

Delphine wandered over, and they stood in silence for a time, watching the two men talk. "This place," Delphine said at last, her voice low, "will be everything to women like us. Everything I never had."

Harriet looked at her, sensing something beneath the words. "That's over now. We have each other. You'll never be alone again."

There was a long pause before Delphine spoke again, her voice so quiet Harriet almost missed it. "He knows. About the baby."

Harriet sucked in a sharp breath. "You told him after all this time?"

"I did. But he already knew. He saw the grave the day we buried little Charlie. He knew."

Harriet reached for her hand. "Oh, Delphine, I'm so sorry. I was so lost in my own grief, it never even occurred to me, but of course he would see it."

Delphine smiled. "Don't apologise for that."

"Did he ask you about it?"

"No, he never said a word, but I saw the way he looked at it. When I told him, he said, 'I know'—and he just held me for the longest time."

The wind rustled through the leaves above them. Harriet squeezed her hand. "Do you feel better?" she said softly.

Delphine nodded, her throat too tight for words.

They stood a moment longer, then turned and climbed back onto the cart to go home.

THE OLD FARMHOUSE took almost a year to transform. It had been hard work, but the barns were unrecognisable now—painted, partitioned, and full of life. Where hay bales had once gathered dust, there were warm little rooms with wooden cradles, white walls and hand-sewn quilts.

Charlie had spent his summer hammering, measuring, and sanding to help Elijah. He moved through the maternity ward that evening with a pride Harriet found contagious. "You'd never know it used to be a cattle barn," he said, running his hand over the smooth edge of a doorframe.

Elijah was down the corridor, adjusting a shutter hinge. Harriet leaned in the doorway, arms folded, watching him with quiet affection. Theodora passed her with an armful of baby blankets, tucking them carefully into the cradle of each room. She hummed to herself as she worked. Her hair was tied back and her cheeks flushed with the sort of purpose Harriet hadn't seen in her for a long time.

The sky outside turned amber as Delphine hurried to put the finishing touches to the rooms: a vase of flowers, a framed picture, and in the common room, a large tapestry with embroidered wording that she had made herself. It read, *'Thou art forgiven, for all have sinned and come short of the glory of God.'*

She stood back, admiring it, then turned to Harriet. "I don't know about you, Hattie, but I could have used a few reminders of that."

Harriet smiled. "I love it." She kissed Delphine on the cheek. "It's perfect."

She took a final walk through the buildings to check everything was as it should be. The delivery ward waited patiently with six beds, wrapped in crisp white sheets. Piles of towels and linens, polished steel instruments, bowls and all manner of paraphernalia that the midwives had requested. They were arriving the next day.

Twelve modest bedrooms and a shared common room filled the largest of the buildings—a place where young mothers could live without fear, without judgement, where they had a sense of belonging, dignity. There were offices too, in one of the buildings and staff quarters for the midwives and the nurses.

Delphine had studied for months, developing a plan to rehabilitate young girls back into society, into work, so that they had means to support themselves. Her idea was that the women would share a job, working alternate days and looking after each other's children. A sort of nursery, where they all helped each other.

She even had work placements lined up—people willing to take them on. That had been the most difficult part. It would be a long time before the world's attitudes caught up with theirs.

Harriet had been working on a secondary charity—The White Lilly Foundation—dedicated to reuniting mothers and children separated at birth. She hired a man who had once investigated cases of missing people for the police. She wasn't sure how well it would turn out, but it was something she had to try—for Theodora.

Later that evening, as the sun fell behind the hills of Lancaster, they gathered in the common room to toast their success. Harriet lit the last of the lanterns, whilst Elijah lit the fire, its golden glow casting flickers across the whitewashed walls.

Delphine poured the brandy and raised her glass. "To the end of one life and the start of another."

"To the women who will pass through these doors," said Harriet, "and to those who never got the chance." They toasted and sat together in comfortable silence, staring at the hypnotic dance of the flames.

Later, when most had gone to bed, Harriet stepped outside, and breathed in the scent of sawdust and crisp winter air. Elijah stood beside her, gazing at the sign over the main door. *'The Bennett Foundation.'* Freshly gilded in smart gold letters. Beneath it: *Harriet Bennett, Delphine De Matthieu, Theodora Davenport.*

He reached for her hand. "You did it, Hattie."

"We did it," she replied, leaning into him.

She thought about how far she'd come. How far they had all come. None of them unscathed but still standing. They'd all lost something—homes, chances, children, love, even innocence. The world had taken much from them, but it had not taken everything. What remained was theirs to shape.

Harriet felt the weight of the past settle. It could not be undone, but it had led them here, to a place of their own making, and in the ruins, they had built something greater, where no woman would ever be turned away again. She thought of all the versions of herself she'd been: the girl with her father's books, the widow, the grieving mother, the woman on the witness stand, and now this.

This was the self she had fought to become.

A PERSONAL NOTE FROM THE AUTHOR

Dear Reader,

If you've reached this page, you've walked beside Harriet through every joy, loss, and hard-won triumph of her journey. You've seen her stumble, rise, and keep moving forward—and I hope that, in some way, her story has touched your heart as much as it has mine.

Stories only truly live when they're shared. If *Standing At The Edge Of Ordinary* spoke to you, made you feel, or stayed in your mind after you turned the page, I would be deeply grateful if you could leave a short review.

It doesn't have to be long—just a few words about your experience. Reviews help other readers discover Harriet's story, and they are one of the most meaningful ways you can support my work as an independent author.

You can share your thoughts on my Amazon Author page.

Thank you for spending your time in this world I created. I hope our paths cross again in the next book.

With all my gratitude,

Lisa-Marie Ainley

ABOUT THE AUTHOR

Lisa-Marie Ainley was born and raised in Lancaster, where she still lives with her daughter. A teaching assistant for children with additional needs, she has always been passionate about history and literature. Her love of classic novels—especially Jane Eyre—has deeply influenced her writing. Drawing from both historical intrigue and personal experience, she crafts stories that explore themes of love, grief, family, and the constraints of societal expectations, always centring on resilient female characters.

www.lisamarieainley.com

facebook.com/lisamarieainleyauthor

STAY CONNECTED

If you enjoyed *Standing At The Edge Of Ordinary,* I'd love to keep in touch.

By subscribing my newsletter, you'll receive:
• Updates on my next book before anyone else
• Exclusive bonus content
• Behind-the-scenes research notes and inspiration
It's completely free, and you can unsubscribe at any time.
Visit my website to subscribe: https://lisamarieainley.com/

I can't wait to share more stories with you.